KU-216-436

The Forgotten Sister

Judy Summers

The Forgotten Sister

WELBECK

Published in 2021 by Welbeck Fiction Limited,
part of Welbeck Publishing Group
20 Mortimer Street London W1T 3JW

Copyright © Judy Summers, 2021

The moral right of the author has been asserted.

*All characters and events in this publication, other than those clearly in
the public domain, are fictitious and any resemblance to real persons,
living or dead, is purely coincidental.*

All rights reserved. No part of this publication may be reproduced, stored
in a retrieval system, or transmitted in any form or by any means,
electronically, mechanical, photocopying, recording or otherwise, without
the prior permission of the copyright owners and the publishers.

A CIP catalogue record for this book is available from the British Library

Paperback ISBN: 978-1-78739-690-6
Ebook ISBN: 978-1-78739-691-3

Printed and bound by CPI Group (UK) Ltd, Croydon, CR0 4YY
10 9 8 7 6 5 4 3 2 1

MIX
Paper from
responsible sources
FSC
www.fsc.org   FSC® C171272

Foreword

I thoroughly enjoyed this book set in Liverpool in the Victorian era, which has been rather neglected by modern novelists but was a very formative time in the city's growth, status and wealth. Beside the magnificent townhouses, mansions, parks and civic buildings, it depicts vividly the terrible, soul-destroying conditions in the slums of the city and those unfortunate enough to find themselves with no other recourse than the dreaded Brownlow Hill Workhouse.

Judy Summers has meticulously researched the period and has included a wealth of detail. Her characters are well drawn and very believable. It is the story of a feisty young girl and her equally feisty family who battle against poverty, tragedy, injustice, discrimination and at times pure malign fate but who, like many Liverpudlians then and now, refuse to give up their hopes and dreams.

I can't wait to find out more about the Shaw family in Judy's next novel.

Lyn Andrews

Chapter One

Liverpool, October 1848

Meg heard the *smack* of her father's knuckles connecting with her face before she felt it.

The pain arrived a moment later, as it always did, exploding into stars, dizzying; she staggered back with a hand to her stinging cheek, reeling from the combination of the blow, the shock and the fumes of cheap gin.

'Pa! Stop that!' That was Delilah, from the other side of the room.

'Got a right to respect in my own house, haven't I?' he slurred, swaying. 'She should have my tea ready if she knows what's good for her.' He aimed another backhanded swipe, but this time Meg was prepared and stepped out of the way. This seemed to enrage him more, and Delilah rose from her chair, but Sam was quicker – he darted in and kicked Pa's crutches out from under him, making him overbalance, and then shoved him down on the sofa. There Pa flailed about, bellowing and cursing, before he subsided into angry muttering and, eventually, snores.

Delilah reached Meg's side. 'Your mouth is bleeding. Here, let me—'

'I'm fine.' Meg avoided her sister's hand as deftly as she had her father's, and scrubbed her face on her sleeve before kneeling to comfort Rosie and Annie, who had both burst into tears when they'd seen him hit her. *At least it wasn't them this time.* She buried her face in their soft necks as they put their little arms around her, making soothing noises that were as much for herself as for them. Annie planted a wet kiss on her cheek.

Once they were quiet, and Meg was sure that she wasn't going to cry in front of everyone, she sniffed, stood up and moved with what she hoped was briskness to the tiny fire in the grate. 'He won't want anything to eat now,' she said, keeping her voice steady, 'but we'd better save him some in case he wakes up later.'

'What is there?' Sam and Jem – Liverpool's champion eaters, Delilah jokingly used to call them, back in their old life – were both looking at her like hopeful puppies.

2

'We've no meat, and I couldn't get potatoes today,' said Meg, poking the pot with their remaining spoon. 'But I've made a broth with those vegetables they were throwing out at the market yesterday, and it'll do to soften the bread.'

Jem was staring at her blankly, and she realised she'd spoken while turned away from him in the dim light. She looked directly into his face and repeated the words 'broth' and 'bread' while making the signs he used for them. He brightened.

There wasn't going to be much between seven – eight, if they saved some for Pa – but it would have to do. Delilah, the almost-adult, and William, who earned a wage, naturally got theirs first; after they had theirs Meg slopped some more broth out for Sam and Jem, smaller portions for Rosie and Annie, and the dregs for herself, leaving the barest scraping and the last crust of the bread for Pa, who probably wouldn't come round until the morning anyway.

Meg found a corner of the mattress alongside her sisters, dipping Annie's bread and feeding her piece by piece to make sure she didn't spill or waste any of the precious hot liquid. Pa was taking up the whole sofa, snorting and sweating despite the cold, so Delilah and William used the two mismatched chairs by the table and the smaller boys sat on the floor with their backs to the door, their dirty, bare feet sticking out in front of them.

Hers was almost cold by the time she got to it, but it didn't matter. As she ate – *shame we couldn't get an onion or a leek to go in it, that would have improved the taste* – Meg briefly allowed her mind to wander back to the time when they'd lived in a whole house rather than one stinking, crowded room. But thinking of the past was no good; it only reminded her of those who were lost. Ma, baby Jemima, Jonny . . . all gone now, just like their home.

She checked herself. Dragging up these memories was no use, and besides, Delilah didn't like them to talk about what had happened. Meg pushed the thoughts away as best she could, seeking to concentrate on something else, on those who were still here.

She watched William. He was fading away, so much thinner and paler than he'd been a year ago, but after Pa's accident he'd had no choice but to leave his beloved school and get a job labouring at the docks. If only she could look after him properly, feed him more nourishing meals, have him look at her and appreciate how much she loved him. He was exactly a year older than her, their birthdays the same day, and by rights he should have been her special friend in the family, but he always looked to Delilah for everything.

4

Delilah. Seventeen, and she'd be eighteen before the winter was out; only four and a half years older than Meg, but it might be a hundred for all they had in common. Delilah, who had been left in charge of the family when Ma died, who had taken on her work and her worries and the thankless task of trying to keep Pa from killing himself with drink. Meg knew she should be grateful, that she should adore Delilah like all the others did, but somehow there was a cloud in the way.

The candle had almost burned down to the halfway mark scratched on its surface. Like everything else, it had to be strictly rationed – one every two days – and as with the food, they had all learned the hard lesson that using too much today would mean less or nothing for tomorrow. She and Delilah wrapped shawls and jackets around the smaller children and hustled them all outside to visit the two privies shared by the whole court, before the shadowy men and the raucous drunks appeared, as they would later. Meg shivered while she awaited her turn. After the almost comforting fug of broth, fire and warm musty damp inside the room, the cold outside was like a knife, even though it was only October, and it made her bruised face sting all the more. Still, at least it kept down the reek from the privies. They'd only lived here a month; Meg couldn't bring herself to think about what it might smell like if they were still here next summer.

Once they were safely back inside their room with the door shut, and a chair pressed against it in case of unwanted nocturnal visitors, Meg busied herself tucking Rosie and Annie up on the mattress. Sam and Jem were at the other end, and Rosie giggled as Jem's cold feet met hers and tickled them. The boys, tired out by the endless miles they covered scampering round the city during the day, were soon asleep. The little girls took longer to drop off, and Meg stayed with them, stroking their hair and singing softly, until their eyes closed and their breathing deepened.

The candle had been blown out by now; the only light in the room came from the dying embers of the fire. Pa hadn't woken up, but he could have his bread and cold broth for breakfast, if he wanted to, and washing the bowls out could wait until the morning when Meg would be able to see better to draw water from the pump outside.

Yawning, Meg gently prodded Rosie until she rolled over, and then squeezed on to the edge of the mattress, cuddling up to her sisters for warmth. Delilah and William were still at the table, pushing round the day's collected earnings, a pile of silver and coppers that Meg knew wasn't big enough.

Pa had gone quiet at last, which meant he was either sound asleep or dead, and Meg didn't much care which. She drowsed, listening to the soft breathing next to her and the low voices from the other side of the darkened room. She wasn't sure whether she was awake or asleep and dreaming when she caught one word that stood out from the rest: *workhouse*.

* * *

It was warm under the blankets with all the little sleeping bodies, but when dawn broke Meg knew she had to get up. She could smell that Delilah had lit the fire, and she came in with water from the pump just as Meg got to her feet.

'Breakfast will have to be a drink of tea on its own,' said Delilah. She set the kettle to hang over the licking flames. 'But I can give you some money to buy food while I'm out. I'll have to go soon. We've a big load of sheets coming into the laundry today – can you manage?'

Was it still early? Meg automatically looked at the mantel over the fire, but the clock that had regulated their days for the whole of her life, one of the few things they'd brought with them, was gone now; it was in the front window of the pawnbroker's on Scotland Road and the mantel was bare.

Before the kettle was even boiling William was ready to go – he had a long walk down to the docks these days, and to be late was to miss the opportunity of being picked for the day's unloading work. Meg hastily reached for yesterday's tea leaves, carefully dried so they could be used again. She spooned some into a cup and poured water over them. 'Here. Something warm before you go out, at least.' William drained the cup, and as he handed it back she pressed the last crust of bread into his hand. 'You'll need something.' She cut short his protestations, looking scornfully at the sleeping figure on the sofa. 'Never mind Pa. If he asks after it I'll tell him a rat took it.'

William managed a tired smile and a brief press of her hand, and then he was gone.

Delilah was putting on her shawl, and she called Meg over to the table. 'I've put aside the rent money already, so this is all for food. It's Sunday tomorrow, so see what you can get for two days. When Sam gets up, that mending', she pointed at some neatly folded linen in a basket, 'is to go to Mrs Walker in Hunter Street on his way. All right?'

Meg nodded. Delilah stepped forward as though to kiss her, but she evaded the embrace. 'I'll see what I can get. Don't worry about us.'

She watched her sister leave and then took the now boiling kettle off the fire again and shook Sam and Jem awake. A few quick slurps and they were out the door, carrying the basket between them.

Meg turned to the table. The coins stacked on it added up to three shillings and sixpence, and her mind began to work. For two days they would need at least four four-pound loaves, at eightpence each, which was two and eight, leaving – she frowned, having much preferred reading to arithmetic during the Sunday school sessions they used to have – tenpence. That wasn't bad; allowing for enough potatoes for Sunday dinner, she might be able to get a bit of salt beef to add to make a stew. She picked up the coins and went to wake Rosie and Annie.

Rough hands suddenly seized her, and she let out a shriek. Dear Lord, she had forgotten about Pa, and had made the catastrophic error of stepping within his reach with money in her hand. He must have woken up while she was counting and waited for her to move away from the table.

She tried to clench her fist tightly round the coins as she struggled against him, but it was no use. The accident that had crippled his legs had left his arms uninjured; the action of dragging himself round on crutches had made them even stronger. He wrapped one round her like a vice, holding her fast, while with his other hand he forced hers open.

'Please, Pa, it's for food. For all of us!'

But she knew he didn't care. His face, close to hers, was sweating, and his eyes were wild and yellow. There was only one thing on his mind. Slowly her fingers were prised apart, and then he had the money.

She wasn't about to give up that easily. She might not be able to move her arms, but he wasn't holding her head; she bobbed it down and bit into his forearm, sinking her teeth in hard. He swore and loosened his hold, allowing her to lash out and send some of the coins flying across the room. 'Quickly!' she shouted to Rosie, who was out of bed and cowering at the sight before her. 'Pick them all up and run outside.'

Rosie scuttled across, keeping well out of Pa's way as he fell back exclaiming at the bite mark. Meg, released from his grip, stayed where she was, glaring at him. She rubbed the bruises on her arm where his fingers had dug in. 'Give that back.'

He made a derisive noise as he looked blearily at the coins in his palm. 'This'll do for now.' He looked up at her. 'Anyone asks, you lost the money, you hear? You dropped it somewhere. If you know what's good for you.'

She was about to retort that she didn't care when his next words, in a more vicious tone, turned her blood to ice. 'Or if you know what's good for Rosie, anyway.'

Meg stopped dead. He wouldn't, would he? He wouldn't threaten to harm an innocent little girl, his own daughter? Of course, he hit Meg, but she was older than Rosie. But then she looked into his eyes and saw the despair and the craving. He would let nothing get between him and his drink. She scooped Annie up and ran outside.

Rosie was already there, with what remained of their coins clasped in her fist. Meg hurried them both away from the door, but stopping in the middle of the court was no good – the place was full of curious faces and the last thing she needed to do was to stand out in the open and count money.

She mustered as much dignity as she could in front of the audience. 'Ah, there you are, Rosie. Come on, we're going to the market.' With Annie balanced on one hip, she held out her other hand to Rosie, who took it. 'Keep tight hold of that money till we find somewhere quiet,' she murmured under her breath.

Once out of the court she had to stop to orient herself, still not used to the maze of narrow alleys and dead ends that pressed together behind the semi-respectable façade of Gerard Street. Eventually she found the one that would lead them to the main road, and they picked their way through it, avoiding the slimy rubbish-strewn cobbles and a few barefoot toddlers covered in sores. There was one particular court entrance they hurried past, the one that contained what Delilah primly called 'a house of ill repute', and what the local men called something far coarser. No respectable woman or girl walked anywhere near it at night, for fear of being mistaken for one of those who worked there – or for fear of being attacked by a drunk who couldn't tell the difference – but there was little danger this early in the morning. All was quiet, and indeed the madam herself was standing outside her door catching the air, her red hair bright against the dingy walls. Still, Meg hustled her sisters past the archway quickly.

Once they were on the public street, Meg stepped into the shadow of a shop doorway. 'Right,' she said, grimly, 'let's see what he's left us.'

She counted each coin into the pocket of her apron as Rosie handed them over one by one. One shilling and tenpence. Not as bad as it could have been, but only just over half what she had started with. Not enough to buy even three loaves, never mind four.

Rosie was crying. That pushed the food shopping out of Meg's mind for a moment. She stooped to give her little sister a fierce hug. 'It's all right, darling. He can't hurt you out here.'

'But I don't like it!' wailed Rosie, with Annie now starting to sniffle too. 'I don't like it, I'm scared of Pa, and I'm hungry. I want to go back to how it was before!'

So do I, thought Meg, and for a moment all she wanted to do was collapse in a heap and join them both in their hopeless weeping. But that would never do; she had to be stronger than that. She bit her lip in an effort to stop it trembling. 'It'll get better, don't you worry, darling. We'll make it better, William and me. And Delilah.'

Rosie raised a woeful face. 'Promise?'

Meg knew she was telling a lie, but what else could she do? 'Promise. Now, wipe your faces, both of you, and we'll go to the market to see what we can get. And when we get home, Pa won't be there.' *Because he'll be at the gin shop all day,* she added to herself. *And then he'll come home drunk again and it will all start over.* But she would find a way past all this, find a way to look after her little sisters. She didn't know how yet, but she would.

As they left the shop doorway and headed in the direction of the market, the sun came out. It was a weak, autumnal sun, without much warmth, but still better than the unceasing grey and the chill wind of the last few weeks. Meg took the hands of both her sisters and lifted her face to the sky as she walked on.

* * *

Two loaves of bread, an onion, a very small pile of potatoes and a tiny offcut of bacon were all that lay on the table once they got home. Meg was hungry and tired, but none of it could be touched until that evening. The whole situation had been made worse by having to walk past the pie shop – just starting to bake the wares that would fly off the shelves when the hardworking dockers, labourers and market traders finished their working week on Saturday night – and now her stomach was growling out loud, while Rosie and Annie made eyes at the food.

The only thing to do was to try to take their minds off the hunger. Some girls were playing outside, so Meg sent the others out to join them, giving Rosie strict instructions not to leave the court and not to let Annie out of her sight. Fortunately their room was on the ground floor – the first one you reached as you came in the building – so she could see them through the window and run out if she needed to. She busied herself sweeping the floor and trying to take a scrubbing brush to the patch of black mould on the wall under the cracked glass and the rotting sill.

She was there, on her hands and knees next to the table, when she heard loud male voices outside. That was unusual during the day. She raised herself to peer out; two men were supporting a third between them, and her heart sank as she recognised her father.

One of the men was addressing the group of little girls. 'Which of you knows John Shaw? We were told he lived here.'

Rosie pointed wordlessly at their door, and the men dragged Pa inside. It was only once they were in the room that they noticed Meg, who was keeping the table and chairs between her and them, just in case, but to her relief they slung Pa down on the sofa, dropped his crutches next to him, and turned to go. 'Early home for him, I expect,' one of them said, gesturing to the prone form, 'but he ran out of money and they didn't want him cluttering the place up no more. Lucky for him the gaffer said to bring him home and not kick him out into the street.'

'Aye,' said the other, looking on the drunk man with contempt. 'But only so he'll be back for more another day. They don't want to lose such a good customer, do they?' He laughed.

The first man must have seen Meg's wide eyes, or noticed her trembling legs, and he spoke more kindly. 'Not to worry, lass – he'll be asleep a good long time, till your mother gets home, at least. Just leave him where he is.'

They left, and Meg heaved a sigh of relief. But the man's words, however kindly he had meant them, had stung: if she could have one wish, it would be that her mother really would come home. But Ma was cold in her grave, dead four months ago after giving birth to a baby they couldn't hope to look after. They'd given little Jemima away, and now they lived without Ma – without her love, her protection or the money she'd earned.

As the autumn dusk drew in Meg called the girls inside and lit the fire again, looking with dismay at the almost-empty coal bucket. But there was no other way to heat water, and the least she could do was to have something hot ready for when the working members of the family came home. She hoped it would be soon, for Pa was beginning to stir much earlier than she'd hoped. How much alcohol would he have got for a stolen shilling and eightpence? How drunk could you get when you robbed the food out of the mouths of your own children?

Sam and Jem were first back, and she made them sit on the floor by the fire to warm up, telling Sam to stay out of Pa's reach and keep any earnings in his pockets until the others got home. He gave Jem a look – they never seemed to need words to communicate with each other – and they sat down, Jem soon delighting in playing a silent game with little Annie that involved a lot of finger waving and her giggling. Meg smiled to see them.

William and Delilah came through the door together, having met each other on the way. They both looked exhausted, but Delilah carried more mending to work on into the evening. Meg was glad to see them, for Pa was now fully awake and attempting to sit up. She bustled round, hoping to get a cup of hot tea into them before Delilah noticed the pitiful victuals on the table.

Her hopes were to be disappointed. Delilah was halfway through a sentence when her eyes fell on the food, and she stopped mid-word.

Meg braced herself.

'Is that all you got? For three and six? That can't be more than two shillings' worth, surely.'

In fact it *had* been two shillings' worth of food – Meg had only got it for one and ten because she'd spent an hour helping the potato seller unload heavy sacks from a cart, even though she could hardly reach up to the tailgate. But what would be the point of attempting to say any of that?

She was desperate to let out the whole story, to tell them about what Pa had done, to see them look on her with sympathy instead of condemnation, but in the room's rapidly dimming light she could see Pa behind Delilah, tapping the side of his nose and casting a significant look at Rosie.

There was nothing to be done. 'I lost some of the money.'

'What?'

'I lost it. It was all in separate coins, and while I was in the market some of it must have fallen out of my pocket. I'm sorry.'

Delilah looked ready to burst with anger – either that or to cry, Meg wasn't sure which. 'You *lost* it?' she repeated incredulously. 'William and I work every hour God sends to try and earn enough to keep us all, and I give you the money and you *lose* it?'

Meg felt a shadow at her side. It was Sam, ready to stand by her. Had Rosie let something slip to him about the events of the morning, while they were sitting by the fire? She looked at him and gave the smallest shake of her head, trying to get the situation across to him without words, and he seemed to understand, slipping away again with a grim face.

William was looking at her in sad disappointment, and that was worse than all Delilah's fury. She waited for the storm of angry words to break, but they didn't come. Delilah sat down, seemingly defeated. 'It doesn't matter,' she said, dully. 'We'll just have to make do with what we've got.'

And that was even worse.

* * *

It was a hungry Sunday. They'd only had half as much bread as usual for their meal the night before, dipped in tea, and they all awoke ravenous. The potatoes and the onion went in the pot, but when dinnertime came there wasn't nearly enough to go round – the meal was gone in minutes, every bowl scraped and licked clean, every eye looking about to see if anyone else had left any. The piece of bacon was so small there had been no point in chopping it up; it had gone in whole and Meg had put it in William's portion, glaring and defying any of the others to argue.

Meg was just clearing the bowls, and Delilah was beginning to tell the youngsters to go out and play, when there was a loud knocking at the door.

'The rent man?' William looked even paler than usual as he spoke.

But Meg could see that Delilah was relieved, rather than afraid. 'Good. I've got it put by and I'd rather pay it over before Pa comes home so he can't get his hands on it. I hid it but I know he's been trying to find out where.' She went to one corner of the room and slid out a brick; she removed a pile of coins and then replaced it. 'All right, open the door.'

The man on the threshold was belligerent, as well he might be given how many of the court's residents were inexplicably not to be found whenever he called. 'Rent.'

Delilah stepped forward and poured the coins into his outstretched palm. 'Eight shillings.'

He counted it laboriously and then grunted his acceptance.

'Write it down.' That was William.

'Eh?'

'I said, write it down. In your book. To say that we've paid you in full for this week.'

The man looked displeased, but Jem had already sidled up to him and removed the book that was sticking out of his coat pocket. He skipped back as the man looked to wallop him.

With great ceremony and a baleful glare, the man took out a pencil, licked it and wrote laboriously. 'There.'

'Thank you.'

Meg now expected that the man would leave, but he did not. He folded his arms and rocked on his heels. 'Rent's going up.'

'What?' Delilah sounded aghast.

He grinned a nasty grin. 'So many people wanting housing these days, it's getting expensive.'

'But it's only a couple of weeks since you put it up last time!'

The man shrugged. 'Ten shillings, next Sunday.' The grin vanished abruptly. 'Or you can get out, and I could have an Irish family in here before you could say Paddy O'Hara.' He stabbed one pudgy finger at Delilah and growled. 'Ten shillings.' And then he was gone.

They didn't light the fire that evening. There was hardly any coal left at all, and there was nothing to cook over it anyway. There was nothing in the morning, either, except cold tea, for the one remaining loaf of bread had to be kept for the evening. Meg rarely went to the market on Mondays, as Sundays, being a 'day of rest', meant that nobody earned any money.

By Monday evening she felt light-headed. Everyone was hungry and irritable. The little ones were whining, Delilah looked exhausted and William was almost dead on his feet. There had not been a full day's work at the docks, and he'd only brought home half his usual pay. Jem was dozing. Sam was the only one still with a spark of energy, but when he looked at his evening meal of one sliver of bread and suggested in all seriousness that he should go out and steal some food or money, Delilah boxed his ears so hard that she sent him flying. She lost her temper, screaming at him that they might be poor, but they were honest and God-fearing and she intended it to stay that way.

Sam nursed his sore ear and looked pointedly at the meagre pile of coins on the table, but Meg pulled him away before he could come up with a retort that would just make things worse. He still looked mutinous, and she poked him in the chest. 'And what will happen to the rest of us when you're caught and transported? What will happen to Jem?' That cooled his anger, and although he muttered for a while he said nothing else out loud.

It wasn't long before Meg and all the younger ones were in bed, for what else was there to do? If they were asleep, they might at least forget how hungry they were.

Meg lay awake long after the others, listening to snatches of William and Delilah's conversation. Pa hadn't come home at all yet, which was a relief, so they could openly move the coins around the table. 'But with the rent going up . . . need to put more aside . . .

coals . . . but we must buy food tomorrow . . .' and finally, Delilah's voice through a sob. 'There just isn't enough!'

William murmured something that Meg didn't catch, but she did hear Delilah's answering statement. 'I know we dismissed the idea before, but we can't avoid it now. Someone is going to have to go to the workhouse.'

This time Meg couldn't tell herself that the word was only part of a dream.

Chapter Two

The workhouse. Meg tossed and turned, dreaming of the huge, forbidding building she had walked past once or twice.

The idea of it, she knew, was to give help to the very poor so they didn't starve; but in reality they tried to deter people from using it by making life inside so horrible that many chose to take their chances on the street. Meg was aware that families sometimes sent their children to the workhouse temporarily, during lean times, and then fetched them when they could; but although some children came back, others never emerged.

In the morning, she tried not to give any hint that she had overheard what Delilah said. But all that day, as she went to the market with the miserable allowance of coins, as she pulled and cajoled her hungry, exhausted little sisters through the streets, she had a stone in the pit of her stomach. For there seemed no question to her as to who the 'someone' to go would be. The obvious person would be Pa, who did nothing and drank what little money they had, but he would refuse, and as he was the head of the family they couldn't make him. Besides, as Meg reluctantly admitted to herself, having a grown man about the place – even a drunk and crippled one – did keep some trouble away from their door.

Neither Delilah nor William could go, of course, for they were the two wage earners. And by the same token, that counted out Sam and Jem; they might be only ten and nine, but they already earned a few coppers. Indeed, Meg had seen them only that morning when she'd passed the entrance to the railway station on Lime Street. Sam ran errands and also worked as a crossing sweeper on the wide expanse of busy road between there and the grand Adelphi Hotel, making sure that the fine ladies and gentlemen didn't have to step in the dirt and dung, for which they often tipped him. Jem, of course, wasn't allowed to do the same because he couldn't hear the oncoming traffic, but he stayed in the area so Sam could keep an eye on him and helped out an elderly street bootblack, which earned him a few farthings. And, of course, they were boys.

Boys grew into men, men earned wages, and therefore they were of more value.

So that left her, Rosie and Annie, all of whom lived in the same room with the others and ate the same food, but who brought in no money. And if anyone thought Meg was going to let them send a tot of two and a half to the workhouse, or that she would agree to Rosie having her sixth birthday there on her own, they had another think coming. No. It was Meg who was of no worth, Meg who would have to stand there while Delilah pointed this out to the rest of the family that evening.

Once she got home she pushed the girls out into the court to play – they would be warmer running around out there than they would be sitting inside the damp, fireless room – and allowed herself a very few tears. But she soon told herself firmly that that wasn't going to help, and she forced her lungs to inhale a deep breath while she composed herself. If she were to be gone tomorrow, there was plenty that needed doing first, so she set to work.

By the time everyone else – except Pa – had got home, the blankets from the mattress had been beaten outside to air them and to dislodge the bugs; several buckets of water from the outside pump had been lugged in and used to scrub the floor and the table; the fire was lit and a pot bubbled over it. The vegetable seller at the market, who had daughters of his own, had earlier looked at her wan and bruised face and the pinched features of the little ones, and had let them have some vegetables that were going over for a knockdown price; they were now flavouring the boiling potatoes, and Meg's mouth watered. Mind you, anything would have smelled delicious at this point; it was Tuesday evening, and she had eaten nothing but a couple of slices of bread since Sunday. They would all have one last hot meal together, at least.

Dinner was slightly delayed by Sam coming home with yet another black eye and a loose tooth. 'Someone laughed at our Jem,' was his only explanation.

'And was he bigger than you?' asked Meg, as she bathed the eye with water, the only thing she had. He shrugged, so she turned to Jem and repeated the question. He nodded and put his hand up in the air to indicate a height taller than any of them, and then balled his fists and mimed a fight, dancing around. He patted Sam on the back.

Sam put his finger in his mouth to wobble the loose tooth, and then pulled it out. 'Only a baby one.'

'Well, try not to do it too often.' Meg took the tooth and threw it in the fire. Who was going to mother the little ones while she was away? Delilah certainly didn't have time to do it.

Before long they were all eating, the only sound in the room that of seven hungry mouths working and seven hungry bellies being filled, and Meg looked round with what she knew would be her last contentment for some while.

After every bowl was licked clean, Delilah cleared her throat. 'Don't go just yet, everyone.'

Meg knew what she was going to say, and she was ready. She waited for the right moment. One thing she had resolved on that afternoon was that she would not endure the humiliation of being singled out by Delilah as the most disposable member of the family; she would jump before she was pushed.

And so, as soon as Delilah had pronounced the dread word 'workhouse', Meg stood up. 'I'll go.'

'What?' Delilah was taken aback.

'I said, I'll go,' repeated Meg, trying to keep her voice level. She ran through the reasoning she had been rehearsing all day, struggling to control the heaving of her chest as she spoke of wages, of earnings, of potential. Of the painful truth that, as far as the world was concerned, boys were worth more than girls.

'And so,' she concluded, 'it has to be me.'

Before she could avoid it, Delilah had folded her in an embrace. 'Oh, Meggy, you're so brave – we don't deserve you!' When she stepped back she had tears in her eyes. 'But . . . I'm afraid it's worse than that. William and I have been over the figures several times, and there's no help for it – two of us need to go.'

There was just half a moment of silence before Sam got to his feet. 'Me. I'll go.'

Both Meg and Delilah shook their heads. 'You can't,' Meg got in first. 'Like I said, after them you earn the next most money. And besides', she pointed at his swollen eye, 'how on earth would Jem manage without you?'

Delilah agreed. Then she did something she had never done before: she asked Meg's opinion as an equal. 'What do you think to taking Rosie with you?'

Meg's heart tore as she looked at her little sisters. But . . . 'Well, at least I could look after her then, couldn't I?'

Delilah nodded. 'They keep boys and girls separate, so you wouldn't see Sam or Jem anyway if one of them went, but you and Rosie would be able to stay together.'

'And Annie is too small.' Meg picked up her youngest sister, who was oblivious to what was going on except that everyone looked sad, and hugged her fiercely. 'But you must *promise* to take care of her. If I'm not here and Rosie's not here, what will she do all day?'

Delilah evidently hadn't considered that. *Perhaps I am some use, then,* thought Meg.

'I'll find someone to mind her. One of the girls in the court. Otherwise I'll take her to the laundry with me when I go to work. I'll find a way to explain it.'

Meg wasn't convinced, but what else could she do? The writing was on the wall. 'All right, then. Rosie and I will go in the morning.'

'I'll take you there, of course, and see that you're settled in before I go.'

'Fine.'

There was a horrible pause, and Meg knew she couldn't keep it all inside much longer. 'Now, if you'll excuse me . . .' She made it out the door with dignity, then fled through the court to the privy, shutting herself in and sobbing so hard she thought she would choke.

She didn't know how long it was before there was a knock on the door.

She jammed her foot against the rotting wood. 'In use! Use the other one.'

There was no reply, and the knocking came again.

'I said . . . Oh, never mind. Who is it?'

She heard a strange sound that might have been the word 'Meg' and might not, which gave away the knocker's identity. She scrubbed her eyes and lifted the latch, feeling the rush of cold air after being shut in the fetid space so long. It was Jem, as she had thought, making one of his very rare attempts to speak. He did have the capability to make sounds, but his words were so ill-formed that people – not family, but others – mocked him for trying, so he didn't bother most of the time.

He took her hand and led her over to the quiet corner near the pump. They sat down out of the chill breeze and he looked at her earnestly. 'M-Meg,' he enunciated.

'Yes, Jem.'

'Meg go.' He made a hash of the next word but Meg interpreted it as 'tomorrow'.

She wiped away more tears. 'Yes.'

'Miss you.'

'I know you will, darling, and I'll miss you too. But it can't be helped.' She tried to smile. 'You'll get more to eat.'

He made a 'pshaw' noise and then said something she couldn't make out at all.

'I'm sorry, Jem, I didn't understand.' And he was trying so hard, bless him.

'What he means is, we'll still look out for you.'

Meg looked up to see Sam standing in front of her. He observed her through one bright and one blood-shot, swollen eye. 'I know you'll be in there and we'll be out here, but we're your brothers, and we'll always be here for you.'

Meg was so overcome that she couldn't answer.

Sam offered her his hand. 'Come on now, back inside before you get too cold.'

She allowed herself to be hauled up. Sam was nearly as tall as her, despite being two and a half years younger; Meg's petite stature had always been some-thing of a family joke. As her brothers led her inside, she wondered how tall they would be by the time she saw them again.

* * *

Meg woke early the next morning. Her heart beat much faster than usual as she roused her sisters, and her hands were shaking. She hugged Annie so much and so often that the little girl squirmed, but then she stopped and put one hand on Meg's cheek. 'Meggy sad.'

Meg felt the tears spring to her eyes, but she would not allow them to fall. 'Yes, my love, I am, to be going away.' She forced a note of cheerfulness into her voice. 'But I'll see you again soon, and in the meantime Delilah will look after you. And Jem.'

Jem came to take Annie off her so she could get up, poking and tickling the toddler until she laughed, while his own solemn face looked at Meg over his sister's shoulder.

It didn't take long to get ready; after all, there was nothing to pack. They all stood about awkwardly, nobody quite sure what to say.

William broke the silence by stepping forward to hug Rosie, and then Meg. She felt herself enveloped, and then released as he put his hands on her shoulders and bent to look in her eyes. 'It's only for a few months. Just while we get some more money in. I'll work as hard as I can, every day, I promise you.'

Meg hardly had time to worry about him killing himself with overwork when the others all came crowding round, and she found herself in the middle of arms, hugs and kisses.

And then it was time. The boys departed for work; a neighbour who was going to look after Annie for the day came to collect her.

'You take Rosie outside,' Meg said to Delilah. 'Just give me one more minute.'

Delilah nodded wordlessly and went out, leaving Meg to take a last look round the room. It wasn't home, not exactly; home had been lost weeks ago. But it was where her family slept, ate and gathered together against the world outside, so it was the nearest thing to it.

Pa was awake. She didn't know how long he'd been staring at her, with his bleary yellow eyes, for it was unusual for him to stir so early – he'd been fast asleep and snoring through everything that had just happened.

A huge anger suddenly surged inside Meg. She normally tried to keep out of his way, aware that he could easily knock her flying or even snap her neck if he got violent enough, but now she strode forward as he heaved himself into a sitting position on the sofa, and stabbed a furious finger in his face. 'This is your doing.'

'What?' His unfocused eyes struggled to meet hers.

'Yours. You had your accident, that couldn't be helped, but you've done nothing since except run Ma into an early grave and drink away the money we need for food and shelter.'

He was still incoherent, but it seemed to be sinking in that his tiny daughter was speaking to him in this way, and it shocked him. 'Now, look here—'

'No, *you* look here. I'm going to the workhouse because of you – if Ma was here she'd die of the shame.

But I'll be back,' she spat, 'and let me tell you, if anything – *anything* – happens to my brothers and sisters
while I'm away, you'll live to regret it.'

She stared in disgust and fury at his disbeliev-
ing expression, and then she drew back her arm and
slapped him, as hard as she could, across his sweating,
bilious face. The *smack* echoed satisfyingly around the
bare room as she spun on her heel and walked out
with her head held high.

*   *   *

Meg's defiance lasted for about two streets. As they
made their way up the wide London Road – walking
past shops they would never go into, and then turning
when they reached the statue of some king or other
on a horse – she felt herself crumbling. From there it
was only another quarter of a mile to Brownlow Hill,
but Meg wished they really were walking to London,
so they would keep travelling for ever and never reach
their destination. But there it was, looming above the
terraced houses.

The workhouse.

By the time they reached the great building her
knees were trembling and she thought her heart would
rip itself out of her chest.

But she had to be strong, for Rosie's sake if nothing else. She grasped her little sister's hand ever more tightly. 'Don't worry. I'll be here to look after you.' And then to Delilah, 'Where do we go in?'

A porter pointed them towards a door that led into a small entrance hall smelling strongly of vinegar. There was a corridor and another door straight ahead that said 'Receiving Room'. There was a bell outside it, so they rang it and waited.

After what seemed like an eternity, during which Meg felt sure the others would be able to hear her knees knocking, a severe-looking woman opened the door, a thin cane and a bunch of keys hanging from her belt. She looked down her nose at them, saying nothing.

Delilah bobbed a brief curtsey. 'Good morning, ma'am. I've come to ask if you will take in my two sisters for a while – just temporarily.'

'Yes, that's what they all say,' replied the woman, in a sour tone. 'In here.' She stepped back to allow them to pass through the doorway.

Inside was an austere, whitewashed room containing a desk with an inkwell and various papers on it, and a hard chair behind it. Wooden drawers lined one wall, some of them open to reveal files and papers. The woman sat down, picked up a pen and dipped it in the ink. 'Names?'

'My name's Delilah Shaw, ma'am, and—'

'I'm not interested in your name, girl, unless you're applying for entry too. I need theirs.'

Delilah, for once, looked flustered. 'I beg your pardon, ma'am. This is Meg and Rosie Shaw.'

'Hmm.' The woman wrote laboriously. 'And your reason for claiming indoor relief?'

'My father worked at the docks, ma'am, a respectable hardworking man until he had an accident that crippled him and they laid him off. And my mother died the year after. My younger brother and I both work, but just at the moment we can't feed everyone.'

'Don't tell me,' said the woman, acidly, 'a horde of other children at home?'

'Other than us here, ma'am, just three brothers and another young sister.'

'Children – of – a – crippled – widower,' said the woman, scratching the words on the paper. 'But why,' she then asked, 'if your father was such a respectable man, who worked hard and was injured through no fault of his own, have you been denied outdoor relief?'

Meg remembered Delilah going to the parish overseer but he had visited, taken one look at Pa passed out in a fog of gin fumes, and turned them down. If a man wasn't deserving, his family suffered along with him.

As Meg watched Delilah open her mouth and then pause, trying to think how best to answer, the injustice got too much again. 'Because our Pa's a drunk,' Meg blurted out. 'A drunk who steals the money his children earn and doesn't care if they starve.'

Meg saw the horrified expression on her sister's face, but she didn't care. The world was so unfair that it had to be said out loud sometimes.

The woman was astonished and displeased at being spoken to in such a manner. 'If you're going to stay here, my girl, you'll learn to mind your tongue. In fact you can both wait outside while your sister goes through the paperwork, instead of standing there making my office look untidy.'

Meg found herself out in the corridor, Rosie clutching her hand as though she were drowning. She hadn't made the best start, she knew, but the injustice of being turned down for relief because Pa was useless had really rankled, and being reminded of such unfairness at the very moment when she and poor, innocent Rosie were about to be dumped here because of it had been too much. She supposed she would have to take more care to mind her words in future, especially if this unsympathetic woman was in charge.

They stood without speaking for some minutes, during which time a few people walked past. Some of them looked at the girls with varying degrees of curiosity, but nobody smiled and nobody spoke. Rosie gripped Meg's hand ever more tightly.

Eventually the door opened and Delilah came out.

'Say your goodbyes, then,' said the woman briskly from behind her.

Delilah crouched so she could hug Rosie. 'Goodbye, darling. It won't be for long, and Meg will be here to look after you.'

Rosie had tears running down her cheeks, and she grasped a handful of her sister's skirt. 'Don't go, Lilah.'

Delilah kissed the top of her head and gently disentangled the little fist before turning to Meg. 'I promise – I *promise* – that I'll come and get you in the spring. Look after Rosie until then.'

Meg's throat hurt so much she could barely get the words out. 'I will. And you promise me to look after little Annie, you hear? She likes her hair brushed, and—'

'How touching,' interrupted the woman, without a shred of compassion in her voice. 'But I don't have all day.'

One more kiss, one more fierce embrace, and Delilah was gone. Meg took Rosie's hand and straightened her shoulders.

The woman sniffed. 'That's better. Back inside now.'

Once they were standing in front of the desk again, she began. 'Now, I'm Mrs Leech, the matron in charge of the girls here, and you will obey my every instruction at all times, is that clear?'

'Yes, ma'am.'

'None of your impudent outbursts like we just had, not if you know what's good for you.'

'No, ma'am.'

'Good. Now, as to where to put you. How old is she?'

Meg squeezed Rosie's hand harder. 'She'll be six next week, ma'am.'

The sound of the pen scratching on the paper. 'And you? What are you, about ten?'

It was a mistake that people often made, due to her height. 'No, ma'am, I've just turned thirteen.'

Mrs Leech stopped writing and looked up in surprise. 'Thirteen? Oh dear, that will never do.'

Meg felt a jolt of shock. Was she about to be turned away? But she would never leave Rosie here on her own. Whatever they had to face, they would do it together. If she were turned away, they would both run out, they would run after Delilah, they would go home, back to the family, everyone would see that it had all been a terrible mistake . . .

She was almost in motion when Mrs Leech spoke again. 'I mean, you can't go in with the younger girls. We have five units for children here: one for infants of two years and under, of both sexes, and then four divided into boys and girls, under-tens and over-tens. Your sister will go with the younger ones; they have lighter work duties and some schooling. But you're far too old for that – you'll go with the older girls who are being trained for domestic service.'

Meg gripped Rosie's hand so tightly that her sister winced. 'But we need to stay together, ma'am.'

Mrs Leech put down the pen. 'Are you', she said, in a dangerously level tone, her eyes boring into Meg's, 'daring to contradict me?'

Meg could feel that she was shaking, but she stared at the woman and made no reply.

'So, it's like that, is it?' Mrs Leech rang a small bell that sat on her desk. 'You will go to your different units, and you may see your sister for two hours a week on a Sunday afternoon.' She took on a dismissive tone. 'That will be all.'

Footsteps sounded outside.

'But please . . .' Meg was desperate enough to beg. 'Please, ma'am . . .'

The door opened.

Rosie had understood what was being said, and was now looking up at Meg with absolute terror in her eyes. 'Meggy – Meggy, don't let them take me away!' There was panic in her voice.

'Separate them,' Mrs Leech instructed the two hefty-looking women who had entered. She threw Meg a look of pure malice. 'Put them both through the entry procedure, then take that one to the younger girls' unit and bring the other back to me.'

Meg felt herself being pulled away from Rosie, and she gripped as hard as she could, but she could feel her hand slipping. 'No!'

But it was no use. Just like Pa with the coins, she was helpless against a strong adult prising her fingers apart. She felt the last, final touch of Rosie's hand and then there was a sudden lurch as she was jerked back. Everything was blurry; she couldn't see properly through the hot saltiness filling her eyes. She was shouting, but she didn't know what; she struggled against the constraining arms.

Then she was dragged bodily out of the room, the sound of her little sister's screams ringing in her ears.

Chapter Three

Mrs Leech drummed her fingers on the desk, considering how to proceed. The younger girl was of no consequence, at least not for now – she could safely be put away and forgotten until she was older, if she made it that far. The elder, though . . . she looked like she was going to be trouble, answering back like that with her bold glare and her sharp eyes. Well, they would soon see about that.

The matron drew out a handwritten list from a drawer of her desk and scanned it. Where did she have a space? What would be the hardest, most exhausting labour for such a small girl, and how could Mrs Leech profit from that? Business was business, after all.

She ran her finger down the list and stopped at a name, tapping it. Yes. She would swap them over during the middle of this very day, seamlessly. Working in the kitchen was one of the hardest physical jobs for female inmates. The girl's tiny frame would hardly be up to it, and it would wear her out, perhaps take some of the impudence out of her. That girl – what was her name again? – needed to learn some hard lessons, and Mrs Leech would very much enjoy teaching them.

* * *

As soon as they were out of the room, Meg stopped struggling. There was no point: better to save her energy for the battles she could win.

The woman had been half dragging, half carrying her, but now Meg found her feet on the floor and only a rough hand holding her arm as they made their way at a brisk pace down a corridor.

'Where are we going?' she asked, the only answer to which was, 'In here.' The woman pushed open a door.

It turned out to be a bathhouse, a number of tin tubs lined up with flimsy partitions in between them. To one side of the room were full buckets of water; the woman picked one up and poured the contents into the nearest tub.

'Well, don't just stand there idling! We need five for a bath, so get to it.'

The buckets were heavy, but Meg was used to lugging water from the pump in the court, so it didn't take her long to go backwards and forwards four times.

'Leave the empties there,' said the woman, 'and the girl will come later and fill them up again. You get undressed and get in.'

Meg looked at her doubtfully, and then at the still-open door that led to the corridor.

'Oh, shy, are we?' Then she clicked her tongue and went on with a hint of more sympathy. 'Not to worry, lass – it's nothing I haven't seen before, and no men come in here.' She pushed the door shut.

Meg took off her boots and placed them neatly side by side. Then she undressed, folding each garment carefully before, red-faced, she took off her shift and stepped into the water. It was cold, but at least not icy; her shivering was more from the embarrassment than the temperature.

'Good girl,' said the woman. 'Now, are you going to be sensible and wash yourself without a fuss, or do I have to come and do it for you?'

Meg picked up the hard bar of soap and the cloth and began to wash herself.

'Your hair, too,' came the instruction, 'and then I've to check it for nits. If you've got any then I'll have to shave your head.'

Thank goodness, that was not a problem Meg had encountered any time recently, but she made sure to soap and rinse her hair as thoroughly as she could. Then she stood to get out and the woman passed her a cloth to dry herself.

Meg thought she had better start understanding how things worked. 'Do you work here, then?' she asked as she rubbed her hair.

'No, luvvy, I'm an inmate, like you. Some of us are called pauper assistants, and we get extra food and privileges for helping to keep things running.'

'And is my sister having a bath too? Will she come in here?'

'No, the kiddies have their own baths, and she'll be taken there. But yes, she'll be washed and checked over, and given her uniform. Yours is there.' She pointed. 'Take one thing off each pile.'

There was a table in the furthest corner of the room, away from the water, and Meg went to it with the towel wrapped round her, to put on a pair of drawers, a shift, a heavier dress made of striped cotton, an apron and a pair of thick stockings. A pile of boots lay on the floor and she tried on several before she found a pair that almost fitted.

'Good. That's it for now, but you get an extra petticoat and a shawl in the winter.'

'What about my own clothes?'

'They'll get disinfected and put away, and you'll get them back when you leave.'

Meg tried to hold on to that thought. Yes, she would leave one day. This was only temporary and she had to get through it. She *would* get through it.

The woman examined and then began to brush Meg's hair. She wasn't exactly gentle, but she wasn't being rough just for the sake of it, and Meg began to feel just a tiny bit calmer.

Her hair tucked up inside a cap that she'd taken from the final pile on the table, Meg squared her shoulders. 'What now?'

'Now you see the medical officer, and then back to Mrs Leech.' The woman paused, then bent so that she was looking Meg in the eye. 'You're about the same age as my youngest girl would be, so I'll give you some advice. Don't cheek Mrs Leech, don't even look like you're going to talk back. Just do exactly what she says.'

'Yes, ma'am.'

The woman laughed. 'Yes, just like that. But there's no need to call me ma'am, bless you. My name's Lizzie.'

They left the bathroom and entered the corridor, Meg walking so demurely this time that Lizzie didn't feel the need to hold her arm. 'Is she in here, too?'

'Who?'

'Your daughter. The one who's the same age as me.'

'No, luvvy. She's dead, same as all my other chicks. Her older sister Eliza was the last one to go; she died here in the workhouse a couple of years ago.' There was silence for a few moments as they walked, and then Lizzie let out a sigh.

Meg felt sad, but she didn't want to ask any more. She had enough to worry about on her own account, she thought, as she was ushered into another anonymous room.

After a brief examination from a man in a scratchy suit, who checked her temperature, looked at her teeth and then at her arms and legs for any signs of skin disease, Meg found herself following Lizzie back the way they had come until the door of the Receiving Room faced her again.

'Remember what I said,' said Lizzie, ringing the bell. And then she was gone and Meg faced the door alone.

*   *   *

I will stay calm, thought Meg to herself as Mrs Leech's sour face confronted her. *For Rosie's sake as well as my own. Whatever she says.*

'Now,' said Mrs Leech, 'as to where we will put you.' She rustled some papers, importantly. 'Some girls your age, of course, are sent to the nursery or the younger children's wards, to help look after them.'

Meg's heart beat faster with hope. Maybe—

'But you won't be doing that,' continued the matron, smoothly and with what Meg felt sure was deliberate spite. 'You'll be working in the kitchens, which will be good practice for when you get sent out later into domestic service.'

Meg wanted to answer that she wasn't going to be here long enough for that to happen, but she managed to keep to her resolution and hold her tongue. Besides, as it happened, the kitchen would have been her own next choice after the nursery – she enjoyed cooking, and it was vastly preferable to being in a laundry, or doing the endless sewing that could turn you blind, or cleaning up after the old and sick. She had already learned enough about Mrs Leech to know that it would be a very bad idea to say that out loud, so she kept her face neutral, even managing to throw in a hint of disappointment as she answered, 'Yes, ma'am.'

'What, no cheek? No talking back?' goaded the matron. 'My, we have changed our tune.'

Meg stared straight ahead and made no reply. *Keep thinking about Rosie,* she told herself, *and how much better it will be for her if her sister doesn't get a name as a troublemaker.*

Mrs Leech made a noise that was part sigh, part annoyance. 'Very well. I'll take you to the kitchen myself, since I have business there.' She stood and strode out of the room, leaving Meg to hurry after her.

Meg tried to keep a track of where they were going as she scurried to keep up, but the place was huge and she was soon lost. They must be approaching the kitchen, however; she could smell food being cooked. Her mouth watered.

Mrs Leech swept into a huge room that was a bustle of activity, full of women tending pots and fires and racks, all wearing the same uniform as Meg. The matron beckoned one of them over. 'Find Ellen Tate and bring her to me. This new girl will take her place.' Then she spoke to Meg. 'Go with her and do as you're told.'

Meg curtseyed, still keeping her stony expression, and followed the kitchen worker. She wondered who Ellen Tate was, and where she was being moved to, but that was not her concern. She was taken to the one woman in the room not wearing the workhouse uniform, who looked her up and down.

'Seriously?' was her first word. 'Why have they sent me a child? How old are you, girl?'

Meg drew herself up to her full height. 'Thirteen, ma'am.'

'And I'm expected to believe that, am I?' Meg made no reply, but none was needed as the woman gestured impatiently. 'Very well, then – I suppose I'll have to make the best of what I've got. Someone will show you what to do in here later, but dinner is nearly ready anyway, so you can start by going out to lay out the spoons and cups.' She pointed to a door, through which Meg could see a large hall containing many long tables.

Several other girls were taking spoons and enamel mugs from a large basket and placing them one by one on the tables. Some of them looked up at her, with varying degrees of curiosity, as she entered, but nobody said anything. She went to the basket, picked up as many as her hands would hold at once and started to lay them on the tables, watching the others to see how far apart they should be spaced. The tables were of an odd design, very thin; benches were not placed around them on both sides, but rather in rows all facing forward. 'So we can't speak to each other at meals,' whispered one girl under her breath as she passed, seeing Meg's confusion.

It took some while for everything to be ready. The room was enormous: the number of places laid was far more than Meg could count, but she reckoned it must be many hundreds. So many poor mouths to feed, so many souls who had lost enough hope to have entered the workhouse.

But one of them, surely, would be Rosie? As she returned to the kitchen to help carry in baskets of bread, as she watched a huge tureen being wheeled in on a trolley, as she saw the doors at the other end of the hall open to admit the inmates, and as she took a bowl and shuffled forward in the queue, Meg looked around her. But she looked in vain. She did see a file of small girls enter, but they were right on the other side of the hall, with taller adults in between, and all she could see as she craned her neck was the top of dozens of identical white caps.

Meg's turn to be served arrived; she held out her bowl to see a ladleful of indeterminate liquid splashed into it, and she was handed a piece of bread. Then she followed the girl in front to take a place sitting at one of the long tables. She was about to pick up her spoon and start eating when she noticed that nobody else was doing so, so she waited. Better to familiarise herself with the rules.

Once everyone had food in front of them, watching it go cold as they looked on it with hungry eyes, several people entered to stand by a separate table at the top of the room. One of them was Mrs Leech, and one was the medical officer who had examined Meg.

A tall, stern-looking man in a suit with a starched collar and tie placed himself by the central chair. At his arrival everyone in the room except Meg – and maybe Rosie as well, if only she could see her – stood up. Meg hastily followed suit.

The man gabbled his way through a grace, thanking the Almighty for the generous bounty they were all about to enjoy, and after the massed inmates had replied, 'Amen,' they sat down again and were finally allowed to start their meal.

It was probably meant to be some kind of lobscouse, which, back in her old life, Meg or her mother would have produced as a thick stew of potatoes, onions and whatever other vegetables were in season, flavoured with chunks of salt beef and mutton. The bowl in front of her, however, was almost entirely greasy warm water, with a few bits of unidentifiable over-boiled . . . cabbage? and maybe beans? and some lumps of gristle that might once have come from an animal. Ma would have scorned to dish up anything like this, but it was more than Meg had eaten at home for a while, and she was ravenous. She scooped it up, soaking up the excess water with her bread and then using the last crust to wipe around the bowl. All around her, other girls were doing the same, putting their spoons down when they had finished and staring straight ahead of them in silence. Meg was still hungry when she had finished, but she told herself to be grateful – after all, she had eaten nothing at noon for weeks except on Sundays.

Once those at the top table had finished their own meal – which Meg couldn't help noticing was very different from their own – they stood. This was the signal for everyone else to do likewise. The inmates began to file out, except for the kitchen workers, so Meg assumed she would need to stay. She copied the others in picking up a stack of bowls, and then followed them through and around the cooking area to a back room containing a number of large sinks.

She hesitated, having no idea what to do next, but a figure standing still amid such bustle was bound to be noticed. 'You – new girl!' came a voice. 'Get one of those kettles off the fire and pour it in there.'

Meg looked around and saw that several enormous kettles were hanging over a fire. She approached. They were very hot – how was she supposed to pick one up? There didn't seem to be a cloth or anything nearby to wrap round the handle. But she needed to do something, so she bunched up her apron and used it to protect her hands as she reached over the flames. She was so taken aback by the weight that she nearly slipped into the fire, and only narrowly avoided spilling the boiling water all over herself, but she managed to regain her balance and staggered over to the sink that had been indicated, which was half full of cold water.

Lifting the weighty kettle up high enough to pour it into the sink was something of an issue, and Meg was glad when rough hands clasped on top of her own and hefted it. 'Honestly,' said a voice, 'what are they doing sending a little tot like you to work in here?'

Meg stepped back and unwound her apron. It now had a black mark on it from where the soot-stained kettle had rubbed against it.

'And you'll catch it for that, too,' continued the voice.

Meg looked up into the red face of the woman who had spoken. 'Well,' she replied, finally unable *not* to stand up for herself, 'I couldn't touch it with my bare hands, could I? What else was I supposed to do?'

'There's a stack of cloths behind there,' said the woman, pointing to a table Meg couldn't possibly have noticed. 'Use one of them next time.'

'I will, now I know they're there,' she replied, tartly.

'What's going on here?' The head cook, the one not wearing a uniform, had appeared. 'Stop gossiping and get to work.'

Meg couldn't help it. 'I will, ma'am, and gladly. But I can't work properly unless someone tells me what my duties are and shows me the tools to do it.'

'Why, of all the cheek—' began the cook, as the other woman stifled a snigger. She took Meg by the shoulders and propelled her over to a double sink with a rack next to it, her fingers digging in uncomfortably. 'These are dirty bowls,' she said, with heavy sarcasm. 'Two sinks: soda in the first one to wash, vinegar in the second to rinse, then stack them there. Is that clear enough for you?'

'Yes, ma'am, thank you, ma'am,' replied Meg, just about managing to keep her tone on the right side of respectful.

The cook harrumphed and left, and Meg rolled up her sleeves.

'Oh, it does me good to see someone talk to her like that,' said the other woman, cheerfully. 'You keep sticking up for yourself, girl.'

Meg picked up the first bowl and looked her in the eye. 'My name is Meg.'

'And I'm Jen,' said the other, smiling to reveal a mouth full of rotten teeth and gaps. She gave Meg a hearty slap on the back. 'You keep it up, Meg. Now, you wash, and I'll fetch more hot water. It'll be quicker that way round. And we'll see if we can do something about that apron afterwards.'

There were four sets of sinks in the room, each with a washer and a water carrier, but, as Jen informed

Meg, there were over a thousand inmates in the work-house, which still meant an awful lot of washing up before they even started on the pots and utensils that had been used for the actual cooking. By the time she had scrubbed out and scoured the last pan Meg was exhausted, and her hands were raw and red from the hot water and the abrasive soda.

Finally the last item was on the drying rack. Meg stepped away from the sink and wearily pushed back some stray hair that had escaped from her cap. 'What now?'

Jen gave her a look of sympathy. 'Now we start all over again to prepare the supper, and heat more water ready to do all the same washing again afterwards.'

*   *   *

It was a long, long, afternoon and evening. By the time the last of the washing-up was done and the kitchen tables and floors had been scrubbed clean ready for the morning Meg was drooping from exhaustion. Once the cook had declared herself satisfied the kitchen workers separated, the older women going off one way and the girls trooping up to their designated dormitories under the supervision of a group of what Meg assumed were more pauper assistants, like Lizzie.

Meg was shown to a long room with bedsteads lined up along both sides. By now it was dark, the only light coming from a single candle at each end of the room and the faint glow of the moon through the windows set high up in one wall. Each bed had a thin mattress and was neatly made up with blankets, tightly tucked, and a pillow at each end; this latter was soon explained when Meg saw two girls preparing to get in each bed. Well, that was no hardship – Meg had shared with her sisters all her life, and lately with Sam and Jem as well.

There was already a girl sitting on the mattress to which Meg was pointed, unaware of her at first as she was concentrating on removing her boots and stockings. Then she looked up, and smiled so broadly that Meg almost smiled back.

'Hello. I've had this to myself for a week so I thought I'd get someone new soon. Have you just arrived?'

'Yes. I mean, I came in this morning.' Had it really only been that morning that she had woken up at home, on the mattress with all the others? Only this morning that she had said goodbye to them all? It felt like weeks ago already.

Meg sat, or rather collapsed, down on to the bed and began to unlace her boots. They were badly made and uncomfortable, and she had aching feet and the beginnings of blisters, which was not helping.

'I'm Sally,' said her new companion, brightly, 'and I'm eleven.'

Meg looked at her in surprise. In complete contrast to herself, Sally was big for her age – she would certainly be taller than Meg if they stood up, which Meg was too tired and uninterested to do. A friendly face, though, was not to be taken for granted, so she should make an effort. 'Have you been in here long?'

There was a pause as Sally had her dress half over her head, but when it was off she replied cheerfully, 'Oh, all my life. I was born here.'

Meg was shocked into something like interest. 'What, really? You've never lived anywhere else?'

'No,' said Sally, standing up in her shift. 'Except in the nursery and then the little girls' section, of course. Come on, we have to go and use the privy and wash-room before we get into bed.'

Meg followed her, her mind churning at the thought that somebody might have spent her entire life confined within these austere walls. Never to have walked in the crowded streets or past the occasional trees and grass, or to have looked in the shops. 'So – you've really never been outside? Never?'

'We used to have to go out on Sundays, to go to church,' continued Sally, hugging herself as they stood barefoot and shivering in a queue in a cold passageway. 'But then they built the chapel inside, so we didn't need to. So I haven't been out since then. We do actually go outside, once a day, in the yard, though.'

Meg was still almost overwhelmed by the idea, but then another thought struck her. 'You used to be in the unit for younger girls? What was it like?'

Sally frowned. 'What do you mean, what was it like?'

'I mean, did it look like this? Beds like this? What did you do there? Were there chores, or did you go to school? What did you eat? Were people kind?'

'Oh, I see.' She frowned. 'The beds looked like ours, but smaller. I shared with lots of different girls. And we went to bed earlier. There was a school where we had to sit and learn to read and all that, but I wasn't very good at it, 'cos I'm stupid and good for nothing.'

Meg was struck by Sally's matter-of-fact tone. 'Who told you that?'

Sally shrugged. 'Everyone. And it's true: I couldn't read 'cos the words kept jumping around, and I couldn't write 'cos I was always trying to hold the pen in the wrong hand. The teacher would crack her ruler down over my knuckles till they fair swole up.' In the darkness of the passageway she held up her left hand and examined the back of it curiously, as though she might be able to see the marks on it still. 'But why do you want to know all this? You won't go there, you're too old.'

'My little sister is there. We came in together and I thought I'd be able to look after her, but they separated us.' Meg could hardly swallow the sob that came unbidden to her throat.

Sally, however, seemed delighted, and she clapped. 'A sister! Oh, I'd love to have a sister. I never had anyone. Was it always the two of you?'

Meg stumbled over her answer, thinking of the losses and the tragedies that had befallen her family. She didn't want to go into all that, not with a stranger, no matter how friendly she was. So she settled on what was currently near enough the truth. 'I've got three sisters and three brothers.'

Sally was almost in raptures, but their turn had come to go through and out to the earth closets, and then back in to a line of water-filled basins. Many other girls had used them already, and the water wasn't exactly clean, but with the stern eyes of various adult women on her Meg splashed some on her face. She was really shivering by now. 'Do we do this every night?'

'What, use the privy and wash? Of course.'

'No, I mean – do all this after we've got undressed. Wouldn't it be better, and warmer, to do it before, while we've still got our dresses and shoes on?'

Sally's forehead creased with the effort of considering the question as they made their way back to the dormitory. 'I don't know,' she said, at last. 'That's just the way we do it. It's not too bad in the summer.'

Please God, thought Meg, *Rosie and I will be gone long before the summer.*

'Anyway,' continued Sally, 'if you need to go in the night you don't have to go out there again – there's chamber pots at each end of the dormitory.' Meg could just about make out, in the dim light, that Sally wrinkled her nose. 'It's one of my jobs to empty them out in the mornings.'

They reached the bed and got into it, one at each end. All round them other girls were doing the same, burrowing under the blankets to try to warm their freezing bodies.

All the adult supervisors now left, except one. She stalked down the centre of the room to blow out the candle at the far end, then back to the door to pick up the other. 'Lights out, no talking, no moving.' Then she was gone.

There were a few minutes of complete silence in the darkness, while Meg thought that everyone was obeying the instruction. She was so tired that she was nearly asleep already, so maybe the others were the same. But then a very quiet whispering started.

She felt the mattress moving; Sally was crawling up to her end so their heads were on the same pillow. 'Can't stay like this for long, 'cos if I fall asleep and we're found at the same end it's the cane. But I wanted to say, I'm glad you're here, and tomorrow I want to hear all about your brothers and sisters.' She put her arm around Meg.

After a few minutes of lying rigidly still, waiting for Sally to move away again, Meg could feel the arm getting heavier. She poked the other girl. 'Sally, go back before you fall asleep.'

With a sleepy mumble, Sally went back to her own end, and Meg could feel their feet touching. She drew her legs up so she was curled into a ball. What was Rosie doing just now? She would be asleep, surely. But what if she was lying awake, crying, because Meg wasn't there for her?

Meg knew it wasn't a good idea to torture herself with such thoughts, for what good would they do? In all likelihood Rosie was fast asleep, full of the milk porridge that had been prepared in the kitchen for the little ones' suppers. And so, probably, was Annie, on the mattress at home with only Sam and Jem for company, no sisters on either side of her to keep her warm. But, thought Meg, in her confused half-asleep state, Annie wouldn't have had any milk porridge, so was it better for Rosie to be in here? But anyway, Meg would see her on Sunday . . . when was that? Today was . . .

She was halfway through the thought when she fell into a deep sleep.

Chapter Four

Meg was awoken the next morning by a loud ringing sound. Panicked, she sat bolt upright before realising where she was; when it all came back to her, her heart sank. But there was no time to mope. All the girls were hurrying out of bed, and Meg followed.

They washed, dressed and made the beds, but instead of then going out to their work, they all lined up down the middle of the room. Meg took her place, about to ask why, but the answer became evident when Mrs Leech entered the room.

There was an immediate sense of tension and fear – Meg could feel it, even though nobody spoke. Mrs Leech made her way down the line, inspecting both the beds and the girls, sometimes barking at one or another to hold her hands out to show clean nails, or to stand up straight.

She continued, with all eyes upon her, and then stopped; the sound of a little sigh from all around the room was quickly stifled. The girl in front of her, one of the half-dozen with dark skin, had a strand of her black, frizzy hair poking out from under her cap.

Mrs Leech pointed at it. 'I've told you about that before. Hand.'

The girl held out a trembling hand, palm upwards, and screwed up her face in anticipation.

Mrs Leech did not hurry to take up the cane that hung from her belt; once she had it in her hand she gave it a couple of experimental swishes through the air. Then she brought it down, hard, on the girl's palm.

Almost everyone in the room gasped or winced in sympathy as the girl bit her lip in an effort not to cry out or let her tears fall. Instead she bobbed a curtsey and said, 'Thank you, Mrs Leech.' Once the matron had moved on, she tucked her hand under her arm and squirmed.

A second girl was treated similarly for having dirty nails, and then Mrs Leech came to Meg. She spent a moment looking her up and down, and then, with a smile, noted the dirty apron. Jen had tried to help Meg clean the worst of the soot off it the previous evening, but inevitably it was still smeared.

Mrs Leech made a tutting noise. 'What have we here? One day, you've been here, and look at the filthy raga-muffin you've become again already. Anyone would think you'd been out on the streets. Hand.'

Meg forced herself to look Mrs Leech in the eye rather than cowering.

The cane whistled down and smacked into her hand. The pain was incredible, almost unbearable; Meg thought she knew about pain from having been hit by Pa so often, but this was different, a whip-sharp cut into the sensitive palm of her hand that made her want to hop about and shriek until it subsided.

And then Mrs Leech brought the cane down again.

This time Meg couldn't stop the tears from flow-ing. She could hardly think past the agony, but she was damned if she was going to give the matron the satisfaction of hearing her whimper. She looked up venomously and met her eye.

'What – do – you – say?' asked Mrs Leech.

Meg stared back defiantly without replying.

'Very well. Hold out your other hand.'

There was a gasp from around the room, one that wasn't suppressed this time.

Shaking with the effort of remaining still, Meg raised her other hand. She was ready for it this time, but the shock and the pain were just as great as the thin cane whipped down and bit into her palm.

'Meg, please, say it!' Next to her, Sally had let the words escape her before she could stop them.

Mrs Leech pounced. 'How dare you, girl! How dare you interrupt?' She raised the cane even higher. 'Your hand, now.'

'I'm sorry!' Meg burst out, horrified to think that Sally, who had been kind and who was already starting to cry, might be punished because *she* had been stubborn. 'I beg your pardon, Mrs Leech.'

The matron paused with her cane still in the air.

'And I thank you for teaching me a lesson, ma'am,' Meg continued, hurriedly. She looked down at the floor in what she hoped was a demure attitude.

'I'm glad to hear it,' said Mrs Leech, before smacking the cane down on to Sally's outstretched palm anyway and walking out.

There were tears in the dormitory, but there was also kindness. Once the matron had left, her assistants made no move to stop the girls as they crowded round to sympathise with those who had been hurt. Meg looked at her hands. The right one had a thin, angry red weal raised on it, while the left had two such, bleeding where they crossed over each other. Both hands were shaking and Meg didn't think the throbbing sting was going to go away any time soon. But that wasn't her main concern.

She turned to Sally. 'I'm sorry.'

Sally looked confused. 'For what?'

'That she hit you because of me.'

Sally blew on her palm and then tucked it in her armpit. 'Well, she often hits me. I don't like it . . .' Her voice wobbled, and a fresh tear ran down her cheek, 'but it's just one of those things.'

Meg felt so sorry for her that she did something she could never have imagined: she hugged Sally, someone she had known less than twenty-four hours.

'Now, then, that's enough. Go on with you or you'll all be late.' One of the assistants stepped forward to shoo them all out the door. Meg obeyed, strengthened for what lay ahead by the solidarity of the girls around her.

* * *

As the morning wore on, Meg berated herself for her stupidity. What had she told herself only yesterday? *Save your energy for the battles you can win.* And now here she was with agonising, stinging hands, and all because she'd been needlessly stubborn. What would it have cost her, really, to lower her eyes and say 'thank you' to Mrs Leech, like the others had done?

Breakfast – a lumpy oatmeal made with milk that smelled like it was on the turn – had not taken long to prepare, for the oats had been left soaking overnight in readiness. But it was when Meg started on the washing up, her hands forced into the hot water with the soda and the vinegar, that the pain got worse and she told herself not to be so foolish again. How was she going to keep well enough to do whatever she could for Rosie if this happened again? And what if she were to be punished for insubordination by being denied her Sunday visit? *Idiot,* she said to herself, as the endless pile of dishes slowly grew smaller.

In the middle of the morning a bell rang. Meg was confused, but Jen explained that it was time for compulsory outdoor exercise. 'I'd rather stay in here where it's warm, to be honest, but there's no point arguing.'

'But what about the dinner?' There were pots bubbling and racks of potatoes steaming.

'We go out half at a time. Come on, I'll show you where to go.'

Meg followed her through a maze of hallways and then out into a yard, where a number of women and older girls were despondently and silently walking around the edge. The cold struck Meg after the heat of the kitchen, but it was good to get a bit of air on to her face. She hugged her arms around herself as she joined the parade.

There was no hope of seeing anything outside; the brick walls were ten feet high at least, with broken glass set in the top. 'Do they think we're going to try and escape?' she asked Jen, under her breath.

Jen smiled her gap-toothed grin. 'No, it's so the men can't get in – their yard is on the other side.' She chuckled. 'Wouldn't mind seeing a man, myself, but most of the girls are happier without them. 'Cept those with husbands or brothers, of course.'

Meg could hear male voices coming from over the wall, some raised in ribald comments or jokes at the women – some of which received replies from this side that made Meg blush – but others calling out names, seeking news.

Under cover of the shouting, which various pauper assistants were attempting to quell, Meg risked another question. 'Are we anywhere near where the smaller children exercise?'

'No, they're right over the other side, near the chapel, boys' playground on one side and the girls' on the other.' Jen attempted to point, but the featureless yard with its high wall was disorientating. 'Difficult to know which way is which in here, so I don't know where they are exactly from here, but you wouldn't be able to see or hear them.'

Meg tramped on in silence. Another bell was heard and the women started to shuffle back inside. Instead of following, though, she paused. She couldn't see out of the yard, but she could look up, and although it was an overcast morning she could make out where the sun was. Now, if it was before noon then the sun would be in the east, so which way was home from here? If she could even just face it for a few moments . . . and which home was she thinking of, anyway? The old one, down on Brick Street near the docks, would have been to the west or south-west, wouldn't it? But that's not where her family were now – they were in the court, a move of a couple of miles north. But which way was north?

She'd got herself all turned around, dizzied again by the high walls, and it was no good. She'd just have to keep thinking about them, even if she couldn't face the right way. Time to go in.

To her surprise, Meg found herself alone in the yard. She had wasted more minutes than she had realised trying to work out which way was which, and somehow the assistants must have overlooked her as they ushered everyone back inside.

She passed through the door and looked left and right, but the hallway was empty. She would be in trouble if she didn't get back to the kitchen straight away – and she certainly didn't need any more physical punishment this morning, nor the threat that she might not get her Sunday visit – but where was it?

She concentrated. Earlier they had definitely turned right to enter the yard, so she needed to go left to head back the same way. Yes. She'd noticed that scratch in the wall as she'd passed it, so she must be correct now.

But when she got to another turning she couldn't remember at all. There was no point in trying to listen out for kitchen noises, either; it had been quite a walk so she would still be nowhere near it yet. She guessed, but soon realised she'd gone wrong. The corridor ended in a door that led outside to a path that snaked between the high walls of different workhouse buildings. Should she go back, or forward? She was bound to be missed when the others got back to the kitchen. Feeling slightly panicky now, she scurried out and across the path and into another door on the other side. Why did everything here look the same? Why did it all smell the same? And why wasn't there anyone to ask?

Finally she heard the sound of voices, and she hurried towards them, hoping she might be able to apologise profusely enough to whomever she met and be returned to the kitchen unpunished.

But then she stopped dead, recognising where she was. She was almost outside the Receiving Room, and one of the voices she could hear was that of Mrs Leech.

Meg flattened herself against the wall in terror, her heart and mind racing as she considered what to do. Could she go back? But she'd only get lost again, and would definitely then be going in the wrong direction: the vague hint of food being cooked met her nostrils, and it was coming from in front of her. But in order to follow it she would have to pass the open Receiving Room door.

In either case she couldn't stand here all day, for eventually the interview would come to an end and Mrs Leech would leave the room. The smell of cooking – something with leek or onion in it – was getting stronger, so she decided she had to take the chance, and sidled nearer the door.

There was evidently someone else in the room with the matron. A woman's voice, but rasping and low so that Meg couldn't make out any actual words. Someone seeking admittance, no doubt.

Mrs Leech's voice suddenly rose, and Meg froze. 'You owe me ten shillings from yesterday before you get any more.'

A murmured reply.

'Yes, yes, I can. But the arrangement was always that you pay for each one before you get the next.'

That was very strange. Perhaps it wasn't someone trying to get in, but some kind of supplier or dealer who bought the goods that the workhouse inmates made – some of the women were set to sewing, and some of the men and boys to making boots, as she'd overheard in a conversation in the kitchen that morning. Which, incidentally, explained why her own were so shoddy – they must keep the ones that weren't good enough to sell.

But anyway, the thing now was to get past the door. It wasn't wide open, so she might get past it unseen if Mrs Leech or the other woman weren't facing it directly. Attempting either to sidle past it or to run would be no good; both were likely to attract attention. Meg braced herself, held her head up and took a deep breath, then walked briskly but steadily past the door, looking straight ahead, for all the world as though it was exactly what she was supposed to be doing.

Thank her lucky stars, no shouts came after her. As soon as she thought she was far enough past the door that her footsteps wouldn't be heard, she ran.

* * *

Her luck was certainly in. The kitchen was so busy that the cook hadn't noticed her absence, and the second group of workers was now trickling back in, so Meg tagged along and was soon back near the bubbling pots over the fire. She picked up a long wooden spoon and tried to look like she'd been there all the time.

Jen wasn't fooled, but she wasn't angry, either. 'You don't want to do that too often, Meg – I can't cover for you all the time. Where have you been? Were you looking for someone over the wall?'

Meg explained that she'd got lost, and said that she'd be sure to follow Jen more closely next time. Knowing she was new, Jen accepted this without question and the subject was dropped for now.

The food they produced for the noon meal was supposedly different from yesterday's, but it was just as tasteless. Meg, however, was just as hungry so she wolfed it down. The calculations in the kitchen as to the number of inmates and the amount of food that constituted a portion seemed to be very exactly reckoned: all the girls and women around her had identical helpings, though presumably the men got more and the children less. There was just enough for everyone, no more, no less.

Meg considered this as she started on the mountain of washing-up. As Jen came over with a full kettle, she asked about it.

'Oh yes,' came the reply. 'It's not for us to worry about, but Cook has a list of how many men, women, children and old folk there are, and the size of portions for each is set down by the Board. So she adds it up and tells us how much to use. Mind your hands while I pour this in.'

Meg wondered what else she could ask. The more she knew about the workhouse the better. She'd taken Ellen's place; would someone take her place one day? When Jen came back with the next lot of water, Meg had another question ready. 'Do you know a girl called Ellen Tate?'

'Yes, she works here. Or she did, until yesterday.' Jen looked round. 'I s'pose she's been moved somewhere.'

'Is that normal?'

Jen put the kettle down for a moment. 'It doesn't happen that often, but some of the girls your age do get moved around a bit, to give 'em experience of different work before they get sent out to service.' She flexed her fingers and took up the kettle again. 'She'll have been sent to the laundry or the sewing room, probably.'

The next time she came back Jen asked Meg, 'Is she a friend of yours, then? Ellen?'

'No, I've never met her. I was just wondering, that's all, because I heard Mrs Leech mention the name yesterday.'

Meg continued to wash up. None of this was any of her business, but she had to think about something, and worrying constantly about Rosie, when she could do nothing about the situation, wasn't going to help. Better to keep her mind off it.

The afternoon wore on. The evening meal was the same as yesterday's, as it apparently was every day: a thin, watery oatmeal gruel with a piece of bread for the adults, and a slightly more substantial milk porridge for the children. Meg hoped that Rosie was eating hers up, no matter how sad or homesick she felt. If only Sunday would come, but as far as she could remember – she had already lost much of her sense of time since entering the workhouse – today was only Thursday.

When she reached the dormitory in the evening, Sally was eager to hear more about Meg's family, but Meg got in first with a question about the mysterious Ellen.

'Oh yes, I know her, she's been here a long time, like me.' Sally looked around. 'She used to sleep in here. Funny, she's not here now – I wonder where she's gone?'

As they left the dormitory to queue in the cold passageway for the privy and washroom, Sally pulled another girl into the line next to her. It was the dark-skinned girl who had been caned that morning, and Meg managed to get a tight smile out of her as they compared the marks on their hands.

'Martha, didn't you used to share your bed with Ellen?'

'Yes, until yesterday. She's not here tonight, either – do you know where she's gone?'

'No, that's what we wanted to ask you.'

Meg joined the conversation. 'If she'd been moved somewhere else for work – from the kitchen to the laundry, say – she'd still sleep here, would she?'

'Oh yes,' said Martha, hopping from one leg to the other to try to keep her feet off the freezing floor. 'So probably she's gone from the workhouse – sent out into service. She was just coming up fourteen. Funny she didn't say anything about it, though – she just went off to the kitchen yesterday morning and I haven't seen her since. I asked Lizzie about her, but she didn't know anything.'

Meg made no reply. The others fell to chatting about something else, but she couldn't help thinking. The workhouse was entirely regimented. Everything was timed to the last minute, everyone's day was scheduled, and the exact number of each type of inmate was known. Records were kept: she had herself seen Mrs Leech writing things down when she and Rosie had arrived, and there were drawers full of papers in her office.

So, thought Meg, as she slipped into bed and pulled the blanket up to her chin, *how is it possible for a girl to disappear so mysteriously and so completely?*

Chapter Five

Sunday finally came.

Meg was jumpy all the morning, fidgeting in the chapel, hoping that Mrs Leech wouldn't come up with some excuse to stop her seeing Rosie. She'd been caned again yesterday, this time for supposedly having dirty fingernails – which was about as far away from the truth as it was possible to get, given that Meg spent at least half of every day submerged up to her elbows in water.

Her hands were sore enough without the cane, red raw from the hot water and soda, her knuckles bleeding in places; all the cane had done was redistribute some of the pain from the backs of her hands to the front. This time she had been careful to act submissively and thank Mrs Leech, which had at least avoided a second and third blow, but Meg had been left fuming by the matron finding an excuse to cane Sally as well, and looking more at Meg as she did it. Meg had seethed with suppressed fury, but realised that any reaction on her part would just make things worse for poor Sally, so she had kept silent and made sure her face was as neutral as possible despite her emotions.

After Sunday's dinner – potatoes on a plate with a small piece of something that might vaguely have been classed as meat – came the two hours of leisure time that everyone looked forward to. Some of the women and girls took the opportunity to gather and gossip; others just wanted rest and sleep. But Meg, following Sally, flew through the maze of corridors and outside paths until they reached the separate building that housed the younger children.

Sally knew the way, of course, having spent many years there herself, and she was proud to be able to conduct her new friend there. She already held Meg in awe, which Meg felt alternately grateful for and irritated by, but she had little attention to spare for Sally's commentary as they ran up the flight of stairs that would bring them to the girls' day room.

To Meg's relief it was at least clean, and not too cold. Her first impression was of small wooden desks and chairs pushed back against the walls, and a sea of faces in cotton caps above identical white aprons.

Before she had even looked properly to identify Rosie, a little figure erupted from the others, cannoned into her and wrapped its arms tightly around her waist.

'Oh, Rosie!' Meg was crying properly now, unable to hold it in and letting fall the kind of big, wet tears that she hadn't allowed herself since she entered the workhouse. She kissed her sister again and again, moving over to one side of the room where they could sit down in relative privacy. She pushed two chairs together, but Rosie ignored the second one, climbing into Meg's lap as soon as she was seated.

Meg put her arms about Rosie and held her close as she snuggled in. All around the room, others were doing the same: she and Sally had hurried so quickly that they had outpaced the many other women and girls heading in the same direction, but now the mothers who were separated from their children for almost the whole week were here to enjoy their two precious hours.

There was a great deal of emotion in the room, but Meg didn't care about anyone else. As far as she was concerned, she and Rosie were the only people in the room, the only people in the world. They hugged each other tight for a while, wordlessly, and then Meg pulled back so she could see her sister's face. 'There, now. Let me look at you.'

Tears and snot were staining Rosie's face, and Meg wiped them carefully with one corner of her apron. She had been issued with clean clothes that morning – as would apparently happen every Sunday – and she didn't want to start the new week with another caning for getting it dirty. 'That's better. Now, stop crying, darling, and tell me what you've been doing since I last saw you. Have you eaten your meals? I've been cooking them for you, you know, in a great big kitchen.'

Very slowly, as the sobs subsided a little, she managed to elicit the full story. Rosie had been frightened when Meg was pulled away. She had been bathed by a rough woman who had taken away her clothes and given her these ones instead. The woman had cut her hair, which had made her cry. She had come here, where there were lots of other girls. She didn't like it. They got up early to make beds and sweep the floors before they could have anything to eat. For the rest of the morning they had to sit at desks, with slate and chalk, and learn their letters. The teacher never smiled. Then they went on a long walk to a big scary room filled with people, adults as well as children, to eat their dinner. After that they went outside for a while, then came back in to sit in rows and learn to sew. She had pricked her finger and made it bleed. They were not allowed to talk to each other. Then they had porridge, said prayers and went to bed. She missed Jem and Annie and Delilah and everybody.

Rosie finished her speech and looked up into Meg's face, and Meg felt the little clutching hands. 'Have you come to take me home?'

Meg wanted nothing more than to gather her up and walk out, and indeed for a moment the urge was so strong that she nearly did it. But wait. *Think*. During her story Rosie had spoken of breakfast, of dinner and supper. Every day. She wouldn't get that at home.

It was difficult, agonisingly difficult, but Meg knew she had to harden her heart. Rosie was sad, but Meg hoped she would get over that a little once she got used to things, and it was better than starving. She tried to explain it, but Rosie, not being particularly hungry now, could not imagine being hungry any other time, and to her the idea of being at home with her brothers and sisters outweighed everything else. And so Meg was forced to use the weapon she didn't want to mention. 'Yes, but as well as Delilah and Jem and everyone, Pa is at home. Don't you remember how scared you were of him?'

She regretted the words when she felt Rosie begin to shake, and hated herself for being such a bully. But she had made a promise at home, and she needed to stick to it. The family, as a whole, needed to get back on its feet, and that was best done if the working members could undertake their labour without worrying about having so many mouths to feed for a while. As soon as they had made some headway, they would come to collect her and Rosie. Dear William would be keeping his side of the bargain: he'd already given up his precious school and taken a job so that she and the others could be fed and housed. How, therefore, could she break her own word by leaving the workhouse less than a week after entering it, and turning up on the doorstep to derail the plans?

She would not. She was determined. She would remain here until the spring, as had been agreed, and she would make sure Rosie did the same. That latter part would be more difficult, she could see that now. The unkindness and canings she received were nothing to the feelings of cruelty she experienced as she looked into her little sister's disappointed and betrayed face, but she would be strong.

Meg swallowed her emotion and attempted a cheerful tone. She rattled on, hardly knowing what she was saying in her desire to be positive. 'Just think, if you learn your letters you'll be able to show William when we get home . . . Delilah will love to know that you can sew; remember how she does it so neatly . . . You get breakfast and supper here, as well as dinner . . . Maybe you'll make some new friends . . . You're a big girl now, six tomorrow! . . . And I can come every week and you can tell me all about it . . .'

She tailed off. Rosie had at least stopped crying. 'My birthday?'

'Yes, darling. And I haven't got anything to give you now except this,' she planted a kiss on top of Rosie's head, 'but when we go home, and everything is better, we'll have a bun from the baker's. How would that be?'

'Really? Promise?'

'Yes. One with currants in. So you think about that, and work hard on your letters and your sewing so that everyone back home will be proud of you. Can you do that for me?'

Rosie looked dubious, and Meg was about to encourage her again when she was stopped by a shadow falling over her.

She looked up to see Sally. 'Sorry, Meg, but it's time to go.' And then, 'Is this your sister, then?'

'Yes, this is Rosie. Rosie, this is my friend Sally.'

Sally glowed at being called a friend. She crouched down. 'Have you got any friends in here, Rosie?'

Rosie shook her head and then hid her face in Meg's apron.

'Well, just you wait there a minute.' Sally went away and then came back, holding by the hand a girl who was probably about eight or nine but who had the pinched, lined face of one much older. She looked like an old woman in a child's body.

'This is Peggy. It's a bit like your sister's name, isn't it?' She turned to the girl. 'Peg, remember how I used to look after you when you were little?' The girl nodded. 'Well, I want you to look out for Rosie, here. All right?'

Peggy held out her hand. 'Come on. They have to go now, but we're allowed another hour before supper. Do you want to come and play?'

Rosie still had a fistful of Meg's apron, and didn't seem inclined to let it go, but Meg knew she would have to. There was no point arguing against the rules – this was one of the unwinnable battles that it was useless to fight.

She gently disentangled Rosie's hand, and kissed it. 'Now, you go and play. During the week you eat your meals and do your lessons, and I'll be back next Sunday to see how you're getting on. And in the meantime Peggy here will look after you.' She looked at the ancient child. 'Thank you.'

Peggy seemed taken aback even by this simple acknowledgement, and she smiled, showing a glimpse of the happy little girl she could have been. 'We'll look out for her, don't you worry.' She took Rosie's hand and Meg felt her sister slide off her lap.

Rosie resisted being pulled away, just for a moment. 'You will come back, Meggy?' Her voice wobbled.

'Yes, darling. Next Sunday.' She put her hands to her sister's ear and whispered, 'And don't forget the bun we're going to have to celebrate your birthday once we leave.'

Rosie seemed a tiny bit happier as she allowed herself to be pulled away to a knot of other girls. Meg stood up. She and Sally, having been the first visitors to reach the room, were now the last to leave it, and one or two of the assistants had started to glare. She moved reluctantly towards the door, but was relieved to see, as she turned for a last look, that Rosie was joining in with whatever it was the other girls were playing.

The door shut behind them, and she sighed.

She followed Sally in silence for a while – would she ever learn her way around the place? And then, for the want of anything else to say, she asked, 'So, did you only come to show me the way, or do you go there every Sunday?'

'Most Sundays,' replied Sally. 'I haven't got anyone else to visit and nothing else to do, and it's a bit nicer in there. Besides, there's other girls like me who've been here since they were born, with no ma or sister to come and see them, so if I go then they're not quite so left out, are they?' And, after a moment's silence. 'I know what it's like not to have anyone visit you when everyone else does.'

Meg's heart was full of Rosie, but there was room in it for Sally as well, and she thought again what a sad, lonely life she must have led up until now. But there was no point getting too involved; she would only be here a few months, and Sally would have to go back to living without her once she left. Unless . . .

Sally was continuing. 'And on First Thursdays, as well.'

'What's a First Thursday?'

'Oh, didn't anyone tell you? Some folks, as well as having their family in here with 'em, have some on the outside. Well, like you, I suppose. They're allowed to come here and visit on the first Thursday of every month.'

'Really?'

'Oh yes. Your older sister will come, I 'spect.'

Meg's heart lifted. If she could keep seeing Rosie every week, and then Delilah once a month, it would keep the lifeline intact, and she could cope. She could talk to Delilah about what progress they had been making on the outside, to keep the goal of her and Rosie's release in mind.

'Nobody's ever come to see me, of course, but I'll be glad for you if you can see your sister.'

Sally sounded so mournful that, just for a moment, Meg took her hand. But their ways soon parted and, with Sally pointing her in the right direction, Meg headed back to the kitchen.

* * *

It was so difficult to judge time. Not so much the hours of the day – for those were regimented down to the last minute, and the kitchen workers in particular always knew morning from afternoon from evening – but the days of the week and the date of the month. They were already all blurring into one shapeless mass. *Think, now.* Yesterday had been Sunday, which meant that today was Monday. It was also Rosie's birthday, so that would make it the sixteenth of October. So in three days it would be Thursday, and the date would be ... and then add on in sevens until the end of the month ... but what day of the week would November start on? It was too difficult. The thing to do was to take one day at a time, and hope that each would pass swiftly enough that November, and Delilah, would be here soon.

The days did pass, and before long Meg was mostly able to tell one from the other by what they were cooking for dinner each day. The indeterminate soups, stews and lobscouse did occur quite frequently, but it was meat and potatoes on Sundays and rice pudding made with milk on Wednesdays, which gave her two fixed points, at least.

The endless washing-up continued, her hands getting more and more sore and cracked, despite Jen's assertions that they would 'soon toughen up'. Meg got into the habit of trying to distract herself from the stinging by thinking of other things. She was worried about Rosie. On her second Sunday visit up to the younger girls' day room she had arrived with hopes that Rosie might have been a little more cheerful, that she might have got more used to the routine and made some friends, but she was disappointed in all of it. Rosie was crying when she got there and spent the whole time sitting on Meg's lap and clinging to her.

The older girl, Peggy, had explained to her that she'd tried hard to cheer Rosie up, to look after her and to get her to talk to some others, but that it had proved impossible. She seemed upset and almost fearful of confessing this to Meg, as if she might be angry, and she kept her eyes on the floor most of the time she was talking.

'It's all right,' said Meg, when she'd heard it all. 'You tried your best, and I'm grateful to you.' Then she noticed Peggy's swollen red knuckles, and a foreboding struck her. 'How did you get that?' she asked, pointing.

Peggy immediately put both hands behind her back. 'I . . .'

'I'll tell you,' said Rosie's voice, somewhere from the depths of Meg's apron. She raised her head. 'She was trying to help me with my letters on the slate, 'cos I couldn't do it, and the teacher hit her hand with a ruler.'

The monstrous injustice hit Meg hard, not least because she felt responsible. Was she to cause everyone around her to be beaten? First Sally had got the cane, and now Peggy the ruler, all because they had tried to help her and her sister. An anger was building up inside her, the same way it had done when she had hit Pa, just before she came away. But she had to keep it under control, for to show it in the workhouse would just cause more trouble.

Her greatest problem was the feeling of impotence. What, practically, could she *do* to help Rosie when they were separated and only able to see each other once a week? If they'd been in the same dormitory, or even the same section of the workhouse, things would have been easier. As an interim measure she settled for teaching Rosie a little clapping game, so that she could practise and remember it while Meg wasn't there, and also maybe use it as a way to interact with the other girls.

'Like this,' she said, holding Rosie's hands up and showing her how to move them. 'But quietly, shh! So the grown-ups don't notice.' As she clapped gently, she added, 'Delilah taught me this when I was little, so now I'm teaching you. And when you're bigger, you can show Annie.'

'Really?' Rosie's interest was piqued.

'Yes, when we get home – and don't forget, that's what we'll be doing in the spring. You just have to stay here with the other girls over the winter.'

Rosie brightened as Meg showed her the clapping sequence and sang the little rhyme that went with it. When Meg had to leave, Rosie ran over to show Peggy and the other girls and Meg hoped that she'd had a positive effect – though it would be another week until she could find out.

The following day, after she had washed up the breakfast dishes and taken her outdoor exercise – being sure to keep close to the others on the way there and the way back, so as not to get lost again – the cook called her over. 'Your hands must be clean, and at your age your fingers should be quick. Sit there and shell that basket of peas.' She was about to walk away, but then she paused, and added, 'Put the peas in that bowl, and the empty pods in the other basket.'

Pleased at being given a much more pleasant job, and one that was properly explained this time, Meg sat down – the luxury! – on the low stool and made a start. She fumbled the first few, her hands cold from being outside, but as they warmed up a little she got into the swing of it and was soon racing through the pods. The bowl of fresh, sweet-smelling green peas was enticing, and she imagined how delicious they would taste. But, of course, they were not for the inmates; they were for the meal at the top table. It was pea soup today for everyone else, but theirs was made with the sacks of dried split peas that had been left soaking overnight, thinned out with plenty of water.

She had just finished when the cook came back. She examined the bowl and baskets, deigning to sniff in what Meg thought was approval, or at least lack of criticism, as she picked up the peas. 'And you're the first girl I've set to that task who hasn't taken advantage to eat some of them for herself. I'll call you again next time we have some.'

When the dining room was full, and Meg was dipping her bread into her soup, she craned her neck to see the top table. They were eating meat, potatoes and vegetables with a thick gravy that Meg had seen – and smelled – in a jug on one of the kitchen tables, and which had made her mouth water. She wondered how it was made, and if she might be able to sneak a look next time it was being prepared.

She was almost humming as she started on the washing-up. Things could be a lot worse. That led her, somehow, on to thinking of Sally, and the sadly stunted life she must have led inside the workhouse. Never to have walked along a street full of people; never to have inhaled the scent as she passed the flower shop; never to have heard the loud whistle of one of the terrifying locomotives at Lime Street station; never to have known the love of a sister or a mother.

But then again, she thought, as she placed the latest bowl on the drying rack, never to have starved with no food for days on end. Never to have lived in a filthy court or to have felt the rising terror at being not quite home yet when the sun went down and figures lurked in the shadows. And Sally might not have had a ma, but she should be grateful she didn't have to put up with anyone like Pa.

Meg's daydream continued. Was there any way, any possible way, that she might be able to take Sally with her when she left, as well as Rosie? She couldn't think of any at the moment, but if there was one then Delilah would find it. Meg had had plenty of time since she entered the workhouse to appreciate just how much Delilah had done for the family, and how she, Meg, had not been grateful enough for it. Delilah had been only sixteen at the time of the accident and seventeen when Ma died, and she had taken on responsibility for the whole family – not just working for wages, but organising, budgeting, keeping them together. It wasn't her fault they couldn't keep up and had had to move out of their house and into the single room in the court.

Meg now realised that she had never said any of this to Delilah, never thanked her, never appreciated her enough. She would put all this right on the day of the visit, would tell Delilah how much she meant to Meg, and to all of them. Even though they were apart, they would be a proper family again.

* * *

Mrs Leech had to hold the paper a little further away from her in order to read the list of names on it. It was a sign of approaching age, she knew, but she wasn't ready to retire yet, not until she had sufficient savings to guard against the possibility of penury and the humiliation of having to ask for help or, God forbid, ending up in the workhouse herself. She had no family of any kind, so she could only rely on herself.

And it was a good thing, she thought, that she was clever enough not to rely solely on her wages, which were pitiful. No, she had taken the initiative and set herself up a very profitable sideline. Another ten shillings had been paid over during the last few days, which she had put with the rest in a safe place. Now it was time to step back from it again for a few weeks; little by little had to be her watchword, not too many all at once or too soon, or suspicions might be raised. But that didn't stop her looking through her lists in the delicious anticipation of choosing who would be next.

Footsteps sounded in the hallway, and she pushed the paper into a drawer of her desk, taking up another which she was perusing with apparent interest when Mr Higgin, the workhouse master, entered.

She eyed him. She didn't like or dislike him, particularly; he was just part of the furniture. Her only interest in him was in making sure he didn't find out about what she was doing, but there seemed little chance of that if she was careful.

'Ah, Mrs Leech, hard at work as usual – how lucky we are to have you.'

The jovial tone was a sure sign that he wanted something. She made no reply except to raise her eyebrows and wait for the rest.

'I have received word that the members of the Board wish to visit and to dine here in two weeks' time. The ladies among them will no doubt wish to visit the female quarters, so may I leave that in your hands? And of course they will need a good meal.'

That wasn't as difficult a request as it might have been; the Board members did occasionally make visits to inspect the place. Having sufficient notice of it was a bonus, allowing her to organise matters so that they appeared to best effect. 'Yes, of course, Mr Higgin. I shall make the necessary arrangements.'

He thanked her and left, and she went back to the paper in her hand. It was a list of the extra clothing to be provided to the inmates tomorrow, the start of November. She felt irritated at the coddling. Why shouldn't they be cold? They were fed, clothed and housed through no effort or virtue of their own. Let them be cold. She felt no pity when she watched the women and girls go to their evening ablutions in their shifts and bare feet. It helped put them in their place. And as for providing them with additional clothing – why, that was an unnecessary expense for the Board, as much as anything.

Mrs Leech pondered for a few moments whether it might be possible simply not to give out the winter clothing this year. But, reluctantly, she decided not to try it. When the members of the Board visited it would be obvious to them that no inmates were wearing shawls or coats, and they would be bound to ask about it. No, she sighed to herself, it was evident that the clothing would have to be distributed. But as she compared the clothing order with the number of inmates to be provided for, she had one small satisfaction at least. She dipped a pen in the inkwell, struck through the number of shawls and petticoats to be provided, and reduced the figure by one.

* * *

There was some excitement in the dormitory the next morning when the assistants brought in a basket just as the girls were getting out of bed. They were made to line up and were each handed a petticoat and shawl, with no choice, but the assistants turned a blind eye to the chattering and swapping that went on afterwards.

Meg had been given a petticoat that was far too long; not only would it look ridiculous but she would trip over it, which would be a hazard in the kitchen. Fortunately Martha, who was much taller, had the opposite problem and she agreed to the exchange.

As she felt the extra weight of fabric under her dress and wrapped the warm wool around her shoulders, Meg was excited for more reasons than one. The clothing's arrival meant that it was the first of November. She was also aware that it was Wednesday today, as they would be cooking rice pudding in the kitchen. That meant that tomorrow would be the first Thursday of the month. *Tomorrow*. She only had to wait one more day until she could see Delilah and pour her heart out to her.

Naturally that made the day almost endless, but finally it was night, and then morning, and today was the day. Breakfast came and went, and so did dinner.

Jen knew how excited Meg was, and lent a hand with the washing-up when the cook wasn't looking. 'And now you're done,' she said, wiping her hands. 'The visiting is in the dining hall, so you haven't got far to go.'

Meg stood in the doorway for a few moments, getting her bearings. Visiting time had only just started, and the first few people were slipping in, mainly parents with thin, sad faces who had come to see their children. Meg scanned them all as they entered. Of course, it was not to be expected that Delilah would be among the very earliest of the visitors; she would have had to arrange time off from the laundry, and maybe someone to mind Annie. Or maybe she would bring Annie with her! Or might the others come too? Meg could hardly stand the anticipation. She slipped into the room and sat on a bench at the back, from where she had a good view of the door at the other end. She would have to wait until the others got here to have Rosie fetched; visitors were asked, when they arrived, whom they had come to see and then the inmates in question were summoned. This stopped the dining hall becoming a scene of chaos – if hundreds of inmates used the situation as an excuse to mill around, the lack of order and discipline would never be tolerated. Meg was only here herself because the hall was right next to the kitchen, and she'd have to sit quietly in case anyone noticed her alone.

After half an hour the type of people arriving started to change. These people were not the respectable poor: they were loud, raucous and sometimes even drunk, come to see their friends and fellow troublemakers who had fallen on hard times. Meg caught glimpses of food and tobacco being passed under the tables.

After an hour the room was full of noise, and one or two of the drunks had been thrown out. The friends they had visited were in no hurry to leave the dining hall, so they joined together with other groups in loud conversation. A few late arrivals – parents, friends, siblings? – rushed in, apologising to their family members for not being able to get away, for having to run through the streets to get here at all . . . but each was instantly forgiven as the face of the workhouse inmate in question lit up.

After an hour and a half, the trickle of new entrants had stopped. Meg stared and stared at the door, *willing* Delilah to appear and truly believing that she would if only she wished hard enough. The room was emptier by now, the raucous visitors gone and only the desperate parents remaining, clutching at their children and making the most of every last moment. The same whispered words echoed from all around the hall: 'It's only for now . . . we'll be back to get you soon . . . just until we get more money in . . . Pa will have a new job soon . . .'

After two hours, visiting time was over. Workhouse children cried as their parents were ushered out by the pauper assistants, and more than one visitor was wiping away a tear.

Meg wasn't crying. She was still sitting exactly where she had been for the last two hours, on the bench at the back of the room, frozen in incomprehension and misery and trying to face up to the fact that Delilah had not come.

Chapter Six

Meg was numb for the rest of the day and for several days afterwards. Both Jen, in the kitchen, and Sally, out of it, tried to cheer her up, coming up with excuse after excuse as to why Delilah might have been prevented from visiting.

Meg knew that they were all wrong. Her sister hadn't come because she didn't care. She had got rid of two members of the family who were financial burdens, and she had realised that the family were better off without them. More space in the one room they all shared, fewer mouths to feed, the chance to put by a bit of money and maybe look to a better home, a brighter future: that was what Delilah was thinking about. All Meg's tender thoughts towards her sister had evaporated, the former bitterness returning. She refused to listen to any arguments to the contrary, reasoning that if Delilah had really wanted to come, she would have made a way; and even if she had been prevented by work, as William no doubt had – Meg would not blame William – they could easily have sent Sam to explain it all to her. He was young, but he wasn't scared of anything; he would have marched into the workhouse on his own to see her without a qualm.

Thank goodness Rosie hadn't been in the dining hall on Thursday afternoon, although Meg worried that she might have heard from the other girls that visitors had come that day and wondered why she hadn't had any. The thought that Rosie might be feeling the same crushing disappointment that Meg was, while Meg was not with her to offer comfort, only made her more determined to make the most of the time they *did* have together.

Meg's next visit to Rosie was three days afterwards, and she was pleased to see that she seemed to have taught the clapping game to several of the others. Meg was also satisfied that her sister was physically healthy. None of the children, of course, could be anything like plump on the diet they were fed, but equally none of them had that hollow, skeletal look that one sometimes saw in children on the streets, and they were kept ferociously clean. Rosie generally spent most of each winter with a hacking cough, but it hadn't come on yet, and Meg had hopes that maybe it might not. She determined that they would wait out the winter, as planned, and then she would make a decision as to what the two of them would do, now that they were so evidently on their own.

* * *

It was early in the morning a couple of weeks later that Meg and a few others among the kitchen hands were summoned by the cook.

'Today the members of the Board are visiting, and they will be dining in the hall along with everyone else at noon. The inmates' dinner will be cooked as usual, but the meal for the top table will be more ambitious. You have all proved to be trustworthy and will therefore move from your regular duties today in order to help prepare it.' She swept them all with her iron gaze. 'Do not let me down, or it will be a disorderly diet for you for a week.'

Meg was pleased to have been selected as trustworthy and had no intention of letting the cook down, but she also had no idea what was going on.

Unfortunately Jen was not one of those chosen for the task, so Meg risked a whisper to one of the others as they began to set ingredients out on the table. 'Who are the Board?'

The woman looked carefully around to see that they were not being overheard. 'The people who are in overall charge of the workhouse and the parish. They come to inspect every so often to see that rules are being followed.'

'And what's a disorderly diet?'

'It's what you get as a punishment – bread and water and nothing else. One of the things you can get it for is lazing around and not working, so I suggest you shut up and start on those carrots.'

Meg didn't mind ending the conversation there. She was too enraptured by the baskets of fresh ingredients that surrounded them all, taking in the colours and the textures, the rich smell of the outdoors.

She was set to peeling and chopping, having been for some time deemed a safe person to be put in charge of a knife. None of the really bad women were ever assigned to the kitchen, she had learned, for precisely that reason; but still, the cook kept an eagle eye on anything sharp, counting the knives out and counting them back in again after every meal.

As Meg worked she kept half an eye on the cook, who was preparing some kind of creamy pudding the like of which she had never seen. Truly, these Board members must be important people. And they were having their meat roasted, rather than boiled: two large joints were sizzling over a fire, and the smell was so thick Meg thought she could eat it.

She was not one of those chosen to carry the fancy meal up to the top table, the cook thinking her too small and in danger of dropping something at the wrong moment. But Meg didn't care: her interest was in preparing and cooking the food, not walking up and down with it. Still, as she took her place on a bench with a bowl of surprisingly thick stew – of course, they would give the inmates a nicer dinner while the Board members were here, to fool them into thinking the food was like that all the time – she looked up to those at the top of the room to see how they were reacting to such luxury.

To her disappointment, they were talking among themselves and eating without really noticing or appreciating what was before them, as though it was the sort of thing they were fed every day. Still, at least they weren't complaining, and she could thus consider that the vegetables she had prepared had passed muster.

Her eye wandered across the figures. It was crowded up there, at least a dozen extra alongside those who normally ate at the top table. Most of them were men, some taller or shorter, or with more or less hair and whiskers, but all alike in their dark suits and superior expressions.

Of more interest were the three women among them. Meg was surprised to see women – ladies, she should say – in such a position of authority, but she guessed that the Board would need some female members in order to inspect the female side of the workhouse, in the same way that it had a matron as well as a master. Perhaps they were the wives of some of the men. Or even their mothers or aunts: two of them were older women, dressed in severe dark colours and the sort of caps that widows wore. The third was different, and Meg's eye lingered on her the longest. She was younger, with a pleasant face; she even smiled once or twice as she looked down at the children in the room. Her gown was of a bright blue, and she stood out from all the others at the top table like a butterfly on a grey stone wall. She was eating delicately, tiny pieces of meat and vegetables being conveyed from the plate to her mouth with a fork held in a small white hand.

'Are you going to eat that?' came a voice from next to her, and Meg realised that everyone else's bowl was empty and that covetous eyes were being cast at hers. Hastily she wolfed down the rest of the stew and her bread before turning her eyes to the top table again. The pudding had made an appearance, and a thousand pairs of jealous eyes watched as it was distributed and eaten.

Once it was finished, the inmates stood respectfully as those at the top table left, and then they filed out in their usual manner, leaving Meg and the others to start cleaning up. She was surprised, as she stood at her sink, to find china plates being brought to her instead of the usual earthenware and enamel; polished pewter cutlery instead of wooden spoons.

'You have a more careful hand than some of the others,' explained the cook. 'Mind you take care of it all, or there'll be trouble – and I've counted those forks.' She swept off, and Meg could hear her berating someone for clumsiness.

Annoyed that the cook had supposed that she wouldn't take care, Meg washed everything slowly and thoroughly, leaving it all gleaming on the drying rack. She wondered who the butterfly lady was, but neither Jen nor any of the others seemed to know or care. Whoever she was, she was as far above them as the moon, and they had no interest in someone whose life was so totally irrelevant to their own.

* * *

There had been even more cleaning to do in the kitchen than usual that evening, Cook finding herself dissatisfied with the scrubbing of the oatmeal pots and the food preparation tables, and insisting on it all being done again. So it was late when Meg left.

As she made her way through the darkened but now more familiar hallways, she heard the sound of sobbing. She looked around a corner to see that she wasn't the only one who was out late: a girl was kneeling on the floor, a bucket of water and a candle next to her and a scrubbing brush lying idle while she wept over her hands and blew on them. She started in terror when she heard footsteps, turning her face upwards, and Meg saw that it was Sally.

She rushed forward. 'What happened? Are you hurt?'

Sally held up her hands, and even in the dim light Meg could see that they were criss-crossed with the marks of the cane – three or four on each palm, at least. Meg sucked in her breath, dropped to her knees and took Sally's hands in her own. And it was only then that she noticed what she hadn't seen at first: a similar red weal across Sally's face.

She gasped. 'Sally! Oh, you poor thing. Did Mrs Leech do this to you?'

Sally nodded through her tears. Between sobs, she told Meg the whole story. She had been scrubbing the floor of the dormitory earlier when Mrs Leech had come in with three ladies, who were there to inspect it. Sally had stood respectfully to answer their questions, but she had been so nervous that it made her clumsy and she had accidentally knocked her bucket of water. The hem of one of the ladies' dresses had got splashed.

Meg winced on Sally's behalf as she imagined Mrs Leech's reaction to such an occurrence, and Sally's terror of it.

'The lady was kind about it,' continued Sally, 'and at first Mrs Leech was all sweetness, about how they had to look after stupid girls as well as the sharp ones, and find them work to do that fitted their cay . . . their cape— I can't remember the word she used, but they all went away.' She looked at her palms. 'And then, when they were gone, she came back, and she gave me such a scolding, and she hit me over and over again . . .' She tailed off, dissolving in tears again.

'And then she set you to cleaning this floor?'

Sally nodded. 'I've to go all the way from that end to this on my knees, without standing up, and clean it so's she can see her face in it. But I'm not halfway yet, and I'm tired and my hands hurt, and if don't finish I'll be in trouble, and if I do, then I'm late to bed, I'll be in trouble anyway.' She tried to pick up the brush, handling it very gingerly. 'And I know I'm clumsy and useless, but I didn't do it on purpose; it was just an accident.'

'I believe you,' said Meg. She looked up and down the hallway. 'There's nobody here now. You rest a minute and I'll do some of it for you.'

'But we'll get in trouble!' whispered Sally, clearly terrified.

'Like you said, you're going to be in trouble whatever you do. So you may as well save your strength for it.'

'But you'll—'

'I know I will, and I don't much care,' snapped Meg, surprised to find that it was actually true. She was so incensed at what had happened to poor Sally that there was no possible way she could go calmly off to bed and leave her there. She needed some outlet for her aggression, and scrubbing angrily at the floor would be just the thing.

She took up the brush and started, while Sally leant back on her heels, still too frightened to stand up.

Meg inched her way across the floor, dipping the brush in the vinegary water that no longer irritated her toughened hands and scratching the bristles as hard and as vigorously as she could.

She had made a few yards' progress when she thought she heard Sally give a little gasp. Still on her hands and knees, Meg raised her eyes from the floor to see that the hem of a dress was before her. She looked up: it belonged Mrs Leech.

'Stand. Up,' said the matron, slowly and deliberately.

Meg obeyed, but she was not frightened: she was seething. The exercise of scrubbing had not worn off her anger, but had rather strengthened it as she had the time to reflect on the injustice of it all.

She stared Mrs Leech in the face, boldly. That was guaranteed to bring all hell down on her head, but Meg didn't care.

'What do you think you are doing?'

'What does it look like I'm doing?' she retorted. 'I'm helping Sally because she's too badly hurt to do it herself.'

'She's hurt because she's a wicked girl who misbehaved in front of our visitors, no doubt to try and get their attention.'

'She's hurt because you beat her,' continued Meg, recklessly. 'Much more than she ever deserved for such a small accident – and much more than you're allowed to, surely.'

She didn't hear Mrs Leech's reply, if there was one, because the next thing she knew the matron had grabbed her by the neck and slammed her head into the wall. Stunned, she was vaguely aware of Sally screaming as she was pulled back and forced downwards, and then she was choking as her face was held under water.

She couldn't think of anything else except the need to breathe, to lift her head out of the bucket, but the hand holding her under was too strong, and she could do nothing other than thrash her arms, trying to get away as the water got into her eyes, her nose ... Then everything went strange and detached, and she stopped struggling. Perhaps it would be better to ...

Meg was abruptly pulled out and dropped on the floor, choking and spitting out filthy water as she gasped for precious air. She was vaguely aware of Mrs Leech's voice sounding from a great distance. 'Take her up to the dormitory, and get to bed. You can finish this floor in the morning after you've done your other chores.'

Receding footsteps sounded as Meg's choking and coughing slowly subsided. She lay on her back, staring hazily at the ceiling. Or, at least, where she knew the ceiling to be – the candle had gone out and it was now almost completely dark.

'Meg?' came Sally's voice. 'Meg, are you all right?'

'I'm not sure,' she replied, still feeling dreamy and detached. She tried to sit up, but was hit by a wave of dizziness and a throbbing agony in her head. She lay back down again. 'Just give me a minute.'

She felt Sally moving closer, felt her hand being taken. 'I'm sorry, Meg. This is all my fault.'

Determination brought Meg to herself a little. 'It's not your fault,' she managed, quite firmly. 'Nobody is to blame for beating us except the person who did it.' Strangely, she recalled something she had once heard Delilah say. 'Whatever happens, we all have a choice about whether to be cruel or not.' She wondered where Delilah was. But her head hurt, and all she wanted to do was to stay lying down. It was cold here on the floor, but she didn't mind.

'Meg, we're going to be really, really late. Can you get up and walk? I won't be able to carry you.'

Just then more footsteps sounded, the light of a candle came round a corner, and Sally let out a little shriek of fear. Then the steps picked up pace, and Meg felt someone leaning over her who was not Mrs Leech.

'What in—' said a female voice, and then, 'It's Meg, isn't it?'

Meg heard Sally reply on her behalf, and then she saw a face bending to look into her own. 'Meg. It's Lizzie – do you remember, I took you to the bath-house when you first arrived? I'm on duty in your dor-mitory and I was sent to find you because you were both missing. What have you been doing to yourself?'

'She didn't do it to herself,' muttered Sally, and Meg, even in her stupor, was proud of her friend for this tiny act of insurrection.

'Hit my head,' said Meg, trying to gesture with an arm that felt like it was made of wet string.

'All right,' came Lizzie's voice. 'I'll carry you. Sally, you take the candle. We'll go to the dormitory first and then see if you need to go to the infirmary.'

Meg felt herself being lifted by strong arms, and then a sensation of movement, of being carried. This went on for some while. Then a door opening, the sound of many breaths being drawn, and she was being laid down on a bed. Her cap was removed and Lizzie's hands were exploring her scalp. She got to where the tender lump was and Meg whimpered. The light of the candle seemed much brighter than usual, hurting her eyes; she wished someone would move it away from her.

'All right,' came Lizzie's voice. 'You've got a big bump there but I think your head's in one piece. Best to stay here and get some sleep, and you'll feel better in the morning.' She moved away. 'You two, help them both get undressed, and the rest of you, back to bed.'

Gentle hands removed Meg's boots, and soon she was tucked up under the blanket with Sally's arm round her. At last, she allowed her eyes to close properly.

* * *

Mrs Leech admonished herself. That girl irritated her so much that she had been drawn into overreacting, but, satisfying as it had been to push her impudent little head into the wall and the bucket, if she had died then Mrs Leech would have been in serious trouble. And if she lost her job before she had enough money saved up . . .

Anyway, she would have to restrain herself in future, and she hoped it wouldn't be too long before she could get rid of the girl: either the dratted sister would come to pick her up, or she would turn fourteen and could be sent out to a position. The quicker the better with one that sharp; she had already cottoned on to the fact that Mrs Leech was overstepping her boundaries with the cane.

Mrs Leech moved over to a framed set of workhouse rules that hung on her office wall, and held the candle up to it. 'No corporal punishment shall be inflicted on any female child,' stared back at her in black and white, and she snorted. As if they could be kept in order any other way.

Anyway, there were greater worries on the horizon than one obstinate girl. An outbreak of cholera had been making itself felt in the city, and was threatening to sweep through the cramped streets with a vengeance. Nobody knew how it spread, but it always affected the poorer areas worst, which would mean many deaths. That would be little loss in general terms, but it would no doubt result in a wave of orphans whom the Board would be forced to accommodate in the workhouse. Those paupers who were already inside would probably be spared the worst of it – the last outbreak hadn't reached this far. They didn't know how lucky they were.

Mrs Leech sighed. Was there any possibility of sending Meg Shaw out into the disease and death of the city? She'd seen this type of girl before – clever, stubborn, rebellious – and knew she would be a danger to her own business interests. Getting rid of her would be by far the simplest solution. But unfortunately that wasn't really an option; Meg was so young it would be difficult to square the paperwork, and if any irregularities were found it might lead someone to investigate further, a risk she could not take.

The evening drew on, and the candle grew shorter and shorter, flickering as the last guttering flame sank into a puddle of grease. Mrs Leech was occupied by two alternating thoughts: her own future, and how to break Meg Shaw's spirit without losing her own job. Eventually she nodded: she knew how she would proceed.

* * *

Meg awoke the next morning with a pounding head. As soon as she tried to move, tried to sit upright, the hammering got so bad that she felt sick.

'Ooh, Meg, look at your face!'

'What?' Meg was only vaguely aware of Sally's voice, and then those of some of the other girls as they gathered round.

'Your eye!'

'What about it?'

'You've got a big black eye.'

There was no looking-glass in here, of course, but Meg gingerly put her fingers to her face. She could feel a puffiness round one eye. She covered the other one and found that although she could still see, everything was blurry. But it wasn't the eye itself that hurt, it was the lump above it— Ow! Her fingers had found it. But – she forced herself to explore it further – it was all in the skin and the swollen flesh, with no apparent damage to the bone. Bad as she felt, it would surely be worse if she had cracked her skull.

She risked putting her feet on the floor and standing up, very slowly and with extreme care. Only Sally and Martha were still with her; the others had all gone out to the washroom, afraid of being late. She swayed a little, but managed to walk through the pounding in her head and the spinning room to get out into the passageway.

She was last in the queue and last back into the dormitory; and so slowly did she have to dress herself that she was only just tying the strings of her apron when Mrs Leech entered. Luckily Martha had helped Sally make their bed, so all Meg had to do was to join the line of girls standing in silence.

Mrs Leech wasted no time in calling her forward, and Meg wondered what she was in for now as she was made to turn and face the others.

'This girl has let me down. More than that – she has let you all down. I had thought this was a well-behaved dormitory, but evidently it is not, and you must all learn what happens when one member is wicked.'

Meg had no idea what she was talking about, but it was evident from their faces that some of the girls did.

'Everybody hold out your right hand.'

Surely she wasn't going to . . . but she was. Meg was forced to follow Mrs Leech down the line, to look into each girl's eyes as the cane smacked down on to their palms. She tried her best to look apologetic, and some of them seemed to understand, but others looked at her with more hate than they were giving to the matron who was actually hitting them.

They reached Sally, who was already crying as she held up her shaking hand, still criss-crossed from yesterday's beating. Meg had to close her eyes, and she heard Sally cry out, unable to stop herself, as the cane bit into the swollen flesh.

Once they reached the end of the line, Meg expected that her turn would come, and wondered how many strokes she was to expect, and how she would endure it when she could hardly stand upright anyway. But instead, Mrs Leech reattached the cane to her belt, said, 'And let that be a lesson to all of you,' and swept out of the room.

There was noise around Meg, and most of it was unpleasant – not just the whimpering and the quiet weeping, but an undercurrent of anger directed particularly at her. 'Why can't you just behave your-self and do what she says? Look what you've done! Things have been much worse since you've been here . . .'

It was Sally, of all people – fearful, quiet Sally – who shouted them down. 'Stop it, all of you! It wasn't Meg who hit you, it was Mrs Leech. And whatever Meg had done, it was Mrs Leech who chose to hit you – she could easily just have beaten Meg and had done with it.' Surprised by her own vehemence, and the attention she had drawn to herself, she took a step back. 'Anyway, all Meg was doing was helping me after Mrs Leech did this.' She showed them her hands and pointed to the mark on her face. 'So I'm grateful to her.' She stood defiant.

She hadn't convinced all the girls, but there was a slight murmur from some of them, and Martha and a few others came to stand by Meg. 'Sally's right,' said the tall girl, firmly. 'You all know as well as I do that if Mrs Leech wants to punish someone – whoever it is – she'll do it anyway; she doesn't need an excuse. All this is just because she's taken against Meg and she wants all the rest of us to hate her too. Well, I won't: I'll stick to hating Mrs Leech, thank you very much.'

The sound of a throat clearing from the end of the room reminded them all that the pauper assistants were still in the room and waiting for them to line up and go out to their chores. Fortunately the sound had come from Lizzie, who shooed them all towards the door without any further scolding.

She came over to look at Meg's head. 'As I thought. You'll have a thick head today, luvvy, but take it steady if you can, and you'll be all right. Off you go, now.'

Meg left the room, looking back at Sally, who was starting on her unenviable task of collecting the chamber pots. She made her way to the kitchen.

She was late, of course, but the cook's rebuke died on her lips when she saw Meg's face. 'What in heaven's name . . . ?' She collected herself. 'I've already heard that you're to be put on a disorderly diet for a week, and it's right that girls need to be punished for doing wrong. But there's punishing and there's rendering a worker unfit for duty.'

Meg couldn't quite work out whether the cook was angry with her or with Mrs Leech, but it didn't really matter either way, did it? 'Yes, ma'am,' seemed the safest answer.

The cook hesitated. 'Well . . . stay away from the fires until your head clears.' Lest she be suspected of feeling any sympathy, she quickly added, 'It will slow the work down and cause trouble for everyone if you trip over and burn yourself. Now, get out into the dining hall and set it for breakfast.'

Somehow, Meg got through the morning. In the lull after the breakfast washing-up was finished, Jen managed to find a spare minute to sit her down and put a cold, wet cloth over her swollen eye, which helped ease the pain a little.

But she hadn't been sitting long when a shriek from the other side of the kitchen made her jump up. The sudden movement made her immediately dizzy and she collapsed back down again, but even from there she could see the commotion going on and the sounds of someone in intense pain. It would appear that a pot of boiling water had somehow tipped over, and the poor woman nearest to it had been scalded as it poured over her leg. *Strange,* thought Meg, blearily, *that's where I would have been standing, normally.* The cries of pain receded as the injured woman was

126

taken off to the infirmary, and the cook restored order with shouts and sharp words.

Then it was time for Meg to get up and force herself to move, because there were over a thousand mouths to feed, and the work never stopped.

Chapter Seven

That evening, in the dormitory, Meg lay still while her head continued to pound. She should probably be feeling sorry for herself, shouldn't she? But she wasn't. Instead a huge anger was building, and she allowed it to grow.

It felt good to have such a fire on the inside. Where had being good and compliant got her, after all? She had worked hard, and she had been beaten for things she hadn't done. She had seen Sally viciously caned for a simple act of clumsiness, and when she tried to help she had been attacked herself and then forced to watch every innocent girl in her dormitory thrashed too. And so, as Meg thought to herself now in the darkness: if they were going to be beaten anyway, then why not do something to earn it?

It was after lights out, but the pauper assistant had gone and some of the girls were whispering. Sally was already asleep, so there was no point in squirming up to her end. No – Meg would start her new campaign with a tiny act of defiance. She got out of bed and tip-toed over to the one Martha now shared with an Irish girl called Bernadette.

Martha sat up. 'Meg? What is it? Is your head worse?'

'No,' whispered Meg. 'I just wanted to talk to you.'

By now they had attracted the attention of several others nearby, and more and more girls were sitting up. Martha did the same. 'Go on. No, wait! Someone should stand by the door to warn us if they hear anyone coming.'

The two girls in the bed nearest the door did so, and Meg began. 'When Mrs Leech caned everyone this morning, she was able to do it because we're powerless.'

There was a grumble from somewhere that Mrs Leech had done it because Meg had misbehaved, but Martha cut it off. 'No, it's like I said this morning, she did it because she wanted to.'

'And that's what I said, too.' Sally had woken up, and she now joined them. 'Meg and Martha are right.'

'But what can we do?' cut in another.

Meg strained her eyes in the darkness – the speaker was a girl she didn't know very well but whom she thought was called Dolly.

'The fact is, we *are* powerless,' Dolly continued. 'So the only thing we can do is keep our heads down and hope she picks on someone else.'

Meg shook her head. 'No. No, that's exactly what we *shouldn't* do. If we all go round hoping that Mrs Leech will bully someone else, we're almost as bad as she is, don't you see? And it means she's divided us. We'll be stronger if we stick together.'

'That makes sense,' said Martha, 'but how?'

Meg thought for a moment. 'We can't stop Mrs Leech but here's how we can start to work together. I think we can agree that what we all want is to get out of here – to have lives of our own, good lives. None of us is going to marry a prince but we can all make our own way if we're given the chance.' She looked round, aware that she now had the attention of the whole dormitory. 'We're all a mixture: we've come from different places and different backgrounds. Some of us have only arrived recently and others have been here their whole lives.'

Sally was by now sitting next to Meg on the edge of Martha's bed, and Meg squeezed her hand before continuing. 'So, how about if we all start by each sharing what we know of the world outside, so that everyone is better informed when they do leave?'

There was a murmur, but it wasn't hostile. 'Bernadette can tell us what it's like to be on a ship, for example,' continued Meg. 'Imagine that! I've been to the docks, and there will be girls in here who know about the railway, about mills and factories, about all the places in Liverpool. Some of us will have had mothers who worked in different jobs – tell the rest of us about that, about what it involves.'

'Do you know,' said Martha, slowly, 'I think Meg might be right.'

'Of course Meg's right!' exclaimed Sally, in a voice so loud that the others had to shush her in case they were found out.

'We're better together,' said Meg, firmly, 'and sharing our experiences will make all of us stronger. We can do it every night after lights out, as long as we're careful. We don't really even need to get out of bed – we could all just sit up, talk quietly, and then quickly lie down again if we hear anyone coming.' She took a deep breath. 'Are we all agreed? Because everyone has to want to do it.'

As far as Meg could see, every girl in the dormitory was nodding. 'Good. Now, who wants to start?'

* * *

By the time the first Thursday in December arrived the lump on Meg's head had long since subsided, and she had heard tales of both wonder and heartbreak from the girls she was now beginning to see as new sisters. Their small act of rebellion, of solidarity, had emboldened even the quietest among them to speak and to be heard.

They hadn't been caught, but Meg's punishments continued anyway – which just made her all the more determined to rebel. She was dizzy from hunger. She had been on the disorderly diet for two weeks now, the punishment made all the worse by working in the kitchen: even the greasy, watery slop they produced for the inmates seemed like heaven. If the situation weren't so horrible it could almost be funny: she'd come to the workhouse because her family couldn't afford to feed her, and now here she was eating no better. She hadn't been allowed to see Rosie for two weeks, either, and her heart tore at the thought of her little sister feeling even more abandoned, with only Sally and Martha to visit her and not Meg. Surely if Meg could tell Delilah all about this, she would agree to them leaving and coming home?

Despite her best efforts to remain calm and detached, Meg had allowed some hope to creep in about this afternoon. Maybe Delilah hadn't come last time because she had been unavoidably delayed, or because she couldn't leave work, or for any one of a host of reasons that would all seem eminently rational when she explained them. Maybe she would be here this afternoon, maybe Meg would be able to talk to her, beg her to take them away, no matter how difficult things were at home, anything to get her and Rosie *out* of here . . .

This time she didn't sit in the dining hall. Instead she stayed in the kitchen, but she certainly found herself hovering by the door more often than would normally be the case. As before, she could see people coming in and out; she could see families being reunited, albeit briefly. And also as before, the two hours passed and Delilah did not come.

* * *

When she was finally allowed to visit Rosie again, Meg flew up to the little girls' day room and looked about her.

But what a difference three weeks had made! This time, no little girl came running. It took Meg some moments to spot her sister sitting on a chair at one side of the room.

She made her way over. 'Hello, Rosie darling.'

Rosie didn't immediately look up; she was busy coughing. Meg's heart sank as she sat down and gathered her sister in her arms.

After a while the bout subsided and Rosie was able to look at her. 'Why didn't you want to come and see me? Have I been naughty?'

'No, darling, of course you haven't. And I did want to come and see you – I just wasn't allowed to. Didn't Sally or Martha tell you? I asked them to, when they came up.'

'I don't remember.'

There was silence for a few moments before Rosie started to cough again.

'How long have you had this?'

Rosie somehow managed to shrug in between the hacking, her shoulders shaking. 'Don't know.'

That was hardly surprising, if Rosie's sense of time was getting as disconnected as Meg's. Meg tried to speak cheerfully. 'I'm sure it's just like the one you often get in the winter. Nothing to worry about.' But she knew she was lying; she could hear how much wetter the cough sounded.

Their allotted time passed very slowly, Meg cradling Rosie on her knee and talking to her gently in between the attacks that left her gasping for air, and trying without much success to elicit any information from her at all about what she had been eating or doing.

And then their time was up and Meg had to leave, having had very little opportunity for proper conversation or regaining any of their former closeness. As she left the room, Meg felt as though all of her sisters were slipping away from her.

* * *

Time had lost all meaning. The days blended together. Meg lived for Sundays, for just a few hours with Rosie.

By now it was nearly Christmas. Back in Meg's old life – when Ma was alive and they had lived in their house – they had celebrated it, in a small way. Money had always been tight, but somehow Ma had managed a goose and a plum pudding each year, and occasionally there had even been little gifts: Meg vividly remembered a bright ribbon that she had proudly tied in her hair every day until it fell to pieces.

There wasn't going to be any of that in here, of course, but the members of the Board would visit the week before Christmas, which would at least mean a better meal.

The day soon came, and Meg was once again moved from her regular duties to help prepare the dinner for the eminent visitors. She peeled and chopped, breathing in the heady aroma of the goose that was roasting for them, a smell so rich that it stopped everyone in their tracks in the kitchen, and probably out in the hallways as well.

Meg tried to pretend that she was cooking a wonderful Christmas meal for her family. How Sam and Jem's eyes would widen as they saw the mountain of fresh, expensive food she was preparing! They would sniff the air as she bustled about the kitchen telling them not to get in the way but secretly delighted rather than cross. William would carve the goose and then sit down to a full plate of juicy meat and steaming gravy. Rosie and Annie would enjoy helping her to stir the pudding, dropping the sixpence in before she wrapped it and set it to steam . . .

'Have you done those yet?'

Meg was jerked out of her daydream. Fortunately her hands had not idled even as her mind had wandered, and she handed over her basket.

When dinner was ready, Meg was almost as keen to look for the butterfly lady as she was to taste the meat and potatoes on her plate. And there she was: in a pale rose-coloured gown this time, a delicate flower among the black and grey thorns at the top table. Meg watched her as they both ate, feeling a connection despite their different meals, different places, different worlds. She, Meg Shaw, had prepared some of the food on that fine plate.

When the meal was finished, Meg expected that they would stand and leave as normal, but something else was afoot: the butterfly lady was saying something to the workhouse master, and he was pointing towards the doors. The lady turned to look, and Meg followed her gaze to see that several of the male paupers were entering, carrying crates. A little murmur went round the room, which grew into a louder cheerful buzz as the lids were lifted to reveal that the crates were full of oranges. The butterfly lady smiled and clapped her hands with joy, and then all of the smaller children were chivvied into a line to step forward and receive one.

Meg was delighted at the thought that Rosie would have such a gift, a treat she would never have got at home. Meg didn't think it was usual workhouse fare, either – not even at Christmas – and she felt sure that the bright fruit was a gift from the butterfly lady herself to the children. She smiled, thinking of the extra effort she would put into her part of the meal preparations next time the members of the Board visited: the lady would never know, but it would be Meg's way of thanking her for her kindness to children who had known so little of it.

*   *   *

Christmas Day itself came around, but it was an anti-climax after the earlier visit of the Board members. It was supposed to be a day of rest with all normal labour suspended, but of course a holiday was never a holiday for those who worked in the kitchen, and they were kept at it just the same, the only difference being that there was even more to prepare as each inmate received a dish of pudding after their dinner. It wasn't exactly a Christmas pudding, which would have been far too extravagant, but it was at least a thick slice of something sweet and stodgy that had a few currants in it.

There were other glimmers of cheerfulness. Sally and Martha had managed to find spaces next to Meg at the bench, and Sally had smiled as she noted that Christmas Day was her birthday, so she always felt as though the pudding was a special treat to mark the occasion. Meg had nothing to offer except her good wishes, but she gave them all the same and then squeezed Sally's hand under the table. 'Twelve, now, is it?' she whispered. 'You'll soon be a grown-up – a fine lady!' This had made all three of them giggle, and such was the general air of goodwill in the room that they were not even scolded for such levity.

The day passed, and after a freezing week during which the wash basins had to have their ice broken in the mornings before the water could be used, it was both Sunday and New Year's Eve. Meg spent the afternoon with Rosie, holding her sister on her lap, partly for warmth and partly to try to ease her cough. Each time she saw Rosie, she seemed worse. Back when Ma was alive she used to sit Rosie over a bowl of hot water so she could breathe in the steam; something that was easy to procure in a household that earned money by taking in washing, but less readily available in the cold expanse of the little girls' day room in the Liverpool workhouse.

As she rocked Rosie to and fro, Meg wondered what the new year would bring. Tomorrow it would be 1849 and a blank slate. Her early years were now a little bit hazy, and some of them ran into each other in her mind, but the last few were very clear: 1847 had been terrible and 1848 worse, so would the downward spiral continue, or would this be the year that the family turned the corner and started on the way up again?

And what would that even look like – a new home, new jobs? A reformed Pa was certainly too much to hope for.

She wondered how the others were spending this last day of December. William would not be at work, of course, not on a Sunday, and Delilah wouldn't be out at the laundry. However, she might well be sitting with a pile of the mending that she brought home to earn a few precious extra shillings and pennies, sitting close to the candle as she sewed with those tiny, neat stitches that Meg could never master. Sam and Jem might be out in the cold streets, but if they were they would at least be running around, ruddy and red-cheeked, and they might even bring home a few coppers if there were any generous ladies and gentlemen risking a walk despite the weather. And Annie? Meg hoped that Annie was well wrapped up next to the fire, watching for the kettle to boil so Delilah could get a hot meal inside her before she went to bed, curled up under a blanket on this cold winter night.

Meg sighed as she buried her face in Rosie's cap and held her tight. Rosie's hair was starting to grow back; she could feel it through the cotton. Next Thursday would be another visiting day, but after her last two experiences Meg had little hope that anyone would come to see her. Perhaps it was for the best that the two parts of the family didn't meet until the day they could all be together again properly. And it *would* happen. This year had been the one during which she and Rosie had entered the workhouse; the one starting tomorrow would be the year they left it. She vowed it to herself as she kissed Rosie goodbye and made her way out.

*   *   *

January was as miserable as January ever was, and the workhouse seemed to be getting fuller and fuller by the day: orphans, starving children, frail old people and even a number of able-bodied men and women arrived every day. The dormitories were full to bursting, and more beds had been squeezed into the one in which Meg slept, so that there was hardly room to walk between them. Meg heard the word 'cholera' more than once and was struck by fear for her family. But Delilah would find a way to keep them out of it, surely – she would protect the members of the family she actually cared about.

Meg's solace was the growing feeling between all the girls in the dormitory. Last night they'd heard from Dolly. She had arrived after Meg, along with her sister Molly; they were twins, and she had regaled them all with tales of the pranks they'd played on people over the years who couldn't tell them apart. Although they were the same age and thus in the same workhouse unit, Mrs Leech had managed to house them in separate dormitories and set them to work in different places.

Dolly had laughed as she told them all of her sister, and then cried as she said she only felt like half a person without Molly around. She was afraid they would never see each other again. That brought Meg's mind to their other main concern: the girls who mysteriously disappeared. Ellen hadn't been the first to vanish without a word. She began to use the evening chats to try to piece together more details of what had happened to whom, and when.

A couple of the older girls in the dormitory had been there for three years, and they confirmed it had been happening all that time.

'But,' asked Meg, 'how do we know who's disappeared and who's just been sent out to a position, like we're supposed to? Is it possible we're making something out of nothing and they've just got jobs?'

'No, I don't think so,' said Martha, shaking her head. She looked at some of the older ones. 'As far as I can see, when a girl gets a domestic service post, she gets told about it one day, then she comes back here in the evening and tells us all about it, then she leaves the next day when they come to sign the papers and pick her up. But the others – they just get up and go out to their workhouse job one morning like usual, and you never see them again, and you never hear what's happened. Like Ellen, who used to share the bed with me.'

The other older girls were nodding.

'There's something else,' said Sally, suddenly.

All eyes turned to her. Sally hardly ever spoke during their evening chats, having no life outside the workhouse to recount, and she preferred to sit enraptured and drink in the stories of others.

'Go on,' said Meg, in an encouraging voice.

'Well, they're definitely all from the oldest girls – nobody who's only eleven or twelve ever just disappears.' Her brow creased with the effort of concentration. 'And they're all a bit alike. I don't mean they all look exactly alike – the ones I can think of had different-coloured hair or skin – but they're all . . . I don't know the word for it. Big girls. Grown-up-looking for their age.'

Sally looked around, ready to shrink if anyone disagreed, but there were more nods. 'Yes . . . Ellen . . . and remember Maud . . . and then there was . . .'

Meg took all this in and continued to think about it as she sank once more into the workhouse's mind-numbing routine. Day after day in the kitchen, which seemed to have become a more dangerous place than it had been before, with mishaps or negligence resulting in several women having to be taken to the infirmary. Sunday after Sunday with Rosie, whose cough wasn't getting any better as January turned to February.

Recalling the date made Meg think of her own and her family's situation. February meant Annie's birthday: she would be turning three, and Meg was not there to make a fuss of her. It also raised the question of 'spring', and when it could fairly be said to start. Delilah had promised to come back for them 'in the spring', but did that mean the first day of March, or Easter, or May Day? When would she come?

Chapter Eight

Spring was not only here; it was almost over. It was light when they got up in the mornings, the sun shone on the little yard as they walked around it every day, and it would soon be midsummer.

Meg had not heard one word from her family since Delilah had left the workhouse on that awful day last October, more than half a year ago now, and hope was ebbing away. What she couldn't understand was *why* she and Rosie should have been abandoned, why Delilah could have been so cruel. Admittedly, they didn't earn money, but what had they ever done to deserve this? To be cast loose into the world with nobody to protect them or love them?

And there was another thing. Poor little Rosie must be feeling even more abandoned, as Meg hadn't been allowed to visit her for weeks and weeks now. She

did know the reason why, of course: pure vindic-
tiveness on the part of Mrs Leech. To all intents and
purposes Meg had done nothing wrong – Mrs Leech
still had no idea about the girls' evening meetings, so as
far as she was concerned Meg worked hard, kept herself neat and tidy and hardly opened her mouth. And
yet every week, without fail, the matron found some
excuse to punish her by preventing her Sunday visit.
It just added more fuel to Meg's fire and increased her
conviction that she was justified in rebelling.

Meg's one comfort had been Sally and Martha.
Mrs Leech, knowing that neither of them had any
family, had not realised that they often went up to
the younger girls' room on Sundays – and what she
didn't know, she couldn't forbid. So each week Sally
and Martha slipped off, ostensibly to see Peggy or
one of their other old friends, but also to talk to
Rosie, to reassure her that Meg loved her and would
come as soon as she could, and then to bring back
to Meg what news they could. That was how Meg
knew that Rosie's winter cough had at last subsided
as the days grew longer and warmer, and this was
some relief from worry, at least. Each season brought
its own dangers, and a summer fever was apparently
now beginning to make itself felt in both children's

units, but Meg was not unduly concerned: surely this was much less serious than the wet, racking cough.

Meg had been surprised by the growing depth of her friendship with the two very mismatched girls. She'd always tended to keep herself to herself, and she had so many family members to look out for that she'd never really had the chance to have a friend her own age. Well, they weren't both exactly her own age, of course. Martha was only a little older but the age gap seemed more pronounced as she was so mature. Sally was a year and a bit younger than Meg, and despite the fact that she was taller she seemed even younger due to her innocence of the world. Poor Sally, never having known anything of the outside, was simple and naïve in ways Meg could hardly even begin to imagine, but – unlike some others – Meg could see that it was in no way her own fault. How could it be, when she had never been taught anything but the regime of the workhouse, when she had spent her whole life being told how stupid and useless she was, when she had never known love?

That last one was the key. Meg often felt sorry for herself but tried not to cry; she was never alone and she didn't want or need everyone else to know her feelings. But as she lay awake at night after their meetings had finished, she often debated her and Sally's relative situations in her mind. She, Meg, had loved and lost a mother and siblings, which was terrible – a gaping, tearing wound that she didn't think would ever heal. But Sally had never known those things at all, and surely that was worse. What filled the space in her heart where her family ought to have been?

As time went by and Meg, Sally and Martha began to know them better, the girls in the dormitory had come to feel almost like a surrogate family. Some of them had stories similar to Meg's own, and had even been in and out of the workhouse several times, but others had horrific histories of neglect, abuse and abandonment. And even those weren't the worst, or so she had heard during night-time whispering sessions; there were children in the workhouse who had been permanently crippled or made into imbeciles by their early life experiences. None of them were housed in Meg's dormitory, which was for girls who worked and who were being prepared for a life in domestic service; this meant that they all had to be fit and strong. But there were many other places hidden away in the recesses of the workhouse.

Meg had certainly got stronger as the months had progressed. She was still tired at the end of each day, but it wasn't the all-encompassing, deathly exhaustion she had felt at first. Her hands had finally toughened up, too, as Jen had said they would: neither the hot water nor the soda and vinegar bothered her any more. Long hours of practice meant that she could scrub a table or a floor until it shone and still have life left in her arms afterwards. She even thought that she might have grown a little taller, although if that was the case it was not so noticeable – she was still the shortest girl in the dormitory.

One night in early June, the girls had been shut up as usual and left lying silently in their beds. Although there were no candles, there was still enough light coming in through the high windows for them to see each other as Lizzie left the room, and several smiles were smothered. Lizzie looked upon them all with a little more lenience than the other pauper assistants and would turn a blind eye as long as they made no real noise, so they all sat up almost immediately, some girls even getting out of their beds to sit with others. They were now all willing to risk punishment in the name of togetherness.

Martha was sitting on Meg and Sally's bed, and Sally was toying with the older girl's frizzy hair. 'So much of it!' she said, wonderingly.

'It's a pain to try and keep under my cap, and Mrs Leech has threatened to shave my head more than once, but it's mine and I like it,' said Martha.

'How will you manage it when you go out to service?' asked Meg curiously, for it really was of a magnificent thickness.

Martha shrugged. 'I'll worry about that when it happens.'

Sally turned to a conversation that was always current in the dormitory. 'I wonder what we'll all do when we get sent out. Where we'll end up.'

Meg knew already that her dearest wish would be to work in a kitchen, a proper kitchen, preparing delicious meals that would make those eating them really happy. So different from the slop she was forced to produce in vast quantities day after day in the workhouse kitchen. Roast meat, tasty sauces, sweet puddings, fine pastries ... but, as ever, she refrained from saying this out loud, on the basis that wishing for something would mean it would never happen. Instead she turned to Martha. 'Do you like working in the sewing room?'

Martha made a face. 'I would if there was better things to sew. It's all workhouse aprons and uniforms – coarse stuff and plain seams.'

'Would you rather be making fine gowns and lace caps?'

'Of course.' Martha sighed. 'What I really want to be is a lady's maid. I could work for a nice lady, doing her hair, taking care of her clothes and all that, and it would be lovely.'

'Well, maybe you will.' Meg tried to sound encouraging, but lady's maids were at the very top end of domestic service, and it was unlikely that a workhouse girl would end up as one. *Or as a cook.*

'I won't though, will I? Not just because I'm in here, but because of my colour. What fine lady is going to want a personal maid who's half and half, like me?' She stretched out her hand, as though they might yet be unaware of its dark shade.

Meg said nothing. Martha was right and there was no point arguing. It was, like many other things, so *unfair*; why should the colour of Martha's skin have anything to do with her abilities? And yet it was a battle that would seemingly never be won.

'Was your Ma and Pa different colours, then?' Sally, as ever, was several steps behind.

Martha nodded. 'He was a sailor she met at the docks when his ship came in. They come from all over the world, you know.'

'Do they?' Sally asked. She settled in, as if for a story.

'Yes,' added Meg. Pa had worked at the docks all his life, until his accident, and Meg had sometimes been sent down with his midday meal if it hadn't been ready for him to take out in the morning. It was a place of grinding hard work, but also of hopes and dreams: the great ships docked there, with their sails like giant birds' wings, had seen faraway parts of the world, places she couldn't even begin to imagine. The men who sailed them were best avoided by respectable girls, Ma had said. Little Meg hadn't understood the overtone and had peeped at them, wide-eyed at their strange looks, their tattoos and the many shades of their skins, from the blue-eyed and pale-faced fishermen of the north, through swarthy and olive and brown and deepest black.

'So,' Martha was continuing to Sally, 'when my ma had me and I came out this colour, Pa – the man she was married to – knew I wasn't his, and he threw her out. She managed for a while, getting bits of work, but eventually we ended up in here – I was about six, I think – and then she died.'

Another lost soul, thought Meg to herself, and wondered again what would become of them all.

'Let's make a pact,' she said, suddenly.

'A what?' That was Sally.

'A deal.'

'What sort of deal?' asked Martha.

'Whichever one of us gets out of here first will do everything she can, on the outside, to get the others out.'

Martha nodded. 'Agreed. If it's me, I'll do whatever I can.'

'I agree too,' said Sally, 'though I can't see that it'll be me. But when you both leave, does that mean you won't forget me?'

'Never,' said Meg, and Martha echoed her.

As they returned to bed, Meg laid her head on her pillow. What would become of her? She was desperate to leave, of course, and for Sally and Martha to get out too, but what about Rosie? She was so much younger. It was becoming ever clearer that Delilah had no intention of coming back for them, which meant that they would have to make their own way as best they could. But what would Rosie do after Meg had left? She would turn into another Martha, vaguely aware in the depths of her mind that she had once had a family and a life, but unable to remember them, having been here from such a young age that she would be unable to recall any existence outside the workhouse. Or worse, she might just disappear one day.

The thought gnawed at Meg as she drowsed, stopping her from falling asleep properly, but what could she do? She was under no illusion that any position she was sent to would allow her to bring a little sister with her, but she must put that to one side and start to make some definite plans for Rosie – for it would appear that Rosie had nobody else.

* * *

A few days after this conversation, Meg was at work in the kitchen when she became aware of an unusual disturbance. She had got so used to the daily routine that it only took something tiny, some small speck sticking in the clockwork, to attract notice.

A woman she didn't recognise had entered the kitchen and was speaking urgently to the cook. Meg tried not to stare as she continued stirring the pot in front of her, but she soon became aware that the cook was pointing at her, and that both of them were making their way over.

In all the months she had worked in the kitchen, Meg had never received what she might call a kind word from the cook, but she had gathered that her work was satisfactory because the sarcasm had ceased and she was only very rarely scolded. Now she was surprised to find that the cook was looking at her with a strange expression on her face. Was that . . . sympathy?

'Meg,' she began briskly – for she had long since ceased to address Meg with the impersonal 'girl' she had used at first. 'You need to go with this woman now.'

Meg's stomach lurched. Was she about to be 'disappeared', as had happened to several other girls one by one? Where was she to be taken? What—

'She is one of the assistants in the younger girls' unit,' continued the cook. Meg realised her mistake and her heart sank even lower. For surely this could mean only one thing.

'I am aware,' said the cook, 'that you have been prevented from seeing your sister for some time. It's not for me to criticise Mrs Leech, but I will say for you that you're a good worker in the kitchen, and I've no idea how you get in so much trouble when you're out of it.'

'Thank you, ma'am,' was the only thing Meg could think of to say, as her mind whirled.

'Mrs Leech won't come in here this morning, so nobody will know that you've gone. I'll get one of the others to cover your work.' The expression of sympathy deepened. 'I think you need to go right now.'

Meg followed the woman through the now familiar corridors and paths, but when they reached the younger girls' unit they did not go up to the day room; instead they turned off down a passageway Meg hadn't used before.

'Children's infirmary,' said the woman, laconically, pointing Meg to a door.

Meg's heart was in her mouth as she entered, hardly daring to breathe. She looked up and down the rows of beds but none of the children there was Rosie. She began to panic.

A much older woman approached. 'You're Rosie's sister? She's through there, in the fever ward.'

Meg almost tripped over her own feet. Part of her wanted to rush to her sister's side, to run as fast as she could, but the other half didn't want to go through the door at all, believing in some way that if she didn't then none of this would be real.

Somehow she was standing at the foot of a bed, with no knowledge of how she'd got there. Rosie lay in it, bathed in sweat and tossing from side to side, almost unrecognisable with her head newly shaven. She was surrounded by other beds containing other small writhing and groaning forms, but Meg only had eyes for Rosie. She knelt by the side of the damp sheets and took her sister's hand. It was boiling, as was her forehead.

Meg looked about her in desperation. 'Please,' she asked the older woman, 'please, have you a bowl of cold water and a cloth?'

'I have, and you're welcome to it, but the medical officer says she's well past that now.' She disappeared and then returned a few moments later with an enamel basin.

Meg dipped the cloth and used it to dab at Rosie's face, trying vainly to cool the fire. 'Rosie, darling, it's Meg. Can you hear me?'

There was no reply. Rosie was too far off in a fevered dream-world.

Meg knelt there for . . . she didn't know how long. She tried her best, but no sooner did she place the cold, damp cloth on any part of her sister's skin than it dried and almost boiled. The heat emanating from the little body was intense. As she tossed and turned Rosie occasionally cried out; sometimes incoherently, sometimes recognisable words, sometimes names. 'Ma' and 'Meg' were the most frequent, and Meg tried in vain to get through to her, to let her know that at least one of her loved ones was with her during her moment of crisis.

After some while, Rosie ceased thrashing about and lay still.

The older woman returned.

'Is this good? Is she getting better?' Meg knew she was begging, rather than asking.

The woman only shook her head. 'You stay there with her. I've heard from Cook, and she says to stay as long as . . . you need.'

Meg nodded and turned numbly back to Rosie. She was lying very still and her breath was coming in short, ragged gasps.

Meg put her mouth close to her sister's ear, feeling the unstoppable heat radiating off her. 'Rosie, darling, my own dearest darling, I'm here. It's Meg. I'm sorry I haven't been to see you for a while, and I'm sorry, more sorry than I can say, that you ended up here in the first place. I should have done more – we all should. But it's me who's let you down. I should have been there to look after you, and I wasn't.'

She felt and saw her tears dripping on to Rosie's stubbly, shaven head, and she wiped them away. With one hand she held Rosie's hot fingers, and with the other she smoothed and stroked her head, murmuring words of comfort that she hoped her sister might hear, wherever she was now.

The afternoon wore on and turned into evening. Meg didn't stir, her legs cramping. She gripped the hand ever tighter, as though she could hold her sister here, keep her in this world, by sheer force of will. But Rosie's gasping breath grew shallower and shallower, and then – so simply, so peacefully that Meg hardly noticed it in between one moment and the next – it stopped.

Meg knelt unmoving for a long time, gazing at Rosie's face in an attempt to imprint it on her mind and continuing to stroke her head. The little hand clasped in her own finally grew colder.

* * *

Meg stared at the ceiling. Everyone else in the dormitory was asleep; she could hear the deep breathing coming from all around her. But the fires of anger were keeping her awake.

Rosie was dead. The little sister she'd sworn to protect was gone, and the terrible scene in the children's infirmary played over and over again in Meg's mind.

She had continued to kneel at Rosie's bedside for a long while after she knew she was dead. Not in any hope that she would, by some miracle, come back to life – because Meg had seen enough death to know that wouldn't happen – but just because Rosie was her last remaining sibling, her last link to her earlier life, and Meg didn't want to let go. And also because she loved Rosie with all her heart and soul, and wanted to spend every last precious moment with her that she could.

Eventually the infirmary overseer's hints to leave had turned into direct instructions, and finally an exasperated cry that they needed the bed for someone else. Meg had kissed her little sister's forehead, taken one last look at her darling face, and walked out in an almost dreamlike state, her mind unable to believe that what had just happened was real. She had not been allowed to attend the funeral, not that 'funeral' was even the right word; Rosie had been buried in an unmarked grave along with several others from the workhouse who had died the same day, with no official service and no mourners. Meg didn't even know where the grave was.

And now here she was, and what was the point of anything? It was tempting to fall into a kind of stupor, to try to lessen the pain by subduing her feelings about everything, but Meg just couldn't do it. Instead she let the anger grow – anger at Mrs Leech, anger at everyone who had let Rosie down, anger at Delilah, Jem, Sam and even William, anger at the injustice of the world. She was going to step up her rebellion, and she was going to get Sally and Martha out of this place. She might have failed Rosie, but she was not going to fail them.

Chapter Nine

Mrs Lydia Lawrence skewered another pin into her hat and looked at her reflection in the glass.

Yes. Neat. Tidy. *Respectable*. That was what the world expected of the housekeeper to such an important man as Mr Harcourt. If she had one hair out of place it would reflect badly on the master and his family, and she was certainly not about to let that happen.

There was a tiny smudge on the glass, and she tutted as she dabbed at it with the corner of her handkerchief. The housemaids were good enough, she supposed, and they did a decent job when they cleaned and tidied upstairs, but down here in the servants' quarters they sometimes let their standards drop, and Mrs Lawrence did not stand for that.

The servants and the composition of the household were the main concern on her mind this morning.

Back when Mr Harcourt had been a bachelor in a modest house, she had run only a very small staff, but once he had married the place simply wasn't big enough; after a few months and with a baby on the way he and his wife had moved to the sort of residence that his money and status warranted. This had allowed Mrs Lawrence to expand the household, and now, six years and a few false starts later, she had almost a full complement for the mansion. Everything was on the whole satisfactory but there remained some irritants, such as those that were currently occupying her.

She would address the question of the dirty mirror when she returned; she had no time to do it now, for the coachman would be waiting and it did not do to be late, even when one's deadline was self-imposed. She pushed in one more hatpin, just to be sure, then nodded at herself before passing through the back door and up the steps to the street.

The conveyance awaiting her was not, of course, the family coach, but the small gig that the master occasionally used for informal trips if he was on his own, and in which the senior servants could be conveyed to the centre of Liverpool when they had business there. James, the coachman, was smartly turned out in his livery and both the gig and the horse's harness shone.

Mrs Lawrence nodded her approval as he assisted her up to the seat.

As they set off at a steady, suitable pace, Mrs Lawrence had leisure to consider the two greatest of the servant problems. The first, unfortunately, she could do little about, because it involved the butler. Back when Mr Harcourt had been a bachelor, Wilson had been his valet – a good valet, she had to admit; but that was not her complaint. When they had moved and expanded the household, Mrs Lawrence had mentioned to the master that he would now need a butler, as the size of the mansion and the company he would be keeping necessitated such an appointment. She had done this reluctantly, because up until that point she had been the senior in the household, and a butler would outrank her. Still, it was in the best interests of Mr Harcourt and his then-new wife, and so she was prepared to make the sacrifice on their behalf. No doubt they would be able to find some sober, experienced man who was accustomed to running a household of that size and could do so with discretion.

However, Mr Harcourt had grown so used to having Wilson as the senior man about the place that he didn't want him outranked, so he had taken the decision to offer him the post of butler. He had evidently not considered it important that Mrs Lawrence would, in turn, now be outranked by a man who used to be her subordinate, with the result that she now had to call him 'Mr Wilson' and defer to his opinion. She *might* have been able to cope with that, were it not for the fact that his lack of experience meant that he was not a very good butler, so the household did not always run smoothly, and also that he still retained his role as Mr Harcourt's valet, attempting to do both jobs and thus letting the household down on both sides. He was also slack in his discipline with the male servants, who answered to him rather than to her, and had rather lower standards about what constituted acceptable servant behaviour. All of this combined to enrage Mrs Lawrence daily, but as both Mr Harcourt and Mr Wilson were happy, there was nothing she could do.

This constant frustration meant that Mrs Lawrence kept everything that *was* under her control on a very tight rein indeed, and this brought her to her other preoccupation, the one she was going to sort out this morning. It concerned the scullery maid. This was the lowest position of all among the staff, and thus one that many people might think was of little import-ance, but not Mrs Lawrence; she knew that a house-hold functioned from the bottom up. Since their move she had employed several scullery maids, and every one of them had turned out to be unsatisfactory. The latest was a girl of ten who had been given the place because her mother was a friend of Nanny's, but she simply could not keep up with the work and was constantly behind and being scolded by the cook, who in turn never ceased complaining to Mrs Lawrence. Mrs Roberts was the first professed cook the household had ever employed, a woman of great experience who had previously worked in a large country house as well as some of the richest town houses in Liverpool. Her accepting the position in the Harcourt household was something of a favour, even a step down from her previous roles, and Mrs Lawrence was extremely keen to keep her happy: she was exceptionally good at her job and invitations to Mr and Mrs Harcourt's dinner parties were much sought after in town society.

Mrs Lawrence had taken Mrs Roberts's point about the scullery maid – who'd run back to her mother – and had decided to fix this situation as soon as possible. She was determined to get it right this time. A ten-year-old, while cheap, was just too young to cope with the hard physical labour of the scullery maid's position, and this one had run away because she knew she had a home to go back to. In order to avoid either of these problems in future, Mrs Lawrence had decided upon a course of action that she had never considered before: she was going to the workhouse. She had been told that girls there were trained for service, and she hoped to get one who was a little older, maybe thirteen or fourteen, and who knew what hard work was. On top of that she would select one who had no family, so there was no chance of her running away to her mother at the slightest little scolding. No, she would choose a girl, offer her the position on trial, and then simply send her back to the workhouse if she proved unsatisfactory. That would leave the whole situation in Mrs Lawrence's control, which was just how she liked it.

By the time all these thoughts had run through Mrs Lawrence's head, James was stopping the gig outside the workhouse entrance. She alighted and told him to wait; he led the horse to stand in the shade cast by the huge building so that it would not overheat in the hot sun on this last day of August. She nodded to herself, both at his consideration for the animal and at the efficient, unfussy way in which he carried out his work. The household had *some* servants who knew how to comport themselves, at least.

Having never visited the workhouse before, Mrs Lawrence was not sure of the correct form, but a porter was able to direct her through the main door to an office that was labelled 'Receiving Room'. She rang the bell sharply and waited.

She was already tapping her foot in impatience when a woman, whom she judged by the keys and the cane hanging from her belt to be the matron, approached. When she saw her visitor, her expression changed from irritation to one of welcome. She introduced herself as Mrs Leech – the title no doubt an honorific, just as Mrs Lawrence's own was – and invited her into a stark but impressively clean office.

At the matron's invitation, Mrs Lawrence took a seat and explained her mission.

The matron nodded. 'Yes, we do train girls for service here and we can easily find you one.' She paused, licking her lips a little nervously. 'There will be a fee to pay, of course.'

Mrs Lawrence hadn't known this, but as she had never had any dealings with the workhouse before, it was not surprising that she should be ignorant of how it was run. 'How much?'

'Ten shillings,' was the reply, a price Mrs Lawrence thought was a little steep, but she hid her startled expression so as not to appear ignorant. 'There is a great deal of administration involved,' added Mrs Leech, a little too quickly, 'and of course you can always take it out of the girl's first quarter's wages.'

'I don't have that with me today, but if we can sort out a girl now, I will return to collect her on Monday and bring the fee with me, if that is acceptable? That will give you time to complete the necessary . . .' she gestured vaguely, 'formalities.'

'That will be fine,' said Mrs Leech, and Mrs Lawrence wondered that she sounded . . . nervous? relieved? But it was no matter.

The matron was already scanning a list that she had taken out of a drawer. 'A scullery maid, you say? Yes, I know just the girl—'

Mrs Lawrence held up her hand. 'If I am to pay ten shillings for the privilege, I think I am entitled to choose one for myself. Please arrange for half a dozen to be brought here so I can look them over.' That brought the conversation back under her control, she thought. The last thing she wanted was this woman palming off an unsuitable girl she was keen to get rid of.

The matron looked sour, but she did not voice any objection. She picked up a bell from her desk and rang it. The two of them waited in strained silence until another woman, this one wearing what was presumably a workhouse uniform, arrived. Mrs Leech reeled off six names to her and told her to fetch them. Then she turned back and, with what was clearly an effort, smiled and offered Mrs Lawrence tea.

Mrs Lawrence declined; she folded her hands neatly in her lap and waited.

It was around a quarter of an hour before the woman returned, ushering six girls into the room before departing. Mrs Leech made the arrivals line up so that Mrs Lawrence could inspect them.

* * *

In the weeks since Rosie died, Meg had been putting her time to good use. She had kept up with her work, of course; she was a model worker in the kitchen and the cook was even showing signs of appreciating her. But she also engaged in a number of less public activities. The nightly meetings in the dormitory continued, each new girl being introduced and welcomed as a sister, and Mrs Leech still had no idea about them. The matron also had no idea how or why various little inconveniences had started occurring, such as the workhouse clocks – of which there were many – all being set to different times so that the smooth running of the place, on which she prided herself, was disrupted. This small mischief buoyed the girls' spirits and gave them a tiny measure of control.

Mrs Leech might, Meg admitted to herself, have some inkling of why the question of disappearing girls was suddenly being whispered not only in the dormitories but also in the women's section, the laundry, the sewing room and the kitchen; but if so, she couldn't pin it on Meg without evidence. That didn't stop the canings, of course, which Mrs Leech had still been undertaking at every available opportunity, but even these seemed to be occurring less frequently. Meg liked to watch the matron's discomfort as every single girl in the dormitory now had the confidence to stare her in the eye and smile when she hit them, instead of lowering their gaze and begging for mercy.

By now Meg was getting the impression that Mrs Leech had decided to get rid of her altogether. Meg feared that she might end up being one of the 'disappeared', but it hadn't happened so far. She had been called to the Receiving Room several times to line up with other girls when someone had come to choose a maid from the workhouse, and Mrs Leech seemed to be pushing Meg's claims each time, but so far she had always been passed over due to her size. Although she had grown a little, she was still much smaller than other girls the same age, and most Liverpool matrons wanted a stout, hearty girl to be a maid-of-all-work.

It was late August – Meg thought – when she was called out of the kitchen again one afternoon. She trailed the pauper assistant around the workhouse as they picked up others from various places, and then made their way to the Receiving Room. She entered and lined up with the others.

Mrs Leech was there with another woman Meg didn't recognise. She was more smartly dressed than some of the others who had come seeking a maid, and Meg's interest was piqued. However, the first thing that happened was entirely predictable. The stranger pointed at Meg: 'That one looks very small. I asked for girls who were at least twelve.'

Meg was already resigning herself to being sent away when Mrs Leech showed the other woman a piece of paper that she had in her hand. 'She's small, I grant you. But she's actually the eldest of the girls in the room – she'll be fourteen in a couple of weeks.'

'Hmm,' was the only reply, and then the stranger turned back to the girls. 'Hold out your hands, please.'

There was some reluctance, for in the workhouse that normally only meant one thing: Mrs Leech's cane. But they all did as they were told, and fortunately it was only so the woman could inspect their hands.

'Far too soft,' was her dismissal of the first girl; Meg didn't know her well but thought she worked in the sewing room. Then the woman continued down the line, stopping at Meg and actually taking up her hands, as if astonished to find they could be so tough. The feeling of being inspected like a horse irritated Meg, but she held her tongue in case there really was a chance of getting out this time. She didn't want to leave her new sisters, but the first step in getting them all out was getting one of them out.

The woman stepped back. 'Tell me, which of you knows how best to make up a solution to clean a wooden table?'

Meg had been doing that for nearly a year, and such was her interest in this woman by now that she had no hesitation in rapping out the details of soda, fuller's earth and boiling water before any of the others could speak.

More questions followed, on subjects such as washing plates, scrubbing pots and floors, preparing and cooking vegetables and blacking a range. Meg could answer them all except the last: they'd never had something as expensive as a range at home, and the workhouse cooking was done on open fires and steam racks. But as none of the others could answer that one either, it was of little matter. Indeed, the other girls were mostly completely silent, and Meg wondered at Mrs Leech summoning girls from the laundry and the sewing room to come here and be questioned about matters relating to a kitchen.

At last the woman fell silent. She walked up and down the line one more time, and then stopped in front of Meg. 'This one looks like the best fit. What about it, girl?'

This was it. But what was on offer and, crucially, would it be something that might help her to help Sally and Martha? Meg risked speaking up. 'I can't answer that question, ma'am, until you tell me what it is that you're asking.'

Meg could hear Mrs Leech's sharp intake of breath and knew that she might just have blown her chance of getting out of the workhouse. However, the woman, although she seemed a little taken aback, was not angry. 'It's a fair question,' she replied. 'I am the housekeeper in a large house with a number of servants, and I'm looking for a new scullery maid. You would live in and be paid four p— three pounds and ten shillings for the year. Half a day off per fortnight, but in return I would expect you to work extremely hard from six in the morning until late in the evening, keep yourself clean and respectable, and do exactly as you're told by all the more senior servants. Especially the cook, to whom you would be answerable on a day-to-day basis.'

Meg could hardly believe her ears. A kitchen! To work in a kitchen – and to be paid for it! And – her mind began to race – a big house. Where there might be other employment opportunities, or a chance to ask the mistress for advice and help.

But the woman was still looking at her. 'Well, what about it?'

'Yes, ma'am. Oh yes, I'd love to, thank you, ma'am.'

To Meg's enormous relief, the woman nodded and turned to Mrs Leech. 'Good. Please see to whatever you need to do, and I'll be back on Monday as agreed with the fee.' The girls were ushered out, Meg almost overwhelmed at the change in her fortune. But, of course, a lot could still happen between now and Monday: Mrs Leech could prevent it from happening if she so minded, and that, rather than the prospect of her new job, was uppermost in Meg's mind as she left the room and returned to the kitchen.

* * *

Mrs Leech sagged with relief once the room was empty. She had tried a new money-making idea, and it had succeeded, which opened up a host of new possibilities. Up until now she had only been paid for her under-the-counter dealings; the regular business of sending girls out to respectable domestic situations was too well known as being free for her to attempt to charge for it. But it was perfectly clear that this morning's visitor had never been inside the workhouse before and had no idea how it worked, so Mrs Leech had thought she would try her luck. And what luck she had enjoyed! From now on she would make a close study of every woman who came looking for a servant girl, to see if she might get away with it again. If it worked, she would be able to save at twice the rate she was at the moment. It was all purely business, of course; any single woman had to make the best of her opportunities if she was to make her way in a world built for men. If that meant sometimes being . . . less than strictly honest, then what of it? Life was cruel to everyone, particularly those in her position, and it was each man – or woman – for themselves.

The Shaw girl, though. It was a shame to be sending her out to such a good situation; a tough maid-of-all-work job in a lower-middle-class terrace with a harsh mistress would have been more fitting. But Mrs Leech needed to be rid of her – she was too sharp by half and a disruptive influence. She didn't respond to being beaten and wouldn't be cowed, and Mrs Leech was suspicious that she knew more than she let on about the . . . special project. And was it her imagination, or had the girl been reading the workhouse regulations on the wall while she'd been standing in the office just now? Specifically, the one about female inmates not being subject to corporal punishment?

No, the best course of action was certainly to get rid of her before she caused more trouble, and to this end Mrs Leech had been putting Meg up for all kinds of jobs for some while, but with no luck. So although it irritated her to see Meg go to a good position rather than a rough one, it was certainly preferable to having her stay here. It had been a stroke of genius this afternoon, she prided herself, to think of filling the room with girls who worked in the laundry or the sewing room when the visitor wanted someone for a kitchen.

Thinking of the visitor caused another thought to burrow its way into Mrs Leech's increasingly strained and paranoid mind. She had first mentioned the fee when they were alone, but the woman had referred to it while the girls were still in the room. Had Meg heard it? Would she put it together with anything else she might know? And in that case . . .

Mrs Leech pulled herself together. The visitor had said 'fee' and then only very quickly; if she'd actually said 'ten shillings' then it might have been a problem, but surely it was not. She was thinking far too much about that one girl, imputing thoughts to the wretched child that had in all probability never occurred to her. It was a sign that she had been working in this godforsaken job for far too long; the quicker she could retire to a nice cottage with a servant or two, the better. In the meantime she was another ten shillings richer than she had been this morning, or at least she would be, and she had finally rid herself of Meg Shaw. The job was too good for her, yes, but in a providential light it had all worked out well: Meg would be sent further away than was usual for workhouse girls, and would be buried in a basement kitchen somewhere, unable to come into the centre of Liverpool and thus incapable of coming into contact with anyone to whom she might spill Mrs Leech's secrets. She was so sharp she must have worked some of it out by now, even though she hadn't let on. As soon as Mrs Leech had seen the girl off with Mrs – what was her name again? – on Monday, she would breathe a sigh of relief.

* * *

Meg spent the rest of the afternoon in the kitchen doing little more than going through the motions of her work. Soon, she would be leaving; she would able to walk out of the workhouse door and start a new life. For herself she was glad to be going, though now it came down to it she was worried about leaving Martha and, particularly, Sally. But, she told herself, the best way to help them was to be on the outside, so this was a positive development and she should look forward to it. The visitor had said 'Monday', hadn't she? Today was Friday, so that just meant the weekend in between; only two more days to endure.

'You look like the cat that's got the cream,' came Jen's voice, breaking into Meg's thoughts. 'Very pleased with yourself.'

'Am I?'

'You're even humming, and I haven't heard you do that for a long time.'

Meg leaned in as Jen poured hot water into the sink and spoke in a low voice. 'I've been offered a position.'

The clap on the back that Jen gave her nearly sent her flying into the sink. 'Good for you, girl! You get out of here and make something of yourself.'

Meg kept her smile to herself as she returned to the dirty dishes, but inside she was churning with a mix of happiness, excitement, maybe a little nervousness. And, most of all, she was planning for a future for all of them that was going to be much better than the past or the present.

Breaking the news that night in the dormitory proved a trying experience. Most of the girls offered good-luck wishes, but telling Martha and Sally was much more difficult, for different reasons.

Martha was a little older than Meg, fourteen already, and she was desperate to escape and be sent out to a position. Indeed, she should by rights have gone already. Several of the town seamstresses and menders were regular visitors to the workhouse, picking out girls who had been trained in plain sewing, and all of them had admired the samples of Martha's work that they were shown – but as soon as she had been brought before them in person their enthusiasm waned, and she had never made it out the door. The time would eventually come, if the situation continued, when she would have to leave the girls' section of the workhouse and be placed with the women, those who would stay here for the long term.

Meg's leaving must have only emphasised to Martha the harshness of her own position, but she was gracious enough to put her own worries to one side and congratulate Meg on her good fortune. Meg could see how much it cost her, and she vowed again that she would keep her promise. She was soon sorry for Sally, too, for the younger girl burst into sobs as soon as she heard the news, and both the others tried to comfort her.

'I know, I know, it's silly, and I should be used to it by now, 'cos people come and go all the time. But you've been my real friend, sticking up for me and everything.' Tears poured down Sally's face.

Meg hugged her. 'I know – and you've been my good friend too, looking after me when I first arrived. And I will do everything I can for you, so just think – only another year and then you'll be nearly fourteen, and you can go out to work as well. And when we're both maids, or whatever we are, there'll be nothing to stop us seeing each other. Just think – we could have our half-days together and go for a walk around the town!'

'Really?'

'Yes, really.'

Sally's eyes were still wet, but her shoulders stopped heaving. She hiccupped. 'The streets, and the shops, like you told me about all those evenings?'

'Yes, and even the big trains,' replied Meg, pushing away the thought that she both did and did not want ever to go near the railway station again, in case she did or did not see two once-beloved figures outside it.

'But a whole year, though! More, really, 'cos I won't even be thirteen until Christmas.'

'Don't worry,' said Martha, with what Meg thought was a huge self-restraint and generosity. 'I'll still be here in the meantime, won't I, and we can look out for each other.'

Meg took both their hands in her own. 'The lady said I'd get half a day off a fortnight. I don't know what day it'll be, but if it's a Thursday then I'll come and visit you, I promise.'

'And tell us all about it?' Sally sounded a little more reconciled to her loss.

'Yes. And I promise I'll be thinking of you in between.' Meg took a deep breath and said it out loud for the first time. 'After all, we're family, aren't we?'

Sally looked thunderstruck. '*Family* . . .' She hardly dared to whisper the word.

Martha smiled her rare, beaming smile. 'Of course we are.'

'Family,' said Meg, firmly. She squeezed their hands.

Later that night, when the lights were out and the evening's chat was over, Sally wriggled up to Meg's end of the bed and put one arm about her. There was a time when Meg would have tensed, unable to move until such unwanted contact had disappeared, but now she welcomed it.

'Tell me another story about the trains,' said Sally, sleepily. 'So I can remember it when you've gone.'

Meg spoke in a low, comforting voice and soon felt Sally beginning to drop off.

They were both dozing when Sally's voice came again in Meg's ear, 'At least you didn't just disappear.'

That woke Meg up again. She managed to nudge Sally back to her own end of the bed and then lay thinking. It was the older girls who disappeared, which meant that Martha would be in danger. And maybe Sally as well, because she was big for her age and could be mistaken for someone older.

These thoughts naturally took Meg's mind back to Mrs Leech. Something that had been said in the matron's office that afternoon was nagging at the back of her mind, but she couldn't think what it was. Maybe it would come back to her after a night's sleep; or maybe it wasn't important at all.

Chapter Ten

Today was the day, and Meg had been jittery since the moment she awoke. Something, surely, was going to prevent her leaving. When Mrs Leech made one of her sporadic appearances in the dormitory as soon as the girls were out of bed, Meg's heart sank and she felt sick, but – wonder of wonders – the matron paid her no heed at all, simply inspecting everyone for clean hands and aprons and caning one unfortunate girl who was new to the workhouse and who cried sufficiently to satisfy her.

That was me, once, thought Meg. *But it won't ever be me again.*

After Mrs Leech had left, Sally, Martha and some of the others gathered round Meg to hug her and wish her luck. Sally bore up bravely, not letting her tears fall as they held each other tight. She whispered in Meg's ear, 'I won't forget you.'

'And I won't forget you,' Meg assured her. She turned to Martha and all the girls. 'I won't forget any of you – and see that you keep looking after each other as much as you can.'

Soon the girls were off to their work, and Meg was left with this morning's pauper assistant, who turned out to be Lizzie.

'I won't have to pick you up and carry you this time, I suppose.'

'No,' said Meg, smiling. 'I'll come of my own accord now that I'm leaving. Where do we have to go?'

'First to the room where everyone's clothes are stored – we have to put you back in what you were wearing when you came here, and then send your uniform to the laundry with the others. Then to Mrs Leech for paperwork, and then you're free to go.'

Free to go. The words echoed in Meg's mind as she walked the familiar, detested hallways.

They reached the place where clothes were stored, a room Meg had never visited before. There were shelves and shelves covering each wall from floor to ceiling, all stuffed not only with clothes, but with the few personal possessions that some inmates had brought with them: there were several clay pipes on the nearest shelves, and Meg spotted a bright hair ribbon next to a small pair of shoes. A lump formed in her throat. She wondered if Rosie's things still sat on a shelf, for ever waiting for their owner to come back.

The usual workhouse efficiency was on show, and the bundle handed to her did indeed turn out to be her own clothes. She spent a few moments touching them almost in wonder until the woman in charge of the room asked her if she was going to be there all day, as she had other work to do? Meg hastened to leave.

As if to emphasise that she was doing everything in reverse, Lizzie next led her to the bath house so she could take off the workhouse uniform. It was at this point that Meg discovered that she had, as she had guessed, grown during the year. She still wasn't exactly tall – the housekeeper had mistaken her for someone younger – but her dress didn't fit. It was an old one of Delilah's that had been too big for her when she arrived, but it was now indecently short, barely reaching mid-calf. She tugged it down as best she could but there was little to be done. And worse was to come: she couldn't get her old boots on at all.

'Hmm.' Lizzie was looking at her. 'Never mind them: just throw yours on the pile there ready for new arrivals, and keep the ones you're wearing. Nobody will know the difference as long as there's the same number of pairs.'

Meg placed her old boots carefully next to the heap of workhouse ones. She sighed as she pulled back on those she had been wearing for the last few months: they did fit better, but they were shoddy in the extreme, the front of one sole flapping off and loose stitching everywhere. If they'd been made by one of the workhouse boys, she didn't think he had much of a career ahead of him.

She looked awful, she knew she did. But what could she do about it? She could only hope that her appearance wouldn't put off the housekeeper, whose name she still didn't know. Meg worried she might look so bad that the housekeeper would turn around in disgust and leave without taking Meg with her.

Lizzie accompanied Meg to the door of the Receiving Room and then stopped. She bent down and put her hands on Meg's shoulders. 'You have a good life, Meg Shaw. Have the life my daughters never had, and make something of yourself.' She gave Meg a little shake and then, as if ashamed of having displayed so much emotion, she cleared her throat, knocked on the door and then walked firmly away down the corridor.

Meg was still looking after her, and the lump was still in her throat, when the door opened, and there – please God for the final time – was Mrs Leech.

'Inside,' was the matron's only word.

Meg entered the office. She braced herself for whatever was to come, but Mrs Leech was pushing pieces of paper around on her desk and writing in complete silence, other than the sound of her pen scratching.

That suited Meg, who had no wish to enter into any kind of conversation with the matron. She stood in an equally stony silence, letting her eye wander around the room. It was the same as it had been on Friday, the same as it had been on the day she had scurried past it in fright when she was lost, the same as it had been when she had first arrived; the only difference now was that she herself was not in a heightened state of panic, as she had been on all the other occasions.

This gave her the chance to see things that she hadn't noticed before, and she gazed at the framed set of workhouse rules on the wall. 'Every Person shall be employed in such labour as their respective age and ability will admit . . . commence their work by six o'Clock in the morning . . . anyone refusing to work shall for the first offence go without their next meal . . . the Poor shall have their provisions in a clean and wholesome manner . . . the House to be swept from top to bottom every morning and cleaned all over . . .' They went on and on and on; no wonder everything in the workhouse ran like clockwork when the rules were spelled out in such minute detail.

But then she gasped, a sound audible enough to make Mrs Leech look up from what she was doing. Meg stared again at the words, wondering if she had read them incorrectly, but there they were: 'No corporal punishment shall be inflicted on any female child.'

Mrs Leech seemed to know exactly what she was thinking, and was surging round the desk in an instant. Despite herself, Meg took a step back, but then she recovered, anger taking the place of fright. 'You're not allowed to use that cane on us! You never have been!'

She felt a sudden intense pain in her earlobe: Mrs Leech was pinching it, hard. 'And what are you going to do about it. Eh? You?'

Meg felt as though her ear was about to be torn off; not content with pinching her nails into it, Mrs Leech was lifting it higher and higher, forcing Meg on to her tiptoes. But she was furious. All that pain, all those tears, inflicted unnecessarily. 'I'm going to find out who the right person is and tell them about it, that's what I'm going to do.'

Mrs Leech shook her. 'And who's going to believe you? A little workhouse brat like you, from the criminal underclass? No doubt a liar since the day you were born?'

Meg's fury burst. She wrenched herself away from Mrs Leech. 'Criminal? We might be poor, but we're hardworking and honest and law-abiding, which is more than I can say for you!'

Mrs Leech's eyes blazed with fury. 'How dare you speak to me like that!' She fumbled at the loop that held the cane to her belt.

'You can't cane me – not ever again,' said Meg. She pointed to the papers on Mrs Leech's desk. 'You've just signed to say I'm not an inmate of the workhouse any more.'

Mrs Leech had got the cane free and was cutting it through the air. 'No, you're right, you're not an inmate. You're the violent mad girl off the street who's come in here and attacked me, forcing me to defend myself. I'll send you to an asylum!'

She made to strike Meg with the cane, but Meg evaded it easily. 'It's not me who's mad.'

This infuriated Mrs Leech even more, and she advanced, trying to back Meg into a corner. 'You'll pay for your impudence, girl.'

Pay. That was the thought that had been nagging away at the back of Meg's mind. 'That's it!'

Mrs Leech was momentarily distracted. 'That's what?'

'Oh, you're even more wicked than I thought. You've been taking money from people to send them girls! You sold me to the woman who came here on

Friday, didn't you? That's why she talked about a fee. Is that where girls have been disappearing to?'

Mrs Leech positively screeched as she flew forward. Meg tried to manoeuvre herself towards the door, but in stepping backwards while still trying to keep her eye on the enraged matron, she tripped over the chair and fell. In an instant Mrs Leech was upon her, slashing down with the cane again and again on every part of Meg that she could reach.

Meg could do nothing but try to defend herself, although she was so angry that she barely felt the whipping cuts as they descended.

And then the door opened.

Meg heard a man's voice. 'What on earth . . . ?'

The slashing of the cane stopped. Meg was able to sit up. She saw that the newcomer was the workhouse master himself and that Mrs Leech was stepping back. Meg hauled herself to her feet.

The master quickly shut the door behind him. 'Mrs Leech, would you care to explain what is going on here?'

Mrs Leech made what Meg saw was a huge effort to compose herself. 'I'm glad you've come to witness this, Mr Higgin. No sooner had I discharged this girl than she went insane, attacking me. Fortunately I was able to defend myself. She's lucky I don't have the law on her before we throw her out. Or maybe we should summon—'

'That's not true!' shouted Meg. She appealed to the master. 'It was her who attacked me with that cane, the one she's not even supposed to—'

'Silence! Nobody asked you,' interrupted Mr Higgin. He turned back to Mrs Leech. 'I am perfectly willing to call a member of the constabulary if you wish.'

Meg glared at Mrs Leech. If she did call a police-man then Meg would shout to the rooftops about what Mrs Leech had been doing. Even if the man they called wouldn't listen, and she was taken away, surely she would get a chance to speak later, or in court, or something? Surely *someone* would listen to her side of the story?

Mrs Leech, evidently thinking the same thing, was shaking her head. 'Thank you, Mr Higgin, that won't be necessary. As you know, I'm always prepared to make sacrifices and endure discomforts in the course of doing my duty.'

'That's extremely magnanimous of you, Mrs Leech.'

Mr Higgin addressed Meg once more. 'I've never seen such an example of base ingratitude in all my life. This workhouse has fed and sheltered you, Mrs Leech is like a mother to all you girls, and this is how you repay her?'

'But—'

He held up his hand again. 'Enough! I have no wish to hear your feeble excuses.' He sighed. 'Girls like you will always revert to their true character, given the chance. But if you've been discharged then it's no problem of ours. Get out now, before I decide to take further action after all.'

'I'll see her off the premises, Mr Higgin,' said Mrs Leech. She took Meg firmly by one arm and marched her out of the room.

As soon as they were clear of the master, Mrs Leech bent to hiss in Meg's ear. 'You see? Nobody will listen to a worthless little good-for-nothing like you.' She gave Meg a firm shake. 'And even though you're on your way out, your friends are still here, aren't they? Dear Martha and poor, stupid little Sally who you like so much?'

Meg gasped. 'You wouldn't!'

'Oh, I would, believe me. Now, you get out of here and never let me see your face again. And if you breathe one word of anything, *one word* to anybody, I'll see that your little friends endure lives of unending misery every day from dawn to dusk.' They reached the outer door. 'Do we understand each other?'

Meg's watchword had always been to save her energy for the battles she might win. And, just for a moment, she had thought she might win this one. But it was no use: the power was all on one side. And to make any further attempt now would only be to harm the others, which she couldn't allow herself to do. Fuming at the injustice, she replied, 'We do.'

'Good.'

Meg met Mrs Leech's eye and glared into it with a suppressed fury so strong that it could have set the workhouse on fire. 'Now. Let. Go. Of. My. Arm.'

Mrs Leech released her and strode off without a word, re-entering her office and banging the door shut behind her.

Meg took a moment to calm down, forcing herself to remain still until her breathing was less ragged and the extreme rage had subsided. She was getting out of here, and she would damn well get Sally and Martha out too, one day. And she would see that Mrs Leech got her comeuppance, however long it took. She didn't know how, but she would.

Meg had entered the workhouse with her knees trembling and her hands shaking. She walked out of it with her head held high.

Chapter Eleven

The housekeeper had probably told Mrs Leech what time of day she would arrive to pick Meg up, but if she had then Mrs Leech hadn't let Meg know. Meg had started on the deregistration process first thing, before breakfast – which she had missed – and it was now surely no later than nine o'clock. Well, she would wait.

By early afternoon she was hungry and really feeling the sting from the many blows of the cane she had endured earlier. She had been so angry at the time that she hardly noticed them, but the passing hours gave her every opportunity to focus on the growing pain. There were quite a few on her back, and also on her arms where she'd raised them to defend herself. Those wouldn't be noticeable to anyone else, at least, though by the feel of it there were also two on her face that would surely be obvious, and her ear was bleeding where Mrs Leech had pinched the lobe and pulled it away from her head. When all this was added to the too-short dress and the terrible boots, Meg knew that she could hardly look worse, and she was genuinely worried that the housekeeper would reject her and choose someone else. And what would she do then? Go home? Turn up on the doorstep of the family who didn't want her, only to be rejected again? Seek re-entry to the workhouse? But no, she would never do that, come what may.

It was around mid-afternoon, and Meg was starting to think she would need to find a privy soon, when she saw a smart-looking little carriage coming up the road, two-wheeled and drawn by one horse. At the reins was a man in a very fancy uniform, and next to him was the woman Meg recognised as the housekeeper.

The carriage stopped and the woman got down. Meg straightened herself and smoothed her dress. The woman approached and seemed about to walk straight past her until Meg stepped forward, almost blocking her path, curtseyed and said, 'Good day, ma'am.'

The woman was about to nod and pass on when she stopped, turned back to Meg and looked at her properly. 'What in the name of all the saints . . . is that you? The girl I engaged? What on earth has happened to your face?'

'Yes, ma'am. My name is Meg Shaw.' Meg hesitated, unsure how to answer the last part without damaging her own prospects.

Thankfully, the woman didn't dismiss her out of hand. Instead she pursed her lips as she looked Meg up and down and glanced towards the door that led into the workhouse and the Receiving Room. 'Hmm,' she said, considering. Then, reaching some kind of decision, she added, 'Wait there,' and strode inside.

Meg stood, knowing that the carriage driver was watching her. She was in an agony to know what was going on inside, what lies Mrs Leech might be telling about her and whether they would influence the housekeeper's decision.

It seemed an age before she emerged once more. She walked briskly over, and Meg waited to hear her fate.

'Meg, you said?'

'Yes, ma'am.'

'I'm Mrs Lawrence, and you may address me as such.'

'Yes, Mrs Lawrence.'

'Well, this whole episode has not proceeded in the way I thought it would, but here we are. You have no luggage, no other clothes?'

'No, Mrs Lawrence. Sorry.'

Mrs Lawrence clicked her tongue. 'Still, I don't suppose that's your fault,' she said. 'We'll take a detour on the way back. Come.'

Meg could hardly believe her luck. Mrs Lawrence still wanted to take her! She still had a position to go to!

The horse and the carriage were both bigger than she expected as she drew near them. The man was of that indeterminate age, neither young nor middle-aged, and Meg didn't know whether to see him as a threat or not. She eyed him warily, but after assisting Mrs Lawrence he held out his hand with a friendly smile. 'Up you get, then, young 'un. Can you manage?'

Meg scrambled up on to the step and then up again on to the seat. She had never sat in any kind of carriage before and felt dizzyingly high off the ground. The man went round to the other side and swung himself up with the ease of practice, and Meg squeezed herself as far as possible to the edge of the bench-like seat to avoid squashing Mrs Lawrence in the middle or crushing her dress.

'It's not really meant for three,' the housekeeper explained, 'but I could hardly bring the family's formal coach to the workhouse, and I remembered you were slight.'

Meg swallowed her surprise at finding that her new employer had a second carriage, and by implication one that was bigger than this one. She was in a new world now, and she didn't want to look ignorant. But surely she was about to start work for a family that was very rich indeed.

Mrs Lawrence was addressing the driver. 'James, take us to the cobblers where we send the boots to be mended. I can't have her in the house wearing those.'

James shook the reins and the carriage set off. Meg was terrified, never having travelled at such a pace, nor so far off the ground. She clutched at the rail to one side of her and held on for dear life, convinced every moment that she was about to be thrown out and dashed on the stones of the road.

Not once did she look back at the workhouse.

The others were talking to each other, and didn't seem to need Meg's attention, so she felt free to watch as the streets and the people went by. Eventually she grew less fearful of falling out, and even began to enjoy the sensation of the ride. What a fine thing it was to be conveyed in a horse and carriage rather than trudging through the streets. Her fingers loosened on the rail.

Some of the words being spoken by the others reached her ears. 'Disgrace' – that was Mrs Lawrence, and Meg was afraid that meant her, but then she caught '. . . treating girls like that' and felt more hopeful.

'Are you going to tell the mistress?' asked James, in a low voice. 'Will she want to know?'

Meg didn't quite catch the reply, as Mrs Lawrence was facing away from her to talk to James, but she thought it was negative, and she sighed in relief. Her best hope, when she reached the house, was to remain as anonymous as possible while she found her feet – the last thing she needed was to be drawn to the attention of the presumably very fine lady who was the mistress.

After some minutes they stopped outside a row of shops. Meg was nearest the pavement, so she climbed out first and waited for Mrs Lawrence to alight and lead the way into the cobblers.

The interior was dark after the bright day outside, and Meg breathed in the aroma of leather and polish while she waited for her eyes to adjust.

The shopkeeper came forward straight away. 'Yes, madam, how can I serve you?'

Mrs Lawrence pointed at Meg's feet. 'Our new maid needs some decent footwear before she starts work. Nothing too new, but if you have anything in the back room that will fit, we'll try some.'

The man bent to look closely at Meg's feet, and she felt embarrassed. 'Yes, well, I can see your point,' was all that he said, and then he went back behind his counter and into another room.

A sudden terrible thought struck Meg. She knew she shouldn't speak unless she was spoken to, but she had to take the chance. 'Mrs Lawrence,' she whispered, 'I have no money to buy boots.'

Mrs Lawrence didn't seem annoyed. 'I didn't expect you to, child. You're a member of our household now, so we'll see you're provided for.' Then, to Meg's great surprise, she smiled. 'Besides, when I saw the state of you I told the workhouse matron I would only pay half the fee, so I've saved five shillings, more than enough.'

Meg returned the smile, pleased at the thought that someone had got the better of Mrs Leech, but she turned her head to hide it.

For a moment the only sound was that of the cobbler in the other room, and then Mrs Lawrence, keeping her face forward and not looking at Meg, said, softly, 'Now that you're under my jurisdiction, I expect you to work hard – very hard. But in return, I promise you that nobody will hit or beat you. Not ever.'

Meg felt tears coming to her eyes and she nodded without speaking.

Mrs Lawrence cleared her throat and continued looking straight ahead.

The cobbler came back with not one pair of boots, but three, and Meg enjoyed the luxury of trying them all on to see which was the best fit. Mrs Lawrence spoke sharply when he tried to name his price, haggling him down to two shillings and elevenpence, and he succumbed, taking the coins. 'Do you want the boots wrapped, madam?'

'No, she can wear them,' came the reply. 'And as for those' – she pointed at the sad-looking workhouse boots lying discarded – 'if you can salvage any of the leather then you're welcome to it, otherwise you can dispose of them as you see fit.'

He inclined his head as though she were doing him a great favour. *Still*, thought Meg, following Mrs Lawrence outside, *he'll get something for them*. Nothing in the city was ever wasted, not clothes nor boots nor food. Everything just gradually made its way downwards until it fell into the hands of someone who was grateful to have it.

'Good,' said Mrs Lawrence once they were again seated in the carriage. 'You'll need a new dress, too, but we have several of those in the house, so there's no need for further purchases.' She turned to James. 'Home now, if you please. We're already much later than I intended.'

Nobody spoke during the journey through Liverpool's streets, but that was fine by Meg. She spent her time alternately watching the buildings and the people go by – at such a speed, with the horse trotting! – and looking down at her well-shod feet. *Two shillings and elevenpence.* Enough to feed a whole family, or pay a day's rent, and all spent on one pair of boots for her. When she thought also of Mrs Lawrence's kind words while they were in the shop, Meg didn't think she could possibly feel more grateful if she tried. She was going to work *so* hard in her new position to repay such benevolence. They would be glad that they took her on, and she would be in a better position to help Martha and Sally.

It wasn't long before they had passed out of anywhere that Meg recognised. The streets grew wider and wider and the houses larger and larger. Meg wondered which one of these fine dwellings was to be their destination, but they kept going, right out of the city streets and into a park. The large open space of grass and trees was so alien to Meg that she stopped thinking about her boots and simply stared. There was even a lake, a great expanse of clean water with ducks swimming on the surface.

Mrs Lawrence noticed her wide-eyed expression. 'Prince's Park,' she said. 'The main park is open to the public for recreation, but the houses and gardens, of course, are private.' She pointed. 'There.'

Meg hadn't thought she could be any more astonished and overwhelmed than she already was, but Mrs Lawrence was indicating a row of the most enormous houses she could possibly imagine. 'And . . . I'm to work in one of these?'

'Yes. Prince's Park Terrace, one of the finest addresses in Liverpool. Ten houses, each of five storeys plus a basement, and each with its own enclosed garden as well as all the necessary stables and so on.' She looked down at Meg, glad to have somebody new to impress, even if it was only a scullery maid. 'All brand new when we moved in six years ago, with all the latest conveniences.'

The carriage passed the front of all the impressive façades before pulling up outside the last one. James handed them down, and then winked at Meg as she whispered a barely audible 'thank you' and stared up at the huge, white building.

'We'll be late for tea by now,' said Mrs Lawrence to him. 'I'll give you some time to see to the horse and then have yours sent across, so you needn't come in.'

He thanked her and took the carriage on a narrower road that led around behind the houses.

Meg followed Mrs Lawrence towards the house. They didn't go up the steps to the imposing front door, but instead passed through an iron gate and down a flight of stairs that led to a basement entrance.

Mrs Lawrence hesitated with her hand on the latch. She cleared her throat. 'The privy is round the back in the yard, if you need to visit it before you come in.'

Meg was glad to do so, finding it clean and with a bunch of some kind of sweet-smelling herb hung up in the corner.

Once she had returned and they were inside the house, Mrs Lawrence led Meg into the nearest room via a door on the right. 'The scullery,' she said. 'You'll spend much of your time in here, but for now just wash your hands and face. We're already late, and I can't abide lateness.'

'Yes, Mrs Lawrence,' said Meg. She approached the sink – something with which she certainly *was* familiar – and was surprised and pleased to see that it had its own pump: indoors! There was a bar of hard soap to one side so she pumped water and lathered her hands, wiping them across her face and wincing as they met the marks of the cane.

When she had finished she looked out into the hallway, where Mrs Lawrence was standing by a looking-glass, patting her hair into shape after having removed her hat.

She looked Meg up and down. 'Now you're cleaner I can see how pale you look, as well as small. I hope this hasn't been a mistake.'

Meg felt confident enough to reply. 'I can work hard, Mrs Lawrence, I assure you. And if I'm pale it's probably just because I didn't get outside much at the workhouse.' As she spoke, the scent of cooked food wafted towards her, and to her embarrassment her stomach gave a loud rumble. 'Or maybe because I haven't had anything to eat yet today.'

'What?' Mrs Lawrence's expression grew annoyed again. 'Why, if I had known that when I spoke to the matron—' She checked herself. 'But no matter. Come in now and you can have your tea before you do anything else.'

Meg followed her down the passage and through another door on her right. As Mrs Lawrence moved from being directly in front of her, Meg could see the whole room at once. Down the middle ran a large table, at which a dozen or so people were seated, each with an almost-empty plate in front of them. There had been a quiet hum of conversation, but that stopped as she appeared, framed in the doorway; the room went silent and every face turned to stare at her.

* * *

After a few moments, the man sitting at the head of the table broke the silence. 'Mrs Lawrence. When you weren't back by the time tea was ready, we ate anyway as otherwise the staff will be late for their evening duties. I've had some put by for you and for the new maid. Ivy,' he addressed a girl sitting towards the bottom end of the table, 'fetch the plates from the kitchen, please.'

Everyone was still staring at Meg, and she swallowed. Although she had at least got rid of the terrible boots, she was still wearing the old, short dress and she was aware that the marks on her face must be visible.

'Meg, you can sit there,' said Mrs Lawrence, indicating a chair at the bottom end of the table, next to the one Ivy had just vacated. 'Everyone, this is Meg, our new scullery maid.' She paused, and then added, with a dignity Meg certainly didn't feel, 'She came with an excellent recommendation.'

Meg heard a few sniggers from the middle of the table, and the whispered word 'workhouse', but she ignored it and sat down. Opposite her was the only person in the room younger than herself, a boy of about twelve. He stuck his tongue out at her, though she noticed that he was careful not to let those at the top of the table see him.

The man who had spoken earlier addressed Meg down the length of the table. 'Now, Meg, you may not remember everyone's names straight away, but we'll start with the introductions. I'm Mr Wilson, the butler and the master's valet. I'm the head of the staff. You've already met Mrs Lawrence, the house-keeper.' Meg wondered why Mrs Lawrence was looking daggers at him, but she didn't have time to think about it as the butler was moving on. 'Next we have Miss Greenwood, lady's maid.' He indicated an elegant woman in her mid-thirties, who nodded graciously.

Mr Wilson pointed to the only other man in the room. 'Samuel, footman.' The name gave Meg a little stab of sadness, but at least she would remember it. Although he was seated, she could see that Samuel was tall; he was also extremely handsome, and several of the maids hadn't taken their eyes off him since Meg had entered the room.

'Then we have May and Dot, house-parlour maids; and Hannah, the kitchen maid. You'll be under her as well as Mrs Roberts, the cook.' Meg smiled at Hannah, eager to make a good impression, but she received only a curled lip and a look of disdain in reply.

'And finally, Robbie, the hall boy.' This was the boy sitting opposite Meg.

'Mrs Roberts is in the kitchen, as she couldn't leave the preparations for the family dinner, but she'll be able to eat now because Hannah will go to take over from her.' He paused. '*Now*, please, Hannah.'

Meg watched the kitchen maid leave the room.

'There is also Nanny, whom you won't see much as she has her meals up in the nursery, and James, the coachman.'

'And I'm Ivy, the tweenie,' said a new voice. 'I've been doing your work since the other girl left, and I'm glad to have you here, I can tell you.' She put a plate down in front of Meg. 'Is James coming in, Mrs Lawrence, or shall I take his tea out to him?'

'You can take it out, thank you.'

Meg vaguely heard Mr Wilson tell everyone else to get up and get about their work, but the meal in front of her was by now absorbing all her attention. On the plate was a thick slice of cold meat pie, with fresh green beans and peas alongside it. The aroma of the meal, after so many months of tasteless slop in the workhouse and combined with today's complete lack of food, was so overwhelming that it made her dizzy. She picked up her knife and fork, and the rest of the room, the rest of the *world*, simply disappeared.

The sensations of taste – the crisp pastry, the well-cooked and flavoured meat, the vegetables that hadn't been boiled into mush – were even better than those of smell, and it wasn't until the plate was completely clean that Meg became at all aware of her surroundings again. The room was empty apart from her and Mrs Lawrence, who was gazing at her in a mixture of horror and sympathy. Her own plate was still half full, and Meg realised that she must have eaten hers rather quickly. She felt her face grow hot.

'I think we'll skip the cake for this evening,' said the housekeeper, nodding at Meg's empty plate. She took another small mouthful and waited until she had chewed and swallowed before continuing. 'Not because I want to deprive you, but because it looks like you'll need to get your stomach accustomed to real food. I don't want you to stuff yourself with too much now if you're not used to it, and make yourself too ill to work tomorrow.'

As Meg hadn't even vaguely considered the possibility that there might be a pudding – on a Monday, a normal working day – this was no loss. Besides, her stomach already felt full, and she could still taste the juicy, perfectly cooked meat and pastry in her mouth, a sensation she wanted to savour as long as she could.

She stood up. These people had been so kind to her already; it was time to start paying back. 'Shall I take your plate, Mrs Lawrence, if you've finished? And if you could kindly point me to the scullery again, I can start with the washing-up.'

The housekeeper nodded in approval. 'Here. And it's out there, back down the passageway, last door on your left before you get to the back door. Ivy will show you what to do.'

Meg found the scullery without a problem, and Ivy in it. She was a little older than Meg, perhaps around sixteen, and she smiled broadly. 'Oh, you're ready to start already? That's good. I told Mrs Roberts you were here and she said to stay by you for a while so you know what to do. At the moment it's the washing-up from the servants' tea, and then after that it'll be the pots from the family dinner, and then later their plates and cutlery.'

She paused, but only to take a breath; Meg didn't get a chance to reply before Ivy was continuing. 'There's an awful lot of washing-up here, what with the family and the nursery and a dozen servants – ooh, thirteen now you're here! I hope you're not superstitious – so you'd better get used to standing by that sink.'

Meg could have laughed out loud. After scrubbing out the pots and bowls every day for so many hundreds of inmates in the workhouse, cleaning for thirteen servants plus however many members there were in the family would almost feel like a holiday. Still, she checked herself, better not get too cocky about it so soon. The family meals would no doubt be more like those enjoyed by the top table in the workhouse, so there would be many more delicate items. She would have to take a great deal more care than she had done with the chipped enamel and wood.

'I see there's an indoor pump,' Meg managed to interject. 'Where do I get hot water from?'

'Oh, didn't I say? It's over there. See those hotplates? They're connected to the kitchen range, which is just on the other side of the wall – there's pipes and things. So we keep those kettles full and sat on the plates all the time, and it keeps the water hot without us needing to light a separate fire in here. It's clever, in't it?'

Mrs Lawrence had spoken of the house having modern conveniences, and Meg could see that this would save a lot of work. She fetched one of the hot kettles, hefting it easily now she was so much stronger than she used to be, and poured the water into the sink. Then she filled it from the pump, and then it was a simple matter of taking six steps to set it on the hotplate again, and all without even needing to light a fire or to clean coal dust off everything. She could hardly believe her luck as she rolled up her sleeves and plunged her arms into the water.

Ivy, as she had promised, stayed by her, passing and stacking items and keeping up a steady flow of one-sided conversation. Meg didn't mind; it made a change from the strict silence of the workhouse and it would give her a chance to learn something about her new surroundings.

There was a window in the scullery, over the sink – high up in here, but ground level outside – which let in sufficient light in the daytime, but as dusk started to fall and Ivy brought in pans and cooking utensils Meg found it more difficult to see properly. 'Are we allowed to light a candle?'

'A candle? Oh, we don't need to do that.'

'I think we do – I can hardly see now and I don't want to miss a bit and risk having something not clean.'

'No, I mean, we don't need a candle. Just wait there.' Ivy disappeared through the door to the kitchen. She returned with a box of lucifer matches, struck one and took it over to a brass-and-glass contraption on the wall. Soon there was a steady, even glow illuminating the sink area.

'Oil lamp,' Ivy explained. 'Robbie fills them up with oil every morning, and then the light lasts all evening; no need to keep fetching candles.'

'And the light is better, too,' said Meg, in some wonder at the steady, clear flame.

Ivy giggled. 'Watch this!' She turned something on the side of the lamp, making the flame brighter and then duller again, enjoying Meg's wonder. Truly, this place was almost too good to be true.

The window had darkened completely by the time the fine china from the family dinner made its way in. 'We don't get the glassware in here,' explained Ivy as she carefully set down the most delicate-looking plates Meg had ever seen, ''cos of the sink being stone and in case we're not careful enough. Samuel does those in a special wooden bowl before he puts them away.'

Meg emptied the sink of dirty water from the kitchen pans, rinsed it and started to work the pump again. Ivy, her fetching and carrying duties done, leaned back against the wall and watched as Meg started on the new batch of items. 'You've got a good hand with that. Much faster than me.'

'I've had a lot of practice,' replied Meg as she admired the pattern on a plate before she immersed it. She thought it might be an idea to continue the conversation, to find out a bit more. 'So, you're the what kind of maid? I didn't catch it earlier.'

'The tweenie. The between maid? Or the running-up-and-down-stairs maid, as I should call it. It means I work between the house and the kitchen – in the morning I help May and Dot with the housework, and in the afternoons and evenings I help out in the kitchen.'

'That sounds like a lot of work.'

Ivy shrugged. 'It is. But everything's hard work, in't it? Anyway, I get to scrub the front doorstep every morning, and I like that 'cos all the other maids from the other houses are doing the same, and we have a bit of a chat. Otherwise it gets a bit close round here – only ever seeing the same dozen people all day, every day.'

Meg nodded, still washing, but before she could ask another question the door to the passageway opened.

'Ivy!' came Mrs Lawrence's voice, making Ivy jump away from the wall and straighten herself up. 'Stop lazing around there. I'm sure Meg can manage those last few bits on her own now. You go and set the supper in the servants' hall.'

'Yes, Mrs Lawrence,' replied Ivy, sidling past the housekeeper out of the room.

Mrs Lawrence walked over to the drainer next to the sink and picked up one of the plates, examining it closely. 'Good. You know how to wash up, at least.'

'Yes, Mrs Lawrence, thank you.'

'Now,' continued the housekeeper briskly. 'I was going to introduce you to Mrs Roberts once the cooking was over, but she's retired to bed early with a headache, so that can wait until tomorrow. You'll need to be down here first thing, ready.'

'I will, Mrs Lawrence.'

'I've looked out some clothes that should fit you, including a proper corset. We need to dress respectably here: just because the workhouse was happy to have you looking like you were wearing a sack doesn't mean that we are. Cleanliness, tidiness and smartness must be observed at all times.'

'Yes, Mrs Lawrence.' Meg put the final plate on the rack and felt around in the depths of the sink to release the plug.

'Now, off to the servants' hall for supper, then there's only a few bits to wash up from that, and you can go to bed.'

'Supper?' It hadn't occurred to Meg that there would be more food this evening.

'Just a slice of bread and jam, with a drink of hot milk for you younger ones. Otherwise it's a long time from tea at five until breakfast tomorrow at eight. After that Ivy will show you where you'll sleep. Your new clothes are in the room already.'

Meg took her place at the bottom end of the table in the servants' hall and tried to remember everyone's names. Ivy, of course. Mr Wilson. And the footman was called Samuel. The lady's maid – Miss . . . what? – wasn't there. The other maids, now – the two in the smarter uniforms – were the house-parlour maids, whatever that meant, and she couldn't recall their names at all. The other one, dressed in a more workaday fashion, was Hannah, the maid who would be her superior in the kitchen. Meg wanted to talk to her, but she wasn't sure enough of how things were done to risk addressing someone who was above her without being spoken to first.

When supper was over, and Meg's belly was full of bread and warm milk, she filled the sink again, still marvelling at the readily available hot water. Once the washing-up was finished Ivy lit a candle, placed it in a holder and showed Meg the way to the staircase that led up from the corner of the servants' hall. 'The back stairs, of course,' she said, as they started their climb. 'So the family don't have to see us.'

On each floor of the house was a landing with a door through to what Meg assumed was the main part of the house. She counted as they went up: the basement, then four storeys . . . this must be the last flight of stairs now, or at least she hoped so.

Ivy opened the door on the final landing, and in the flickering light Meg could see a long passageway with a bare wooden floor, with doors opening off it. 'Servants' bedrooms,' explained Ivy, unnecessarily. 'The men's ones first, so they don't have to walk past ours on their way in and out.' A shadow passed over her face, or perhaps Meg was only imagining it as the candle fluttered in a draught. 'Which is for the best.'

Ivy walked briskly down the passageway to a door at the end – *Last one on the left,* thought Meg, trying to remember her way around – and opened it. Inside was a room with a sharply sloping ceiling containing two metal bedsteads with a small table between them, on which stood a clock. There was a wardrobe in one corner and a washstand under the window.

'It's not much,' said Ivy, making a deliberately extravagant gesture, 'but it's home. And there's nobody in here to shout at us for being lazy!' She put down the candle and threw herself on one of the beds.

Meg turned to the other, which had a neatly folded pile of clothes at its foot. She still couldn't believe her luck, not least because she had never, in her life, had a bed to herself. This was honestly, honestly, too good to be true – she hoped she wasn't going to wake up and find she'd been dreaming all along.

'So,' said Ivy, as they got ready for bed, 'I forgot to ask earlier. Have you got any family?'

Meg had already thought to herself that this was a question someone might ask, and she had prepared an answer. 'I used to have,' she replied, keeping her voice steady, 'but not any more.'

Chapter Twelve

Meg was aware, as she got into bed, that Ivy was waiting for a further explanation. But she didn't feel inclined to give one just now, not to a girl she'd only just met. Talking to Sally and Martha about her family was one thing, but she wasn't about to spill her deepest thoughts and feelings to a stranger. Ivy would probably assume that Meg meant they had died, and Meg didn't mind that if it meant that she wouldn't have to face any more questions.

As she lay in bed listening to Ivy's deep breathing, Meg reflected that this was not how she had envisioned spending her first night out of the workhouse. In her mind she had always seen a family reunion: Delilah would come to collect her and Rosie, and they would go home – either to the court or to some other, better dwelling that had somehow appeared while she had been away – and she would spend the evening surrounded by her happy brothers and sisters, warm in the embrace of family love. And yet here she was, in a strange house in a strange part of town, up in an attic bedroom with someone she'd only met that afternoon. She had been abandoned, forgotten, and Rosie was gone.

That thought hurt Meg so much that she finally allowed herself to do what she hadn't done during all her months in the workhouse, where she was never alone: she cried.

She wasn't alone now either, of course, but Ivy was fast asleep and there was nobody else in the room, so it was as near to privacy as Meg was going to get. She allowed the sobs to overtake her, racking her entire body and shaking the bed while she struggled to do it quietly so she didn't wake the whole house.

Meg didn't know how long it was until the storm of weeping abated. Ivy was still asleep, the house was still quiet and the room was still dark, so she lay on her back and stared up. Whatever had happened she was now, quite definitely, on her own, and she always would be. She could rely on nothing and nobody but herself, so the quicker she got used to that fact, the better. It was time to put the past behind her.

For what she told herself was the very last time, Meg conjured up pictures of Delilah, of dear William, Sam, Jem and Annie. She also had room in her heart for those who were dead or gone: Rosie, Ma, Jonny and baby Jemima. She didn't and wouldn't spare a thought for Pa.

Meg lay awake all night, listening to the ticking of the clock and waiting for morning. While it was dark and she was lying in bed, she told herself, she could grieve for what she had lost. But as soon as the morning came, as soon as she put one foot on the floor, it was the start of her new life and she wouldn't allow herself to look back. She would swallow the tears and bottle up the sadness until it dried up and went away. That was the bargain she made with herself.

The hands of the clock moved slowly, but eventually it was half past five and the dawn light was starting to filter in through the window. Meg had been told that she needed to be downstairs 'first thing', but now she realised that nobody had actually specified a time.

On the basis that it would be better to be early rather than late on her first day, she sat up. The sadness weighed heavily upon her and she allowed herself to sink into it for one final moment. She said, in her mind, the names of all her sisters and brothers, living and dead, and then, with aching slowness, turned to sit sideways on the bed and stretched out one leg.

Her foot touched the floor.

* * *

By ten to six Meg was washed and dressed, wincing as yesterday's cane marks made themselves felt. The corset over her shift wasn't laced too tightly but it still felt strange, as she had never worn one before; but then again, she felt strange in all sorts of ways in any case. In some respects it was a good thing, she supposed, her new garments marking the start of her new life. The corset forced her to stand very upright, and it made her feel more grown-up. More like D— More like a woman.

Yes, that was it: as of now, she was no longer a girl but a young woman, and one who was going to make her own way in the world. She would be the best scullery maid anyone had ever seen, she would be promoted to kitchen maid, and one day she would be the best cook in Liverpool. She would get Martha and Sally out of the workhouse, somehow. And it all started today.

She shook Ivy. 'Which room does Hannah sleep in? I'm supposed to go down with her so she can show me what to do.'

'Next door,' said Ivy, sleepily.

Meg had no idea what time Ivy herself was supposed to get up, but that wasn't her concern. She opened the door quietly and tiptoed to the next one along, the new boots making no noise even on the bare wooden floor.

She knocked. 'Hannah?' There was no reply, so she knocked again a little more loudly. 'Hannah.'

'Who's there?' came a sleepy voice.

'It's Meg – the new scullery maid. I was supposed to go downstairs with you this morning.'

'Well, it's too early. Go back to your room and I'll come and get you when it's time.'

Meg hesitated. But Hannah would know best, and besides, she was Meg's superior in the kitchen, wasn't she? Perhaps best not to start her first day by disobeying an order. She went back to her room.

Ivy was now stirring. Meg didn't want to be seen to be watching her as she got up and dressed, so she crossed to the window. She was disappointed, for the only thing visible was the stone balustrade immediately outside – there was no view of the park.

'You can see it from some of the picture windows on the front side of the house,' said Ivy, apparently reading her thoughts, 'but you probably won't ever be there. I'm in the family drawing room early in the morning to sweep out the fireplace, so I sometimes peek out.'

'I expect I'll be downstairs in the kitchen and the scullery all the time, will I?'

'Oh yes,' said Ivy. 'The whole house would fall down if a scullery maid was seen above stairs.' She giggled. 'Imagine the master and mistress's shock!'

She smoothed her apron, a rough hessian one, and pointed at the other clothes on Meg's bed. 'For first thing in the morning you'll need the sacking apron, so you don't get your cotton one too dirty. But take both down with you, and then it'll save you the stairs when you need to change it. There's a hook on the kitchen door to hang it. And you can put your spare dress in the wardrobe – there's plenty of room.'

Meg did so and then tidied her already pristine bed again, wondering how long it was going to be before Hannah came to collect her.

'I'll get off now,' said Ivy, picking up the clock to wind it. 'Hannah'll be here in a minute, I'm sure. She's a bit of a sleep-head, but she won't want to make you late on your first day.'

Then she was off, leaving Meg to perch on the edge of her bed and count the minutes as they ticked by.

It was a quarter to seven by the time she heard a banging on the door and Hannah's voice calling, 'Are you ready or not?'

Meg picked up her second apron and went out.

She followed Hannah down the many flights of stairs – at least she wouldn't be able to get lost here, as she would need to go from top to bottom every day without stopping off at any of the floors in between – and emerged into the servants' hall. Then they made their way down the passageway and into the room Meg had not seen last night even though she desperately wanted to: the kitchen.

Two things struck her immediately on entering. The first was that the room was large, spacious, clean and stacked with every kind of pan and utensil she could possibly imagine. And the second was that standing in the middle of the room, next to a scrubbed wooden table, was a very angry-looking cook.

Mrs Roberts, for she it must be, looked sternly at them both. 'Late, Hannah? And on the day you're supposed to be showing the new maid the ropes?'

Meg expected Hannah to apologise, but instead she tossed her head and replied, 'You can blame your workhouse girl, Mrs Roberts. I don't know what they teach 'em there, but I've been waiting for her this half-hour. Lazy, that's what I call it.'

Gaping at the audacity of the lie, Meg stared at the kitchen maid. But Mrs Roberts was now turning to her: 'You should know, my girl, that I don't think much of lazy maids – there's too much to do in this kitchen. You'd better smarten your ideas up or you'll find yourself back where you came from.'

Meg deemed it wisest not to begin her acquaintance with the cook by contradicting her or starting an argument, so she merely curtseyed and said, 'Yes, Mrs Roberts, sorry Mrs Roberts, it won't happen again.' But inside she fumed at the injustice. Just as she had been hoping to make a good impression!

'Hmm. Well now, get to work. Hannah will show you how to black the range and re-light it while I make the dough and set the morning rolls. I've no time now to have a cup of tea first as there's no hot water.'

The none-too-pleased cook bustled off through an archway on the other side of the room, and Meg followed Hannah over to the range. 'What did you say that for?' she whispered, furiously.

'You keep your mouth shut, or you'll know about it,' was the only reply, spoken under Hannah's breath, which soon turned into, 'No, look, like this,' in a louder tone as soon as Mrs Roberts reappeared.

Fine, thought Meg. *If that's the way you want to play it.* She would remain silent for now, until she had found her feet a little and knew what was what. Besides, the range was the most incredible thing she'd ever seen in a kitchen, sleek and black and complicated-looking, and she couldn't wait to find out how to work it and what sort of cooking results could be achieved from it.

Hannah took up a stiff brush and handed it to Meg. 'You start by cleaning off all yesterday's soot and dust.'

Meg set to the task enthusiastically, very glad that Ivy had recommended that she wear the sacking apron rather than the cotton one, while Hannah stood back and watched.

That took a good few minutes of work. Meg coughed and turned her head to take a breath that wasn't filled with soot. 'What next?'

'Then you sweep all the ashes out – you can use that same brush and there's a dustpan there – and you drop them in that metal bucket.' Meg did so, but then jumped back in surprise as a hot spark landed on the back of her hand. 'Oh, yes – you have to be careful, sometimes it's still warm from yesterday.'

'Thanks for letting me know,' said Meg, drily, as she started sweeping with a little more care. She dropped the ashes in the bucket. 'What happens when it's full?'

'The gardener takes it, and then brings it back empty.'

'Gardener?'

Hannah rolled her eyes. 'Yes. Who else do you think looks after the garden and grows the vegetables?'

This place was even bigger than Meg had thought it was. An actual garden, growing fresh food! *But* – she checked herself – *one thing at a time.*

Hannah was now picking up a pot containing a thick black liquid. 'This is the blacking. There's a separate brush for it – that one there – and you sort of paint it on all over the outside.' Again she stood watching, her hands on her hips, not bothering to try to help.

'What's it made of?' asked Meg, as she smoothed the first brushful along the cast iron of the range.

'Full of questions, aren't you?'

Meg paused and stared flatly at her until she was forced to continue.

'You boil black lead and a bit of soap with a pint of beer,' said Hannah, at last and with reluctance. 'Then you pour it in the pot and leave it to cool down, and it goes thick and gloopy like that.'

That sounded so odd that Meg couldn't quite work out whether or not Hannah was joking with her, but she put the question aside for now – she could always ask someone else. She concentrated on painting all of the black surfaces.

'Do we leave it like this to dry?'

Hannah made a derisive noise. 'Were you born in a barn? No, you take that hard brush and you rub and scrub it all until it shines.'

Meg took the brush and began to scour and burnish as hard as she could. By the time she'd finished she was filthier than she'd ever been – especially when compared to Hannah, who didn't have a speck on her – but the range was gleaming. She stood back to admire it.

'Not bad for a first attempt,' said a voice from behind them, and Meg was startled to find that Mrs Roberts had been watching them while she worked – and for quite some time, based on the advanced state of the dough in the trough before her. 'It might have gone quicker if you'd actually helped her, Hannah, but get on now and light it, or breakfast will never be ready in time.'

Under Hannah's supervision, Meg laid the fire with the dry paper, straw and twigs that were stored ready, then put some larger sticks and pieces of coal on top.

As she made to light it, the vigilant cook called, 'Stop!' and pointed out something called the chimney damper. 'That one open, all the rest closed, otherwise the whole kitchen will be full of smoke.'

Hannah looked sulky. Meg wondered if she'd been waiting for her to do something wrong, but surely the smooth running of the kitchen would be more important to the kitchen maid than making herself look good at the expense of the new girl? Anyway, the range was now lit, and Meg admired it once more.

'That'll be your job every morning – and earlier than today,' said Mrs Roberts to Meg. 'Now, take those kettles and fill them from the pump in the scullery, and we'll set them to boil.'

Meg took two bright copper kettles – *I wonder how these are kept so clean and shiny* – and filled them. Despite their weight, she was able to bring them both back at once, one in each hand, and the cook showed her where to set them on the range.

Meg looked around. 'What next, Mrs Roberts?'

'Under the sink in the scullery you'll find a wooden bucket and a scrubbing brush. The floor in here and in there needs scrubbing, as well as the pantry and larder.' She pointed to the archway through which she had passed earlier. 'And the passageway.'

'Will the water on the plates in the scullery still be warm? Or is it all right to use cold? And is there any vinegar to put in it?'

Mrs Roberts nodded approvingly. 'I'm glad you've some idea of what you're doing, at least. Cold will do for now – they're done twice a day and you can use hot in the evening – and the vinegar is also under the sink.'

Meg hummed to herself as she got to work, but she hadn't reached the end of the passageway when she was being called to lay the table for the servants' breakfast. She looked in dismay at the unfinished floor, the dirty water and her filthy apron.

'I'll do it, Mrs Roberts,' called a voice, and Meg was grateful to see Ivy coming in the back door. 'Thought you might be a bit pushed for time, on your first day,' she whispered, 'so I've done the servants' chamber pots for you and left them outside to dry.'

Meg started to thank her, but was cut off. 'You'll get up to speed soon, and I daresay you'll do me a favour one day.'

'Thank you,' said Meg, really meaning it. 'Now, have I just got time to finish this and clear up?'

'If you're quick. Make sure you stow all that in the scullery before you come in.' She started to hurry off down the passageway but turned and spoke again. 'And change your apron for having breakfast!'

Meg was the last person into the servants' hall for the meal, but it was close – the others were only just sitting down – so it didn't look too obvious. A bowl of thick, milky porridge was passed to her and soon downed and appreciated, along with a cup of tea, and then she was clearing the table and starting on the day's first washing-up, a task augmented when Ivy brought in more dishes.

'From the nursery,' she explained. 'They have their breakfast at eight, same as us, but it's the same porridge so it's easy. Mrs Roberts is making the eggs and bacon and whatnot for the master and mistress's breakfast now.'

'Is that later?'

'Yes, at nine. So as soon as you've finished on those, go in the kitchen and fetch the pans to wash up while they eat, and then there'll be the dishes from the dining room afterwards.' She started to fly off again, backing away even while she spoke.

'How on earth did you manage to do all my work *and* your own since the other maid left?'

'Practice, my girl, practice,' said Ivy, in a mock-pompous tone. 'Seriously, though, I thought I might die, and that was with not doing half of everything properly.'

'Well, I'm here now,' said Meg, plunging her arms into the sink once more.

'That you are. And I'm made up about it, I can tell you.'

So am I, thought Meg, left to herself. From the evidence of the crockery and cutlery she deduced that there were probably three children in the nursery, as well as the nanny, and that one of them was small enough to require a baby spoon. She turned it over and over in her hand and sighed, before scrubbing it along with the rest.

After the family breakfast it was not Ivy who brought the plates in but Samuel, the footman.

'Alone at last,' he joked, as the door to the passage swung shut behind him.

Meg said nothing, concentrating on getting the last bit of bacon grease out of a large frying pan.

'I'm talking to you,' he said, coming closer and setting the food-soiled items down next to the sink. 'It would be polite to answer.'

Meg murmured a vague greeting, hoping he would simply go away, but he lingered. She was uncomfortable, not having been this *close* to a man, or alone with one, since the day she left home almost a year ago. The memory of Pa's fists made her shudder, and although Samuel didn't seem threatening in the same way – and would surely not be violent, here in this nice house – he was standing unnecessarily close to her, and her instinct was to sidle away.

'Anyway,' he continued, either not noticing her discomfort or ignoring it, 'you look a different girl from the one who arrived here yesterday. Much more . . .' he looked her up and down, 'grown-up.'

Meg couldn't help herself: she looked at the door.

He laughed. 'Oh, someone'll be in soon, no doubt. There's never any privacy round here. But sometimes it's nice to have a chat, just alone with someone, don't you think?'

'I've got work to do,' was Meg's only reply, and she picked up the first china plate.

He laughed again, but it wasn't a particularly nice sound. 'Oh, you're a tough one, aren't you? But not to worry – we're both going to be in this house a good long time, so there'll be plenty of opportunity for us to get to know each other better. I'll look forward to it.'

The door to the kitchen began to open, and Samuel sprang up from where he had been lounging against the sink. 'Until later, then.' He disappeared back into the passageway.

The new entrant was Hannah, but Meg would have been glad to see anybody.

* * *

The rest of the day passed in a blur. In some ways it was similar to being in the workhouse: everything ran according to a strict schedule, and everyone – well, everyone except Meg – knew exactly where they were supposed to be at all times. But in many other ways it was completely different. For one thing, talking was allowed as long as it didn't interfere with duties; Meg could overhear cheerful chit-chat as she worked, although she didn't feel the need to join in with it herself. And, of course, the number of people was much smaller. She still hadn't met the nanny, who ate up in the nursery, nor the gardener and his boy, who didn't live in and therefore weren't entitled to an indoor meal; but by tea time, when she had been in the house twenty-four hours, she knew everyone else's name and their accustomed places at the dining table.

The other, very material, difference from the work-house was the food. It was what Mrs Roberts described as 'good, plain food for working people', but to Meg it was such a luxury that she was hard put to stop tears from falling every time she sat down. Breakfast at eight; cooked dinner at twelve; tea at five; supper at nine. All of it perfectly cooked and in ample quantities, and there had been an apple tart after dinner that had almost sent Meg into raptures.

The work of the kitchen was more complicated than it had been in the workhouse, from the necessity of cooking three different sets of meals each day, for the servants, the nursery and 'the family'. It turned out that this last was just two people, the master and mistress, who were called Mr and Mrs Harcourt.

It was made very clear to Meg, in the course of a mid-afternoon lesson in her duties from Mrs Lawrence, that she should never expect to meet her employers.

'The scullery maid is *never* seen upstairs,' said the housekeeper, firmly. 'It just wouldn't be right. If by any chance you ever do see the master or mistress, you are to curtsey and lower your gaze so you don't look at them. There should be no reason for them to speak to you, but if they do you are to address them as "sir" and "madam", and confine yourself only to answering their questions. Is that clear?'

'Yes, Mrs Lawrence,' replied Meg, not sure if she was more glad about not having to come to the master and mistress's notice, or annoyed that she wasn't considered good enough even to look at them. And never seeing them would certainly put a dampener on any plans to ask them for help for Sally and Martha; she would have to find another way once she had got a better idea of how the household worked.

They were in the servants' hall while this conversation was going on, and Mrs Lawrence now pointed to two rows of bells on the wall. Each was labelled with the name of a room in the house, and Meg wondered how two people with three children could possibly need so many; why, some of them must hardly be used.

'You need not concern yourself with most of these,' continued the housekeeper. 'But it is your job to open the back door when it rings. Can you . . . I mean . . . it's the last bell on the right in the bottom row.'

Meg assured her that she could read well enough to understand the words 'Back Door', and added, 'Before I was in the workhouse, I went to Sunday school every week.'

Mrs Lawrence looked surprised. 'But I specifically requested . . . never mind. Anyway, where was I? The back door. The bell rings in here, but of course if you're in the scullery then you're right next to it, so you'll hear it anyway.'

'Who is likely to call, Mrs Lawrence?'

'All sorts of tradesmen and deliveries – anyone who doesn't use the front door. If it's the postman, you take the letters and bring them to Mr Wilson's office. If it's a delivery boy, from the butcher, the grocer and so on, you can let them in; they will carry their wares into the kitchen, where Mrs Roberts will inspect them for quality before accepting. If it's anyone else then you're to ask them who they need to see, tell them to wait outside, and then fetch me, or Mr Wilson, or whomever is most appropriate. Clear?'

'Yes, Mrs Lawrence.'

Just as Meg was saying the words, the bell marked Back Door sounded.

'May I be excused to answer that, Mrs Lawrence?'

'Yes, off you go.'

Meg made her way to the back door to find that it was the afternoon post – a nice easy one to start with. She ran the letters up to the butler's room, at the far end of the corridor past the servants' hall, and returned to the scullery.

There was, of course, always plenty to do at the sink, but it was not so monotonous as it had been at the workhouse; the bouts of scouring were broken up by answering the door and also by trips to the kitchen to clear up after Mrs Roberts and Hannah as they worked.

Meg took every opportunity she could to watch the cook. Mrs Roberts was . . . well, Meg wouldn't exactly use the word 'plump', but she was certainly rounder at the edges than anyone else she'd ever met. She was agile and alert, seemingly everywhere in the kitchen at once as she mixed, prepared, stirred, boiled and baked in a flurry of activity, all the while making tiny adjustments to the levers on the range or tasting something to make sure it was perfectly done.

Meg was in awe. Despite having worked in a kitchen at the workhouse, and cooked at home before that, she now realised how much she didn't know. She had never even heard of some of the ingredients that Mrs Roberts was continually telling Hannah to fetch, never mind cooked with them. But she was determined to learn, and she listened carefully to every instruction the cook issued to her kitchen maid, storing up as much information as she could.

By the time supper came round again, Meg was flagging. The labour at the workhouse had been hard, but it had finished early as the girls were expected to be in bed by eight o'clock in the summer and seven in the winter. Besides, she hadn't slept at all last night so she had plenty of catching up to do, and the restrictive corset wasn't quite so welcome now as it had been that morning when it was still a novelty. She was glad to drink her hot milk, clear up quickly and get to bed.

The following morning Meg was out of bed and washing in the cold water at half past five on the dot. She didn't bother waiting for Hannah or knocking on her door to wake her, but instead descended to the kitchen alone. It was almost dark in the cavernous room, the dawn light not yet having made its way through the north-facing windows, so she struck a light from the box of lucifer matches and lit a candle. The kitchen was fitted with oil lamps, their glass tube chimneys now reflecting the flame of her candle from various corners, but Meg was still a little suspicious of them and especially the way the flame could be turned up or down at will. She had no desire to cause an accident through clumsiness or lack of experience, and besides, the candle would give ample light for what she needed to do.

She turned to the range, touching it reverently. Such a device was almost inconceivable to her, allowing cooking to take place simultaneously via ovens, hot-plates and warming shelves, as well as heating water *in another room*. Meg did not yet understand what all the levers and pipes did, or exactly how to control the range, but she would learn; and in the meantime, she could certainly clean it.

Within half an hour the range was swept, black-leaded, burnished to within an inch of its life, and alight. Some old habits died hard, so as soon as there was another source of light in the room Meg blew out the candle to conserve it. By the time Hannah came down, yawning, Meg had scrubbed halfway across the floor, and by the time Mrs Roberts appeared at seven o'clock, only a few minutes later, she had finished it.

Hannah rushed forward to the cook. 'The kettle's on for your early tea, Mrs Roberts – shall I fetch your cup and saucer?'

'Yes, thank you,' came the reply. 'I don't know what's made you more efficient all of a sudden, but well done, and long may this continue.'

Meg stood aghast. How could Hannah . . .? But now was not the time. She gritted her teeth and went to empty the bucket in the scullery sink.

By that time, Ivy had brought down the female servants' chamber pots. Meg didn't have to deal with those of the men, thank goodness, for that was the job of Robbie the hall boy, but even so she knew that this was going to be her least favourite part of the job. They had to be emptied outside rather than in the scullery, and then washed at the pump in the yard before being wiped out with a vinegar-soaked cloth kept only for the purpose, and left to dry.

By the time Meg got back into the kitchen Mrs Roberts was just finishing her tea. She placed the cup carefully back on the saucer and, for the first time that Meg had seen, she smiled. 'Right, girls. We've made a good start to the day – let's get to work, shall we?'

Meg rolled up her sleeves.

Chapter Thirteen

The first Thursday of Meg's week in the house was also the first Thursday of the month, but she dared not mention the subject of her promised half-day so early in her time there; visiting Sally and Martha would have to wait. As she spent the afternoon at the sink she thought of them, wondering how they were getting on and hoping they would be safe without her. She hoped that Mrs Leech hadn't taken out any of her anger with Meg on them; logically there would be no reason for her to do so, because there was no point if Meg wasn't there to be forced to watch it – but then again, you never knew with Mrs Leech. She was quite capable of being cruel without needing a particular reason. Meg did her best not to think about the disappearing girls, for there was nothing she could do about them. For a moment in Mrs Leech's office, she thought she'd worked it out: Mrs Leech was selling the girls into service, just as she had sold Meg. But that didn't quite ring true. Meg hadn't disappeared, she'd been offered a place, had time to say her good-byes and then left. There had to be something more going on.

The washing-up was light: Mr Harcourt was out at his business, so the mistress had eaten her meal alone. 'Luncheon', they called it, as the family had their main meal of dinner in the evening, the other way round from the servants and the nursery, who had dinner in the middle of the day and tea later on. Meg had there-fore already finished and was wiping her hands when she heard the back doorbell ring.

As luck would have it, it was the one delivery boy she didn't really like. Although 'boy' was the wrong word: the others were all youths of about her own age, but Walter from the grocery was a grown man, prob-ably around twenty if Meg was any judge. However, she wouldn't have to put up with his superciliousness for long: he had been sure to mention several times on his previous visit that he was about to be promoted to shop assistant, so he would pass the deliveries over to a new, younger boy. He barely acknowledged Meg as he swept past her now, taking his crate of goods into the kitchen, thumping it down on the recently scrubbed main table and unpacking it for Mrs Roberts's inspection.

Her work in the scullery done for now, Meg lingered in the kitchen to watch. She had caught glimpses of Mrs Roberts's inspections before, and was fascinated by the different methods she used to check all sorts of goods. Meat was weighed, of course, before it was taken to the cold shelf in the larder, and examined for signs of having gone off; fish were poked to see that the flesh was firm, and the cook even checked the eyes, noting to Hannah – and overheard by Meg – that they should be bright if the fish were fresh. 'Any sunken eyes, or if the fish is flabby or smells bad, we send it straight back,' she had said briskly, and Meg had stored the information for future use.

The inspection of the grocer's delivery was different, of course, for they were mainly dry goods rather than fresh. Mrs Roberts opened a packet and took a spoonful of flour, mixing it in a teacup with some lemon juice, another of those ingredients Meg had never seen before entering the house, but one she now loved the scent of. The cook was showing the cup to Hannah, who didn't seem particularly interested, and Meg edged a little nearer so she could see into it. 'Now, if the flour's pure, it stays like this, at rest. If it's been adulterated with whitening or chalk it will start to ferment or bubble up when you put it in the juice.'

'Like yeast?' asked Meg, without thinking. She took a step back, thinking she was about to be sent out the room, but Mrs Roberts seemed pleased by her interest.

'Yes, that's right. And, of course, if that happened we'd send it back.' She turned to Walter. 'Not that we don't trust Mr Jones, of course – he's been supplying the house for a good while – but you never know who else has been at it during the process.'

Walter sniffed. 'If that's all, Mrs Roberts, I'll be off. It'll be a new boy from now on; I've been promoted to Mr Jones's assistant so I'll be serving in the shop.'

'Yes,' said Mrs Roberts, drily. 'You did mention that.'

Meg smiled to herself as she followed Walter back to the door and watched him stride off. Hopefully his replacement would have better manners.

Just as she was about to shut the door, she heard the sound of voices from the pavement at the top of the outside stairs. Excited, high little voices. She risked taking a few steps up so she could see the speakers.

Meg was well aware by now – for one could not but be aware of everything once Ivy started talking about it – that she had been right in her surmise about there being three children in the house. They were

Miss Amelia, who was nearly six; Master Francis, who was three and a half, and the baby, Master George, who was one year and three months old. She could see the two older ones now, both in their white dresses – for Master Francis was as yet some way off being breeched – with Miss Amelia holding carefully on to her brother's hand while they waited for Nanny. She eventually came into Meg's line of view, being helped by Samuel to carry down the front steps an enormous wheeled baby carriage in which she would push Master George around the park while the others walked. It looked awkward in the extreme, and Meg wondered, as she had done the first time she'd seen it, why Nanny didn't just do what all normal people did, and carry the baby tied to her in a sling. That way she would always have him close, and she'd have both hands free.

But it wasn't Meg's place to wonder why her betters did things in the way they did, and she had work to do. She took one final look at the children, smiled at their excitement at the thought of going to feed the ducks, and went back inside.

She ran into Hannah in the passageway.

'Taking your time about showing Walter out, were you? Didn't take you long to get sweet on him, did it – is that what they teach you in the workhouse?'

Meg didn't bother dignifying that with an answer, merely saying that she needed to get back to work.

'Well, you can put all that grocery delivery away before you get back to your scullery. Mrs Roberts has asked *me* to go out to talk to the gardener about the vegetables for tomorrow, which is much more important.'

'I'll be happy to,' replied Meg, refusing to be drawn and standing politely to one side so that Hannah could pass her.

Hannah tossed her head and walked out, leaving Meg to shut the back door behind her before she returned to the kitchen.

Mrs Roberts was sitting in the chair that was kept for her use in the corner of the kitchen. Next to it stood a low table on which there were various books of receipts. She was consulting one now, running her finger across the page. She spoke distractedly as Meg moved to the table. 'Yes, yes, put that all away, there's a good girl. I just need to go and ask Mrs Lawrence something.' She stood up and went out, taking the book with her.

Meg took up the first few packets of flour and sugar and moved towards the archway. The pantry and the larder were both accessed via a small inner lobby, so that they could only be reached through the kitchen and not from the passageway or the servants' hall – sensible, of course, with so much precious food lying around. Meg had stared in wonder at each room the first time she had seen them, overcome by the sight of so much food in one place. Now she'd been in the house a few days she felt herself to be an old hand, accustomed to such things, but she still loved to go in there, feeling a sense of safety and security when she looked at the large quantities of foodstuffs all arranged in regimental order.

As it was a grocer's delivery, she needed only the pantry: the colder larder was for the meat and dairy produce delivered daily. She stacked the packets of flour neatly – newest ones at the back, as she had been taught – but the sugar was stored on the high shelf, the one she couldn't reach, so she dragged out the wooden stool that was kept in the corner.

She was standing on it, on her tiptoes and with her arms up to place the sugar, when a voice came from behind her. 'Need any help?'

Meg spun round on the stool, nearly falling off it, for she knew it was Samuel. 'What are you doing in here?'

'Came in with a message for Mrs Roberts, but she's not here, and neither is Hannah.' He paused. 'So it's just us.'

He was standing in the only doorway, leaning against the frame with his arms crossed. Meg didn't think him exactly dangerous, but she had the acute sense of discomfort that she had often felt when she'd had to walk past the entrance to the court that contained the brothel, back in the old days. The groups of lounging men had made the public space their own and thought they were entitled to the attention – or, worse, the person – of any women and girls who had to walk near them.

'Yes,' she said, with a confidence she didn't exactly feel. 'I could use your help. Those bags of rice are quite heavy. You can bring them in here to save me the job.'

His expression was amused, but he inclined his head and came back with the two sacks. He moved very close to her in order to hand the first one over. He was still taller than her, even though she was standing on the stool.

'Anything else?' he drawled.

Meg could see that he was perfectly aware of her discomfort, and that he was enjoying it, which was actually worse than the discomfort itself.

'No, thank you – I can manage the rest myself.' She wanted to get down and walk past him, but he was still filling far too much of the space.

'One good turn deserves another, don't you think?'

'And I'll be glad to do one, whenever the situation should arise,' she replied, firmly. She looked over his shoulder. 'Ah, Mrs Roberts.'

Samuel jumped back as though he'd been stung, and turned. He'd barely had time to take in the empty doorway before Meg was past him and out of it, back into the kitchen. That was also empty, but it was a much larger space, and Mrs Roberts or Hannah might be expected back at any moment, so it was safer.

Meg busied herself at the table with the remaining items from the delivery, pushing the jars of treacle around and keeping her back to the archway. She heard Samuel come through it and felt him approaching behind her.

'Don't worry,' said a low voice in her ear. 'I like a girl that's hard to get.'

And then he was gone. For now.

As Meg went back and forth putting away the rest of the items, she tried not to reflect on the fact that there was going to be no way to get away from Samuel, not properly. They lived in the same house and she would see him multiple times a day, every day, and she would never be able to guarantee that she wouldn't be left alone with him.

She sighed. Funny – it was completely the opposite problem from the workhouse. That had been huge, impersonal, full of people whose names she didn't know and who she might see one day and then never again. But now, here, everything was close and the same faces were to be seen all day every day. Well, she would just have to find a strategy to deal with it, she told herself. *Would you rather be back in the workhouse? No? Then deal with what you've got here.*

Mrs Roberts returned. 'Is that all away yet? And where has Hannah got to? It surely doesn't take this long to find one gardener.'

'I don't know, Mrs Roberts, and yes, it's nearly all away but I couldn't do the spices as I didn't have the key to the cupboard.'

'Oh, yes, of course. We'll do that now.'

Meg collected up all the incredible-smelling packets and followed the cook back to the pantry. The spices were expensive and were therefore kept under separate lock and key in a small press.

Mrs Roberts unlocked it and then smiled as Meg took in a huge breath. 'You're just like I was at your age. Come now, we'll have a little test and see how you do, even though you've only been here a few days. Close your eyes.'

Meg did so, and Mrs Roberts held something up below her nose. 'What's this?'

'Cinnamon, Mrs Roberts.' That one was easy, as it was not uncommon in the bakeries around the town that she used to visit.

'And this?'

'Nutmeg?'

'Right again. Now, I won't be cruel enough to make you breathe in pepper or ginger, so here's a more difficult one.'

A very pungent aroma met Meg's nostrils, and she shook her head. 'Sorry, Mrs Roberts, I don't know that one.'

'All right. Open your eyes now and look.'

Meg saw a packet of an orangey-brown powder.

'Ground cloves,' said the cook. 'Versatile, but only to be used in small quantities so it doesn't overpower everything.'

Meg took one last sniff. 'I don't think I'll be forgetting that one in a hurry.'

The cook folded over the top of the packet, stowed it away and locked the cupboard. 'There, now. Really we haven't got time to be idling like this, but I do like to see a young person who's interested in her work.'

The sound of the door between kitchen and passageway sounded, and when they came out of the pantry it was to find Hannah in the kitchen. She was looking at her reflection in the bottom of a bright copper saucepan and rearranging her cap.

'Right, girls, just to let you know before we start on the tea and the family dinner.'

Meg stood to attention; Hannah reluctantly looked away from the saucepan.

'On Sunday it's Miss Amelia's birthday, so there will be a tea party in the nursery in the afternoon, with ten guests plus their nannies.'

'But this Sunday's my half-day!' burst out Hannah.

'Yes, I'm aware of that, just as I was aware it would be the first thing you would say,' replied Mrs Roberts. 'However, I'm sure I can manage a nursery tea without your assistance, especially as it's a Sunday.'

Meg knew that the family had their main dinner, a roasted joint, in the middle of the day on Sundays, so in the evening they simply had a cold collation – this was why the cook and the kitchen maid had alternating Sundays as their afternoon off. And as to Hannah being away on the day of the tea party, she desperately wanted to put herself forward, to say, 'I'll be here to help, Mrs Roberts,' but she dared not.

As she moved away to the scullery, however, she thought she caught a glimpse of the cook watching her and giving a satisfied nod.

*   *   *

That night, while Meg and Ivy were getting ready for bed, Meg mentioned that she'd seen the Harcourt children that morning. The reply, predictably, came in a torrent.

'They're lovely, aren't they?' said Ivy, from over by the washstand. 'I see them quite a lot, you know, as it's my job to take all the nursery meals up and bring the plates back down again after – all those stairs! – but I don't mind, it's nice up there. Always warm, too, what with having a fire going all day every day.'

'I hear that it will soon be Miss Amelia's birthday – Mrs Roberts says we have to prepare for a tea party on Sunday.'

'Yes, she'll be six – how quickly time flies! She was only a tiny tot when I came here. Oh, it's fun when they have little tea parties. All dressed up in their best, with the visiting children and their nannies. And Miss Amelia acting like such a perfect little hostess, with her best manners!'

'It sounds like you've been to these parties before?'

'Oh, yes, it's such a treat. Because there's more children than usual, I'm allowed to help serve the food.'

'I don't suppose you noticed if there's anything particular that is Miss Amelia's favourite to eat?'

Ivy finished splashing water on her face and skipped over to her bed. 'Ooh, now, there's a question. Let me think. She's a good girl, of course, eats whatever is on her plate, but I think – yes, I'm sure I remember that she loved the custard pudding. Yes, that was definitely it, because one of the other nannies mentioned to Nanny that a lot of children didn't like the flavour of vanilla.'

'Good, I'll remember that.'

'Ooh, you're going to be such a good cook one day. Not like Hannah – she doesn't really like working in the kitchen.'

'I've noticed,' replied Meg, getting into bed herself and pulling the covers up to her waist as she sat. The sensation of having a smooth cotton sheet in between her and the rougher blankets was still a novelty, and she ran one finger over it. 'What would she rather be doing?'

'She wants to be a lady's maid – I heard her say so. But the problem is, if she stays in the kitchen her hands will get rough and then she'll be no good for fine sewing.' A thought seemed to strike Ivy. 'Maybe if she leaves to find a different position somewhere, you might get to be kitchen maid!'

Meg drew up her knees and hugged them. 'I'd like that.' The mention of fine sewing reminded her of Martha, and she sighed. But there would be a way, somewhere – she just needed to find it. She wouldn't talk about it now, though; she might confide in Ivy about the others later, but not until they knew each other better and Meg knew she could be trusted.

She looked over at Ivy. 'And what about you? What do you want to be?'

Ivy sighed. 'I'd love to be a nanny. A nursemaid first, of course, but then a nanny when I'm older. Looking after the children and the babies would be such fun, much nicer than sweeping floors and carrying things up and down stairs all day.'

Meg smiled wistfully. 'There's a bit more to it than that.'

'How do you— Oh, yes.'

There was silence for a few moments. Meg wanted to change the subject, wanted to ask Ivy what she knew about Samuel and if she'd ever had any problems with him, but she had no idea how to bring up the topic. She would have to talk about her own experiences, her own feelings, and those were best kept locked down inside.

'Shall we blow out the candle? It's getting late.'

She lay down in the darkness, her thoughts her own.

* * *

Sunday came. The morning was a whirl of activity in the kitchen with the family roast to prepare, which generated a large amount of greasy washing-up, but once that was done Meg had leisure to consider how she might approach Mrs Roberts. She was at least safe in the knowledge that there would be no unpleasant disturbances, for it was Samuel's half-day as well as Hannah's, and Meg had seen them both leave with a sigh of relief.

Meg stood in the scullery, facing the closed door that led through to the kitchen. She could hear the cook bustling around inside, having made a start on the party preparations while Meg was at the sink. She decided that the best way was to be direct, so she squared her shoulders and pushed open the door.

It all came out in a rush. 'Begging your pardon, Mrs Roberts, but is there any way I can help you with the cooking for Miss Amelia's party? I'll still do all the washing-up and my other normal duties as well, but I'd love to watch and learn, if you don't mind.'

Mrs Roberts looked up from a saucepan she was stirring on the range. 'Well, there's something to be said for being keen. You didn't make the best start to your position here, back on your first morning, but you're making up for it now, I'll give you that.'

Meg wasn't sure whether that was a yes or a no.

'The little sponge cakes will be the easiest for you to start on. Flour, eggs, sugar and butter are already there on the table. Fetch a mixing bowl and I'll tell you how much to weigh out – I can't leave this custard just now or it'll spoil.'

Meg could hardly contain her excitement as she weighed, measured and stirred according to Mrs Roberts's instructions. The mix looked and smelled all right, and she brought the bowl over for the cook to see.

'That's fine. Now, out the way for a moment while I take this over to the table – it's hot, mind – and then I'll show you how to spoon out your mix and put the cakes in the oven.'

The early part of that afternoon was the most pleasant time Meg had experienced in years, if not ever. She cooked and she learned and she delighted in the results, all in the knowledge that nobody was going to fly into a rage or intimidate her or hit her with anything. She hummed as she flew around the kitchen.

It was the bowl of oranges that spoiled everything.

The party tea was ready; they were arranging the cold chicken, tiny sandwiches and delicate cakes on plates. Mrs Roberts expertly turned out a shaped custard pudding and Meg couldn't help clapping her hands. 'Miss Amelia and the children will love it!'

Mrs Roberts smiled. 'I hope so. Now,' she looked at the clock, 'we'll be expecting to hear the front doorbell soon. Just one more thing and then we're ready to have it carried up.' She disappeared into the larder and came back with a covered bowl. 'I ordered these specially as an extra treat.' Placing the bowl on the table among the other dishes, she flicked off the cloth to reveal a heap of bright oranges.

Meg was suddenly hit with a vivid memory of Christmas dinner in the workhouse, and the crate of fruit that had been brought in for the children. How pleased she had been that Rosie should have such a gift. And now here she was, surrounded by mounds of delicate treats for another little girl who was turning six, while Rosie had died without even having the currant bun Meg had promised her.

A wave of dizziness and nausea came over her, and she staggered back with her hand to her mouth.

Mrs Roberts didn't notice to start with, still checking that everything on the table was perfect, but then she turned around. 'Meg? What . . . ?'

From a great distance, Meg heard the sound of the front doorbell.

Mrs Lawrence entered the kitchen. 'It's time to—' She also noticed Meg.

Meg had at least managed not to back into the hot range; she now leaned against the jamb of the scullery door, trying to keep her heaving stomach down and to stop the whole room from spinning.

Mrs Lawrence stepped forward. 'Meg! I don't know what's got into you, but we won't have this sort of behaviour in the kitchen. Pull yourself together, please.'

Meg was trying hard to do so, but the oranges were still there, looking at her, accusing her, and she could feel Rosie's cold, dead hand clasped in hers. Distantly, she saw that Ivy was also in the kitchen, and was whispering in the ear of the concerned-looking cook.

Mrs Roberts now stepped forward. 'I'm sure she'll be fine, Mrs Lawrence. It did get very hot as she was standing next to the range, and she's probably not used to that corset. Also, you know, girls of that age . . . Anyway, perhaps you could supervise Ivy taking up the plates – we can't have Miss Amelia's party affected, can we? I'll deal with Meg.'

Mrs Lawrence looked at the clock, just as the doorbell sounded again. 'Very well,' she said, giving Meg one last glance. 'Come along, Ivy.'

Once they were gone, Mrs Roberts spoke gently to Meg. 'Ivy told me that you said you used to have a family, and now you haven't. Is that what it was? Something I said reminded you of them?'

Meg didn't know how to answer, so she gave a tight nod. Thank goodness, the oranges were gone; Ivy had taken them. She was starting to come to herself now, and a feeling of extreme foolishness and embarrassment was sweeping over her. 'I'm so sorry, Mrs Roberts. I – I don't know what came over me. It won't happen again, I promise.'

The cook didn't attempt to pry further. 'Now,' she said, in a brusque but not unkind tone, 'perhaps the best thing to do is to concentrate on work. You get all this out to the scullery and get started, and if you're quick with it all we'll have time for a cup of tea before we start on the cold cuts for the family supper.'

Meg nodded and began mechanically to collect up the mixing bowls and baking pans.

Chapter Fourteen

It was some days before Meg could remember the episode without blushing a deep red. How had she let her feelings come to the surface like that? She must try harder. She kept herself to herself in the scullery, only leaving it when she was needed to fetch and carry, scrub floors or answer the door.

In the middle of the morning the back doorbell rang, and Meg went to answer it. On the step was a boy she'd never seen before. She guessed him to be around a year older than herself. Naturally, he was taller than her – everyone was – stocky, and with eyes of an unusual hazel-green colour. He was exceedingly nervous. As soon as the door opened, he whipped off his cap, twisting it in his hands before pushing it into his jacket pocket. 'Morning, miss. I'm from Mr Jones, the grocer. I hope I'm in the right place – party by the name of Roberts?'

'Yes, Mrs Roberts is our cook.'

'Well, that's a relief! This is my first delivery, miss, and to be honest with you I was dreading it.' He paused, a little awkwardly. 'Er . . . what do I do now?'

Meg, amused at meeting someone even newer in post and more unsure than herself, stepped back to allow him entry. 'You need to bring everything into the kitchen, so Mrs Roberts can check it. Do you need me to carry anything?'

He seemed horrified. 'You? No, miss, of course not – I can manage it, if you'll show me the way.' The full crate was by his feet, and he picked it up with ease. 'Walter packed it all for me – he's been here lots of times, so it should all be right.'

Meg led him to the kitchen, pointed him to the table and helped to unpack the goods. She frowned as she took out some of the packets. 'I'm not sure . . .'

By then Mrs Roberts had appeared. 'Groceries? You must be the new boy.' Then she stopped as she looked at the items on the table. 'Is this some kind of joke?'

The boy was taken aback. 'No, ma'am, of course not. It's—'

'It's not what I ordered, that's what it is. Something has gone amiss.'

The boy's face fell, and Meg felt sorry for him. And on his first day, too.

'Still, there is some flour, so we'll keep that once I've tested it. Meg, pack the rest away again and he can take it back.'

Meg helped the boy put the packets of unwanted ingredients back in the crate. 'I'm so sorry, miss,' he mumbled to her, miserably. 'Walter swore it was right. I must have mixed up the boxes or something.' A thought seemed to strike him. 'You won't get in any trouble, will you? I know it's not your fault, but, well, the wrong people do get blamed for things sometimes, especially if they're at the bottom of the heap.'

He was looking at her anxiously, and Meg felt a stirring of – what? She didn't know. But the idea that this youth, who was surely going to be in deep water himself, was more concerned about *her* gave her a little warm glow. 'I'll be fine. And not to worry – I'm sure it's not as bad as . . . oh.'

Meg turned on hearing Mrs Roberts's expression of annoyance. She was testing the flour in a teacup, as Meg had seen her do many times before, but this time the mixture was bubbling and frothing up.

Mrs Roberts set the teacup down, put her hands on her hips and turned to face the horrified boy. 'You should know,' she said, in a tone harsher than any Meg had heard her use, 'that I do not appreciate jokes, nor unsatisfactory service. Cooking is a serious business, and I don't have the time to deal with idiot boys who think it's funny to fool around and waste my time. You can take the whole lot of this back, and you can tell Mr Jones why. And if a replacement order isn't here by this afternoon, then—'

The boy was by now white-faced and horrified, and Meg was convinced of his innocence. She recalled two things: Hannah's behaviour on her own first morning, and Walter's smirk on his last visit.

Mrs Roberts was still in full flow, and Meg surprised herself by daring to interrupt. 'If you please, Mrs Roberts,' she began.

The cook stopped mid-sentence, turning to Meg in some surprise.

'If you please, Mrs Roberts,' continued Meg, boldly, and picking her words with care. 'As it's his first day, I wonder if someone else hasn't done this deliberately, to play a prank on him. To make him look bad in your eyes, on purpose, because he's new.'

Mrs Roberts gave Meg a sharp look, one that encompassed more than the present situation, and pursed her lips. 'Hmm,' she said. Then, still not exactly kindly but sounding at least a little mollified, 'Perhaps there may be some truth in that.' She turned to the boy. 'Take it all back, and if the correct order is here by this afternoon, we'll say no more about it.'

'Oh, thank you, ma'am, that's very kind of you.' He fumbled the last few things back in the crate and picked it up. 'I'm sure I don't know what happened, ma'am, but I'll put it right, I swear . . .'

'All right, all right.' Mrs Roberts waved an arm, and Meg could tell that underneath the stern exterior she was beginning to thaw. 'Be off with you.'

'I'll see him out, Mrs Roberts,' said Meg, as she followed the boy to the back door.

Once he was outside, he turned. 'I can't thank you enough, miss,' he said. 'Sticking up for me like that, when you had no need to.'

'I don't like to see people treated unfairly,' replied Meg, who could still hardly believe her own boldness. 'And really, there's no need to call me miss – I'm only the scullery maid. My name's Meg.'

'Never mind "only" anything,' he said, with feeling. 'To me you'll always be the brave girl who stood up for me. I'm Tommy.' He put down the crate, wiped his hand carefully on the front of his jacket, and held it out. 'Pleased to meet you, Meg.'

Amused at the formality, and touched by the gesture, she took his hand, which dwarfed hers. 'Pleased to meet you too, Tommy. And I'll look forward to seeing you again.'

He grinned and jammed his cap back on his head. 'Likewise.'

He picked up the crate and Meg watched as he made his way up the steps, whistling.

*   *   *

Meg didn't get much chance to speak to Tommy when he came back that afternoon, but from then on she knew she would see him regularly, as they had grocery deliveries three times a week.

The days passed, perhaps not exactly pleasantly, but certainly without any particular trouble. Meg's birthday came and went. She didn't bother mentioning it to anyone in the house, but she marked it in her head and in her heart; not so much as her own fourteenth, but as William's fifteenth, wherever he was. She wished she could stop caring.

Meg had a stroke of luck when it came to arranging which day was to be her fortnightly afternoon out. She was initially allocated Wednesdays, but it turned out that Ivy, who had Thursdays, was desperate to swap:

her sister had started in service somewhere in town and she wanted to have the same day so they could take their afternoons out together. Meg had met Ivy's sister, Bella, who was about her own age – with prior approval, the servants were occasionally allowed to invite a guest to tea, and Bella had been at the last one. Meg was happy for them both, and would have swapped to help Ivy even if it hadn't benefitted herself. As it was, it worked out perfectly and they begged so earnestly, with so many promises of covering each other's work, that neither cook nor housekeeper could see grounds to refuse.

Of course, visiting at the workhouse was only once a month, and so Meg would have every second afternoon off to herself. The first such day arrived in late September, at which point Meg realised she had absolutely no idea what to do with herself. For a year she had been locked in, confined, her every waking moment scheduled, and the idea of a free afternoon was, oddly, quite intimidating.

There was a temptation to spend those hours simply lying on her bed and resting, but Meg gave herself a talking-to as soon as she realised that the prospect was tempting not because she was tired, but because she was too scared to go out. Honestly, she, the girl who had walked boldly around Liverpool since her earliest years, who had shopped and haggled with market traders!

As the moment arrived, Meg faced the back door and told herself not to be foolish. It was a fine day. She would walk around the park, which was open to the public; she would look at the lake and the trees, stopping whenever she liked to enjoy the view and the fresh air. She would. Nobody could stop her. Everything would be fine.

She was actually reaching for the door latch when she heard Mrs Lawrence calling out behind her, and she wasn't sure whether she was annoyed or relieved.

But, 'Meg, surely you're not going out without a hat?' was the housekeeper's only question, to which Meg's honest reply was that she didn't own one. Such an item had not been considered necessary in the workhouse, and before that she'd always just pulled her shawl over her head when she was cold, or gone bare-headed if she was not.

Mrs Lawrence shook her head. 'That might have been all right then, but it certainly isn't now. You're a young woman, not a little girl, and moreover you're a member of this household. I don't care if it's your half-day; you're still representing the family and it's not decent or respectable to be seen out without a hat.'

Meg nodded and turned to come back. An afternoon napping on her bed it was, then, and now she knew, from the feeling of disappointment, that deep down she had been looking forward to going out.

Mrs Lawrence saw her disappointment, made a tut-ting noise and relented. 'There must be a spare one in the house somewhere, or one of the girls could lend you one just for today. It's quarter-day next week, and although you've only been here a few weeks you'll be due *some* wages – you can spend them on a hat ready for next time you go out.'

Meg thought she should go and find Ivy, but it was Miss Greenwood, of all people, who came to her res-cue. The lady's maid was the household servant Meg knew least well, as she was often upstairs with the mistress rather than in the servants' hall, and she never came into the kitchen or scullery at all. But she had been doing some quiet mending and had over-heard the conversation. She came into the passage, instructed Meg to wait, and reappeared some minutes later with a bonnet that she and Mrs Lawrence both declared plain but serviceable and fit for the purpose.

'There,' said the housekeeper, tying the ribbon under Meg's chin. 'Not so fine that you look above yourself, but smart enough that you won't disgrace us.'

Meg looked at herself in the glass in the passage-way, and a stranger stared back at her. Not a little girl, not a pauper from the alleys and courts, not a workhouse inmate; rather, a respectable and smartly though modestly dressed young woman.

Overwhelmed with appreciation, she couldn't help dropping a curtsey to the other two women. 'Oh, thank you, I'm so grateful.'

Miss Greenwood's usually expressionless face broke into a smile. 'Off you go now, Meg – the fresh air will do you good.'

Meg went out, walking on air as she ascended the steps, crossed the street and entered the park.

That such a place should be open to the public, should be available for the use of ordinary people, seemed barely credible, and at first Meg had to talk herself into the fact that she was permitted to be there; indeed, that she *belonged*. As she walked along the path that led to the lake she saw that she was approaching a park keeper in a uniform, and she was almost afraid that he was going to see right through her, see that she wasn't worthy of being in such a nice place, and throw her out. But when she passed him he barely gave her a second glance other than actually to touch his cap to her, as though she were a lady.

Meg walked on, conscious not only of the bonnet, but also that she had by now become accustomed to wearing the corset and that it had changed the way she walked. On a weekday afternoon the park was not crowded, the other people there being mainly nannies with children or the occasional couple or respectable-looking individual out for a stroll; none of them gave the slightest indication that they thought she was out of place.

After an hour wandering around the paths and admiring the leaves just starting to change colour – she'd never seen so many trees all at once – Meg stopped to take a seat on one of the park's many benches, this one affording a fine view of the lake. How she would love to show all this to Sally and Martha. But she would, one day. She smiled as she watched prettily dressed children feeding the ducks and sailing toy boats under the watchful eyes of their nannies.

'Do you mind if I sit here for a moment?'

Meg looked up to see that she was being addressed by an elderly woman.

She jumped to her feet. 'Why, of course, ma'am. Would you prefer if I moved on somewhere else?'

'Why, bless you, no – there's plenty of room for us to share it. Though I must say, it's pleasant to meet a girl with such nice manners. Sadly lacking in so many of today's young people.'

She started to lower herself on to the bench, grimacing, and Meg held out an arm to steady her.

'Thank you,' she said, finally settled. 'These things aren't as easy as they used to be. I'm supposed to be meeting my son, but I'll just have a rest for a while first.'

They sat in silence for some while, and then the woman, seemingly inclined to chat, spoke again. 'Are you waiting for someone, dear?'

'No, ma'am,' replied Meg. She was going to leave it at that but realised it might sound a bit abrupt. 'I'm in service, and it's my afternoon out.'

'And you decided to spend it in the park? Good for you. So many young women these days would be gadding about the town.'

'It's nice to be in this open space. Actually, I'm not sure how long I've been here – I don't want to be late back.'

'Ah, but on quiet days like this you can hear the church clock: I'm not quite sure which one it is, but it strikes the hour. In fact, it must be nearly . . .'

As if on cue, Meg heard a bell strike four. She had plenty of time, but the woman seemed flustered.

'Four o'clock was the time I was meant to meet my son. He'll worry if I'm not there . . .' She started to get up from the bench, but was evidently struggling.

Meg stood up. 'May I help you, ma'am?' She offered her arm, and, when the woman was safely on her feet, added, 'I'd be happy to walk with you until you find him.'

'That's very kind, dear, but I don't want to put you out of your way. I don't suppose you get much time off.'

'It's no trouble,' said Meg, and she meant it – she didn't like to think of an older person being in danger of falling, and besides, the woman had a nice face and had spoken to her kindly. 'Now, where are we heading?'

They walked off together, the woman's arm through Meg's. Meg was on the lookout for someone who might be her son – a man in his twenties or thirties, perhaps – and was taken aback when her companion's, 'Ah, there he is,' indicated a mere youth. She was even more surprised to see it was Tommy, the grocery delivery boy.

He rushed forward. 'Ma, are you all right? I beg your pardon, miss, I—' He stopped short as he realised who she was.

'This is my son, Tommy,' said the woman, oblivious to their mutual recognition.

Meg looked at her again and realised her mistake: Tommy's mother was not old, but ill.

Tommy grinned broadly. 'Ma, you couldn't have found a better girl to walk with. This is Meg, who was so nice to me last week. Do you remember me telling you?' He turned to Meg. 'Sorry, forgetting my manners. This is my ma, Mrs Hopkins.'

'Well,' said his mother, 'this is a happy coincidence.'

Meg, still holding her arm, could feel her swaying a little. 'Would you like to sit down again, ma'am? There's another bench just over there.'

They moved to it and lowered Mrs Hopkins down, taking a seat one on either side of her.

'Well now,' she said, as soon as they were all settled. 'It seems I need to thank you on two counts. So kind of you to stand up for Tommy. It was a shocking trick to play on a lad on his first day – it might have cost him his position, and then I don't know what we should have done.'

'Now, Ma,' said Tommy, awkwardly. 'Meg doesn't want to hear about all that.' He looked past his mother. 'Is it your half-day today, then?'

'Yes. I've been enjoying the air here.'

'It's lovely, isn't it? And I can hardly believe we're allowed to walk around here, such a smart place. But it's good for Ma to get out of the city when she can, and Thursday afternoons Mr Thompson brings his coal deliveries up here, so he gives her a lift and she can spend an hour here.'

Meg was liking him more and more now that she could see his evident love and care for his sick mother. 'Is it your half-day, too?'

'Ah.' He blushed. 'Not exactly. But I'll work an hour later when I get back to the shop, to make up.' He looked at Meg. 'You won't tell anyone?'

'Of course not.' She grinned. 'Our secret.'

The three of them sat on the bench for another half an hour or so, and Meg felt happier and more relaxed than she had done at any time since her afternoon preparing party food with Mrs Roberts. And to think, she had nearly been too afraid to come out, nearly decided to spend the afternoon in her room, and she would have missed all this!

Eventually, though, she realised it was time to go. She would have to retrace her steps across the park, and she didn't want to be late back on her first afternoon out. She stood up and said goodbye to Mrs Hopkins, who was by now looking very tired.

Tommy also stood. 'Can I walk—' He checked himself and spoke again, awkwardly. 'It would be polite of me to walk you back, wouldn't it, but it's too far for Ma and I shouldn't leave her. Mr Thompson will be by soon to pick her up.'

'Of course you can't leave her – and I can easily find my way back.' She paused. 'I've had a very nice afternoon.'

A smile spread over his face, and then he looked at the ground. 'Me too.'

He seemed on the verge of saying something else, but Meg thought that was enough for one day. She said her goodbyes again and was aware that Tommy was watching her as she walked away. It was probably a good thing, she reflected, that Tommy wasn't going to walk her back to the house, that there was no danger of anyone there seeing them walking together, just the two of them. Mrs Lawrence had strong views on 'followers', as she called them, and Meg had heard her scolding both May and Dot on separate occasions.

But still. Meg's next afternoon out, of course, would be spent at the workhouse visiting Sally and Martha, but the one after that would be free. If she happened to walk in the park again, and happened to come across Mrs Hopkins, and happened to meet Tommy once more because of that, where would be the harm in that?

As she reached the house and opened the back door, Meg found herself calculating when the next grocery delivery was due to arrive.

Chapter Fifteen

If her Sundays in the kitchen alone with Mrs Roberts, while Hannah had her afternoon out, were Meg's favourite time, then it was fair to say that the alternate Sundays were the worst.

It was the last Sunday in September, and no sooner had Mrs Roberts departed, issuing instructions even as she went, than Hannah turned on Meg. 'You seem to have been having an easy time of it lately – I don't think you work nearly hard enough. Well, you're not to be lazy while I'm in charge. You can start by peeling and chopping those potatoes for making hash for the servants' tea, and then you can take every one of those saucepans down off the dresser and scrub and polish them until I can see my face in them.'

Meg made no objection, although preparing vegetables was Hannah's job, and she could already see her face in the bright copper of the pans. The potatoes didn't take her long, and she soon started collecting up the pans while Hannah sat herself down in Mrs Roberts's chair.

Samuel came in, but fortunately Meg was already halfway through the scullery door, so she didn't have to speak to him. She piled the pans on the scullery table and took up a lemon – lemons were part of the grocery delivery, and she made a mental note to tell Mrs Roberts that they were running low – in order to cut it in half and dip it in salt.

She was hard at work scrubbing away any tiny smudge of grease she could find when Robbie clattered in. He put down a collection of oil lamps on the table. 'Move up.'

Meg was concentrating so hard on her pans that she didn't really notice Robbie again until he gave a cry of pain and some oil slopped over the table in front of her.

She looked up. Robbie was holding his ear and Samuel was standing behind him.

'Tsk, clumsy boy,' said the footman. 'Better get that cleared up.'

Robbie said nothing, making his way over to the sink with the sort of tight, unhappy movements that Meg recognised all too well from her time in the workhouse.

They denoted an expectation of further punishment. She watched as Robbie bent to take a cloth from under the sink and, inevitably, Samuel followed up with a kick to the backside that sent the boy sprawling.

Meg couldn't help it. 'Leave him alone.'

'Oh, leave him alone,' repeated Samuel in a mock, high woman's voice. 'You need a girl to stick up for you now, do you, Robbie?' Robbie had just got to his feet and Samuel smacked him on the back of his head, looking at Meg all the while.

Meg knew from bitter experience that the best thing to do would be to shut her mouth and walk away, but such casual bullying angered her. It was just so unnecessary. 'Why do you treat him like that all the time?'

Samuel now had Robbie by the ear. 'Natural way of things, isn't it? The footman did it to me when I was a hall boy; I do it to Robbie; and he'll do it to someone else when he's a footman, if he ever gets that far.' Still holding the ear, he gave the boy a shake, and Meg winced in sympathy. 'Won't you?'

'Yes,' squeaked Robbie.

This only elicited a further squeak. 'Yes what?'

'Yes, sir.'

Samuel dropped him. 'That's more like it. Now, get back to your work.' He clipped Robbie round the ear as a parting gesture and returned to the kitchen.

Meg was ready with words of sympathy as Robbie wiped up the spilled oil, but he spoke first. 'Just keep out of my way, won't you? As if I need a girl to look out for me.'

'Somebody ought to – he's a bully.'

'Course he is! Everyone kicks out at those below them. I can't wait until I'm a footman and there's someone smaller than me.' He threw the dirty rag in the general direction of the sink. 'You'll do it too when you're higher up – you're just sore 'cos there's no girl lower than you, so you've got nobody to take it out on.'

He lapsed into a sullen silence, concentrating on filling up the lamps with oil and then furiously polishing the brass.

Meg returned to her pans, Delilah's words floating back to her once more: 'We all have a choice about whether to be cruel or not.' *And no*, Meg thought. *No, I'll never be like that, like Robbie thinks I will.* And, in a sudden insight, she added to herself, *Because that's how I would turn into Mrs Leech.*

Robbie finished with the lamps and left. As she took up the cloth from where it had landed on the floor, and did a rather better job of wiping the oil stain on the table, Meg wondered that Mr Wilson should let Samuel behave in such a way. But then, he was very rarely seen; he was often upstairs with the master, or dealing with the master's clothes, and even when he was below stairs he spent most of the time in his own butler's room.

Meg had heard Hannah banging around in the kitchen, so it was probably time to put the gleaming copper pans away and then make a first sweep of the dirty bowls and utensils. Hannah never seemed to be able to cook without using every single thing in the kitchen.

As Meg put out her hand to the door, she heard her own name mentioned.

'Meg?' Samuel's voice sounded incredulous.

'Well, why do you pay her so much attention, then? Skinny little thing, she is.'

'I'm only playing – a scrawny little workhouse girl like that is of no interest, but she's funny when she gets scared. Like a rabbit.'

Meg didn't catch Hannah's murmured reply, but it sounded like she wasn't convinced.

'Ah, you know you're the only girl for me,' said Samuel in quite a different tone.

There was a moment of silence before Hannah's voice came again. 'Not in here!' She giggled.

'Well, when and where, then? Come on, you know you want to.'

Meg reminded herself both that eavesdropping was beneath her, and that this was a place of work. She banged a few pots together loudly and unnecessarily before opening the door.

Hannah and Samuel were standing separately, though giving the strong impression that they had only just moved away from each other. Meg pretended not to notice anything, stacking the pans back on the dresser and collecting up some forks, spoons and bowls. She went back to the scullery.

She had filled the sink and started on the washing-up when she became aware that Samuel was also in the room. She ground her teeth in exasperation. Honestly, why wouldn't he just leave her alone? Didn't he have any work of his own to get on with?

She tried to ignore his presence, but she could feel him coming closer and closer. He loomed over her, and she could feel his breath on the back of her neck. Still she said nothing and kept washing.

'Still playing hard to get, then? You should be glad to get some attention from a man like me – who else would be interested in a little bit like you?'

She scrubbed at some cutlery and put the dripping items on the drying rack.

'Well, if you won't *talk* to me, then . . .' Meg felt his hand on her waist, moving down towards her hip.

The next moment he was leaping back with a yelp of pain. 'What did you do that for, you bitch?'

'So sorry,' said Meg, not looking round. 'You made me jump and I completely forgot that I had that fork in my hand.'

But if she thought that this would make him retreat, she had miscalculated. Badly.

The next thing she knew, he had grabbed her and slammed her back against the wall, hard, knocking the breath out of her. Before she could catch it back he had his hand over her mouth, pressing her head back against the bricks.

'Fine – you don't want to sigh over me like the other girls? You don't like me? Then I'll settle for you being afraid of me.'

She struggled, but he was so much bigger and stronger than her that she could hardly move. She tried not to panic. Surely someone would come in.

Deliberately, he put one hand on her breast and squeezed. Harder and harder, looking her in the eye, his face close to hers, until she couldn't help it: tears came to her eyes and she whimpered with the pain.

'That's more like it,' he said, his mouth close to her ear. He pinched her nipple and it was all she could do not to cry out, even beneath the suffocating weight of his hand on her face.

He looked down. 'Not quite up to Hannah's stand-ard, I have to say, but there's enough there to show that you're growing up.' He put his mouth to her ear again and whispered. 'Just *think* of all the things we could do, whenever I can catch you alone. You'd like it. And even if you didn't, I certainly would.'

She was panicking now, she knew she was. Her arms were free, and she tried hitting him, tried push-ing him away, but he only laughed. Then she saw that she was close enough to the sink to reach the items that were still waiting to be washed; she swung her arm and knocked the whole lot on to the floor.

The sound of several enamel bowls hitting the tiled floor made enough of a clatter to be audible in the kitchen and the passageway, surely?

Her prayers were answered when the door to the passage swung open. Like lightning – and with a reaction no doubt born of long practice – he removed his hands from her. But he didn't quite have enough time to step away, and he was still looming over her, Meg still pressed against the wall, when Mr Wilson saw them.

The butler made an exasperated noise. 'Get about your duties, Samuel.'

'Yes, Mr Wilson.' And, blessedly, he was gone, out the door.

Meg sagged with relief and opened her mouth to pour out the story of the assault to the butler.

She was forestalled. 'I'm extremely disappointed in you, Meg.'

Meg stopped in her tracks as though he'd slapped her. 'What?'

'I thought you were different. Mrs Roberts speaks highly of your work, and you didn't seem to be mooning after Samuel like the others.' He shook his head. 'But you girls are all the same when it comes to it.'

The absolute, shocking injustice of this took Meg's breath away. She tried to command herself. 'Mr Wilson—'

He held up his hand. 'I don't want to hear it. You should know that I don't think much of girls who spend their time distracting men from their work. I don't want to see it again, you hear?'

'But Mr Wilson—'

'That's enough. The other thing you should know, as I'm sure you do, is that footmen are difficult to come by. Scullery maids, on the other hand, are ten a penny.'

The threat was clear, and Meg had just enough reason left to realise that back-chatting the butler was likely to result in her dismissal. And what would she do then?

But the effort of remaining silent was so great that she bit her lip until she could feel it bleed.

'Well then,' said Mr Wilson. 'That's better. Get about your work and we'll say no more about it for now.' He stabbed a finger towards her. 'But none of this business again, you hear? I'll be watching.'

He left, and Meg's knees gave way beneath her. She sank to the floor among the spilled bowls and buried her head in her hands. Why did life have to be like this? Why was it so unfair? And why didn't she have anyone – not one single person in the world – to take her part?

She couldn't help it; she thought of her family. Having a Pa to protect her had always been a useless hope, but if Ma had found out how Samuel had treated her she would have waded in and given him a hefty slap, boxing his ears and screeching fit to wake the dead. And Sam would have had his fists flying by now, even though he was only half the size of his loathsome namesake. Even William, dear William, who had no love for fighting at all, would have been on her side. If Delilah were here now, Meg would have flown to her, hugged her, cried into her shoulder, sought comfort from her, never let her go.

But Delilah isn't here, is she? Meg told herself, eventually. *She hasn't been here for a long time.* And neither were any of the others. That was what really hurt: even if Delilah didn't want Meg, surely William or Sam could have stood up to her and said they were going to collect their sisters from the workhouse? But they hadn't and Meg was on her own – and once more she would have to cope with it, just as she had to cope with missing Sally and Martha. They might not have been able to stop Samuel, but they would have been on her side at least. Until she could get them out, Meg must push all this down inside her along with the rest.

Meg pulled herself up on to her hands and knees, and began to pick up the scattered bowls. Thank goodness these were the enamel ones – if she'd knocked over and broken anything earthenware or china she'd be in even more trouble.

She managed to stand upright. For a moment she thought she was going to be sick. The moment passed, but she was then overtaken by a kind of panicked over-breathing that made her gasping and dizzy. She was sucking in great lungfuls but somehow getting no air. She held the side of the sink and leaned forward, huge racking gasps shaking her shoulders. Her hands were trembling. *Force it down,* she told herself. *Get yourself under control.*

The door to the kitchen banged open. 'Haven't you finished with those yet?' came Hannah's voice. 'Lazy, that's what I call it. There's more for you to collect in here.'

'Yes,' Meg managed, in a strangled tone that Hannah didn't notice. 'Sorry. I'll start on those now.'

*   *   *

Meg remembered with great clarity how she had sat in the workhouse dining hall nearly a year ago, waiting for a visit that never came, frozen in misery at the first hint that she had been abandoned by her family. She wasn't going to do the same to Sally and Martha.

She hovered in the kitchen until the cook noticed her. 'Aren't you on your way out?'

'Yes, Mrs Roberts, but I was wondering if I might ask a favour.'

'A favour?'

'Yes, Mrs Roberts.' Meg knew it was cheeky, but the fact that it was for the benefit of someone else rather than herself gave her courage.

'Go on, then – you can ask, at least.'

'At teatime tonight, would I be having a slice of that pound cake?'

'You would, yes – it needs eating so I've put it aside for the servants' tea.'

'May I please have my piece now?'

Mrs Roberts smiled. 'Are you planning a picnic? It's not the best weather for it.'

'No, ma'am.' Meg hesitated, but then decided that honesty was the best policy. She spoke in a rush. 'I'm going to the workhouse, to see my friends Sally and Martha who are still there. They don't ever get treats like that – workhouse food is nothing like what you cook – and I thought that if it was a piece that was going to be for me anyway, I could take it with me and they could share it.'

There was a brief silence, and Meg was worried she'd annoyed the cook. But she'd had to ask.

Mrs Roberts pursed her lips, considering. 'And I expect they're as underfed as you were when you first came, are they?'

Meg nodded.

The decision was made. 'Fetch me that bit of paper that we unwrapped from around the cheese,' said the cook, briskly, reaching for a knife.

Meg hurried to get it, bursting with joy that Sally and Martha would have such a treat.

'Two of them, is there?' Mrs Roberts cut a generous slice of cake and placed it on the paper that Meg had smoothed out on the table. 'That's the piece you were going to have at teatime, then.'

Meg was stammering her thanks and about to wrap it up when Mrs Roberts added, 'Ah!' and held up a finger to stop her. To Meg's astonishment, she cut another slice and added it to the first. 'And that's mine. Now they'll have a piece each and they won't have to share.'

Meg's eyes filled with tears.

'Now, off with you, then. You've quite a long walk into town. Do you know the way?'

'I should be all right, Mrs Roberts – I asked James the coachman when I took his dinner out the other day. He knew it well so he explained it all to me.'

'Good. Don't get lost on the way – or on the way back.'

'I won't, Mrs Roberts. And . . . thank you.'

Meg set off on the walk into town. Knowing that she was smartly dressed, well shod, and having borrowed the same bonnet again, she was not afraid of walking past the large houses on the outskirts. Nobody would think she was there for suspicious purposes and attempt to chase her away. As she got further in and the houses got smaller and meaner, the streets narrower, and as the forbidding workhouse building loomed closer, she clutched the parcel of cake to her chest. But she kept going.

She was here. She was in front of the workhouse.

She swallowed.

Of course, now she was visiting and not seeking admittance, it was a different door. It must be slightly after the hour, for Meg could see others making their way in.

The workhouse.

Meg took a deep breath and stepped over the threshold.

Chapter Sixteen

Meg followed the crowd towards the dining hall. On the way each visitor had to stop and tell one of the pauper assistants whom they wanted to see, and Meg boldly gave both Sally's name and Martha's.

The dining hall was just as Meg remembered it, and she shivered as she walked through the main door. She took a seat, resolutely turning her back so she couldn't see the kitchen, and sat like that for some while.

'Meg? Meg, is that you?'

Meg looked up to see the girls approaching, and Sally gave a squeal of delight.

'It is! It is you! Oh, I knew you would come!' She rushed forward, tripping over in her hurry, and threw herself at Meg. 'I've never had a visitor before, never, and when they called me I thought it was a mistake!

But then they said for Martha to come too, and she said, "I wonder if it's Meg," and here you are!'

Such simple delight, such overwhelming happiness, could not be withstood, and Meg hugged her back, laughing at the torrent of words.

Sally eventually pulled away and held Meg by the shoulders. 'Now, let me look at you. How grown-up you look! What a smart dress, and a hat! Where did you get it all from? Did they give it to you, where you're working? What's it like there? Are you—'

'Stop, stop!' said Meg, still smiling. 'Sit down, both of you – I've brought you a present. And then I'll tell you all about it.'

'A present!' Sally clapped her hands. 'I've never had a present before! What is it?'

Martha shared an amused look with Meg, as she was finally able to shoehorn a word into the conversation. 'If you sit down, Sally, I expect you'll find out.' She now took her turn to hug Meg. 'I'm glad to see you.'

'And I you.'

Martha sat down. 'You'd better tell us what it is, or I think Sally is going to burst.'

Meg put her parcel down on the table and unwrapped it with a flourish. 'Pound cake. From the cook where I work. And she's the best cook anywhere, so it's delicious.'

Martha was looking hungrily at the cake, and Sally's eyes had nearly fallen out of her head.

Meg felt a pang of sympathy and sadness for them, of guilt at her own good fortune. 'Better eat it now,' she said, gently, 'before anyone can see it and take it away. We'll have plenty of time to talk afterwards.'

She watched them as they ate, Martha savouring every mouthful and trying to retain some dignity in breaking her cake into small pieces, while Sally wolfed hers down as though the world was about to end.

When she'd finished, Sally licked her finger and dabbed it at the paper to pick up every last tiny crumb. 'That was the best thing I've ever tasted!' she exclaimed. 'Oh, Meg, I'm so glad you've gone to a nice place. They must be kind, if they give you cake to take out.'

And that was Sally all over, thought Meg. No self-pity at all, no jealousy at Meg's good fortune while she had none; just pure, unadulterated happiness for her friend.

Meg felt her eyes beginning to prickle. 'So,' she said, hastily, 'are you all right? How have you been getting on since I went away?'

'Oh, you know,' Sally shrugged. 'Same as usual. I do my jobs and everything. Oh, and Peggy's moved up to our room from the little girls' section, so we share the bed.'

Meg remembered the ancient, hollow-eyed child who had once tried to help Rosie, a lifetime ago now, or so it seemed. 'That's good,' she said, brightly. 'And I'm sure she's glad to have you there to look out for her. You're good at that.'

Sally beamed.

'And . . .' Meg didn't quite know how to phrase it, couldn't bring herself to say the name. 'And are you keeping away from punishments?'

Martha had now finished her cake, and she spoke. 'If you mean, is Mrs Leech still a horrible bitch who canes everyone whenever she feels like it, regardless of what they've done, then yes, she is.'

'Martha!' said Sally, in a horrified and yet admiring tone. 'Don't say such things, not here! Somebody might hear you!'

'I don't care if they do.' Martha made a face. 'Looks like I'm stuck here for ever, or at least for now, so they'll be moving me in with the women soon, I expect.'

Meg looked at her. Even through the shapeless workhouse uniform she could see that Martha had blossomed into a woman's form. She would be nearly fifteen by now, too old to remain with the girls. 'Maybe something will come up,' she tried, in a tentative attempt at comfort.

'I doubt it,' said Martha, bitterly. 'No matter how well I sew.'

Thinking of Martha's age gave Meg another pang of apprehension about the missing girls. 'I don't suppose you've managed to find out anything more about the girls? I thought it was happening to me, you know, but that wasn't it. I went to a line-up and got picked, there in the office for everyone to see, and then I came back to you. So it wasn't like being "disappeared" at all.'

Sally was beginning to look frightened, but Martha had a thoughtful expression on her face. 'There might be . . .'

'What?'

'It might be nothing. But the other day I was taking some dishcloths we'd finished making over to the kitchen, and I passed by Mrs Leech's door.'

'And?'

'She had someone in there with her – I didn't see who, because I didn't want to risk getting too close and her seeing me. A woman – quite a deep voice for a woman, but definitely female. Mrs Leech said, "You're back very soon. It's only a couple of weeks since the last time," and the visitor said . . . hang on, it'll come back to me . . . yes, she said, "I'm careful to do it on different days at different times, so as not to be so noticeable. Besides, I need more girls."'

Meg gasped. 'That must be it! It can't be anything else, surely. The girls aren't just disappearing – Mrs Leech is getting rid of them somehow.'

'But what for? And where are they going?'

'That's what we'll need to find out next. Did you hear anything else?'

Martha screwed up her face in an effort to recall. 'Mrs Leech said, "Again? You seem to be going through them at quite some speed just at the moment." And then, and then . . . yes. The other woman said, "Some of them last and some don't. You might call it an occupational hazard. Anyway, what's it to you, as long as you get paid? What have you got for me?" And I remember thinking that if it was our girls she was talking about, she didn't care for them very much.'

'Doesn't sound like it, does it? Anything else?'

Martha shook her head. 'Mrs Leech just said something like, "Let me see," and then I could hear her moving, so I ran off – I didn't want her to see me and know I'd been listening outside her office.'

Meg needed to think all this through, but perhaps now wasn't the time. Visiting time would be over soon, so she needed to concentrate on Sally and Martha while she was here – she could always go through this new information while she was walking back afterwards.

There was a moment of silence, and then Sally rushed to fill it. 'But Meg, tell us all about your new place. What's it like? What do you have to do?'

Meg trod a narrow path as she told her tale, careful to balance it between seeming to brag at her good fortune and not complaining about all the bits she didn't like. She would not think about Samuel today, she told herself.

'And they gave you these nice clothes?' Sally rubbed the fabric of Meg's skirt between her forefinger and thumb.

It was a sign of how far she'd come, and how quickly, that Meg's first instinct was to laugh at anyone calling a scullery maid's dress 'nice', not when they could compare it to the housekeeper's, or the finery of the lady's maid. But it was only a few short weeks since she would have said the same, and she reminded herself of how overwhelmed she'd been at the purchase of a pair of boots that now looked no more than plain and serviceable.

Martha was examining the seams and hems. 'Nicely done, though I could do it better.'

'It was a spare one in the house,' explained Meg. 'I expect one of the housemaids made it – the lady's maid does very fine sewing, but only for herself and the mistress.'

'What's she like?' asked Sally, eagerly. 'The mistress, I mean? Is she pretty? Has she got lovely clothes?'

'I don't know,' replied Meg, honestly. 'I've never seen her.' She wondered idly if the master and mistress were even aware of her existence or her name; if they knew how much frantic work went on below stairs every moment of every day to keep their lives sailing serenely on, how a dozen people's lives were spent doing nothing but supporting theirs. 'To start with I thought I might be able to ask her for help in getting you out of here, finding you jobs, but that's not going to work if I never see her. Don't worry, though – I'll find another way as soon as I can.'

The time flew by, and it was sooner than Meg would have believed possible that the end of visiting hours was being called.

Sally hugged her tightly. 'Oh, it's been so nice to see you. Will you come again next time?'

'I'll try.' Meg was struck by a thought, and added, 'But if I don't, it's not because I've forgotten about you, you hear? It's only that I couldn't leave work, or wasn't allowed to come.' She looked Sally in the eye. 'I would never forget about you.'

She turned to Martha and hugged her too. 'Maybe you won't be here next time I come. Maybe you'll have found a place. If so, we can meet up outside of here – you know where I am now.'

'Maybe', said Martha, in a dull voice. 'And maybe not.'

Meg bade them one last farewell and left the dining room, at which point she almost ran straight into Mrs Leech.

She forced herself not to step back.

Mrs Leech's astonishment was obvious. But she soon recovered herself enough to sneer. 'Here to see your little friends?'

'Yes,' said Meg, calmly. 'Some of us have friends.'

She made as if to walk on, but Mrs Leech's voice brought her to a halt. 'Oh, so hoity-toity we are now! Well, you remember where you came from – and remember who's still here.'

Meg turned, slowly.

'Yes, that's it,' said the matron, knowing she'd scored a hit. 'You think very carefully. And now I know you're coming I'll be able to have a little treat ready for you next time. I wonder what poor little Sally will look like next time you see her?'

Furious at Mrs Leech, and fuming at her own powerlessness to do anything about it, Meg walked off. The matron had done it again – managed to get under Meg's skin and to threaten her by threatening someone else. After she thought she had escaped. But there was no escape, or at least not at the moment. She could leave, but Sally and Martha had no such luxury.

As she walked out the workhouse door, Meg swore to herself again and again that she would fix this, somehow. *Now, what was it Martha had said?*

She was just orienting herself for the walk back to Prince's Park when she was surprised to hear her name being called. It didn't take her long to spot James the coachman, standing by the little two-wheeled carriage that Meg now knew was called a gig.

She made her way over to him, through the dawdling and curious groups of other visitors also leaving the workhouse.

'James? Is Mrs Lawrence here? Is something the matter?'

He smiled down at her in a way that Pa never had. 'No, nothing the matter except that Mrs Roberts suddenly discovered that she was short on some vital ingredient or other, and nothing would do but it needed to be fetched now. She recalled that you were already in town, so I'm to take you to get it, and then bring you back.'

'That,' said Meg, 'is the worst story I've ever heard.'

He chuckled. 'It is, isn't it? But it's hers, not mine – I just do what I'm told.' He became more serious. 'And it's no bad thing that she's worried about you. When I think of what you looked like the day we came to get you . . .' He shook his head.

'Well, those days are over now,' said Meg, firmly, wishing she believed it herself. 'So, what is it Mrs Roberts needs?'

'Ground cloves, apparently,' replied James, handing her up on to the gig's seat. He moved round to the other side. 'So we're off to the grocer's before they shut.'

That settled the question: Meg knew perfectly well that there was already a stock of ground cloves, for she had smelled the pungent aroma in the pantry only that morning. She glowed at the thought that Mrs Roberts had been so kind, putting all this in place just for her. Part of Meg was embarrassed to be leaving in such style – picked up by a liveried coachman, indeed! – when all those around her were on foot and many in rags; but, on the other hand, the day was very much looking up.

She checked that her bonnet was tied on firmly, and then held on to the rail as James flicked the reins to stir the horse into action.

* * *

The weeks passed, and soon the house was full of preparations for Christmas. This meant even more work in the kitchen than usual, but Meg didn't mind: the place was full of the most heavenly smells imaginable, of cinnamon, of dried fruit, of mulling wine. Mrs Roberts seemed to be everywhere at once, flying about the kitchen and producing batches of perfectly turned-out treats for the many visitors upstairs as well as all the normal meals in a day. Meg was learning all the time: the autumn had been a practical time of clearing up after the cook as she took in huge amounts of produce from the garden and made pickles, preserves and jams, and now she picked up what she could about rich fruit puddings and cakes.

If life had been only about her work in the kitchen and the scullery, Meg would have been happy. But she was worried about the girls back in the work-house and she was also in constant fear of Samuel appearing every time she was alone. As the days grew shorter and the servants' quarters became a place of cold, dark shadows, she jumped almost out of her skin every time she heard the scullery door open when she had her back to it. Samuel had not, actually, made any further attempt at assault; he seemed to be occupying himself with the girls in the house who were more willing. He spent rather a lot of time with Hannah, and May and Dot were always hanging round him as well whenever they got half a chance. Only Ivy seemed to share Meg's wariness, and Meg wondered if she too had suffered at the footman's hands. But it was a subject she still couldn't bring herself to broach, for fear of the feelings and emotions that might break loose.

Meg was also desperately worried about Sally. She had been back to the workhouse on the first Thursdays of November and December, bringing more of Mrs Roberts's cake each time, and she had been almost brought to tears by watching Sally hardly able to pick it up due to the vicious cane marks on the palms of her hands. Sally had tried, as usual, to put it down to 'just one of those things'; she never expected kindness, which was just as well given that so little of it ever came her way. But in a murmured conversation with Martha, while Sally was concentrating on her cake, Meg had learned that Mrs Leech had specifically found an excuse to beat Sally on the day before her visits. She felt sure that the matron had done this on purpose as a warning and a taunt to herself, and on her walk home she could have shrieked with the frustration of being able to do nothing about it. She held firm to her belief that she would get both of her friends out one day, but she was aware that time was passing and she hadn't found a way to do it yet – and, in the meantime, Sally was suffering the consequences.

At this time of year the kitchen was a hive of activity, and the washing up seemed almost as endless as it had been in the workhouse. Meg had been running through all these thoughts in her mind as she scrubbed, and then she stopped on one word. *Home.* She had walked *home* from her visits to Sally and Martha.

Meg paused for a moment, a dripping mixing bowl in her hand. She supposed it was, really; the house contained the people who had come to stand in for her family – even though she hated and feared at least one of them as much as she had done her Pa – and it was the place where she ate and slept and dreamed. Where she *lived*, not just where she existed. She had even started to put down what might be classed as roots, spending some of her wages on a proper servant's box to keep under her bed, which made her feel more permanent. She would not be leaving any time soon, not if she could help it.

The back doorbell sounded and Meg went to answer it. Deliveries from the butcher, fishmonger, dairy and grocer had all become more frequent, and Mrs Roberts had even deigned to have some from the baker, pushed for time as she was and unable to keep up with the daily baking on top of everything else. She had been heard grumbling about having such a small kitchen, with so little space to work properly and so few staff. Meg had surveyed the large, well-equipped room and wondered how it could possibly be improved, at which point she received a short lecture, from behind a waving wooden spoon, about the benefits of a proper country-house kitchen with its own dairy and still room. Mrs Roberts wasn't angry with Meg, only flustered, and she finished by handing over the spoon to be washed and adding, 'So let that be a lesson: working hard and becoming a good cook can open all sorts of doors that were closed to you before.'

Meg smiled as she opened the back door to find Tommy on the step. Their friendship had blossomed in the last couple of months – not that she would ever say that out loud to anyone – and she looked forward to his visits as a chance for a quick chat, a smile and a warm glow inside. On her second afternoon out in the park she had met up with his mother again, and then on her third she had actively looked out for Mrs Hopkins, enjoying the peace of sitting on a bench watching the world go by while they talked of this and that, and of Tommy. Tommy himself had managed to turn up for a few minutes each time, which just made for an even greater treat.

Tommy looked harassed this morning, as well he might given how busy he was. But he still had time for that smile, for those hazel eyes to light up when he saw her.

'I'll have to get this lot in quickly,' he said, hefting the first of the two crates by his feet. 'I'm running late as it is.'

'Let me help, then,' said Meg, stooping to pick up the other.

'But you shouldn't – oh, thanks, Meg, you're a trooper and no mistake. Nobody else on my rounds helps me carry anything, I can tell you that for nothing.'

'Been busy, have you?' she asked, as they made their way to the kitchen.

'Not half. Things coming into the shop to put away, deliveries to go out . . .' He thumped the box down on the kitchen table. 'Honest to God, I've never seen so many oranges in my life.'

Meg laughed, looking in the crate. 'There's two dozen in there, or there should be – surely you're used to seeing that many all together?'

'No, I didn't mean these ones, I meant—'

'Ah, Tommy, there you are,' interrupted Mrs Roberts, emerging from the archway. 'Did you bring everything? I'm almost out of raisins.'

'Yes, ma'am,' he replied. 'All present and correct.'

'As it always has been, since that unfortunate incident on your first day,' noted the cook. Tommy opened his mouth to say something, but she forestalled him. 'Not to worry about it – that's over and done with and you've made good since then. Now, you're already late, so you'd better get going. I'll take it on trust, this once, that everything is correct without checking it over.'

Tommy stammered his thanks, already halfway back out the kitchen door, and Meg followed to show him out.

On the doorstep he paused. He looked about him to check that nobody was watching, and lowered his voice. 'Will you be in the park, on your next afternoon out?'

'Yes, I should think so. I have one more before Christmas.'

'My Ma really likes seeing you,' he said. 'And so do—'

Footsteps sounded on the outside stairs, and the butcher's boy arrived.

'Anyway,' said Tommy, blushing a deep red. 'I'll be off. See you soon!'

Meg watched him go, before turning her attention to the chops and joints Mrs Roberts had been waiting for.

*   *   *

Mrs Roberts, Hannah and Meg – and Ivy, who was to spend all her time in the kitchen for the next few days – had been on the go since half past six in the morning on Christmas Eve, taking it in turns to snatch a few minutes for something to eat without ever sitting down. By three o'clock there was a slight lull, and Mrs Roberts was just starting to say that they might be able to put the kettle on when Mrs Lawrence popped her head around the door.

She was smiling. 'If you've a few moments to spare, you might want to come and see this.'

Curious, they all followed as she led them out the back door and up the steps to the pavement. It was freezing out here, especially after the warmth of the busy kitchen, and Meg hugged herself as she watched her breath mist in front of her.

A wagon was parked outside the house, and from it the delivery man, with the help of Mr Wilson and Samuel, was unloading an awkwardly shaped tree.

'What in heaven's name are they going to do with that?' asked Mrs Roberts. 'It's got no roots for planting, and it's far too green to burn.'

To Meg's astonishment, the men carried the tree up the steps and in through the front door. *What . . . ?*

Mrs Lawrence smiled at their incomprehension. 'Ah, you're obviously not up with the latest Christmas fashions. As I wasn't, until a couple of days ago. But apparently it's been the latest craze in London these last few years since the queen and Prince Albert started it. Mrs Harcourt showed me a picture in a magazine.'

'But what are they going to do with it?' asked Mrs Roberts.

'They will decorate it – the children will be brought down from the nursery to help, because that's what the royal family do – and light it up with candles. Then they will put their gifts for each other under it ready for tomorrow morning.'

Meg had never been in the main part of the house, but she had just glimpsed a spacious, tiled hallway inside the open front door, and the start of an elegant staircase. 'Won't it look beautiful!' she cried, forgetting that she wasn't supposed to speak to Mrs Lawrence without being spoken to.

'And won't the children love it!' That was Ivy, clapping her hands, equally forgetful of her place.

The Christmas spirit prevailed. 'Yes, I'm sure it will,' was all Mrs Lawrence said. 'Now, let's get back inside before you all catch a chill – but there was no time for you to fetch your coats and hats.'

There was just time for a warming cup of tea before preparations needed to be in full swing again, both for the servants' tea and that evening's dinner party upstairs. Meg smiled as she worked, thinking of the family all together round the tree upstairs. She wouldn't see it, of course, but nobody could stop her imagining what it would look like with its candles and decorations.

The evening went on and on, endless dishes of stunning, elaborately presented food going up and an equally endless stream of washing-up coming down.

By the time the last item was washed and dried, it was very late. The only light in the scullery was from the oil lamp by the sink; the rest of the room was in darkness.

Just as Meg was wiping her wrinkled hands dry, the door to the passageway opened, and the shadow of Samuel stood framed in it.

Meg froze, her heart in her throat. *Not now! Not on Christmas Eve!*

He took a step inside the room, but they were both startled by the kitchen door opening and Mrs Roberts appearing. 'Meg, have you—'

She stopped and took in the scene. Meg didn't know if she could bear it if the cook was going to jump to the same conclusion as the butler had last time.

Mrs Roberts put her hands on her hips and surveyed them both. 'Samuel – you've no business in here at this time of night. Off with you.'

The footman disappeared and Meg sagged with relief.

'If you've finished in here, you'd better step through to the kitchen.'

Meg turned the oil lamp down, so that the only light came from the soft glow of the kitchen though the door that Mrs Roberts was holding open. She went through.

There was nobody else in the kitchen; all was quiet. Meg moved to the range, which was cooling down from the fierce heat of the day, but still warm.

'Bless me, child, but you're shivering,' said Mrs Roberts. In a businesslike way she took down a small pan. 'You missed your hot milk earlier, so no reason why you shouldn't have some now. The range is still warm enough.'

'Oh, Mrs Roberts, that's—'

'No arguing,' said the cook, crisply. 'There's still plenty of today's left, and it's kept fine in the larder, at this time of year. You fetch some.'

Meg did as she was told, then came back and stood in silence while the cook heated it and poured it into a cup. 'There, now. Drink it all up. You've worked hard today.'

Meg drained it all, feeling the hot liquid soothe her.

Once it was finished, Mrs Roberts cleared her throat. 'It's late, and we've another long day tomorrow. You get yourself to bed – I've already sent Hannah and Ivy.'

'But I haven't scrubbed the floor yet, Mrs Roberts.'

The cook looked at the kitchen floor, which did show the signs of the day's work. She wavered between sympathy and professionalism for a moment, but then professionalism won out. 'All right. You get that done.'

Meg's eyes automatically strayed to the door.

'I've got to look through my notes for tomorrow, anyway, so I'll sit here and do that while you're busy, and then we'll go upstairs together.'

Meg was grateful both for Mrs Roberts's words and for the ones she hadn't said out loud.

By the time the floor was clean and the water poured away, the kitchen clock was striking midnight.

Mrs Roberts yawned. 'Definitely time for bed now. Merry Christmas, Meg.'

Meg was so tired she could hardly stay upright. Thank goodness for the comfortable boots, or she would have been dead on her feet by now. 'Merry Christmas, Mrs Roberts.'

* * *

Meg was down in the kitchen again six hours later. At first she shivered, but by the time she'd vigorously swept, blacked and lit the range she had warmed up.

After the early morning work and breakfast, most of the servants put on their coats and hats to go to church. But, as ever, a holiday was not a holiday for the kitchen workers, so Mrs Roberts, Hannah, Meg and Ivy watched them all go out and then got back to work. Meg didn't mind; the smell of roasting meat was so tantalising that she didn't want to leave it for a chilly church pew and a lecture about how everyone's place in life was divinely ordained.

The day passed in a blur, but it wasn't an unhappy blur: there was a distribution of gifts sent down by the family – a length of cloth each for Meg and the other junior female servants, to make a new dress – as well as a lovely meal in the servants' hall and the satisfaction of having supplied a stupendous Christmas dinner for upstairs. The afternoon was a little quieter, at least; the family would not have another cooked meal in the evening, so they could all afford to relax just a little bit. At the servants' tea there was a small glass of wine, well watered for the younger ones, and a toast to the queen and to Mr and Mrs Harcourt, followed by singing. Meg was surprised to discover that Mr Wilson had a very fine voice.

And then, after the usual evening tasks, the day was over, and Meg took her sturdy cotton cloth upstairs to the icy bedroom, wondering how she was ever to find either the time or the skill to make a dress. She thought of Martha and Sally, and wished she could share her Christmas with them.

The rest of the week, while not as busy as Christmas Day, was still full of social engagements for the family, which meant plenty of work below stairs. Soon it was New Year's Eve, and Meg lay in bed, contemplating all that had passed since last year. It hardly seemed possible that only twelve months had elapsed. What would 1850 bring?

She was halfway through a thought about hazel eyes when she fell asleep.

Chapter Seventeen

It was the second half of the century, but as the first half of the year passed Meg had little time to wonder about how the modern world was faring. She already had two worlds of her own: the workhouse, where her friends were still trapped, and the house, encompassing the even smaller world of the downstairs part of it. She had still never entered the upstairs rooms, never seen Mr or Mrs Harcourt in person.

She had, however, met the children. Miss Amelia, Master Francis and Master George lived on the top floor of the main house, immediately below the servants' bedrooms in the attic, where the nursery was situated. It was a whole complex to itself, with a day room, a night room where the two older children slept, and a separate bedroom for Nanny, which also contained a cot for Master George.

Meg knew all this because in the first weeks of January Ivy had gone down with a bad cold, necessitating a couple of days in bed and a ban on her entering the nursery for a week after that, lest she should infect the children. This meant that Meg had carried up the meals three times a day, at which point she began to sympathise with Ivy's continual grumbles about the number of stairs in the house.

She passed Robbie many times as she went up and down, as one of his duties was lugging up the many buckets of coals that were needed to keep the nursery fires burning continuously during the cold weather. Meg felt a bit sorry for him. He was the youngest member of the household staff, and the only boy; she might be the lowest of the low, but at least she had Ivy to talk to, and the other three maids weren't all that much older. But Robbie had nobody except Samuel, who continued to bully him, and Mr Wilson, who more or less ignored him unless he'd done something wrong. Meg smiled at Robbie whenever she could, and was sure to greet and speak to him when their paths crossed, but he ignored all her overtures of friendship; indeed, if Samuel happened to be in the vicinity he would be actively nasty to her and play tricks, tripping her up or hiding something she was looking for in a vain attempt to amuse or impress the bullying footman he both feared and adored.

With so much extra work to do Meg often found herself having to stay up late to finish her own. One evening it was nearly eleven o'clock before she was satisfied with the state of the kitchen, and she was wary as she carried her candle down the dark passageway in case Samuel was lurking about somewhere. As she approached the servants' hall she could see a light burning in there, and she hesitated, but she had no choice: it was the only way to reach the back stairs.

Fortunately the person in the room turned out to be Miss Greenwood, bent over some sewing at the table. She looked up as she heard Meg enter. 'You're up late.'

'Yes, Miss Greenwood. I had some chores to finish and it wouldn't do to have Mrs Roberts coming down to a dirty kitchen tomorrow morning.' The lady's maid had seemed more human since the episode of the bonnet, so Meg ventured to add, 'And you're up late too?'

She received a tired smile. 'Mrs Harcourt hasn't gone to bed yet, so I'm waiting for her to ring for me. But even after she's retired I'll be back down here, I'm afraid. The dressmaker we use is short-staffed at the moment, and there is a great deal to do to make sure Mrs Harcourt's spring wardrobe is ready in time.' She indicated a basket of what Meg could see, even in the dim light, were gorgeous fabrics.

Meg hovered for a moment, torn. 'I . . . I would offer to help you, Miss Greenwood, but my sewing is so terrible that I think it might make things worse. But can I get you anything else while you're working? More light, or a warm drink?'

'You're a good girl, but thank you, no. I'll manage.' But the lady's maid sighed as she looked at the overflowing basket.

The idea struck Meg like a thunderbolt. Why hadn't she thought of it straight away? Her exhaustion must be her excuse. 'Miss Greenwood . . . do you happen to know if the dressmaker might be looking to take on anyone else? Someone who can sew beautifully and is prepared to work really hard?'

The lady's maid paused for a moment. 'I suppose she might be. Why, do you have a candidate in mind? Not yourself, surely.'

'Oh, no, not me – I couldn't be happier here. But one of my friends from the workhouse, Martha, she sews all day and she's keen to find a position. And she's very good at it.'

'Well, I can ask, but if she's that good then I'm sure she'll find something sooner or later without my help.' Miss Greenwood started to turn back to her stitching, but something about the way Meg shuffled must have caught her attention. 'What?'

Meg wasn't quite sure how to phrase it. 'The problem is, Miss Greenwood, she does beautiful sample work, and people are often coming to the workhouse to ask after her, but as soon as they see her, they . . . judge her on her appearance. She has dark skin, you see.'

To Meg's surprise, the elegant Miss Greenwood actually snorted. 'And what, pray, has that to do with needlecraft skill?' She thought for a moment and then spoke firmly. 'Madame Joubert's only interest would be in the quality of the work, I can tell you that – I worked for her before I was fortunate enough to secure this position with Mrs Harcourt. Can you arrange for any samples?'

Meg tried to think to herself whether it might be possible for Martha to smuggle something to her without Mrs Leech finding out, but it would be tricky – the usual workhouse efficiency meant that every scrap of cloth and reel of thread was accounted for in the same way as every spoon or loaf of bread.

Miss Greenwood saw her hesitation. 'Workhouse life must be difficult.' She turned to her basket and rummaged around. 'Not that . . . Too precious . . . Need that one by Monday . . . Ah.' She picked out a plain apron of her own that had a rip in the middle. She examined it for a moment and then additionally pulled one of the strings loose and unpicked a hem. 'There.' She stuck a needle into a reel of white thread, put them in the apron pocket, rolled it all up and held it out. 'Get this to her somehow, ask her to make all that damage good, then bring it back to me and I'll take a look.'

Meg was stammering out her thanks when Miss Greenwood held up a hand. 'I can't promise anything, and I can't make a recommendation to Madame Joubert just because this girl is your friend – the quality of her work must speak for itself. But,' she added after a moment, 'I can tell you that I will judge only the work, not anyone's appearance.'

'Oh, thank you, Miss Greenwood, thank you so much. And Martha will do you proud, I know she will.'

They were cut off by the sound of a bell. It was the one marked 'Mrs Harcourt's Bedchamber', and Miss Greenwood rose. 'Off to bed with you now, and we can speak more once your friend – Martha, is it? – has completed the sample.'

* * *

Ivy returned to work, and Meg was able to redouble her efforts in the kitchen. It was there that she continued to find warmth, both physical and emotional, to support her while she worried about Sally and Martha. She was able to pick up what tips and instructions she could while she was cleaning up after the others, and she was so attentive that Mrs Roberts had unconsciously started to address her as well as Hannah when she was trying to teach something.

By the time the blossom had appeared on the apple trees in the garden, Meg had occasionally been allowed to prepare the nursery meals herself if the others were occupied with a higher calling such as dinner-party food. This proved to have both its advantages and its disadvantages. On the one hand, Meg loved stirring creamy porridge or rice pudding, or boiling mutton until it was tender enough for Master George's little teeth; she imagined the children sitting cosily in the warm nursery enjoying the taste while Nanny told them not to put their elbows on the table. But on the other hand, it made her sad. She remembered cooking for her own family, especially Rosie and Annie, soaking the bread and breaking it into tiny pieces so it wouldn't hurt their sore little mouths when they were teething. Added to this was the further pain of knowing that they had never, in their short lives, tasted anything as luxurious as the meals that were served to the children here, not even the fare that was considered plain nursery food.

Meg was still, on occasion, blindsided by sudden, brutal memories that would come upon her without warning, set off by an unexpected sight or sound or smell. At such times she didn't know whether she wanted to scream or cry or simply run away as fast as she could, but of course she did none of these things: she had to keep working and appear normal while she was doing it. She hoped – she knew – that both Mrs Roberts and Mrs Lawrence appreciated her hard and efficient work, but the spectre of being returned to the purgatory of the workhouse if she did anything wrong still hung over her.

Meg kept up her visits there every month without fail. On her next visit she was able to pass the torn apron to Martha under the table and explain the situation to her, happy and relieved to hear her friend's gasp of joy and assurance that she'd find a way to carry out the work and that she could hide it under her mattress. 'The other girls won't tell,' she added. 'We still try to get one over on Mrs Leech when we can, in remembrance of you, and we enjoy it even though she doesn't know anything about it.'

It would be a month or more before Meg would be able to see Martha again, of course, to collect the completed mending, and it might be many weeks after that before Miss Greenwood could get it to the dressmaker and then wait to hear back, but in the meantime at least they could hold on to the sliver of hope that it provided. They were *doing* something rather than just hoping.

Sally, unfortunately, was a different matter. She was less and less able to put on a cheerful face, even for a couple of hours and with cake in front of her, and she was still the target of Mrs Leech's spite. Meg felt guilty every time she visited, guilty at having escaped, guilty at being well dressed, well shod, well fed. Guilty at being able to get up and walk out at the end of visiting hours when Sally and Martha couldn't, guilty at knowing that a comfortable home awaited her. Terrified that they might disappear before she came back next time, just like the girls whose names they sometimes whispered to her across the table with fear in their eyes.

And comfortable her home was: although Samuel still made token efforts to intimidate or belittle her, it had been months now since he had attempted anything more, and Meg was almost starting to relax – although she still didn't like it if the door between the passage and the scullery opened silently when she had her back to it.

The reason for Samuel's lack of interest was evidently that he was getting what he wanted from

Hannah. They took their afternoons out together, and whenever Mrs Roberts was away he spent as much time as he could in the kitchen, his arm around Hannah's waist when he thought nobody was looking. Both Meg and Ivy had seen them at odd times coming in from the yard together, or standing very close to each other in dark corners, and Meg wondered that Mr Wilson hadn't put a stop to it, in the name of Samuel not being 'distracted' from his duties. But it seemed he hadn't said anything, and as it was none of Meg's business, and she wasn't a snoop or a snitch, she felt it wasn't her place to mention it. Besides, she couldn't help hoping that if they really loved each other they might decide to leave and get married, which would be best for everyone all round.

Meg also continued her afternoons out in the park, her meetings with Mrs Hopkins now being regular and by appointment, and happily spent by both. Mrs Hopkins was growing frailer each time, hardly able to walk at all now, or only with the greatest effort, and they spent their afternoons sitting on a bench near the entrance to the park where she was dropped off, rather than walking round it. Sometimes the older woman tried to chide Meg, to tell her that she didn't want to keep her from having a nice healthy walk, but as Meg generally spent sixteen hours a day on her feet she was not sorry to have a lazy afternoon with such a pleasant companion. Occasionally she would see Nanny and the household children out and about, though of course they didn't acknowledge her.

It was during a beautiful afternoon in May, blossom everywhere, that Meg reached their regular seat to find a discarded copy of the *Liverpool Mercury* lying on it. She picked it up to look through while she waited – she didn't get much chance to practise her reading these days, but it was an indispensable skill for a cook who wanted to find new receipts, so she took any opportunity that she could. She made her way through the front-page announcement of a performance of opera at the Theatre Royal – Mr and Mrs Harcourt sometimes went there, she knew – and the various advertisements for everything from jewellery polish to baby linen to the sale of 'a live male ostrich', whatever that was, just arrived from somewhere called Buenos Ayres.

The news items were inside the paper, so she turned the pages while the awkwardly large sheets flapped and fluttered in the slight breeze. It was while she was scanning down a column that her attention was arrested by a name that she recognised.

Body in Alleyway Identified

read the headline, but it was the two sentences after that which made her heart beat faster:

> The young woman who was found dead in an alley behind Gerard Street last week has been identified as one Ellen Tate, aged sixteen, a native of Liverpool. Her family had seen nothing of her since she voluntarily left the Brownlow Hill Workhouse alone last autumn.

There was little detail in the rest of the short article other than some veiled references to the dubious and immoral way in which Ellen had been earning a living since that time, and a quote from somebody important about appalling levels of violent crime in that part of the city.

Ellen Tate. The girl who had been removed from the kitchen on the very day that Meg had entered the workhouse, and sent to Mrs Leech. Meg was certain that the article was wrong and that Ellen hadn't left of her own accord. Mrs Leech had sent her somewhere – sold her, probably, the same way she had taken money for Meg. But the poor girl had not fallen on her feet as Meg had.

Thinking of feet made Meg belatedly aware that footsteps had been approaching and that they had stopped. She looked up, ready to greet Mrs Hopkins with a smile.

But it wasn't Mrs Hopkins. It was Tommy, crying, wiping his eyes angrily and trying to pretend that he wasn't.

Meg had known that this day was fast approaching, but still she felt a surge of sadness. 'Oh, Tommy, has your mother . . . ?'

He nodded and sat down, heavily.

There was little comfort Meg could give. She well knew what it was like to lose a mother, and the complete sense of wrenching disbelief that came with it. She said nothing, but reached out to take his hand; he held it as though it was the only thing stopping him from drowning.

She spoke quietly and gently to him, and then listened with sympathy as he wept out his feelings of loss, holding her hand all the while.

When they got up from the bench an hour later, Meg left the newspaper where it was, forgotten.

* * *

Meg had the usual pounding in her head and sick feeling in her stomach as she passed through the workhouse door on the first Thursday in August, but she gave Sally and Martha's names confidently enough.

She smiled when she saw them approaching her in the dining hall, but something about them made Meg's face fall, even before they were near enough to speak to each other. 'What is it?' she asked, a deep feeling of misgiving coming over her.

Sally sat down, leaned forward and whispered. 'They've disappeared.'

'Who?'

'Bernadette, and Dolly, and I heard Dolly's twin sister went too. All at once!'

'Disappeared? You mean, like the others?'

Martha spoke. 'Yes. It was just like we said before – they didn't hear that they had a post and then come to tell us all about it before going out the next day; they just left the dormitory one morning and never came back.' She shivered. 'And all three at once? I don't know what's going on, but I'm worried. Anyone could be next.'

Sally was shaking. 'Meg, I'm scared.'

Meg swallowed, the words *found dead in an alley* coming back to her. Something was going on, and Mrs Leech was at the bottom of it, she was sure.

She wasn't going to let this happen, not to Martha and Sally.

She stood up. 'Stay here.'

'Where are you going?' Sally's voice was fearful.

'I'm going to have a look round Mrs Leech's office, if I can. She's not normally in there on visiting afternoons. But I have to do it now, while there are lots of people around who aren't inmates. Stay here, and try and look like you're in one of those big groups, so nobody spots that you're here without a visitor.'

Sally clutched at her hand. 'But what if you get caught?'

'What can she do to me?' replied Meg. 'I'm not one of her inmates, so she can't cane me or push my head in a bucket, can she?'

Dear Sally seemed satisfied with this woefully poor explanation – workhouse punishments being the worst she could imagine – but as Meg moved quietly off through the crowds, she knew that a lot more was at stake. Mrs Leech might not be able to beat her, but she could certainly call the police. The trouble that would cause would result in her instant dismissal. Without references she would end up back in the workhouse, as she had nowhere else to go.

The thought was all but overwhelming, unbearable, but Meg forced herself to keep putting one foot in front of the other. She was doing this for her friends, the girls who had become her sisters when she was at her lowest point. How many times had Sally and Martha been beaten for something Meg had done? It was time to repay the debt.

Once out of the dining hall, Meg took the well-known route to the Receiving Room. She made herself walk normally, as if she had every right to be where she was. The respectable and sober way she was dressed would set her apart immediately from any inmates, so anyone who saw her would either think she was a visitor who was lost or someone with business to attend to.

Her luck was in, to start with; she reached the relevant corridor without being stopped or questioned. But as soon as she entered it she could see that the door to the office was open, which meant that Mrs Leech was inside it.

Meg looked about her. There was nobody else in the hallway. She sidled nearer to the door as quietly as possible, and stopped to listen.

The first voice she heard was Mrs Leech's. The other was one she recognised from somewhere, but where? Ah, she had it – it was the same woman the matron had been talking to on that day many months ago when Meg had got lost on the way back from the exercise yard. And perhaps the same one Martha had overheard?

'You're coming here too often.'

'I told you, I need more girls. Demand's going up, and some of them have either left or . . . been lost.'

'I saw, in the paper. How could you let that happen?'

'I told you, I can't be responsible if anything . . . *untoward* happens to 'em.'

'I didn't mean that.' Mrs Leech's voice dropped, so Meg had to strain to hear it. 'I meant, how could you let her be left in a state where she could be identified? And linked to the workhouse, for heaven's sake? Surely you know someone who could have . . .'

She trailed off, and Meg wondered if she could possibly be hearing what she thought she was hearing. They were dispassionately speaking of a girl who was dead, a girl Mrs Leech had sent out of the workhouse deliberately. Surely this was some kind of nightmare, and she would wake up any minute now?

But there was worse. 'Anyway, the twins are an interesting money-maker, and that Irish girl you sent last week has proved popular – not surprising, I suppose, with so many of them over here these days and the men looking for company that has a familiar voice. I'll take as many of them as you can send me. But no younger than that, mind – there might be some establishments that cater for men who like that sort of thing, but mine isn't one of them.'

'No, that's why I never sent you . . .' Mrs Leech tailed off and then began to sound flustered. 'I can't send more than one at a time. And even then, not so often. It was very risky to send you three at once, and I don't want to do it again.'

The other voice took on a threatening tone. 'Don't forget how much money I'm making you. Nor how easy it would be for me to let slip where I'm getting these girls from. And where's your retirement money then, eh?'

Mrs Leech mumbled something that Meg didn't catch, and there was the sound of a drawer opening.

'That's better,' said the other voice. 'I'll get off now, but I want at least one girl this week and another next week. You see to it.'

That sounded like a cue to leave, and Meg looked about her in a panic. She felt sick to her stomach. There was no mistaking what Mrs Leech and this woman were up to, and it was so much worse than Meg had ever imagined. The corridor was long, and there was nowhere to hide. She would just have to brazen it out and make the best of it. She set off at a brisk walk away from the door as she heard the woman come through it.

But it was no good. 'Oi!' came the call. 'You there!'

Meg hesitated for a fraction of a second over whether to run or whether to turn and pretend to be offended at being thus addressed. But her indecision was disastrous, and she felt her arm being grabbed. She was swung round to look up into a face covered in a thick layer of make-up and topped by a mass of flaming red hair.

One of Meg's old memories came back to her like a punch in the stomach. Of Rosie and Annie clutching her hands as she rushed them past the entrance to the court they had to avoid; of the men lounging around; of that very distinctive hair. For it was unmistake-able – the woman currently gripping her arm was the madam of the brothel.

Chapter Eighteen

Mrs Leech was in too deep. She knew that now, but it was too late to back out so she would just have to keep going.

Her hands shook as she shuffled papers on her desk. It had all started so simply: a way to earn some extra money to top up the pittance she received from the workhouse. It had been galling to find out that she was paid less than half Mr Higgin's wage even though their jobs were very similar, but fortunately she had it in her to be enterprising. Indeed, if the girls she was sending out to the brothel had any sense, they would be thanking her for the opportunity. What would their lives be, otherwise? An existence in the workhouse as a burden on society before a lonely death and a pauper's funeral. No, she was doing them a favour. She gathered that the brothel madam – whose head for business matched Mrs Leech's own – had started her career as one among many working girls, so there was no reason these workhouse brats couldn't do the same.

To start with there had also been a small amount of personal satisfaction, she had to admit. Mrs Leech had once been in love; she had thought that her affections were returned, and had naively planned to herself a wedding, a life together, a family . . . all of which had been cut off in the cruellest fashion when she had over-heard her beloved laughing about her, saying quite openly that he could never be attracted to a girl so thin and bony. Soon afterwards he had gone off with a plump, buxom young woman, and the next thing Mrs Leech had heard was that they were married.

Mrs Leech – or Miss Leech, as she had been then, and would have been destined to remain had it not been for her current position – had been by turns devastated and filled with a white-hot rage. The fault for everything, of course, lay not with him but with the girl who had lured him away with her wiles and her fuller body shape, and from that day forward Mrs Leech had held such girls in contempt, seeking her revenge in the only way she could. When the brothel madam had first come to her, under the guise of wanting 'a good-looking maid for a boarding establishment', Mrs Leech had seen through it straight away. Rather to her visitor's surprise she had stated out loud that she knew exactly what sort of job was really on offer, and that she had no objection to it as long as the financial arrangements were right.

All of that, that . . . *emotion* – she felt disgust even at thinking the word – had long gone, and frankly Mrs Leech couldn't even remember now what her one-time beloved had looked like. Business was just business, and what she wanted was to make enough money so that she herself could escape the fate of all too many older single women. She had no intention of being a poor old maid, the object of pity or ridicule.

The problem was, of course, that not many people were as enlightened in their views as Mrs Leech, and so she had been forced to keep her dealings secret lest she be discovered and sacked – such an eventuality would be a terrible injustice, of course, but what was life but injustice? It was all she had ever known. And so she had been running her little business arrangement under the counter all this time, so secure in her own cleverness that she did not fear being discovered.

However, the demands from the madam had become more frequent and more insistent of late, and this was dangerous – Mrs Leech was hard put to cover everything up. She had become increasingly paranoid at the thought that someone might find out, and convinced that it wouldn't be long before it happened. The members of the Board were the ones most to be feared, of course: they had the power to dismiss her, so when they visited she tried to focus their attentions on the practical aspects of the workhouse's activities, to show them the work going on rather than to let them in her office to view any paperwork. Mr Higgin was not a particular problem – he was a nobody who knew he was lucky to have such a shrewd head managing the women's side of the workhouse, so he kept out of her way.

No, the real danger that had been growing over the last year was from subordinate staff, pauper assistants and even some of the inmates themselves. The cook had directed one or two questions to Mrs Leech lately that had, in the matron's own mind at least, raised the suspicion that she knew something. The pauper assistants who fetched the girls and brought them here ready to be sent off had exchanged some looks that Mrs Leech didn't trust. And, of course, the girls, with their constant whispers in the dormitory about their friends 'disappearing'. Thank heavens, she had at least managed to get rid of that Shaw girl, who was so sharp she could cut not only herself but everyone around her. She had been the real danger. As long as Mrs Leech never set eyes on Meg Shaw again, she could slowly start to regain her confidence in the arrangement.

Mrs Leech had been so lost in her thoughts that she only belatedly became aware of a commotion in the corridor outside the office. She hurried out. The blasted madam was still here, making a spectacle of herself in an altercation with a much smaller woman who looked to be a visitor. Mrs Leech felt her heart rate rise in anxiety. What on earth was she playing at?

She stepped forward to intervene. She would send the madam away and get round the visitor somehow, use some excuse about undesirables finding their way in on visiting days. At that moment, the smaller woman was swung round, and Mrs Leech received a jolt that almost knocked her off her feet when she recognised Meg Shaw.

And then she panicked.

* * *

Meg squirmed and twisted in her attempt to get away from the brothel madam, but the woman was just too strong.

'What are you doing here? How much did you hear?' The woman was shaking her.

Meg was still too overwhelmed by her realisation to be able to form any coherent thoughts, but she knew that she had to get away. She pulled again. 'Let me go! You've got no right—'

'What in God's name is going on?' came an urgent, hissing whisper, and Meg found herself pulled around to look directly into the face of Mrs Leech.

For one moment the matron looked as horrified as Meg felt, but her face soon shut down as she in turn grabbed Meg, pinching her arm hard with those bony fingers.

'You get out of here, quickly,' she ordered the madam. 'Before you attract any more attention. I'll deal with her.'

Meg saw the red-haired woman pass through the outer door even as she herself was dragged back to the office. Once they were inside, Mrs Leech shoved Meg into the middle of the room before turning the key firmly in the lock. Then she faced Meg, breathing heavily.

Meg was not frightened. She could feel the anger building inside her, the anger that always came when she felt something to be unjust, and now it was boiling up to such an extent that her head was spinning. Finally, she let it erupt.

She didn't wait for Mrs Leech to speak first, but instead pointed an accusatory finger and spat out the words, 'You've been sending girls to the brothel! All this time! For *years*!'

Mrs Leech's eyes were wild. 'Yes, yes I have. I knew that you knew – sharp little minx, poking your nose in.'

'All those girls – all sent there when they could have had a respectable position somewhere. They could have had a *life*!'

'Oh, don't be so ridiculous!' snapped Mrs Leech, her evident panic honing itself into a cold fury that was much more dangerous. 'Those girls were nothing, the children of beggars and whores who ended up here because nobody wanted them. It's no more than they deserved – they would never have been respectable. They'd either die in here, or as soon as they got out they'd be selling themselves on street corners and then dead in an alleyway within a year.'

'Like Ellen Tate?'

That seemed to shock Mrs Leech. 'How did you—? But it's no matter.' She began to advance towards Meg.

This time, Meg stood her ground. 'I'm going to report you.'

Mrs Leech paused, but then only laughed. 'Oh, really? Who to? Because that worked so well last time, didn't it? What do you think will happen if I call Mr Higgin in here now?'

'It's different now. I have other people in my life, people who value me and who will listen.' Meg wished that she felt as confident as she sounded. Because, in all seriousness, who would listen to her? The household wouldn't want to be involved in any kind of scandal – she'd be tainted by association and out on her ear before she knew it. But Mrs Leech wouldn't know that. 'You can't stop me,' Meg added boldly, and she moved towards the door.

Once again she was grabbed, this time to be pushed back against a wall. Horrible memories of Samuel doing the same thing started to surface, and Meg tried to push them down. *Not now!*

'Oh, I can stop you,' said Mrs Leech. 'I can stop you the same way I've always stopped you.' She gave Meg a shake. 'Your friends from the dormitory are already there. But at least they're grown women, or almost – and the twins no better than they should be, just like their slut of a mother.' She paused, and then leaned in. 'But how do you think Martha will cope? Or little Sally?'

Meg froze.

Mrs Leech sensed her advantage. 'They won't know that she's still a child on the inside, one who won't understand what's happening to her. And nor will they care. All they'll see is a well-grown girl who's never been touched before.'

Sally. Poor, poor Sally. And Martha. Meg felt her nausea rising at the thought of how they would suffer, the one in terrified and total incomprehension at the wickedness and cruelty being visited upon her, and the other only too aware of it.

Mrs Leech knew she had won. 'So, one word from you, to anybody, and Martha and Sally will be the next to go. And once they've gone you won't get them back, not even if they take me away. It will be too late.' Her mad eyes bored into Meg's. 'So, every time you think of opening your mouth, Meg Shaw, you think of poor dear Sally and Martha in that place, day after day, night after night, man after man. And I hear they can be quite brutal sometimes . . .'

Meg couldn't help it. She vomited.

* * *

Meg had no idea how she got home. She had some vague memory of Mrs Leech springing back in disgust, which gave her the chance to unlock the door and escape; after that she must have run through the streets, but she had no memory of anything before scrabbling to open the back door and collapsing.

She had been found shortly afterwards by May, one of the housemaids, who had raised the alarm, and then there had a been a blur of stairs, and washing, and bed.

Meg didn't know how much time had passed, but now she became aware she was being gently lifted and a cup was put to her lips. She sipped, and warm beef tea slid down her throat. After a little more her nurse seemed satisfied, and she was lowered back down to the pillow.

Her eyes closed. She was in a kind of half-awake, half-asleep state where she could not move or speak, but she could hear.

'What can have happened to her?' asked a voice that Meg vaguely recognised as that of Mrs Roberts. *But that couldn't be right, surely? Was she lying down in the kitchen? Or was Mrs Roberts in her room? Neither was right.*

'She must have been attacked in the street,' responded a whisper that sounded like Mrs Lawrence.

'Oh, I *knew* I shouldn't have let her go there and back on her own,' came the reply, the cook sounding agitated. 'But after that first time she seemed fine.'

'Never mind walking there and back alone – we should never have let her go there at all. I thought it a fine thing that she didn't want to abandon her friends, but none of them seem to have been let out to take up a position, so perhaps they're not . . . respectable. In any case, it's time she forgot them.'

'Yes, maybe putting it all behind her is for the best. Anyway, I must get back down.'

'So should I, but I don't like to leave her alone, not at first. I can manage without Ivy for a few hours if you can.'

'Agreed. I'll find her on my way and send her up.'

Meg heard the sound of the door. Then all was quiet, except for breathing and the sense that someone else was still in the room. Hands smoothed the covers of the bed and touched her forehead. She started to doze off, but was jolted awake by some of the words coming back to her. *It's time she forgot them.* No. No, she would never do that. She would not forget, she would fight, she would find a way . . .

She slipped into a feverish sleep, filled with guilt. She dreamed of Sally and Martha, left behind and in danger. And even when she saved them, the faces of Molly, Dolly and Bernadette stared at her accusingly. Why wouldn't she save them too?

* * *

Meg was soon up and about again, sooner than Mrs Lawrence advised, but she resolutely refused to say one word about what had happened to her: not to the housekeeper, not to Mrs Roberts, and not even to Ivy when they were alone in their bedroom.

She tried hard to concentrate on her usual tasks, but this new fear was one she couldn't push down, and she was constantly worried sick to the point that her hands trembled and her work became sloppy. The problem was that her tasks, while hard and time-consuming, occupied her body and hands but all too often left her mind free. Over and over, round and round, went the worries in her head. Every day that passed was another during which the threat hung over Sally and Martha. Another day that the girls already sold had to suffer. Was it too late for them? Was she right to keep quiet to protect her friends?

How could Meg address it? To whom could she relay her fears? Even if she found someone, would they listen and believe? And, crucially, would they be able to act swiftly enough to catch Mrs Leech before she shipped more girls off? Meg had a vague idea of trying to contact the owner of the one sympathetic face she'd seen during her stay in the workhouse, the one she called the butterfly lady, but Meg had given her that epithet because she didn't know her real name – or indeed the names of any of the members of the Board. Could she find out? And if she did, what would such a fine lady think when an unknown scullery maid turned up on her doorstep with such a wild tale about one of the Board's employees? It was all impossible, and Meg often wept into the sink in anger and frustration.

If she kept her mouth shut, Sally and Martha would have a measure of safety. If Mrs Leech were to send them to the brothel anyway then she would have no further hold over Meg, and must know that Meg would then make everything as public as she could. Meg's hope was that Mrs Leech's sense of self-preservation would be stronger than her spite, and that this would last until Meg could get Martha and Sally out of there. But once again her sense of the injustice of the world – the injustice for girls in particular – threatened to overwhelm her. She was so lost in her thoughts about her friends that she even dropped a few pans as she collected them, spilling the remains of the contents on the floor, much to Mrs Roberts's annoyance.

To add to the cook's dissatisfaction with the less-than-perfect running of the kitchen while Meg was preoccupied, Hannah was also being inexplicably clumsy. As she spilled the porridge one morning, right in front of Mrs Roberts, the cook put her hands on her hips. 'I don't know what's got into you girls, I really don't.'

Hannah opened her mouth to reply, and then seemed to change her mind. 'Sorry, Mrs Roberts, I—' She ran out into the scullery, and Meg could hear the sound of her being noisily sick. Selfishly, she hoped Hannah had managed to do it in the sink and not on the table or the floor.

Mrs Roberts's expression changed. 'So that's it,' she said, grimly. She turned to Meg. 'Run to Mrs Lawrence and ask her if she would come here, please, as soon as she can.'

Meg did so, fortunately catching the housekeeper as she was heading for the kitchen anyway. When they reached it, Meg busied herself about the breakfast duties.

Mrs Lawrence took one look at the weeping Hannah and the grim face of the cook, and sighed. 'Is this what I think it is?'

'It is. She's in the family way. A couple of months gone, I should say.'

The housekeeper shook her head, sadly. 'Oh, Hannah, how could you do such a thing? You'll have to go, you know that.'

Hannah looked up through her tears. 'It's Samuel's,' she said. 'I told him, and I thought we might get married, but he said it's nothing to do with him and he never wants to see me again.' She broke down into more sobs.

Meg didn't think she could despise Samuel any more than she already did, but here was yet more proof that a handsome face could hide a black heart. Hannah had never been particularly kind to her, but her heart swelled on behalf of her fellow maid. It wasn't fair.

Mrs Lawrence and Mrs Roberts had exchanged a glance and a nod. 'I'll fetch Mr Wilson and have him bring Samuel,' said the housekeeper.

While she was gone, Mrs Roberts spoke briskly to Hannah. 'Now then, dry your tears – they won't help. Go and wash your face, come back and we'll see what can be done when they get here.'

Hannah obeyed. Mrs Roberts looked round. 'Meg? Oh, you're a good girl. We can't have nursery breakfast being late. Can you manage that on your own?'

Meg was already stirring porridge on the range, a new batch to replace the one Hannah had spilt. 'Yes, Mrs Roberts. Unless you'd rather I left the room while . . .'

'I know it's not nice for you to hear, but the kitchen work comes first. You concentrate on that so it's ready for Ivy to take up on time.'

Meg turned back to the range, aware that the kitchen door had opened behind her and that the room was full of people.

'What is this, Mrs Lawrence?' came Mr Wilson's voice, sounding tetchy. 'I haven't got time to waste.'

'Hannah is with child, Mr Wilson.'

The butler made an exasperated 'tsk' noise. 'Well, get rid of her, then. I'm glad you informed me, but you don't need my permission to let a kitchen maid go.'

He sounded as though he was about to leave, but Mrs Lawrence forestalled him. 'The thing is, Hannah says that Samuel is the baby's father.'

'It's not true, Mr Wilson.' That was Samuel, of course. Meg's fingers tightened around the spoon.

'Samuel, how can you say such a thing!' Hannah's voice was distraught. 'All those times we were together, and you said we'd leave here, we'd get married . . .'

'The girl's deranged, Mr Wilson,' came the footman's smooth tones. 'She's got herself in trouble and she's trying to find someone to blame.'

'Well, that's that, then,' said Mr Wilson.

'Pardon?' In their surprise, both cook and housekeeper had spoken together.

'You heard him – it's nothing to do with him. Get rid of the girl and we can all go about our business.'

The porridge was ready. Meg would much rather stay where she was, invisible, but if she kept it on the range any longer it would spoil. She took the pan off the hot plate and crept around the outside of the group, trusting that their attention was on each other, and placed it on the trivet standing ready on the table. Then she sidled back to the range to fetch the serving dish from the warming shelf. She was angry, angry that any girl should be treated so; it didn't matter that Hannah had never shown her any friendship. But what could she do? And what would the repercussions be if she tried to intervene? *Stay out of it,* she told herself. *Keep your head down – it's safer.*

But everything she could hear was increasing her sense of injustice, of rage at the way the world worked. Even here in this beautiful house there was no justice for women. What chance did the likes of her and the workhouse girls have? Nobody was listening to Hannah; nobody believed her. Or, at least, neither of the men in the room did, and it was their opinion that counted.

'Do you have any idea how difficult it is to get a trained footman these days? Especially one as tall as that?' was Mr Wilson's latest. 'Of course I'm not going to sack him just on the word of one slutty girl.'

Mrs Lawrence was attempting to remain calm, Meg could see, but she was losing the battle. 'And what if the footman we already have is disrupting the smooth running of the household? This isn't—'

'But he's not, is he? You heard what he said. The simple fact is that this girl has no morals. She went out looking for trouble and she ended up getting what she deserved.'

Getting what she deserved. Meg recalled the very similar words Mrs Leech had used when she had spoken dismissively of sending girls to the living hell of the brothel. The rage grew. She tried to keep it down, to push it back inside, but her hands shook as she poured the porridge into the serving dish.

It was Samuel's words that pushed her over the edge, and the expression on his face as he looked at Hannah – Hannah, whom he had previously smiled at, cajoled, and no doubt made promises to. Whom he had tricked in order to get what he wanted. Now he was looking at her with contempt, his lip curling as he addressed not her but Mr Wilson.

'Like I said, Mr Wilson – she's got herself pregnant, the hussy, and now she's trying to take an easy way out by blaming it all on me. I'm not having it.'

'There, you see—' began the butler to the other women.

Meg experienced a brief internal struggle between doing what was safe and doing what was right. But there was no question which would win out.

She stepped forward. 'But she didn't, did she?'

There was a moment of silence as everyone in the kitchen took in the fact that the scullery maid had dared to interrupt her superiors, had just addressed the butler in this fashion.

'I beg your pardon?' was all that Mr Wilson could manage to splutter, in his outrage.

'She didn't "get herself pregnant", did she? I don't think it can happen without a man.'

Mrs Lawrence now gasped. This was not the sort of thing she would consider 'respectable' conversation in a maid, Meg knew. But – *In for a penny, in for a pound,* she thought.

She addressed them both, butler and housekeeper. 'I know that I'll lose my place for saying this. But dismissing Hannah and not Samuel is unfair. I've seen them together, and so has everyone else if they only cared to look. Of course the baby is his. It couldn't be anyone else's. I know that men are allowed to run away from their responsibilities, to desert their families, at least out there,' she gestured at the wider world, 'but it's shocking that you're going to let it happen here, in this lovely, well-run house.'

Mrs Lawrence had by now recovered the power of speech, and Meg waited for the outburst. But, 'I didn't know you were such friends,' was all that came out.

Hannah was looking at Meg in amazement, and Meg took her hand in solidarity. 'You don't have to be friends with somebody to know what's right and what's wrong, ma'am.'

The outburst, when it came, was from Mr Wilson rather than Mrs Lawrence. He lunged forward, making everyone jump, although Meg did not take a step backwards. 'The only reason,' he almost spat, waving a finger in her face, 'the *only* reason you're not packing your bags right now is that I won't give Mrs Roberts the inconvenience of depriving her of both maids at once. But you're on your last warning, you hear?'

He addressed the housekeeper. 'You will discipline this girl, Mrs Lawrence. As to the rest: I've only Hannah's word for it that the baby is anything to do with Samuel, and she's already proved to be a slattern who can't be trusted, or she wouldn't be in this condition in the first place. I can't afford to lose a trained footman, and the decision rests with me anyway.' He turned. 'Samuel, get about your duties. Hannah, pack your bags and leave.' He stalked out.

Hannah was sobbing again, the hand in Meg's shaking. 'Oh, Samuel, how could you be so cruel?' she wept, moving forward to plead with him, as if it would make the slightest bit of difference, as if she still thought he had a heart. 'Your own child!'

Samuel shook her off and walked towards the door. As he reached it, he turned, but not to look at Hannah, the girl whose life he had ruined: his eyes were fixed on Meg. The sheer malevolence in his gaze almost knocked her backwards, and she knew that she had gambled and lost – not only would Samuel remain in the household, but he was now, more than ever, her enemy. And he would want his revenge.

Chapter Nineteen

It didn't take long.

Meg tried as far as possible to stay out of Samuel's way and never to be alone. She stuck close to Mrs Roberts and Ivy whenever possible, but she found it hard to be aware of her surroundings, to do her job and to keep functioning while being tied in knots about Sally, Martha and the rest of the girls. Her nights were sleepless, as she imagined ways she could save her friends – all of them.

Her anxiety and tiredness made her less alert, so it was inevitable that Samuel would catch her alone and unawares one day. Hannah, of course, was gone; and on this particular morning Mrs Roberts had been summoned upstairs to talk to Mrs Harcourt about menus at the same time as Ivy was four floors away in the nursery.

The butcher's boy had just called and Meg, having weighed everything carefully as she had seen Mrs Roberts do, was storing the joints and chops in the cool larder. She came out, then put her head briefly into the pantry to check all was in readiness to receive the grocery delivery that was also due. Then she turned to pass back through the archway to the kitchen, and came face to face with Samuel.

Or not face to face, of course; her face was no higher than the level of his chest. The physical size difference between them had always been one of the ways in which he intimidated her, and he used it now, blocking the arch and pushing her back into the shadows of the inner lobby.

'Thought you'd get rid of me, did you? Sully my good name? Bitch.'

Meg knew straight away that this was not a situation she would be able to talk her way out of, so she attempted to evade him. He caught her easily. 'Oh no, not this time.' He glanced back into the kitchen, aware that they would be visible to anyone who entered the room, and began to propel her backwards into the pantry.

Meg was about to scream when the kitchen door opened behind him. It was Robbie. He stopped in astonishment, his eyes widening. Samuel saw him, but made no move to stop what he was doing.

'Don't just stand there!' shouted Meg. 'Do something! Stop him – or fetch someone!'

Samuel laughed. 'Oh, do be quiet. You girls talk far too much.' He put his hand over her mouth, and all the memories of when he'd done the same thing before flooded back to her. She began to struggle.

He looked over his shoulder at Robbie. 'You can stay if you want – it will do you good to see what happens to girls who get above themselves.' He grinned. 'If you help me hold her down I might even let you have a bit of a feel yourself. It'll make a man of you.'

Meg screamed against the palm of his hand, but no sound escaped. She could see that Robbie's face was white, and she hoped against hope that he would step forward, that he would do something, but he was terrified of Samuel, she knew. Then he turned and fled.

Samuel laughed. 'Maybe just as well. He's not enough of a man yet.'

They were now fully inside the pantry and invisible to anyone outside the inner lobby. He kicked the door shut behind him. 'This won't take long.' He leaned down to whisper in her ear. 'You probably won't enjoy it – but not to worry, because I will.'

She struggled and she kicked, but she could not get away from him. There was a brief pause when he realised he didn't have enough hands to do everything at once, so he removed the one from across her mouth, but before she could even draw breath to scream he had stuffed in a wad of her apron, making her choke.

'That's better. Girls should keep quiet.'

He had both of her wrists pinioned above her head, easily held in one hand and his body pressing hers against the wall.

Meg couldn't move, couldn't scream, couldn't hit, couldn't bite. She tried kicking her feet, but it was no use. He thrust his free hand under her skirts, and she writhed and struggled as she felt his hard, cruel fingers move up her thigh. She could hear her own voice rising as she shrieked into the folds of choking, suffocating cloth, but no sound escaped. She closed her eyes and tried to brace herself.

And then there was a movement, a strange sound like a sort of soft explosion, and an exclamation.

Meg opened her eyes. Samuel was covered in a white powder, and in the shock of the moment he had loosened his grip on her. Meg managed to push him away a little, and then, with every ounce of strength she possessed, she brought her knee up between his legs.

She wasn't tall enough to hit him with the force she intended, but the contact was sufficient to make him cry out and double over, and finally she could push past him.

'Come on!' shouted a voice she recognised, and a hand took hers and pulled her back through to the comparative safety of the open kitchen.

She tried to breathe in, retched, and felt hands helping her to pull the wads of apron out of her mouth. Then she sucked in a huge gulp of air and faced Tommy.

They stared at each other for a moment, breathing heavily.

Tommy was also covered in white powder. Meg had no idea what was going on. 'What—?'

'Nobody answered the door,' he said, in between heaves of his chest. 'But I was late, so I pushed it open and came in. Thought it was odd the kitchen was empty. But then I heard . . . so I came to see . . . just panicked and used the first thing that came to hand . . .'

Realisation dawned on Meg. 'You hit him with a bag of flour?' she asked, incredulously. Despite her shaking, or perhaps because of it, she began to laugh. But she couldn't control it, and it scared her.

Tommy looked over her shoulder. 'He's coming out!'

Samuel had staggered in. He couldn't move very fast but picked up a nearby saucepan and threw it at them. Tommy pushed Meg out the way, and it hit the wall harmlessly with a loud clatter.

'Quick!' Meg felt her hand seized again, and Tommy was pulling her towards the door. It opened as they approached it, and Mrs Roberts, Mrs Lawrence and Mr Wilson all poured in. Meg could see Robbie and Ivy behind them.

'What . . . ?' Mrs Lawrence was standing aghast at the sight before her, the mess, the powder-covered figures, almost unable to form a question.

Samuel threw himself forward, addressing the butler. 'They attacked me, Mr Wilson. Both of them. I caught them at it, dirty slut that she is, and they turned on me.'

'That's not true!' shouted Tommy, hotly. 'He was attacking Meg, and I had to stop him.'

Mr Wilson now found his voice. 'I told you . . .' he was starting to say to Meg, when Tommy's interjection surprised him. 'And who on earth are you?'

Everybody started shouting at once, but to Meg they all seemed further and further away, echoing from a great distance. She was vaguely aware that Ivy had pushed her way through the crowd and was supporting her, which was the only thing stopping her from falling.

The noise intensified, until everyone was shocked into silence by a sudden loud sound.

It was Mrs Roberts, who had picked up the fallen saucepan and banged it hard on the table several times in order to get their attention.

'That's better,' she said, into the hush. 'Now, this is my kitchen and I will have some order.' She turned first to Ivy. 'Sit her down in my chair. If there's tea left in the pot, give her some with sugar. I'll find the brandy if I need to.'

Meg felt herself being gently propelled, and she subsided gratefully into the chair. She forced herself to swallow some of the sugary warm liquid through her chattering teeth, and came to herself a little.

Mrs Roberts was pointing at Tommy. 'You first. What happened?'

Both Samuel and Mr Wilson opened their mouths, but the cook silenced them with a look. Meg had never seen her so magnificent – and she hadn't seen two men succumb to a woman's instruction like that since Ma was alive.

Tommy's voice was wavering now, as the full force of what had happened – of what had nearly happened to his dear Meg – hit him. He explained again how he'd come in, what he'd seen, and how he'd acted. 'And I'm sorry about the flour, Mrs Roberts, but I didn't know what else to do, and I had to stop him somehow.'

'He's a liar!' shouted Samuel, who was still covered in white and standing very awkwardly. 'Are you going to take his word over mine? It was me caught them at it, in the pantry, and then they both went for me.'

'I did not!' retorted Tommy. 'Meg would never— And don't you call me a liar! My Ma brought me up to tell the truth.' His fists were clenched, his nervousness turning to fury at the man who had dared to attack Meg, and he made a movement as if to step forward.

'And what does Meg have to say about all this?' interjected Mrs Lawrence.

Everyone turned to look at Meg, and she blushed deep red. How could she possibly say out loud . . . ?

Mrs Roberts saw her discomfort. 'You can hardly expect the girl to recount such a thing in a room full of men, Mrs Lawrence.' She gave Samuel a look full of daggers. 'But I know who I believe.'

'Well,' said Mr Wilson, 'I don't. You just can't trust these girls. Once again we only have each person's word for it. And—'

'No, Mr Wilson.'

Meg looked up in surprise, having forgotten that Robbie was in the room. He stepped forward, shaking visibly.

'Well?' asked Mr Wilson, impatiently.

'It's like Meg and Tommy said, sir. Or at least what Meg said – I didn't see Tommy come in. But I was here earlier, and Samuel had hold of Meg, and he was dragging her into the pantry, and he said—' He gulped and looked round. His ears were bright red. 'Well, it wouldn't be proper to repeat what he said. But there's no doubt about it.' He looked directly at the footman for the first time. 'Samuel's a bully, sir, and he's always had it in for Meg, even though she's so kind.' He stopped and looked at the floor.

'Well, there you have it,' said Mrs Lawrence. 'Three words against one.'

'Four,' said Ivy. 'I wasn't here, but I believe the evidence of my own eyes.' Gently, she pulled back Meg's sleeves so everyone could see the angry red marks on her wrists. Cheeks burning, Meg hastened to cover her wrists again, but everyone had seen.

All eyes were on Mr Wilson.

He cleared his throat. 'This is all as may be,' he said, 'but my job is to make sure that Mr and Mrs Harcourt are well served, and Samuel's a good footman. Whereas, as I've said before, scullery maids are ten a penny.'

Meg's heart sank, and tears sprang to her eyes. So this was how it was going to be – again.

But wait.

'And what about professed cooks, Mr Wilson? Are they ten a penny too?' Mrs Roberts was standing with her arms folded.

'I'm afraid I don't quite understand . . .'

'Let me spell it out for you, then. I'm losing my patience with you, Mr Wilson. You constantly offer justification and defence for this . . . *excuse* of a man, while girl after girl is ill-treated and sent away. And in this case the facts simply couldn't be plainer.' She looked at Meg, her tone softening. 'This particular girl is the hardest worker I've ever seen, and she has rare talent, Mr Wilson. I know it when I see it, and she'll be a great cook someday.'

She turned back to the butler and her voice hardened again. 'To put it bluntly, if she goes then I go too. And then you can serve Mr and Mrs Harcourt by doing the cooking yourself.'

She stared the butler down, defiantly, as he opened and closed his mouth like a fish.

Meg was properly in tears now, at the thought of such kindness. And then, to her utter, *utter* astonishment, Mrs Lawrence moved to stand side by side with the cook. 'And you can include me in that too, Mr Wilson.'

He spluttered. 'But—'

'No,' said the housekeeper, firmly. 'You've let the household down, Mr Wilson. You've been slack in your supervision of male staff, with the result that this is no longer a respectable household. Mrs Roberts will leave if you dismiss Meg; I will leave if you *don't* dismiss Samuel.' She looked at the footman as though he was something unpleasant she'd trodden in. 'I suggest he leaves to make an honest woman of Hannah, though I suspect even she's too good for him.'

By this time both Ivy and Robbie had made their way over to Mrs Lawrence's side of the kitchen, leaving Mr Wilson and Samuel on their own. Tommy crouched by Meg's chair. His solid presence next to her was a comfort as she watched the extraordinary scene play out. She noticed, somewhat to her own surprise, that she had taken hold of his hand, and knew that she ought not to do such a thing in front of the senior servants. But she didn't let go.

'Well?' Mrs Roberts had not taken her eye off the butler.

Mr Wilson squared his shoulders and pulled together the shreds of his dignity. 'Meg, you are to stay,' he said. 'Samuel, you are dismissed. You are to be gone before the end of the day.' He looked at the cook, to discover that her steely eye was still upon him. 'And,' he added, 'you will receive no reference.' He nodded at Mrs Roberts and made his escape from the room.

Samuel attempted to glare, opened his mouth to speak, but Mrs Roberts took a single step forward. 'Get. Out. Of. My. Kitchen.'

Meg wanted to cheer as the footman turned on his heel and left, but she was too exhausted, too over-whelmed . . . the room was slipping away.

'Here!' called Tommy, his voice rising. 'Help! Meg, are you all right?'

There were a few moments of commotion, and then Meg felt a cup being put to her lips. Reflexively she swallowed, and then almost choked at the intensity of the unexpected brandy, feeling as though her throat was on fire. She gasped. But it jolted her back to her-self.

She looked, a little groggily, at the circle of faces around her. Friendly faces. Faces she was coming to love as a second – no, wait, third? – family.

She started to struggle to her feet. 'Nursery dinner,' she croaked. 'I'd best get on with it – can't be late.' She staggered past them and set a pan on the range.

* * *

Tommy was back with a regular delivery just a few days later, now even more of a welcome visitor in Mrs Roberts's kitchen; she chatted to him and even turned a blind eye when Meg took a little longer than was strictly necessary to show him out the back door. One day soon after he turned up, blushing, with a little posy of flowers, and Meg was so touched that she kept it in her bedroom until long after the blooms had faded and crumbled. It was bitter as well as sweet, though: every day that the flowers aged was another day during which she was safe and the other girls weren't.

Meg was kept so busy that she didn't immediately have the time to devise new plans; the lack of a kitchen maid meant additional work for her, helping with actual food preparation rather than simply clearing up. She now had almost complete charge of the nursery meals and had delicately experimented with a few flavours, pleased to hear from Ivy that the children enjoyed her creations.

She did occasionally still think of her own family, and those sudden, vivid memories of her past life did still appear from time to time, but it was now two whole years since she had seen or heard from them. She wasn't quite sure whether she was resigned to never seeing them again, or so angry with them that she didn't want to. If they weren't dead, she reasoned, and they did want to see her again, someone would have tried to find her by now, would have enquired at the workhouse and found out where she'd gone. And if they were alive but hadn't bothered to do that, well, they didn't care and were dead to her anyway.

No, the 'family' on her mind was Sally, and Martha, and their terrible situations. The same questions turned over and over in her head: how could she get them out? How could she stop Mrs Leech without putting them in even more danger? How could she rescue all the girls?

These thoughts plagued Meg one afternoon as she stood at the range making bread and milk for nursery tea. Mrs Roberts now trusted her with the key to the spice cupboard, so Meg sprinkled into the thickening mix a pinch of cinnamon and nutmeg. The milky nursery meals were so bland that a tiny bit of additional flavour made all the difference, and last time she had done the same she had even received a passed-on compliment from Nanny herself, who knew nothing about the spices but had noticed the children eagerly eating up their meal without wasting a drop. It was now ready, and Meg poured it into the serving dish. Ivy had not yet arrived to transport it, so Meg placed it back on the warming shelf.

Several minutes passed, and Ivy still did not appear.

Meg looked at the clock. 'Mrs Roberts, shall I take this up the stairs and meet Ivy halfway, if she's running late? Otherwise nursery tea will be late and it'll spoil.'

The cook looked up from the complex fruit tart she was assembling. 'Yes, you do that. And tell her to keep a better eye on the clock next time.'

Meg took up the dish and made her way through the passage and the servants' hall to the back staircase. She expected at every moment to hear Ivy clattering down, but in fact she made it all the way to the nursery landing at the top of the main house without encountering anyone.

She pushed at the door and poked her head round. 'Ivy?'

She received no reply, but there seemed to be some kind of commotion going on. This was unusual, as was Nanny's raised voice.

Then all was explained. 'He's been sick again, Ivy. Where did he get all those plums from?'

'He must have had them in his pockets when you came back from the park, Nanny.'

Meg stepped through the door just as Ivy came out of the day room, flustered and carrying a basin and some cloths. She spotted Meg. 'Oh! Is it teatime already? So sorry, but we've . . .'

'It's all right. It sounds like you're busy.'

'Yes – yes we are. Master Francis has somehow got hold of some plums and eaten so many he's made himself sick; we only just got him out the drawing room in time earlier, and—'

She was interrupted by a sudden scream from the day room. 'Nanny! Ivy!'

'That's Miss Amelia,' said Ivy, now more flustered than ever. 'Let me take these to Nanny and I'll see what she wants. Could you be a love and take that in to the table?'

'Of course,' replied Meg.

As she entered the day room and set down the meal, she was met by the sight of little Master George staggering around, clutching his throat and on the verge of turning blue. Miss Amelia was crying and attempting to shake him. She looked up. 'Help him!'

Meg looked at the choking toddler. Another one of those sudden, visceral memories came back to her. It was Jem, when he was about the same age. He was staggering round just like that and waving his arms, making no sound. But because Jem very rarely made sounds anyway, everyone had thought he was just play-acting. It was only when he really seemed to be struggling for breath, his lips turning blue, that Ma had looked up properly from her ironing and given him her full attention. 'He's not playing, he's got something stuck in his throat,' she had said. And then Ma had . . .

Meg strode across the room, sat down in one of the small chairs, and pulled the boy towards her. Quickly she tipped him over her knee, just as she could picture Ma doing, so that his head was lower than his waist, and gave him several sharp blows between the shoulder blades.

This made Miss Amelia scream loudly and try to grab at Meg's arm. 'What are you doing!'

Then everything seemed to happen at once. First, a *ping* sound was heard and Meg could feel Master George retching and then – blessedly – gasping in air. Next, both Nanny and Ivy came in the door from the night room, Nanny squawking words Meg couldn't make out and flapping her arms around in an attempt to deal with everyone and everything at once. And finally, the door to the main part of the house opened.

Meg felt the shock and its associated energy slowly ebbing away, to be replaced by an overwhelming relief. With shaking hands she set Master George back on his feet and looked closely at him. Yes, he was breathing a little heavily, but otherwise normally.

'Look, Nanny,' came Miss Amelia's voice. 'He must have picked this up and put it in his mouth.' She held out a plum stone.

'Well,' said a calm voice that Meg didn't recognise. 'It's a good thing this girl was here, while nobody else was attending. But who are you, and what are you doing in my children's nursery?'

Meg looked up, and received a jolt so hard that she nearly fell backwards off the chair. This must be Mrs Harcourt, whom Meg had never met in person during her whole time in the house – and expectedly so, given that fine ladies did not associate with their scullery maids.

That wasn't what gave her the shock. The thunderbolt and the tingling she now felt all over were caused by the fact that she was looking at the butterfly lady.

Chapter Twenty

Meg was speechless.

Nanny wasn't, though. 'Stand up, girl,' she hissed, pulling at Meg's arm, 'when the mistress is talking to you.'

Meg had a moment of respite to pull herself together, as Mrs Harcourt moved first to her little boy. 'Poor Georgie,' she said, picking him up. 'Are you all right?' She kissed him.

By the time she put him down, smoothing his hair, Meg was ready. She curtseyed deeply. 'My name is Meg, madam. I'm the scullery maid.' She kept her eyes on the floor, as Mrs Lawrence had told her to do, long ago. The hem of Mrs Harcourt's beautiful rose-coloured gown was formed of stitches so tiny that they could hardly be made out.

'Well, Meg, it seems that we owe you a great debt of gratitude,' came the kind voice. 'But I would like to know *exactly* what has just happened.'

Nanny went to check on Master Francis, returning to report that he was now asleep. Ivy settled the other two at the table with their now sadly congealed bread and milk. At Mrs Harcourt's request, Meg remained where she was, though she knew Mrs Roberts would be wanting her back in the kitchen.

Once they were all at leisure to talk, the situation was explained to the mistress. She knew some of it already; the reason she had come up to the nursery in the first place was because Master Francis had been taken ill during the children's daily hour with their mother in the drawing room. Nanny, as she now heard, had put him to bed, but he had then been sick again. Nanny had then called to Ivy, but one discarded plum stone had escaped Ivy's attention as she left the day room. Master George had picked it up and put it in his mouth, as children of his age often did, and it had got stuck in his throat.

'This I understand,' said Mrs Harcourt. 'But what were you doing here?' she asked Meg.

Meg explained about the bread and milk, all the while turning over various fantastical possibilities in her mind. *The butterfly lady was Mrs Harcourt. Could she—?*

'But how did you know how to . . . ?' Mrs Harcourt gestured.

'If you please, madam, the same thing once happened to my br—' She stumbled over the word, but she *would* say it out loud. 'To my brother when he was little. And I remember that's what my ma did to help him.'

'And you did it very well.' Mrs Harcourt smiled, and Meg was transported back to that day in the workhouse, the sight of all those bright oranges. 'Now, you may go. Mrs Roberts is a hard taskmaster, I know, but if she's cross about the length of time you've been away you may tell her that the delay was because I wished to speak to you.'

'Thank you, madam.' Meg curtseyed and was halfway back to the stairwell door when she realised she had missed her chance to say anything else. But Mrs Harcourt was already addressing Nanny in a firmer tone: 'Now, Nanny, as to procedures in the nursery . . .'

Clearly that was not to be interrupted, so Meg made her exit. Of course, Master George's life was the most important thing, and she was pleased and thankful that she'd been in the right place at the right time, but she could kick herself at missing the one and only chance she might ever get to address the question of the workhouse.

* * *

It was about mid-morning the following day when Mrs Lawrence entered the kitchen to announce that Mrs Harcourt wished to see Meg.

'Me? Upstairs?' was Meg's first exclamation.

'Yes,' replied the housekeeper. 'Whenever Mrs Roberts can spare you, she said.' She looked enquiringly at the cook.

Mrs Roberts looked round at the three different meals in various stages of preparation. 'If you can find someone to mash those potatoes for the servants' dinner, Mrs Lawrence, she can go now. Best not keep the mistress waiting, even if we are as short-handed as I don't know what.' She appraised Meg. 'No time to change your clothes, but tidy your hair and straighten your apron. And your hands should be clean already – let me see? – good. Yes, off you go, then.'

Meg got as far as the door and hesitated. 'Er – Mrs Lawrence? I don't know where I'm going.'

The housekeeper was, to Meg's surprise and not a little amusement, rolling up her sleeves prior to mashing the potatoes herself. 'Oh, of course. Mrs Harcourt's morning room. Dot is in the servants' hall doing some mending – get her to show you.'

It wasn't long before Meg was, for the first time, on the other side of the baize door on the house's first floor. The difference could be felt immediately underfoot, the bare floorboards of the back stairs giving way to a soft, thick carpet that was like walking on air. Meg double-checked to make sure the soles of her boots weren't leaving a mark.

She knocked softly on the door that Dot indicated, and heard an answering, 'Come in.'

The room was the most luxurious place Meg had ever seen. She would have loved to look at everything in hungry detail, to remember it always, but she needed to concentrate on Mrs Harcourt and on what she wanted to say herself, so all she allowed herself was an impression of soft comfort, of carpet, polished furniture, light from the large window and a bright, welcoming fire in the grate.

'Now, Meg,' began Mrs Harcourt, 'I have two things to say to you.'

Meg knew she should speak only when spoken to, but she wasn't sure whether that actually required an answer, so she kept quiet. Better to hear what was going on before she made any attempt to raise the subject that was eager to escape from her. She put her hands behind her back so that the mistress wouldn't see them shaking.

'The first,' continued Mrs Harcourt, smoothly, 'I would normally leave to Mrs Lawrence, but I said I would tell you personally given that you would be here anyway.' She smiled. 'You've only been here a year, but both Mrs Roberts and Mrs Lawrence are very happy with your work, so we have agreed that, rather than appoint a new kitchen maid, we will offer the position to you and then seek a new scullery maid instead.'

Meg's jaw dropped.

Mrs Harcourt laughed, a light, tinkling sound. 'I'll take that as a yes, shall I?'

'S-sorry, madam, I was taken aback there. Yes, of course I'd like to accept, and I'm very grateful for the opportunity.'

'A pay rise, too – six pounds a year, which will be a very useful addition if you send it back to your family. I think you mentioned a mother and brother yesterday?'

'I . . . I used to have a family, madam, but I don't any more.' Meg stared straight ahead.

There was a pause, then, 'I'm so sorry,' Mrs Harcourt said, in a gentle tone. 'If I had known I would not have brought it up.'

'It's fine, madam, really – I'm used to it now.'

'Well then,' said Mrs Harcourt, with an evident desire to change the subject, 'we can move on to the second reason I wished to speak to you.' Her voice became serious. 'My husband and I owe you a great debt of gratitude. There does seem to have been some negligence in the nursery yesterday, but of course none of that is your fault. Your presence there might have been coincidental, but your quick thinking almost certainly saved my son's life. Our doctor visited yesterday evening, and when the circumstances were related to him he shared that opinion.'

She stopped, and Meg felt that was an opening to reply. 'I hope Master George is well today, madam, if you don't mind me asking? And Master Francis too?'

'They are both well, thank you, though Master Francis will certainly be deprived of his puddings for the rest of the week. But,' she continued, 'Mr Harcourt and I have determined that you deserve some extra reward for your actions. We weren't sure what might be most useful to you: a bonus paid in cash, some treat for your fam— Maybe a tea party with invited friends, or a day out?'

This was Meg's big chance. *Don't waste it.*

She took a deep breath. 'Madam, I'd like to ask something that won't cost you anything, but you might think it's unusual.'

Fortunately Mrs Harcourt seemed intrigued rather than irritated, and her well-bred manners carried her through. 'Do continue.'

'Madam, you're a member of the Board at the workhouse. I know that because I was there and I saw you – I even cooked your dinner once.'

'Did you? And yes, that's correct, but I'm not sure what relevance it has to the present situation.'

Another deep breath. *This is it. Last chance.*

'Madam, I'd like to tell you something about the workhouse. And if it's not too much to ask as a reward, could you please sit and hear me out until I've finished, and really *listen* to what I've got to say.'

* * *

Mrs Leech was in her office when she heard the sound of heavy, male footsteps approaching.

The door opened without warning, and in walked Mr Higgin, three members of the Board and two police constables.

Mrs Leech sat in silence for a moment. She put her pen down, and then straightened it with the tips of her forefingers. When it was precisely parallel to the edge of the blotter, she looked up.

'Mrs Leech,' began the chairman of the Board, 'we've received information that you have for some time been acting in a manner which is not only contrary to the regulations of the workhouse, but also illegal.'

The pen rolled a little to one side.

He cleared his throat and continued, perhaps surprised that she hadn't said anything. 'We are here to tell you that you are dismissed without notice or character, as of this moment. And these gentlemen,' he indicated the police constables, 'will be taking you to their cells pending a criminal investigation.'

Still she didn't move.

'Please stand up, Mrs Leech.'

Nothing.

'Stand up, now, please – or I shall ask the constables to remove you by force if necessary.'

Mrs Leech felt something in her mind . . . *snap*.

It was an odd sensation. 'Don't you dare touch me.'

'Well then, stand up.'

'You have no right to touch me,' she said, aware that words were going to come pouring out and that she could do nothing to stop them. 'I don't know what you're talking about.'

'Mrs Leech, please do not make this more difficult than it needs to be. We know what you've done. We've found the girls.'

'I have done nothing wrong. It was all just business – and besides, I saved the Board a great deal of money by finding situations for those girls. You should be grateful, *thanking* me for my work.'

'You're making this needlessly unpleasant for all of us, Mrs Leech.' The chairman nodded at the constables, who came to stand on either side of her.

'Unpleasant?' she suddenly heard herself shrieking. 'I'll tell you what's unpleasant! Having to sit here, day after day, and see these vermin as they crawl in, dirty, filthy, the men useless, the women all tarts with a line of runny-nosed brats trailing after them, and all because they couldn't keep their legs shut!'

'Madam, please! Such language.'

He sounded shocked and offended, which only made Mrs Leech laugh. 'Oh, don't give me that. You and your sort know all about women and back alleys, for all you pretend to be so respectable. I've heard some of the names that visit madam's *establishment*.' The constables were closing in, and she began to flail her arms even as her voice rose. 'I had to take steps to secure my future – it was a business arrangement, do you understand? And those girls? They deserve it! With their pert eyes and their inviting figures. They'd all end up on their backs for a living one day, and they should be grateful I've sent them somewhere with a roof over their heads to do it!'

Spittle had somehow appeared on the desk in front of her, sprayed over the blotter and the precious lists.

She grabbed at the papers. 'But I'm not finished yet! These are the next ones to go, and I have to sort it out before I can leave!'

The constables now had hold of her arms and were lifting her out of her chair. She struggled and kicked out.

'Mrs Leech! Restrain yourself, please.' That was Mr Higgin, useless nobody that he was – why did he think he could speak to her like that? She spat in his face as she was dragged past him, and had the satisfaction of seeing him recoil in horror.

But they had prised the lists out of her hands, the precious lists. And there were two names in particular for whom the moment had come. She screamed and writhed in their grip as they half dragged, half carried her out of the room and towards the outer door.

'Just let me send two more! Or even just one!' For some reason there was a crowd of onlookers in the hallway – what were they doing there? 'You get back to where you're supposed to be, or it'll be the cane!' she cried, but they only laughed. Why would they do that? How dare they? She looked down, but somehow the cane had disappeared from her belt, as had her keys. Frantic now, she jerked her head from side to side as she struggled. 'Get back to work!' But they didn't. Her eye caught one face in particular – a wide-eyed, white-faced Sally. Why did that remind her of something?

She was nearly at the main door now. She could see the black prison coach standing outside. Something – there was something very important . . .

'I told her I would. I said so. To punish her. She knew! So let me back, just for a minute. I just need to send one more.'

The coach door, with its barred window, was right in front of her. It opened wide, ready to swallow.

'One! more!'

Chapter Twenty-one

Meg felt an unfamiliar sense of pleasure and anticipation as she entered the workhouse, rather than the usual foreboding. She skipped up the steps.

In an unexpected development, no sooner had she given Sally and Martha's names to one of the pauper assistants than she was swept off her feet by a hug. Meg started to exclaim, but she was soon put back on the ground by the woman who had embraced her.

It turned out to be Lizzie. 'It's all down to you, Meg!' she crowed.

'What is? Oh, you mean Mrs Leech.'

'Not just that, luvvy. They raided that brothel, you know, and arrested the madam. They took all the girls away, but they didn't bring charges against any who could show they'd been sent against their will from the workhouse. And one of them was my Eliza!'

'Your – your daughter?'

'Yes! I thought they was all dead, but it turns out Mrs Leech lied about one of 'em 'cos she'd sent her off there. And she's back!'

'Here?'

'Yes! She's been put for hard labour, o' course, but she's here and she's alive. My daughter's alive!' Lizzie picked Meg up and swung her round again, laughing, and her joy was so infectious that Meg couldn't help joining in. She'd been so worried about the girls, those she knew and those she didn't. Being found wouldn't fix everything, but now they were safe. She couldn't save poor Ellen, but the others had a chance and that was more than she'd hoped for.

She was happy when she went into the dining hall and even happier when she saw Sally and Martha coming towards her, hugging herself at the thought of what was to come.

She ran to embrace her friends.

'Oh, Meg, we've got so much to tell you!' exclaimed Sally, as they took their seats.

'And I you – but you go first.'

'Mrs Leech is gone!' Sally almost squealed in her excitement. 'I mean, really gone – for ever!'

Martha interrupted. 'Sally says they came and took her away in a police cart, but I reckon she's having me on.'

'I'm not, I'm not! Honest – I saw it. Anyway, we've got a new matron, and she's not nearly so bad.' Sally leaned in. 'She passed me scrubbing the floor the other day, and she stopped, and I thought, *Oh, here we go again,* but she said to me, "Good work." I mean, really! Can you even imagine?'

Her delight was irresistible. Meg was already full of joy; now she felt as though she could fly.

'That's wonderful, Sally. And she really is gone, Martha. The police took her away and they even found the missing girls. Molly, Dolly, Bernadette . . . they're all safe.' Meg updated them on everything that had happened. There were gasps, sadness and then finally happiness and relief. But Meg wasn't finished yet. 'Now, I've got something to tell you both.'

'Did you bring any cake?' Sally asked, spotting the package peeking out of Meg's pocket.

'What? Oh yes, hold on. Here.'

'What type is it?' asked Sally, unwrapping it eagerly. 'Ooh, that pound cake again.' She tucked in and had got halfway through it before she looked up. 'What were you going to say?' she asked, with her mouth full.

'First I have news for Martha.' Meg turned to her. 'It's come through – your job offer.'

'What!'

'Miss Greenwood finally heard back from Madame Joubert, and she was pleased with your work and wants to take you on as an apprentice.'

Martha's expression was like the rising sun.

'It's only on a trial, mind – we couldn't get her to promise more until you've actually been working for her in person. But she did say she didn't care if you were English, Irish or French, or white, black or purple, as long as your stitches were neat.' Meg took a breath. 'It's not all that we dreamed of, I know – it's not a lady's maid, and it's not in our house, but it is . . . something?'

Martha smiled, her eyes shining with tears. 'None of that matters, Meg. It's a *chance*, and that's all I've ever really wanted. You've given me this opportunity, and it's up to me to seize it with both hands, to make my own way. And I will, I promise!'

They hugged, and then both turned to look at Sally.

Sally had heard and understood, and realisation was now dawning that she was about to be left on her own in the workhouse. But she was still – *still* – trying her hardest to suppress her own sadness and rejoice in the good fortune of others. 'Oh, Martha, I'm so happy for you!' she cried, even as her lip wobbled.

Meg smiled. 'Ah, but I've left the best news until last.' She winked at Martha, who stifled a gasp of delight as she caught Meg's meaning.

'What news is that, then?' asked Sally. She looked from one to the other, perhaps picking up that something was going on although she didn't know what.

'Our kitchen maid – the maid in the house where I work – left a few weeks ago.'

'Oh,' came the disappointed reply. 'That's not news. I think you said that last time.'

'But that's not all,' said Meg, her excitement rising. 'Instead of getting a new one, they've decided I can have the job.'

Sally brightened. 'Oh, Meg, that's wonderful! So you'll be able to cook, and everything. That's what you always wanted – I'm made up for you!'

Meg shook her head. 'I haven't got to the best bit yet.' She paused. 'Can't you guess?'

'No – what?'

'So, if I'm going to be the new kitchen maid, they need a new scullery maid to do the job I used to do.'

'Yes?'

Sally still didn't get it. Meg thought she would burst. 'It's you!'

'What is?'

'Our new scullery maid. It's going to be you. Mrs Lawrence – the housekeeper – said I could tell you today, and she'll be here tomorrow morning to sign the papers.'

Sally's mouth was hanging open. 'Me?' she said, eventually. 'Me? I can come out with you, and go to work at the house you work at? Leave the workhouse? For ever?'

'Yes, as long as you do a good job, which I'm sure you will.' Meg grinned. 'Aren't you pleased?'

To her surprise, Sally burst into tears. Through loud sobs, she bawled out how happy she was. 'I never thought I'd leave . . . and with you . . . to work in a nice house . . . and, oh, everything!'

Meg put her arms around Sally while she let her emotions flow free, and thought back to the conversation she'd had with Mrs Roberts and Mrs Lawrence.

They had been in the kitchen, and the two women were discussing the subject of a new scullery maid – and, specifically, whether they should find another girl from the workhouse. 'Could do . . . lucky to get Meg . . . not all like that . . . but easier . . . new matron . . . or any friends' daughters . . .'

Meg hovered near them, and then curtseyed politely when they noticed her.

'I take it you wish to say something?' asked Mrs Lawrence.

'Yes,' said Meg, deciding that the best approach would be to come straight to the point. 'I would like to recommend my friend Sally, from the workhouse, as the new scullery maid.'

Neither woman interrupted or said 'no' straight away, so Meg plunged on. 'She's nearly fourteen, and she's a big strong girl, much bigger than me, and used to hard work.'

Mrs Lawrence and Mrs Roberts exchanged a glance. 'Well,' said the housekeeper, 'we can certainly take her into consideration. We can't just employ a girl because she's your friend, though – she has to be suitable for the position. Does she know anything about cooking, or working in a kitchen?'

Meg reluctantly shook her head. 'No, Mrs Lawrence. But she's been scrubbing floors and washing out chamber pots all her life.' She could hear that her voice sounded anxious.

Mrs Roberts was still considering. 'Not knowing anything about cooking isn't necessarily a bad thing – and it would at least mean she wouldn't have any bad habits we'd need to break her of. And we must remember, not all scullery maids are like Meg – the last two we had before her had never worked in a proper kitchen, either.'

Mrs Lawrence winced. 'Don't remind me.' She paused. 'But, to be fair, the problem with them was that they were too young and too cosseted.' She addressed Meg. 'And you'd vouch for this girl, would you? That she would work hard?'

'Ma'am,' replied Meg, firmly, 'Sally would work for you all day and all night in return for one kind word. If you say you'll feed and pay her as well, she'll think she's died and gone to heaven.'

Another look was exchanged. 'I don't have any other specific candidate in mind,' said Mrs Roberts, slowly, 'so there would be no harm in fetching her here to take the position on trial?'

Mrs Lawrence was nodding. 'Yes, a trial would be the thing. And if she's as hardworking as Meg says she is, there won't be a problem.'

Meg almost skipped with joy.

'And,' added the housekeeper, 'as we've seen recently, an unhappy household is not an efficient one. If having girls who are friends makes everything run smoothly, there's no harm in it.' She turned to Meg again. 'But be in no doubt, I expect you both to *work*, not to spend your time chatting or larking about, do you hear?'

'Oh yes, Mrs Lawrence,' replied Meg, fervently. 'Of course. I'll work harder than ever, and I'll show Sally what to do, and she'll learn, and it will be the best-run scullery ever. Oh, thank you! I'm so grateful to you both.'

They must have noticed the tears coming to her eyes, but all Mrs Lawrence said was, 'Very well. Get along with you now and we'll make the arrangements.'

And they had been made; Mrs Lawrence was even now talking to the workhouse's new matron, while Meg was here in the dining hall with Sally and Martha.

Sally's tears of confusion and joy had, at last, abated. 'And it's really true?' she asked. 'I mean, really? You're not just teasing me?'

'Oh, Sally, of course I'm not. That would be a terrible, cruel thing to do. And nobody's ever going to be cruel to you again.'

That brought fresh tears to Sally's eyes, and they all embraced and laughed and cried together.

When visiting time was over, Meg started to get to her feet. Sally grabbed at her arm, suddenly fearful. 'And – you will come back tomorrow, won't you? I'll get out of here tomorrow, and come to live with you?'

'Yes,' said Meg. 'Yes, you will.'

* * *

Tomorrow came. Meg sat in the gig with Mrs Lawrence, by turns hugely excited and then in terrible fear that something would happen to prevent Sally coming with them. She wished she could rescue all the girls, despite knowing that wasn't possible, but saving Sally as well as Martha was in reach. *What if the matron had changed her mind? What if something had happened to Sally since yesterday? What if—?*

'Here we are,' said James, pulling up.

'You know the way well,' said Meg. 'Of course you do. It never occurred to me to ask you, that first time I needed directions to get back here, why you should know it *well*. How could I not have realised it was because you were bringing Mrs Harcourt here when it was time for Board visits?'

'Well, there's no reason you should,' he replied, handing her down and then performing the same office for Mrs Lawrence. He winked behind the housekeeper's back. 'Good luck.'

Meg followed Mrs Lawrence into the dreaded Receiving Room, her heart in her throat, and was relieved to see that it looked very different. The new matron had – perhaps in a deliberate attempt to erase the traces of her predecessor – rearranged the furniture. There was a vase of flowers on her desk. She herself was younger than Mrs Leech and with a much kinder face. At her belt hung a bunch of keys, but no cane.

Sally was already in the room, dressed for the first time that Meg had ever seen in something that wasn't a workhouse uniform. It struck Meg that Sally wouldn't have owned any clothes at all, having been born here, so they must have found her something from the workhouse stores. The new matron obviously had some standards, because Sally's dress, although old and faded, was neatly mended and the right size. She was also wearing a pair of very serviceable boots; Meg saw Mrs Lawrence glance at them and nod.

The formalities were soon over, and they left the Receiving Room for what Meg sincerely hoped would be the last time in their lives.

'Meg! Sally!' Martha was making her way up the corridor in the company of a pauper assistant. She too was dressed in non-workhouse clothes that were plain but serviceable. 'Oh, I hoped I'd see you before we left.' She approached and bobbed a curtsey to Mrs Lawrence. 'Good morning, ma'am.'

Mrs Lawrence smiled at them all. 'I'll wait outside,' she said to Meg, 'but don't be too long. It won't do to be late back.'

'Just two minutes, Mrs Lawrence, I promise.'

The three girls all joined hands. 'Well,' said Meg, 'here we are.'

Sally was so overcome by it all that she was incapable of speech, but Meg felt her fingers being squeezed.

'I'll see you again as soon as I can,' said Martha. 'Maybe I'll get an afternoon off now and then, and even if not I know where you are, at least.'

'You'll be able to come for tea, sometimes,' said Meg.

'And then we can all eat cake!' Sally's voice was squeaky with joy, making the others laugh.

Then there was one last moment, one last heartfelt hug, and it was time to go. Martha disappeared into the Receiving Room, and Meg led Sally out of the workhouse door.

The gig would not seat four, and Mrs Lawrence, having learned a little more about Sally's background, did not in any case want to overwhelm her with too many new sensations at once. She had therefore settled it that James would convey her back to the house while the girls walked. That would give them the chance to catch up and talk through anything they wanted in private, walking off their feelings, so that they would be refreshed and ready for work by the time they got back. She gave them many injunctions about safety and timeliness before she allowed James to assist her up to her seat, ending with, 'Don't dawdle, now,' but it was said with kindness.

Meg watched the gig as it reached the end of the road and turned smartly, and then they set off through the gusty autumn wind. Walking with Sally, for whom every step, every sight, was a new experience, gave Meg a feeling of excitement herself. She wanted to show her friend everything and rejoice in her delight.

As the streets grew broader and the houses bigger, Sally's eyes opened correspondingly wider. 'To think', she breathed, 'that people really live in such nice places!'

'Wait until you see our house,' replied Meg, mentally hugging herself at the thought of Sally's reaction. 'And the park.'

The effect on Sally of seeing them both was all that Meg had hoped. She seemed to lose the power of both speech and movement as she absorbed it all.

'And . . . and I'll really be allowed to walk around here and look at the trees and things? Whenever I have an afternoon . . . *out*?' She could still hardly believe the words she was saying.

Meg laughed from pure joy. 'Yes!' Then she was more serious. 'But look, Sally, I just want to say one important thing before we go in. It's going to be lovely having both of us here, but it's only a trial, and it could all still go wrong. So we have to work really hard, understand?' She took both of Sally's hands and looked her squarely in the eye. 'If we want to be here, together, like we always dreamed about all those nights in the dormitory, we have to make it happen ourselves. All right?'

Sally looked from Meg to the house and back again. She nodded and spoke with resolution. 'Yes.'

*　　*　　*

Meg needn't have worried.

Sally was the perfect scullery maid. She was big for her age, robust, and had grown even stronger thanks to her continual labour at the workhouse. She worked without stopping every day from dawn to dusk, and indeed beyond, with a cheerful goodwill that soon won over all the servants, even Mr Wilson. She thought so little of her own claims to comfort that she showed not the slightest hint of discontent with even the dirtiest jobs. She made friends with Robbie, who was about the same age, and Meg sometimes heard them giggling together over their work. And, convinced as Sally was – wrongly, in Meg's opinion – that she was stupid, she listened with extreme care and attention to every instruction, which meant that she learned quickly. With Meg in the kitchen and Sally in the scullery, Mrs Roberts had never presided over so efficient or so cheerful an empire.

Meg now had alternate Sundays as her afternoon off, the prerogative of the kitchen maid. As this was also Tommy's one day off during the week, they were able to meet and walk in the park. He had grown a great deal during the last year, and although he remained stocky he was much taller than her. She couldn't help noticing that he was also filling out into his man's shape, the muscles he had developed from hefting all those heavy crates bulging beneath his shirt and jacket. Since the day of – *that* day, as Meg always thought of it, contemptuously refusing to let it have a name – he had been ever more protective of her. When they met, he was careful to let her lead in such matters as how close they would be to each other when they walked or sat, and whether or not they would take each other's hand. This was so different from any male behaviour Meg had ever seen or experienced that she wondered if it could possibly be normal.

One afternoon in late November they were strolling about the paths when he suddenly said, 'I won't be coming to the house much longer.'

'What?' Meg was upset at the thought, taken by surprise as she realised just how much her thrice-weekly encounters with him meant to her.

'It's good news – well, sort of – I mean good apart from not seeing you so often – but what I mean is—' He stopped. 'I've got confused. Where was I?'

'You won't be coming to the house much longer.'

'That's right. Now I'm older I'm not to be the delivery boy any more. I'm going to work in the shop. Starting in January.'

'That's what happened to the one who used to deliver before you did, isn't it? Is Mr Jones going to have both of you there?'

'Walter? Oh, no, he's gone. So there's an opening, and Mr Jones says I'm presentable as well as reliable, so I'm to be his assistant there and he'll find a new delivery boy.'

'Congratulations!'

'It's more money, too, so my sister's pleased – you know I give her most of my wages for my board now I live with her.'

'Even better.' Meg paused. 'So why don't you look happier about it?'

'I am – I am happy. Steady work and all – not daily paid like my sister's husband down at the docks. It's just . . .'

'Yes?'

'Oh, you must know.' He blushed and looked at the floor. 'Because I'll miss seeing you.'

Slowly, Meg reached out and took his hand. It was warm. 'And I'll miss you too.'

Those hazel eyes met hers. 'I don't suppose . . .'

'Yes?'

'Well, what I mean is, I'll still have Sundays off, so if that's still your afternoon out, we could walk out.'

'Of course we can. The park will still be here.'

'But what I mean is – not just meeting by accident or whatever, but a regular thing.' He faced her. 'Meg, will you walk out with me regular, and be my girl?'

Meg was silent for a moment.

He misinterpreted and started to slip his hand away. 'But if you don't want to . . .'

She squeezed his fingers before he could let go. 'It's not that. I'd love to. But I'll have to ask Mrs Lawrence's permission, you know. I can't go behind her back.'

'I wouldn't want you to!' He seemed horrified at the thought. 'Why, back on that day – you know – I've never seen anything like her and Mrs Roberts. Like queens! They told that butler and footman what was what – I've never seen women like it.'

'You never met my ma.'

He laughed, and everything was all right. They set off again, and as she walked Meg slipped her arm through Tommy's.

* * *

Christmas this year was going to be a very different experience, thought Meg. Once more the whole basement was filled with the rich aroma of fruit and spices and good things, but now Sally was here to enjoy it too; she spent most of her time walking around with her nose lifted high in the air, trying to inhale as much of the scent as possible.

Meg was almost completely happy. The new footman, Henry, was young, inexperienced and eager to please, nothing like his predecessor at all, which meant that the household was now a safe, welcoming and friendly place and that dark corners were no longer to be feared. The incident in the nursery, coupled with the fact that Mrs Harcourt was expecting another child, meant that she had decided to add a nursemaid to her staff to assist Nanny; to her immense delight, Ivy had been offered the position starting in the new year, as soon as the Christmas rush in the kitchen was over. This meant that the household would be short of a tweenie maid, resulting in a heavier workload for Meg and Sally, but neither of them minded – they were happy for Ivy's good fortune, and even happier that they now shared a bedroom, as Ivy had moved up to sleep in the nursery already. They had heard from Martha, who was doing wonderfully well in her job at the dressmaker's and was to be taken on permanently. And sometimes all three of them visited their friends at the workhouse, sharing what they'd learned in the hope that more girls would get out. Mrs Lawrence had, with many strictures and injunctions about respectable behaviour, allowed Meg to walk out with Tommy on her Sunday afternoons out, and he was accepted as her guest on the occasions when the servants were permitted to invite a friend to tea. And, of course, Meg had her job in the kitchen: cooking, assisting, learning, enjoying every moment.

So why, she thought to herself one dark December afternoon as she stirred a cheese sauce, *do I still feel like something is missing?*

What Meg didn't know was that her friends, both inside the house and out, had noticed. 'It's a shame for her,' commented Mrs Roberts to Sally one day, as they watched Meg drift out of the kitchen towards the larder, 'not knowing what happened to her family.'

'I can't understand it, Mrs Roberts,' replied Sally, her arms full of dirty pots. 'If Meg was my sister, I'd have come looking for her no matter what. Nothing would have stopped me.'

She went through to the scullery, and the cook stayed where she was, staring into space. The sight of Meg returning with a dish of cream reminded her that she had work to do, but the subject remained on Mrs Roberts's mind for the rest of the day.

* * *

The kitchen had been a hive of activity all morning, as it always was on the day before Christmas Eve, but such had been the efficiency of all concerned that there was a lull in the middle of the afternoon. Unfortunately for Meg, this didn't mean a nice sit-down: Mrs Roberts had recalled that she had promised to send a new receipt over to the cook at the house two doors down, and now she passed it to Meg. 'Don't just hand it over to the maid who answers the back door – make sure you take it right in and give it to Mrs Hay in person.'

Meg, of course, was happy to oblige, and she wasn't sorry to have the opportunity to have a quick look at another kitchen. It would be interesting to see the similarities and differences from their own.

What she didn't know, as she shut the door and made her way carefully up the frozen steps, was that Mrs Hay had been specifically asked to keep her there for at least half an hour, as Mrs Roberts wanted her out of the way.

Once she had seen Meg disappear up to the pavement, the cook called to the other girls. 'Ivy, go and fetch some chairs from the servants' hall. Sally, go to the back door and see if Tommy's here yet.'

Tommy arrived just as the chairs were being set out, having deliberately hurried through the rest of his round and left this delivery until last.

When the four of them were seated, Mrs Roberts outlined why she'd called them. 'There's something not quite right with what's happened to Meg's family. I suppose there's a possibility they might have died in the cholera epidemic a while back, but we don't know that for sure. What if they're out there somewhere, and they don't know about her and she doesn't know about them?'

Between them, they pooled their knowledge of Meg's family and tried to reconstruct a possible course of events.

'But this is all just speculation,' said Mrs Roberts, eventually, in frustration. She looked at Sally's blank face. 'I mean, we don't really know what happened.'

'Then why don't we just look for them?' asked Sally, in all innocence.

The cook smiled. 'Liverpool's quite a big place, dear,' she said. 'I know you haven't seen much of it, but there are hundreds of streets each with hundreds of families living on them.'

'Oh. But Meg's been so kind to me, I don't mind trying, even if it takes ages.'

'Thinking about it, though,' said Ivy, thoughtfully, 'Sally has a point. There can't be all that many people around called Delilah – it's quite an unusual name.

And her last name must be Shaw, same as Meg's. How many Delilah Shaws can there be in one town?'

'That's true,' replied Mrs Roberts, 'but we wouldn't know where to start asking.' She looked at Sally. 'And I absolutely *forbid* either of you to walk round the streets and ask. Do you understand?'

Ivy did; Sally probably didn't. But she wouldn't disobey a direct instruction, so Mrs Roberts was satisfied she wouldn't end up in any danger.

'On the subject of asking around, though,' continued the cook, 'I can't help thinking there's something about that wicked matron. It was in the papers last week – she's come up for trial.'

Sally started to shake.

'She can't come anywhere near you, not ever again,' Mrs Roberts said, firmly, and was pleased to see Ivy taking the younger girl's hand. 'And I'm not intending to ask her myself, of course. But I haven't been a cook in and around Liverpool for thirty years for nothing – I have a few contacts about the place, some of whom have had dealings with the workhouse. I can start some enquiries, at least.'

She turned to Tommy. 'You're fidgeting. What is it?'

'I've got an idea.'

'Which is?'

'It's not the matron or the sister you need to look for, ma'am. Meg used to talk about her family to my ma, God rest her, and I've got an idea.' He started to get up.

'Where are you going? You can't possibly know where to look for them, surely.'

'I don't, exactly,' he replied. 'But I do know where to start.'

Chapter Twenty-two

Sam pocketed another halfpenny and scowled. He hadn't done badly today; it was Christmas Eve and there had been plenty of ladies and gentlemen about who didn't want their shoes soiled in the slushy mess of the road. But he was too old to be sweeping the streets for coppers. He was twelve, twelve *and a half*, even, and he needed to find a proper job. So far, he knew, he had done nothing but let the family down.

When Delilah had set off for the workhouse to collect Meg and Rosie on that dreadful day, over a year ago now, Sam had been filled with happiness at the thought of seeing his sisters again. Little Annie had looked odd on her own all those months without Rosie next to her, giggling and chatting and whatever else they used to get up to. And Meg's absence had left a huge hole in the family, one that couldn't be filled no matter how hard they tried. He couldn't wait to have them back.

We're your brothers, and we'll always be here for you. Sam recalled the exact words he'd spoken to Meg on that last evening. And although he knew he couldn't see her while she was in the workhouse, he had kept his word as best he could by working long hours, taking on extra jobs where he could, and bringing every last farthing home to Delilah to put in the pot. He'd even taken on a few errands he knew she wouldn't approve of, and kept his mouth shut when she asked why he'd sometimes come home with an unexpectedly large pocketful of coins.

And it had all been for nothing. Delilah had returned without them, her face such a picture of frozen misery that at first they couldn't get a word out of her. And then the truth had come out: they had left Meg and Rosie in the workhouse, and now Meg and Rosie were dead. He, Sam, had known that he should have gone in their place, that he should have worked harder so they could be released earlier, that he should have done something – anything – that would have avoided the tragedy. His sisters were dead, and all because he hadn't looked out for them properly.

Delilah had been in tears every day for months. Sam also reckoned he'd seen William wiping his eyes once or twice, though it wasn't fitting for a man to cry. He hadn't cried, but the knot in his stomach and in his heart had tied itself a little tighter. He worried every day about Annie being left with the neighbouring children while they were all out at work – they weren't *family* – and he never let Jem out of his sight. The concentration required to keep them both safe from all the traffic and the other trouble on the streets meant that his mind ended up playing tricks on him. He thought of Meg often, her face burned on his memory, and once he would have sworn blind that he'd actually seen her. But the girl he'd noticed was in a smart two-wheeled gig being driven by a liveried coachman, so that was hardly likely to have been Meg even if she had still been alive.

Sam sighed, and reflexively looked round for Jem. He was on the pavement, out of the way of the traffic, helping old Alf. Most of the shoe-shine work came in the mornings, with the gentlemen on their way out to offices and shops and such, but at this time of year there was often plenty in the afternoon as well, what with shoes getting so dirty in the mucky streets, so they hadn't packed up yet. There was a youth standing with them now.

413

Sam's sharp eye narrowed. That wasn't the sort of fellow who paid to have his boots cleaned. Looked about sixteen or seventeen, dressed in respectable gear, to be sure, but nothing like smart or well off. And he wasn't talking to Alf or putting his feet forward; he was shouting at Jem and waving his arms around.

Sam started to make his way over. As he walked, he sized the fellow up. Not tall, but stocky and looked pretty strong and well built. And a good four or five years older than himself. Sam didn't fancy his chances in a fist fight, but when had that ever stopped him before? Family had to be protected.

He reached the others and barged in front of Jem. 'What do you want with my brother?' he asked belligerently.

Strangely, the youth smiled. 'And you must be Sam.'

Sam was immediately suspicious. 'How do you know my name? What's this about?' His hands began to ball into fists.

'The others wanted to look for your sister,' continued the youth, bafflingly. 'But I remembered: two brothers who work outside the railway station, and one of them is deaf. Shouldn't be too hard to find. I came yesterday but you'd already gone.'

Sam's fists were now fully formed, and he brought them up. 'You watch what you say about my brother.'

For some reason, Jem was pulling his arm. Probably to try to stop him fighting someone so much bigger, but Sam didn't care. The stranger's odd words and behaviour were setting off alarm bells in his head, as was the very unnerving fact that he knew their names.

The youth laughed. 'No need for all of that,' he said cheerfully. 'I'm here with good news. About your sister.'

'Delilah?' Sam's fists dropped a little.

'No, not Delilah – Meg.'

* * *

This Christmas Eve had been just as busy as the last one, but it was enjoyable too. They had all been allowed to slip outside to the pavement to watch the tree being brought in the front door, and Meg had rejoiced not only in the sight but also in Sally's delighted reaction to it. Meg had remembered that Christmas Day was also Sally's birthday, and she had spent some of her saved wages on buying her a proper servant's box to keep under her bed, one the same as her own. James the coachman, who always had a kind word for Sally when she brought his meals out, had even carved the letter 'S' into the top for her and hidden it in the stable so that Sally wouldn't spot it in their bedroom before the big day. Sally would imminently be paid her own first wages, and Meg hoped that soon she would have something to put in the box.

All this was going through her mind as she took a cake from the oven and turned it out, a treat for tomorrow in the nursery. It was only as it was cooling that she became aware of a commotion at the back door.

Meg was just looking enquiringly at Mrs Roberts, to see if she should go and investigate, when Sally burst in.

'Sally!' called out the cook, quite sharply. 'What have I told you about running in the kitchen?'

'Yes Mrs Roberts, sorry Mrs Roberts, but, oh my. Meg, you have to come and see.' Sally was so excited about something that she couldn't stop herself from skipping.

Mrs Roberts wiped her hands and a strange look of understanding came to her face. 'Is this . . . ?' she asked Sally.

'Yes, oh yes!' squeaked Sally. She grabbed Meg's hand. 'Come on!'

Meg looked at Mrs Roberts, confused by this strange behaviour and wondering that the cook should put up with it on such a busy day. But she, too, was now smiling. 'Off you go.'

Sally pulled Meg towards the kitchen door. Whatever it was, it had made her happy, probably some little surprise she had for Meg, so Meg allowed herself to be towed along with good grace.

The passage was empty. 'Mrs Lawrence saw them and took them all into the servants' hall,' said Sally.

'Took what?'

'Oh, you'll see.' They reached the door to the servants' hall. 'Now then.'

Meg felt herself being propelled into the room. What was all this about? There seemed to be quite a few people—

Her heart stopped.

It couldn't be.

Could it?

She couldn't move. She was seeing things.

She rubbed her eyes. They were still there.

Delilah, for it really *was* Delilah, took half a step forward. 'Meg?'

Meg opened her mouth, but no sound came out. So she opened her arms, and within half a moment she was in her sister's loving embrace, feeling the tears falling on to her head.

'Oh, Meg!' was all that Delilah could manage, but it was enough, and then Meg felt three other pairs of arms around her, she was surrounded, she was cocooned in their warmth. She didn't want the moment ever to end.

Eventually they loosened themselves so they could look at each other. Delilah, a little older – a real grown woman now – but as pretty as ever. William, unfeasibly tall and somehow all elbows and knees. Sam and Jem, excitedly hopping around. And, hiding behind Delilah's skirts, the only one who hadn't joined the embrace, a little girl of four years old.

Meg wiped the tears from her eyes and crouched down. 'Annie? Annie, darling, do you remember me?'

Delilah tried to give Annie a gentle push forward, but Meg put out a hand to stop her. 'It's all right. It must be scary here with all these people, and she can hardly remember me. If she doesn't want to come, it's all right.'

The little girl was frowning in concentration. And then, after a long moment, she said, 'Meggy?' She moved away from Delilah and held up her arms in the unmistakeable gesture of wanting to be picked up.

Meg swept her up and held her tight. 'Oh, Annie, darling, how I missed you!' She really was crying now, big proper tears.

She wasn't the only one, either. Sally and Ivy both had tears pouring down their faces, and Mrs Roberts, who had followed them in, was wiping her eyes with the corner of her apron.

Still holding Annie, Meg took a proper look at her family, now seeing things she hadn't noticed in her first shock. Sam and Jem were both wearing boots. William was in a collar and tie. Delilah was wearing a lovely, thick woollen shawl that Meg hadn't seen before.

Many, many questions bubbled up into Meg's head, but the one that came out first wasn't the one she'd meant to start with. 'Why didn't you come for us?' she blurted out.

Delilah wiped away her own tears. 'She told me you were both dead.'

'Who?'

'The matron at the workhouse.'

Meg heard a gasp, and knew it was Sally. 'But . . .'

'It's true, I'm afraid.'

Everyone turned at the sound of a new voice, to see Mrs Lawrence on the stairs that led up from the servants' hall to the main house. 'I've been talking this all over with Mrs Harcourt during our morning meetings for some time. As a member of the workhouse Board she has a duty to investigate what's been going on there, and since her talk with Meg she's been asking particular questions about Mrs Leech and her activities.'

Mrs Lawrence descended and took a seat at the table. 'But perhaps the best thing for now, Meg, is if your sister tells you what she knows.' She indicated that they should all sit.

Meg drew Annie on to her knee in the same way that she used to do with Rosie on her Sunday visits, and the memories came flooding back. 'I'm so sorry, so very sorry! I tried to look after Rosie, I really did, but they pulled us apart and we were separated, and I kept trying to visit her, and they kept stopping me, and she caught the fever and . . .' Meg couldn't prevent the sob escaping. 'She died! She died, Delilah, and I should have done more to help her, there must have been something else—'

She was cut off by Delilah, who was sitting next to her, putting her arms around her. 'It's not your fault, Meg, it isn't. You did everything you could.'

Meg looked at her brothers, but she saw nothing but sympathy on all of their faces. 'Really? You really don't blame me?'

'Yes, really,' said Delilah. 'It wasn't your fault, and we all forbid you from thinking so.' She bit her lip. 'If anything, it's mine, for taking you there in the first place. But it was only meant to be for a few months while we earned some money to feed you.'

'That's what I've never understood,' said Meg. 'You said it wouldn't be for long, but then you never came back.'

'But I did.'

'What?'

'I came back twice. The first time was at the beginning of May, in the spring after we'd left you there – a little bit later than I intended, but not much. I asked if I could see you, but the matron said that wasn't allowed, so I asked her to pass on a message to you both. It was to say that we'd made some money, but still not enough, but that we'd keep going and that I'd come back to get you on the first of September, no matter what.' She paused. 'Are you saying she didn't tell you?'

Meg shook her head. 'But there were all the other times you could have come to see me – on the first Thursday of every month when it was visiting time.'

Now it was Delilah's turn to look incredulous. 'Nobody ever told me I could visit!'

Meg and Delilah stared at each other.

Mrs Lawrence had been thinking, and now she spoke again, turning to Delilah. 'You said that you had told Mrs Leech that you would return on the first day of September. Did you?'

'Of course I did! We'd promised, and we were all looking forward to it so much, and I was so happy as I walked up there. But then when I went into that office, the matron told me you were both dead.'

There was a moment of shocked silence.

Meg was beginning to feel thoroughly ashamed of herself. All this time she'd been blaming Delilah, when her sister had done everything she'd promised. But all the trouble, the heartache, the whole lot of it, was down to Mrs Leech and her cruelty.

'But I don't understand why she would do such a thing,' continued Delilah.

'I think I can,' said Mrs Lawrence. 'Meg, do you remember the day I first came, when I saw you and the other girls and chose you to be our new maid?'

'Of course, Mrs Lawrence.'

'Well, that was the last day of August. It was a Friday, and I said I'd come back to collect you on the Monday, bringing the fee the matron asked for.'

'The fee that was illegal,' said Meg, nodding slowly as she began to piece everything together. 'So when Delilah came the next day, Mrs Leech knew that she'd lose her money if she let me go.' She could hardly believe it. Even by Mrs Leech's standards, this was . . . 'She was willing to separate me from my sister for ever so that she would get paid!'

Once again, Meg and Delilah stared at each other, this time in mutual horror at what had nearly happened. At what *would* have happened, if it hadn't been for Meg's friends.

Mrs Lawrence cleared her throat. 'Meg, I feel that I owe you an apology. I didn't know that what Mrs Leech did was illegal – I assumed she was telling the truth when she said it was an administration fee. But if I had only questioned further . . .'

Meg interrupted. 'Please, Mrs Lawrence, don't blame yourself. How could you possibly have known?' She was silent for a moment, and then added, daringly, 'And, if I may say so, I'm glad that you did what you did. You saw me, even in the state that I was in, and you took me on anyway. You gave me this job, this chance and if you hadn't then we wouldn't all be sitting here now.'

Delilah embraced Meg again. 'I'm so, so sorry. I should have known, I should have found a way round it all, I should—'

Meg hugged her back, awkwardly, with the arm that wasn't holding Annie. 'It's all right. I did think . . . but it's all right now.' And then she couldn't go on, her breaths coming in gulps, tears pouring down her face. She must look a mess, but she didn't care.

Mrs Lawrence looked at them. 'There will be much for us all to consider, but I would suggest that everybody needs time to reflect before reaching any decisions, and that now might not be the best time to do any of that.'

Mrs Roberts, who had been sitting silently by all this time, squawked. 'Christmas Eve! I'd almost forgotten. And still with tonight's family dinner to finish and the rest of the preparations for tomorrow . . .' She was already halfway out the door.

'One moment, if you please, Mrs Roberts,' called Mrs Lawrence.

The cook paused. 'Yes?'

'I have no doubt that the dinner we'll be having down here tomorrow will be as delicious as that for upstairs. Do you think it would stretch to a few extra mouths?'

Mrs Roberts looked at Meg, with her family clustered closely about her. 'Why, yes, Mrs Lawrence, I do think it would.'

'That's settled, then,' said the housekeeper. She turned to Delilah. 'As soon as you all arrived, I went to apprise Mrs Harcourt of the situation, and she gave me permission to extend an invitation to you all to have Christmas dinner here in the servants' hall tomorrow, if you are not otherwise engaged.' She smiled. 'I think your sister would be glad of your company, along with your brothers and this charming little lady.'

Meg's heart was ready to burst.

Delilah was delighted to accept, and William added his thanks. They all made their way down the passage to the back door, where Delilah ushered the boys outside and then held out her arms to Annie. 'Time to go home now, darling.'

Annie wrapped her arms more firmly around Meg's neck. 'No. Want to stay here with Meggy.'

If Meg's heart hadn't already been thoroughly melted by the events of the last hour, it would have done so now. 'I love you, Annie,' she said, 'but you have to do as Delilah says. Anyway, I'll see you tomorrow.'

Annie put her hands on either side of Meg's face. 'Promise?'

Meg looked her in the eye. 'Promise.'

* * *

It was Christmas Day.

It was still dark when Meg got up, so she fumbled for the box of lucifer matches she had left ready and lit a candle. Then she shivered her way over to the wash-stand and had to break ice before she could splash some of the freezing water on her face. But she didn't care; she was warm on the inside.

By the time she had finished washing, Sally was awake.

'I've got something for you,' said Meg. 'It's in the wardrobe there – I brought it up last night after you were asleep.'

Sally clapped her hands and ran, barefoot on the cold floorboards, over to the wardrobe. Her delight at seeing the box made Meg even happier. 'For me? Really?'

'Yes. Merry Christmas, Sally – and many happy returns of your birthday.' Meg hugged her. 'This will be the best one you've ever had, and from now on they'll only get better.'

Sally was so overcome that she was speechless. She thumped back down to sit on the bed, the large box held awkwardly on her knee. 'I can't believe how lucky I was to ever meet you, Meg,' she eventually managed. Then her delight turned to hesitation, just

426

for a moment. 'Now you've got your own sisters back, I know you won't . . .'

Meg flew to her. 'None of that!' She put out an affectionate hand to straighten Sally's cap and tuck away a stray strand of hair. 'You're my sister too, and so is Martha, and you always will be. Do you hear me, Sally? *Sisters.*'

Meg looked at Sally's face and felt herself in danger of being overcome, but it was far too early in the morning for that. She stood. 'Now, come on. We're career girls now, out to make our way in the world, and there's work to do.' She moved the box aside and hauled Sally to her feet, and they left the room hand in hand.

It was still dark in the kitchen when they made their way down, but soon the oil lamps were lit and the range was going, and the whole place was warm and welcoming. Meg got out Mrs Roberts's cup and saucer while Sally fetched the tin of tea. As Meg put the kettle on, she could still hardly believe that yesterday had been real. Had it? Was she really going to spend this Christmas Day, this day of all days, with the family she thought she'd lost?

Mrs Roberts was down early, ready to sip her tea even as she put on her apron and got to work. The early part of the morning passed in a blur of work, but once all the other servants had gone to church, she beckoned Meg, Ivy and Sally to her.

'You're all good girls,' she began, 'and hard workers. I wanted to get you all something, but I wanted it to be a sign of your work, your profession, not something frivolous. So no hair ribbons or bonnet trimmings from me!'

She turned first to Sally. 'You've been here the shortest time, and I don't yet know which way you'll want to turn when you're older, so this is just a token for now.' She presented Sally with a small leather purse. 'I know Meg has got you a box, so here's something to put in it so you can save your wages. You're a woman in paid work now.'

To Ivy she gave an embroidered case that proved to contain needles, thread and a smart little pair of scissors. 'We'll miss you in the kitchen, dear, but you'll make a very good nursemaid, and having a sewing kit at hand will prove useful.'

And finally, to Meg, 'And you're going to be a cook, no doubt about it. In any decent position you should have everything provided, but it's always good to start your own collection of favourite tools.' She held out a shiny, new, copper milk pan, out of which protruded a wooden spoon and a packet of some kind of brown powder.

Meg was overcome. 'Oh, Mrs Roberts! I'll treasure it!'

'It should last you a lifetime if you take care of it.'

'I will, I promise I will.' She sniffed at the powder. 'That smells wonderful – what is it?'

'A new-fangled thing that Mrs Harcourt decided to try after she had it at a friend's house. It's called chocolate – you mix a couple of spoonfuls in the pan and it flavours your hot milk. You can try it tonight and see what you think.'

The girls were all profuse in their thanks, but she waved them off. 'That's that, now. You all make my life easier in the kitchen and I wanted to say that. But now – back to work!'

Later, as the downstairs dinner was being transported to the servants' hall, Meg began to feel oddly nervous. *What if they didn't come? What if—*

The back doorbell rang.

* * *

The dinner had been amazing. Even by her own stand-ards Mrs Roberts had surpassed herself. Delilah and William had enjoyed every morsel, and Sam and Jem's eyes had nearly fallen out of their heads at the sight of the spread before them; they had both wolfed down generous portions and then seconds as well. Meg sat with Annie on her knee and thought about how she couldn't possibly be happier.

There had been moments of sadness, of course; Meg had told them in detail of Rosie's last moments, and she thought wistfully of how there might have been one more face round the table.

Jem had watched her as she spoke, his face solemn. Then he made a series of signs to her – quite sophisticated-looking ones, not like the vague gestures she remembered.

'I'm sorry, Jem – I've been away from you so long that I've forgotten how to understand you.'

Mr Wilson broke into the conversation. 'Does he talk with his hands? How interesting. I was reading something in the paper recently about education for the deaf.'

'He's been learning, sir,' said Sam. 'Only a bit, mind, 'cos he has to work, but it turns out you can say almost anything if you know how.'

Jem had paused while all this was going on, but now he repeated himself, looking at Sam.

'He says – hang on, Jem, you're going too fast – something about giving and taking . . . oh, that's it.' Sam turned to Meg. 'He says, don't think about what's been taken away. Think about what's been given back.'

Meg hugged them both, while Mr Wilson clapped admiringly.

After pudding there was a general air of relaxation, and the party split into groups. Meg found herself drawn to one side with Delilah, Mrs Roberts and Mrs Lawrence. Annie was happy, as both Sally and Ivy were making a fuss of her. Sam and Jem were playing some sort of game with Robbie, while William spoke to Mr Wilson and Henry. Meg could hardly believe how well her family was fitting in, how respectable they all looked. She clearly had much to catch up on, but now there would be time. They had for ever to get to know each other again.

Just to cap Meg's perfect afternoon, Tommy arrived; he had spent most of the day with his elder sister and her family but had dropped in because he was desperate to find out what had happened after he'd spoken to the boys yesterday. His happiness on Meg's behalf had been a thing of wonder for her to behold.

'You don't have to decide anything now, Meg,' said Mrs Lawrence. 'Not while it's all so new to you. Mrs Roberts would – we would *all* be sorry to lose you, but of course you must go back to your family if you want to, now you've found them again.'

'Oh, Meg, yes,' said Delilah, taking her hand. 'Come home with us. Things are different now – I've got so much to tell you.'

There was one huge question that Meg had to get out of the way. 'Is Pa still with you?'

'Well, yes, but—'

Meg was already shaking her head. 'No.'

Delilah looked surprised at such a definite negative.

Meg looked her in the eye and gripped her hand. 'I love you, I love you all – well, except *him*. But that's only part of it. After all, I'd have to work anyway, and where could possibly be better than here?' She thought of Mrs Roberts's words that morning: *You're going to be a cook, no doubt about it*. She would lose all that if she went back.

'I can send you my wages, so you can use them for whatever you need, or keep them for Annie – maybe she can even go to school. But I know what my path is: I'm going to be the best cook in Liverpool.' She blushed. 'Apart from you, obviously, Mrs Roberts.'

The cook smiled. 'You'll get there one day.' She addressed Delilah. 'Your sister has a real and genuine talent, and it would be a shame to waste it.'

Delilah's expression was torn, but she nodded. 'Meg, you're a grown woman now and you can make your own decisions. And I can certainly admire someone who knows what she wants and works for it. But,' her fingers tightened, 'you won't forget us, will you? After all, we're your family.'

'Of course I won't, and you are my family. But . . .' Meg looked around her. At Mrs Lawrence, who had looked at her in that terrible state on the day she came out of the workhouse, and who had decided to take a chance on her anyway. At Ivy, who had welcomed her into the home. At Mrs Roberts, who had trusted her, taught her and come to rely on her. And at dear, dear Sally, whom Meg loved as much as she could love anyone. 'There's more than one kind of family,' she said.

'There is.'

Meg was surprised that Delilah should agree so readily, but her sister was smiling. 'We weren't there for you, were we? Oh, I know it was because of all those reasons, and it might not have been anyone's fault except that horrible woman's, but the fact is, we weren't. And we can't get that time back, we can't change it. So I'm glad, truly glad, that you found another family to help you through it all.'

Delilah wiped her eyes. 'Look at me, I'm being all silly. But I mean it. And now, you can have all of us. You can have family here *and* you can have family with us.'

'Yes,' said Meg. 'I'd like that, more than anything. And of course I'll still have my Sunday half-days.'

'Of course you will. So you can work here, and learn to be a cook, and spend your Sunday afternoons with us. It'll be lovely.'

Just at that moment, Tommy looked across the crowded, noisy room and his eye caught Meg's. His face lit up in a smile.

'It will.' Meg was speaking to her sister, but she was thinking of a warm hand on hers in the park. 'Although, maybe not *every* Sunday . . .'

Find out what really happened to the Shaws
after Meg and Rosie entered the workhouse
in Judy Summers' next book,
coming soon.

Dear Readers,

I've always been fascinated with the past – what it looked like and how people lived their lives – so when I came across a copy of Rudolph Ackermann's *Panoramic View of Liverpool* from 1847 I was hooked. This amazing image is part map and part picture, drawn in such detail that you can see every city landmark, every shop frontage, every mast on every ship in the docks. It immediately catapulted me into the bustle of the city's Victorian era, and I was even more delighted to find that an early nineteenth-century tourist guide to the city was available: *The Picture of Liverpool, or, Stranger's Guide* from 1835 is a treasure trove of descriptions of churches, civic buildings and institutions.

Many of the richer citizens of Victorian Liverpool demonstrated both an intense civic pride and a care for those less fortunate than themselves, and as I was looking through the *Panoramic View* and the *Stranger's Guide* I admired and thanked them for their forward-looking endeavours. They established charities, created libraries and bath-houses and parks for everyone to enjoy, and built schools for the poor as well as for the education of deaf and blind children – among the first of their kind in all of Europe.

I drank it all in and immersed myself in it, making (in my head, at least) a wonderful visit to Victorian Liverpool. I strolled around the streets, both wide and narrow; I passed rich houses and poor ones; I stopped to gaze in trepidation at the forbidding workhouse building, shivering a little before I moved on. I heard the noise of the trains, still a novelty, and I watched the ships sailing into and out of the docks as they carried goods and visitors from all over the world. I browsed the shops and stood for a while outside the baker's, peering in the window and inhaling the scent of fresh bread while I listened to the rumble of carriages and carts all around me.

And I knew that I had to write about this city, at this time.

But wait. The most important part was missing: the people. Victorian Liverpool was a wonderful and growing built environment, but a city is made by its inhabitants. Who were the people who lived and died here, working, dreaming, loving, bringing up their families? Who were the people who made the city live and breathe?

There were, of course, citizens of Liverpool in the 1840s who were prosperous and well-off. Their lives could be very pleasant indeed as they designed mansions, attended theatres and concerts, and donated to philanthropic enterprises. But, I reminded myself, these people were only a tiny percentage of the population. I wanted to find out more about everyone else; the people who had to struggle to get by and who filled the teeming, dynamic city with their hopes and dreams. If I'm perfectly honest I have to say I find these lives more interesting than those of the upper classes – I don't know about you, but if I ever visit a stately home you'll find me in the kitchen, not the posh upstairs rooms.

And so the Shaw family were born. They're completely fictional, but they represent the people of their time and place, and they're proud to stand up for themselves. They've experienced both the middle and the bottom of Liverpool society, but the siblings are all determined to make the best of themselves no matter what hurdles fate might throw in their path.

These hurdles were always greater, of course, for women. This was a time when the law, far from working towards equality, actually enshrined the principle of male superiority, and it was women who were at the sharp end of family hardship. This is why I decided to focus my attention on the girls of the Shaw family and their female friends. The boys all have their own stories too, of course, their own hopes and dreams; but during the Victorian era women were so often pushed into the background that I wanted Meg, Delilah and other girls to be able to stand forward proudly and show us what they could do.

As it happens, I actually started writing Delilah's story first – she's the eldest, and I suppose I had some notion of going along in order of seniority. But as I got to know them all better it was Meg to whom I felt most drawn. Maybe it's because I was the middle child in my own family; maybe it's because she loves to cook and so do I. But whatever the reason, I sat down and had a chat with my lovely editor and we decided to tell Meg's story. That was what I called the book in my head, at first: just *Meg's Story*.

I knew I wanted her to experience the workhouse, cruel as it might seem to create a character only to put her in such a horrible place. I'm sure we all know the basics of workhouse living. Families were fed and kept from starvation – just – but they were also separated, institutionalised and forced into a regime that brutalised and broke them. The cruelty wasn't an accidental by-product of the system; it was a deliberate part of the punishment for being poor. This I knew, but as I did more research it was actually the smaller, more mundane things that jumped out at me and that I knew would be important for Meg. The meagre and bland weekly menu that she would have to cook, over and over again. The incredible amount of washing-up that such a large institution would produce. Even the uncomfortable standard-issue boots, for who can concentrate properly on anything when they're limping from bleeding blisters on their feet? And what if the workhouse matron decided to ignore the rules completely and embark on a campaign of cruelty? Who would be able to stop her? How would the girls cope with the injustice?

Meg, I knew, would be determined to get out and to get away from all this. But I also knew that she'd want to take the others with her – not just her sister but the friends she'd made. There would be no freedom or joy for her if Rosie and Sally and Martha were still suffering. But could a poor, powerless girl save her fellow inmates?

Victorian women were not just housewives (not that there's any 'just' about being a housewife, particularly in an era when there were no labour-saving devices). They also worked for pay, just as women always have. But labour opportunities were strictly divided along male and female lines, on top of class divisions, so it was hopelessly unrealistic to expect that Meg would walk into anything comfortable and well paid. But the tough physical job of working in a kitchen? That was plausible.

Cooking in the Victorian era was even more of a skill than it is now, as I found when I went down more research rabbit-holes. A range was a beautiful object – and the height of domestic technology in the 1840s – but you couldn't control the heat at the touch of a button. Victorian recipes also tended to be vague ('use a good quantity of butter ... add sufficient flour ... bake in a fairly hot oven ... leave until thoroughly cooked'), so simply working from written instructions wasn't enough. You needed some kind of feel for the food and its qualities; you needed skill and experience, and if you were new to the kitchen you needed a good teacher. And here I will confess something to you: for me, the most impressive feat in the whole book is actually the turning out of a perfect vanilla custard pudding. I was applauding along with Meg, I can tell you, because when I tried it the result was a presentational disaster . . .

*　*　*

I hope that you like my picture of 1840s Liverpool and the girls and women who built their lives in it. Those of you who are well acquainted with the city and its history may spot the odd small anachronism, and if so then I hope you will forgive me. One or two of them are actually deliberate, such as Meg talking about locomotives at the railway station (at this time the engines didn't come all the way into Lime Street; they were detached at Edge Hill and the carriages made their way in via gravity and brakes, to be hauled out again by rope). But my choice to do it this way was all for a good cause: dear Sally, as she lay in bed in the cold, comfortless workhouse dormitory, would much rather hear tales of the incredible fire-breathing locomotives than of the carriages on their own. I didn't have the heart to deprive her of the treat and neither, if she knew the truth, would Meg.

Yours truly,
Judy Summers

WELBECK

PUBLISHING GROUP

Love books? Join the club.

Sign up and choose your preferred genres to receive tailored news, deals, extracts, author interviews and more about your next favourite read.

From heart-racing thrillers to award-winning historical fiction, through to must-read music tomes, beautiful picture books and delightful gift ideas, Welbeck is proud to publish titles that suit every taste.

bit.ly/welbeckpublishing